AGAINST
ALL ODDS
JEFFERY H. HASKELL

aethonbooks.com

AGAINST ALL ODDS
©2022 JEFFERY H. HASKELL

Aethon Books
www.aethonbooks.com

Print and eBook formatting by Steve Beaulieu. Artwork provided by Vivid Covers.

Published by Aethon Books LLC.

Aethon Books is not responsible for websites (or their content) that are not owned by the publisher.

ALSO IN SERIES

ACKNOWLEDGMENTS

For my lovely wife, without her none of this would be possible. I also want to thank Jennifer Lynn Collins, Coast Guard. She did an amazing job helping life aboard ship feel authentic.

CHAPTER ONE

22SEP2931 PASCAL SYSTEM, CONCRU21, FRINGE
ALLIANCE SPACE.

Officer of the Watch, Lieutenant (JG) Jacob T. Grimm, leaned back in the center chair, cradling his hot tea and enjoying the warmth in his hands. He squirmed a bit, trying to find a comfortable position in the command chair, finally settling on leaning to the side and using his elbow for support. It wasn't his first watch, but each one filled him with excitement. At ten years of service in the United Systems Alliance Navy (including four at the Academy), he was still a newbie, though he felt like an old hand some days. He liked to imagine how, one day, it would be his ship, his command.

As he sipped his tea, warding off the cold from their most recent heat dump, he realized the rest of the bridge was surreptitiously rubbing their hands together.

He pushed a yellow button on the con and leaned down to speak into the pickup. "Wardroom, Watch, can you send up some coffee to the bridge?"

"Aye, aye, sir. It will be right up," a young woman said.

He felt the approving glances of the bridge crew. Whoever had the watch set the tone, and he wanted to make sure they were comfortable and alert. Coffee would achieve both.

"Lieutenant?" Chief Jimenez asked. The bridge of the light cruiser *Orion* was situated with a sunken helm in front of the command chair nicknamed the "Pit." The helmsman, in this case, Chief Petty Officer Jimenez, had full control of the ship's course.

ConCru21 consisted of the USS *Chameleon*, *Hercules*, *Orion*, and *Dorado*, all light cruisers. They flew through an area of space one hundred twenty thousand cubic kilometers, the ships close enough that their computers could coordinate sensor sweeps and point defense.

"Go ahead, Chief," Jacob replied to his reflection in the mirror, which the helmsman used to make eye contact with the con.

"Sir, I'm getting a weird sensor echo up ahead. Can you double-check it for me?" Chief Jimenez hit a few buttons on the flat-panel display next to him, sending the sensor readings to the multifunction display attached to the con. The MFD could mimic any station, along with providing the Officer of the Watch with all the baseline stats on the ship at a glance.

Jacob tapped a button on the MFD, accepting the incoming screen. The sensor display from the helm was the basic version of what CIC looked at, which was nothing more than the ship's course superimposed over a map of their current area with any relevant features highlighted.

In this case, A-575 was highlighted a little over two million kilometers ahead of them. Part of their mission was cataloging possible live-fire targets for a fleet-wide training exercise coming up in a month. 575 was the eighteenth celestial object they would map as they circled the system along the ecliptic. The only enemy in Pascal was boredom.

"I'm not seeing anything—" Then the asteroid blipped. A flicker really, as if the screen refreshed.

"There it is," Jimenez said, pointing at his own screen.

"Got it." Jacob pushed a button on the screen, replaying the flicker every five seconds. It could be an echo... but something in his gut told him to check it out. He reached across himself and pressed the button giving him a direct line to CIC.

"CIC, Ensign Sabina," she said.

"Officer of the Watch Grimm. We're seeing a flicker on the forward sensor array. Can you confirm?" he asked.

"One moment," Ensign Sabina replied.

Jacob looked back at the screen and checked the distance. Their formation cruised along at nearly six thousand kilometers per second with no acceleration. They were on a scanning mission after all and the wake of their gravcoils would disrupt the ships' combined sensors.

Still... his gut told him something was hinky. 575 was about... three and a half minutes away at their current speed. He had that much time to figure out what was going on.

An idea formed in his mind. He could pop the ship up to use the keel sensors for a better look at the asteroid and compare them against what they already saw.

"Chief, bring us up ten degrees at two-five-zero gravities for one-zero-seconds," Jacob ordered.

"Aye, ten degrees up bubble at two-five-zero gravities for one-zero-seconds." The rest of the crew on the bridge stiffened as the tension told them something was up. It was almost imperceptible, but not to anyone who had served on a ship for years. They all sat up straighter, paid closer attention to their screens, and were generally more alert.

"Bridge, CIC," Sabina said. "It could be a sensor echo. 575 is classified as a high-density core of osmium. It's possible we're seeing a reflection bouncing around the northern pole."

"We're adjusting course to let the keel sensors get a better look. Keep an eye on it," he ordered.

"Aye, sir," Ensign Sabina replied.

The ship rumbled as the gravcoil kicked in, sending out a wake of condensed gravity from the stern. As the bow angled up from Jimenez's deft touch, Jacob felt the pull of the wake as it put a strain on the ship's internal gravity. He fought it, leaning forward in his chair, as did the rest of the crew.

"Course corrected," Jimenez said after ten seconds. In that time, they had traveled sixty thousand kilometers, and each passing second brought them six thousand klicks closer to the lifeless rock.

Another ten seconds went by as the lightspeed sensors bathed 575 and were reflected at the ship. By the time the computer spat out a reading, they were two minutes, fifteen seconds from zero to the asteroid.

"Bridge, Captain. What's going on, Lieutenant Grimm?" Captain Blagojevich's grumpy voice sounded from the speaker on the con. Jacob winced. It was the middle of the "night" and his maneuver must have woken the captain.

Jacob leaned over and hit the comm button. "Sir, there's a sensor anomaly on the upcoming asteroid we're checking out. I ordered a course change to confirm it is an echo," he said with more confidence than he felt.

"Did you run it by CIC?" Captain Blagojevich asked.

"Yes, sir. They confirmed the possibility," he said.

"And?" he asked. Jacob heard the impatience in the man's voice.

"I wanted to be sure, sir." Did he tell him about his gut feeling? It was a tough call. He was just a lieutenant and he'd only served on the *Orion* for a few months. He didn't have a tight relationship with the command crew. Captain Blagojevich was the kind of CO who had dinner with his officers once a month and the rest of the time everything went through the XO. Blago-jevich himself preferred to keep a hands-off approach with his crew.

Jacob swallowed hard, suddenly second-guessing himself. Had he disrupted the skipper's sleep to confirm a hunch? Now the *Orion* was out of formation and all he had was "my gut said so."

The readout on his MFD updated and tagged an object close enough to the surface of 575 that it couldn't rightly be called separate, but it reflected the lightspeed sensors at a different rate.

Then it moved.

"Condition Zulu!" he yelled. All doubt vanished. There could only be one reason to hide a ship that close to the surface of a rock.

The bridge crew didn't miss a beat. The ensign at comms slammed down the alarm, activating the automated systems for battle stations. Across the ship, bulkhead hatches unlocked, waiting for the crew to close them as they ran—not walked—to their stations. From the speakers, an automated voice spoke calmly along with the klaxon. "Condition Zulu. Battle stations, all hands, battle stations. This is not a drill."

"What the hell are you doing, Lieutenant?" Captain Blagoje-vich demanded.

In the thirty seconds it took Jacob to explain, the ship had moved a hundred and eighty thousand kilometers closer to 575 and the ambush that awaited them.

CIC confirmed with red icons the appearance of hostile ships tagged as Tangos One through Four. As the crimson dots flared to life, they accelerated away from the ecliptic. From the light cruiser's perspective, they headed straight "down." Which didn't make sense to Jacob since, even with the Tangos' obscene acceleration of 600 gravities, the cruisers would overrun them in a few minutes and have a perfect "look down" shot with the Long 9s. They didn't even appear to be performing any evasive—

"Launch, launch, launch!" Ensign Ping shouted, her tactical screen lighting up with threat warnings.

Jacob's stomach dropped as a cluster of smaller objects separated from the fleeing ships and rapidly accelerated toward the four light cruisers. Sixteen torpedoes cut through space at over 700 gravities of acceleration in their mad dash at the formation.

"I'm on my way," Captain Blagojevich said. Jacob only heard him distantly.

Fear welled up in him and he had to push through it to do his duty. In all the time he'd spent in the Navy, he'd never experienced an actual battle. No weapons fired in anger, only in simulation and practice. His mouth went dry and he blinked several times before resolve took hold, replacing the fear with determination.

"ECM, drop decoys," he said. He went down the list of commands that were the same for almost every engagement. "Helm, evasive. Bring up point defense." The *Orion* had six 20mm quad-barreled coilguns arrayed over the top of her hull. She could send a hell of a lot of rounds down range.

The torpedoes shot through space faster than the crew of the other three ships could react. Had Jacob not altered course, it was likely the enemy ships would have waited until they were on top of them before firing. Forcing their hand early gave the Navy ships a better chance of survival. Light cruisers were the smallest of the capital ships in the United Systems Alliance Navy. They were fast, maneuverable, and state-of-the-art.

Torpedoes, though, were best used against large, slow-maneuvering targets.

However, any ship caught unaware was vulnerable to an ambush by torpedo.

Automated signals went out to the rest of the ships, but they were a full minute behind *Orion* in readiness and it cost them.

Jacob held his breath when the first of *Orion*'s turrets fired. Point defense engaged as soon as the ship's radar gave them a trajectory to shoot at. They would get one volley off, maybe two, before the torpedoes closed the distance.

As the ship shook from the turrets firing, Jacob prayed silently to God for his crew and shipmates to make it through in one piece. Looking around at the bridge, he realized the only experienced hand besides himself was Chief Jimenez. No doubt the bridge crews of the other three cruisers were of similar makeup.

Of the sixteen torpedoes, two veered off course thanks to *Orion*'s countermeasures. Five more were obliterated by tungsten rounds accelerated to ten-thousand KPS from the rapid-firing multi-barrel coilguns *Orion* triggered. The remaining nine homed in on their individual targets.

He was a spectator watching the screens, the warships invisible to the naked eye. The blips that were the torpedoes separated at the last second, like fragments from a broken bottle.

Four of the deadly weapons homed in on *Hercules*. Jacob willed their point defense to take out at least one of them, but the turrets never came on line. Even at this distance, the brilliant blaze of superheated plasma and a detonating fusion reactor blossomed on their screen. After a moment, *Hercules* vanished from the scope.

Two homed in on *Chameleon,* disgorging their deadly

payload in her path. Sixteen magnetically contained bottles of plasma reached out for her. All but two missed. At least they were able to accelerate, and one smashed into the gravwake generated on the prow of the ship. It exploded in fire, scorching the bow, and scorching deck plates all the way to the first turret. The second one nearly killed her, impacting on the hull directly, exploding in superheated fury and vaporizing the fore of the ship, sending her off in a wild spin as they lost all control.

Dorado flailed like a drowning man as her helm attempted evasive. Her point defense struggled to come online, taking out one torpedo at point-blank range. The other detonated a few hundred meters from the bow. Most of the plasma bottles missed the ship. The other detonated on her prow wake, scorching her nose and peeling paint all the way back to the midsection.

The final torpedo detonated three kilometers off *Orion's* keel, at the very edge of its effective radius. Bottles of plasma sprayed out toward *Orion* like rain in a storm. Either by luck or Chief Jimenez's ship-handling, they detonated on impact with the gravwake, leaving superheated plasma burns along her stern and gravcoil but otherwise unharmed.

Alarms wailed as the ship bucked and rolled. Gravity harnesses held the crew fast, protecting them from being flung across the vessel.

"Helm, status?" Jacob said as his head cleared.

"Unaffected. We still have full power."

Jacob pushed the yellow button on his con. "Damage control to all stations." He heard his voice echo throughout the ship.

"CIC, where are those ships?" he asked.

He waited a moment then leaned down to the mic to make sure he was heard. "Ensign Sabina, where are those ships?"

She coughed for a second before responding. "They—

they're heading away at six hundred gravities on course two-seven-five mark one-eight-zero. Their current speed is twenty-seven hundred KPS," she said.

"Are you okay?" he asked.

"Shaken up, sir. No casualties." Ensign Sabina's voice was distorted through the speaker, but she sounded confident.

Jacob did quick and dirty math in his head. In twenty seconds, *Orion* would shoot past the Tangos' sterns, with a perfect look down shot as they fled. Despite their acceleration, from *Orion*'s perspective, they would be sitting still as they ran straight "down." Checking the plot revealed they were making no attempt to evade either. Which was weird, but he didn't have time to contemplate their mistakes.

"Sir, *Chameleon* is calling for us heave-to and render assistance," the midship at comms said. Jacob checked the screen. *Chameleon* still had power, but she was slowing down and changing course away from the Tangos.

Dorado was the ship he truly worried about. She was decelerating, but her course was erratic. However, even if Jacob ordered a full deceleration, he couldn't render aid for at least an hour. By then, the enemy ships would be gone and he wouldn't —he *couldn't*— allow that to happen.

"Tactical, do we have a torpedo solution?" he asked Ensign Ping.

She shook her head. "They're small, fast, and using a lot of ECM. If I had to guess, I would say they're gunboats. Barely more than engines strapped to life support. We might get lucky, but I doubt we can hit them at this angle before the torpedoes run out of power."

There were men and women, his Navy brothers and sisters, who were dead because of these people. He had a duty to the fallen to make sure the bastards didn't get away with it. He couldn't let them go. Not if he had even a small chance to take them out.

"Bring up the Long 9s. One shot each. We won't be in range for a second shot."

"Aye, sir. Long 9s, one shot each," Ensign Ping repeated. The Long 9s were the ship's main cannon, a hypervelocity coilgun capable of accelerating nine kilos of nano-hardened tungsten to half the speed of light out of a twenty-nine-meter barrel.

"Tactical, call the ball," Jacob said.

"Roger, Tactical has the ball. Helm, ninety degrees down bubble," Ensign Ping said.

"Aye, ninety degrees down bubble, zero acceleration," Chief Jimenez replied. He used the manual controls to maneuver the ship into the angle needed. If they had more time, they could program the correct course, but this was faster, and exactly what the chief spent his career training for.

"Solution locked in. Firing in ten seconds..." Ping looked up to Jacob for the final order.

"Confirmed. Fire when green," he said.

The USS *Orion* was pointed "down" but still flying along on her previous course at a velocity of six thousand kilometers per second, while the enemy ships were moving at three thousand kilometers per second and climbing. At the moment their paths crossed, *Orion*'s computers fired the four batteries.

The entire ship shuddered as four rounds blasted away, one right after another, so close together, the ship shuddered nonstop until the last projectile left the barrel. Nine kilograms of nano-hardened tungsten fired at half the speed of light. At their range, the results were instantaneous. Three of the ships exploded as the arrow-shaped projectiles obliterated their hulls.

Tango Four's acceleration and emissions died, but the hull

remained intact as it spun out of control. Radar showed it remained together but obviously without power.

Behind Jacob, the hatch opened, and Captain Blagojevich marched onto the bridge in his stark white ELS suit, helmet cradled under his arm.

"You stand relieved, Lieutenant," he growled.

"Aye, sir. I stand relieved," Jacob said. He stood immediately, relinquishing the chair to the captain.

"Sir, the four—"

"I have eyes, Grimm," Blagojevich said. Jacob snapped his mouth shut. It was difficult, going from in command to not in the space of two seconds. It would have been easier on him if he had interacted with his captain for more than a couple of formal dinners. The man was a stranger to him.

Blagojevich looked up at him and gave him a small smile. "Well done, son. You may report to your damage control station."

It wasn't much of a congratulations, but for Jacob, it felt like a parade.

"Yes sir," he said sharply. He glanced at the main screen one more time as he left the bridge. The four Tangos were toast, and he was glad of it.

———

It took the *Dorado* hours to decelerate to zero. Hours more for the *Orion* to come back around and stop relative to them and render assistance.

Without Jacob's gut to tell him to alter course for a better look, it would have ended far worse. *Hercules* was lost with all hands. Another one hundred and thirty-three were killed on *Dorado*. Twenty-seven more, including her chief engineer, were lost on *Chameleon*. The only success story came from *Orion*, which, despite a few bumps and bruises, had no casualties.

And everyone alive knew who to thank: Lieutenant Junior Grade Jacob T. Grimm.

For three days, the crews worked around the clock. *Dorado* was a wreck and too unstable to tow home. She had to be abandoned, and the crew integrated into the remaining two ships. *Chameleon* could fly, but only at half speed. Once the surviving crew were evacuated from *Dorado,* the remaining two ships of ConCru21 opened fire and scuttled her.

After that, *Chameleon* headed in the direction of the jump point home and *Orion* accelerated toward the sole remaining enemy ship. Since it would continue the same course and speed, it was relatively easy to follow.

By the time the light cruiser was ready to pursue, the enemy was seven hundred million kilometers away. At top speed, the *Orion* caught up in little less than six hours.

Once their velocity matched the tumbling ship, twelve Marines, armed to the teeth, loaded into one of *Orion*'s three Corsairs and flew over and boarded her.

Normally, Jacob would find out through the most reliable intelligence agency in the known universe—the ship's grapevine—what had happened when they boarded the enemy ships. However, since he was instrumental in stopping the attack, the captain invited him to the bridge to observe.

Jacob climbed up the ladder leading to the bridge deck. Two Marines in their white-grey uniforms stood abreast of the closed hatch leading to the bridge.

"Skip, Lieutenant Grimm for you," the Marine on the left said. Both men looked like they could wrestle a bear with one hand tied behind their back. Grimm tried not to be intimidated; after all, he was only ten centimeters shy of two meters. With broad shoulders, he was as strong as any man in the Navy... but these were Marines, not mere men.

The one who spoke waved his hand over the sensor and the hatch buzzed open, sliding apart to reveal the bridge. During non-combat stations, the hatches remained open. While approaching the enemy ships, the captain had ordered Condition Zulu, and all airtight hatches were closed when not in immediate use.

Jacob walked in and stood behind the con, not wanting to interrupt the captain's conversation with the XO.

"Ahh, Grimm, you're here. Good. Gunny Tuha is breaching the airlock now," the XO said. He pointed to the spot opposite of the captain. Jacob nodded and moved next to the command chair. Excitement roared through him.

For the last three days, despite the hard work and over-whelming sadness of the lost lives, an undercurrent of excitement ran through the ship. What award would they honor the hero of Pascal with? He'd tried not to let the rumors get to him, but it wasn't easy, and he found himself looking forward to the hero's welcome he would receive once they reached home. Maybe even his dad would attend the ceremony.

The main screen flickered to life, showing the view from Gunny Tuha's helmet. The HUD showed several readings, including atmosphere and radiation—there were neither.

"*Orion*, I'm breaching the hatches now." The gunny's hand flashed in front of the camera, and there was a burst of light. The solid outer hatches to the ship's airlock glowed red for a moment before melting into slag and cooling almost immediately. A hole big enough to walk through remained. There was no air to escape, no atmosphere to depressurize.

With all the damage a Long 9 could do, they were lucky to have one intact. Jacob couldn't see the damage from the Marine's camera, but if he had to guess, the shot hit at a glancing blow, which was why the ship was in relatively good shape.

As the gunny moved, he shouldered his MP-17 rifle, clearing each room with deliberate precision. Inwardly, Jacob mocked their over-cautious maneuver. Clearly, no one was alive on the gunboat. There were no heat or power sources on the sensors. No one could spend three days on a ship with no life support.

"Oh God," he heard a Marine mutter over the comms.

"Cut the chatter," the gunny replied. "Captain, you're gonna want the bridge cleared of non-essentials."

The gunny glanced away, his camera flashing by small floating objects so fast, they were indistinct blurs. When he stopped moving, he faced the bulkhead.

"Say again?" the XO replied for the captain.

"Sir, you aren't going to want the ratings to see this," the gunny said.

The executive officer looked down at the captain, who shrugged. "Do as the gunny suggests, XO."

"You heard the man. Clear the bridge. All ratings out," the XO said in a bellow.

Within a few seconds, the only people on the bridge were the officers of the watch and Jacob. What could the gunny have seen to cause that reaction? Sensitive information? Perhaps there was some link to who these ships belonged to.

Then he turned the camera back to the small floating objects covered in ice. Whatever they were, they'd frozen solid in the days since the ship was hit.

The gunny moved forward and gently caught one of the objects and held it still for the camera to see. Confusion filled Jacob's mind. His brain could not, *would not*, process what he was seeing.

"Sweet mother of God," someone said. A choked sob from the Tactical station caught his ear. He looked over to see Ensign

Ping gripping the console tight as tears streamed down her face.

"I don't..." Then it hit him. The floating objects weren't pieces of the ship or loose debris... they were people... children. Maybe six or seven years old.

He'd killed children.

The last thing he remembered was the deck coming to hit him in the face.

CHAPTER TWO

TWO YEARS LATER

Fleet Admiral Noelle Villanueva rubbed the spot on the back of her neck where it perpetually ached. She leaned back in the oversized chair she favored and stared at the plain white ceiling tile in her office. Who knew accepting the promotion would fill her with so much regret?

She shook her head, smiling slightly at the irony of an unsolicited promotion that took her from the thing she loved, to the thing she loathed. Her job went from commanding ships to commanding paper.

The Alliance Navy had operated without a Fleet Admiral for the last twenty years. Technically, the chief naval officer could perform the duties of a Fleet Admiral. However, the CNO had the entire Navy to run. Having a high-ranking admiral whose only responsibility was the operations of the fleet was a smart move, one they hadn't used since the last Fleet Admiral was relieved in disgrace. Something Noelle wasn't eager to repeat.

The last few Secretaries of the Navy had resisted the use of the Fleet Admiral title, for what reason Noelle was unaware.

However, the Secretary was incapable of running the fleet. They dumped it on the CNO.

Noelle was one of a shrinking pool of high-ranking officers who had seen combat. She was the only officer who had commanded a ship in the last war. It gave her an expertise the CNO couldn't match or ignore.

President Axwell had pushed for her appointment to the office, and she intended to do her very best for him. With a little luck and hard work, she might even keep the job long enough to turn the Navy, and its ailing reputation, around.

If she could work her way through the hundreds of messages on her NavPad. Including one from the CNO marked *Urgent*.

He hadn't exactly given her a glowing endorsement and she couldn't shake the feeling he resented the pressure exerted on him to give her the office. Any admiral would jump at the chance. It was both a military appointment and a political one. Like it or not, she was the face of the Navy. The buck stopped with her.

Tapping her desk with the pads of her fingers, she debated opening the message. While she'd served the Systems Alliance as an officer in the Navy her whole life, she was two weeks into the job of Fleet Admiral and already felt in over her head. It didn't matter that her wall was adorned with citations and awards. Combat was a cakewalk compared to the political minefield she had to navigate daily.

Despite her uniform, there were politics involved in every move she made. The CNO and SecNav had made it abundantly clear they were watching her for failure. However, failure could be anything they twisted to use against her. She couldn't go to the head without a step-by-step plan. A single misstep and she would find herself promoted... to civilian.

With enemies on all sides, she felt the political situation in the Alliance was hazardous to say the least. She'd much rather be staring down the plasma guns of a Caliphate ship than reading a letter from the CNO.

"Ma'am," her assistant said. She looked up, grasping for his name like fruit just out of reach.

"Parker, ma'am," the CPO said to her with a kind smile. He stood half in the doorway, letting light from the small reception room spill in.

"Sorry, Chief, I'll remember it once I have my head on straight. Go ahead?"

"Admiral DeBeck is here to see you," he said.

Noelle raised an eyebrow at the name. While she'd never met the head of Naval Intelligence, she certainly knew who he was. "Send him in," she said. Parker turned to do just that. In the few seconds she had, she made sure her uniform was spot on.

Rear Admiral Wit DeBeck cut a dashing figure with his broad shoulders and narrow waist. His movie-star good looks were out of place in a uniform, she thought. Despite genetic aging tech, he had a touch of grey at his temples and a few crow's feet around his blue eyes. His entire demeanor put her at ease... which immediately alerted her to stay on her toes. He wore the white semi-dress uniform officers favored when planetside, along with a stiff-brimmed hat tucked under one arm.

She stood, holding out her hand, and he took it, firmly, but without trying to impress her with an overbearing grip. Noelle appreciated his constraint. DeBeck, though, was a big man, a good twenty centimeters taller than her own one eighty. He smiled pleasantly and sat in the chair opposite her, folding his legs and plopping his hat on his upturned knee.

"Admiral, it's a pleasure to meet you," he said.

She sat as well, eyes narrowing expectantly. She didn't trust easily, and he sent all the signals of a person trying to put her at ease. "Do you prefer 'Admiral' or something less formal?" he asked.

"Wit, right?" she asked. He nodded. "Noelle is fine. If we walk around saying 'admiral' to each other, it won't be long before we have no idea who we're talking to, or about," she said. Her smile was genuine but guarded. She wasn't sure about Wit DeBeck yet and didn't want to make the mistake of putting her trust in someone who didn't deserve it.

Of course she knew who he was and everything about him —at least what was available to her rank and clearance. But the files weren't the man. Cliché as it was, he headed ONI and lied for a living. Everything in the files could also be a lie.

"How are you finding everything? I see you still haven't fully unpacked?" He motioned to the half-empty open box in the corner with her personal effects. Photos of her husband and children. She'd thought about putting them out, but she could never decide between displaying them for guests or herself.

"As you can imagine, it's busy around here. I feel like the entire Navy is in crisis mode," she said, gesturing to the map of the Orion Spur dominating her far wall. It was a digital 2D map, but with the correct information for distance and time between star systems displayed as it slowly rotated clockwise.

The United Systems Alliance was eighteen solar systems with four protectorates. Their position was as ideal as it could be, on the eastern end of the Orion Spur, almost three months from Earth by the most direct route. Ideal for trade but insulated from most conflicts—except the last one, the ramifications of which the Navy still dealt with on a daily basis.

"I don't have to imagine," he said with a semi-serious tone. He looked at the map and Noelle felt like every movement with him was calculated... or maybe she was paranoid?

Could be both, she mused.

"Can I offer you some coffee?" she asked. "It's a very good blend."

He grinned. "The doctors tell me I drink too much... so yes, please."

She signaled her assistant and asked for two cups. Once they had the steaming mugs, she sipped hers, waiting for him to make the first move.

"Damn, this is good stuff. Consortium?" he asked.

She nodded. "I stopped a pirate attack on a freighter when I commanded the *Victory*... God... fifteen years ago? He still hasn't forgotten. Whenever he's in-system, a few pounds of the good stuff find their way to my mailbox."

He perked right up. "I'll need to come up here more often."

"You're always welcome, Wit. However, I am pretty busy, so if you could get to the point...?" She raised one eyebrow to emphasize her question.

"Oh, I like you. I wasn't sure, with your connection to the war, why President Axwell would push for you as Fleet Admiral, but now... yes. I can see it," he said.

The Systems Alliance had joined the last war, the biggest the galaxy had ever seen, and it had amounted to a huge disaster, both in lives lost and resources squandered. While the Systems Alliance had only joined to aid their allies, they had taken a huge hit. Then everyone collectively decided to stop fighting and sign an armistice that punished the allies more than anything else. Since then, Congress had made damn sure to let the Navy know the blame was on them. Not on the elected politicians who ordered them to war.

"I want to talk about the Corridor and the Protectorate Systems," he said plainly.

She kept her face neutral, or she tried to, but her lips tightened at the mention of the place. "My hands are tied," she said automatically. She'd had a private and off-the-record conversation with both the CNO and the SecNav after her appointment by the president. They were unhappy with him for bypassing tradition. Normally, the CNO appointed fleet admirals. They made it clear there was absolutely no reinforcing the protectorates—something Noelle was on record as supporting.

"Oh, but they're not," he said, hiding a grin behind his coffee cup.

"I wish they weren't, believe me. Commodore Xin asks for more equipment and ships monthly. I'll tell you what I told him: I have orders specifically limiting the ships and supplies I can send. 'Can't have the Navy starting *another* war' is how the senator from Seabring put it when I was in front of Congress last month. Even the president, if he wanted to, couldn't do more than send an emergency force, and then he would have to justify it to the oversight committee..." Why are you grinning?" His boyish delight perturbed her.

He put his coffee down and walked to the map. Pacing for a second, he turned and pointed at the farthest system of the Protectorate, Zuckabar.

"The vast majority of our shipping comes through the protectorates, but we're not allowed to do our job because of our tenuous political position here at home." He said the last word with such a sneer, it surprised her. No one got to admiral without playing *The Game*, herself included.

"I'm aware," she said.

He nodded, more to himself than her. "Of course you are. I'm thinking out loud here. The Corridor is kiloparsecs of sparsely populated planets, independent outposts, and pirate havens. Nineteen stars and thirty days to cross in either direction, with ten of those days in real space where piracy is the problem. Not to mention, once they're in the Protectorate, they're only nominally safe until they reach MacGregor's World."

Noelle waited patiently for him to get to the point. A great many people spoke this way, laying out their argument step by step before finally asking the real question. If he really did have a solution to their mutual problem, she was all ears and willing to let him build his argument.

"My assets around Zuckabar tell me something big is going down. Something involving the system as a whole. Possibly even the governor. Enough to make Pascal look like a footnote in history," he said.

She winced. Two years since the massacre and the Navy was still trying to put the truth out to the public. The Caliphate's news network, *Al'akadhib*, had done a fantastic job of painting the Systems Alliance Navy as brutal child-killers.

It galled her that the watch officer didn't have the decency to resign like the other officers on the bridge that day. It put her hackles up. He was everything they were trying to weed out of the Navy. There was a time for aggression, and if they were at war, maybe he would be a decent officer, but now wasn't that time. As long as officers like him were in uniform, the enemy would be able to take advantage of them at every turn. She needed thinking, calculating men and women in uniform, not anachronistic cowboys shooting from the hip!

Part of her, a distant part, acknowledged she might be wrong about him. However, the damage done to her Navy was too great to ignore. Even for a man who saved hundreds of lives. In the long run, the results of his actions were far more damaging.

She shook her head. It was too easy to get worked up and she had more immediate concerns.

"Are you saying the Caliphate is making a move on Zuckabar?" she asked, her interest piqued.

"No. Not exactly. I can't be specific, as we don't have detailed intel. Besides, it's too far for them to hold it and they know it. The most they could hope for would be to destroy the infrastructure and raid some shipping." He held up his hand to forestall her complaint. "If I had a smoking gun, I would be in front of Congress, not here with you. What I need is an excuse to put a task force on the border. Hell, maybe even some way to push public favor to the point where we actually bring those systems into the Alliance instead of leaving them with their junk swinging in the wind," he said.

For a second, she thought he was about to tell her something actionable, something she could use. When nothing was forthcoming, she realized how excited she was about fixing the problem the politicians had created.

"What do you want from me?" she asked cautiously.

"Commodore Xin's picket is on a rotation. Currently, they're not due back to Zuckabar for two months. Delay them. If something were to happen in the system, or on the planet... something catastrophic... something the Navy would have to send a larger force to deal with. Then Congress couldn't say no... What do you think?" he asked, turning around and presenting his hands wide open like a stage magician.

"That's great and all, but I don't see how you could predict such a disaster. It would have to be newsworthy for the president to justify overruling Congress. Bloody enough that no one in the Alliance could reasonably object too. I don't think you're suggesting we orchestrate an event...?"

He shook his head. "No. Not at all. But things *are* happening with or without our help. I say, let them happen. Maybe... *maybe*...nudge them in the right direction," he said as if he were testing the waters. He played a *very* dangerous game. What he suggested was borderline illegal, and certainly immoral.

Noelle didn't like the idea of turning her back on people who needed help. Leaning back, she pressed her hand to the bridge of her nose. She *hated* this decision. Do nothing and allow possibly millions of people to suffer, or do something and cause hundreds, maybe thousands, to die.

"I'm not saying I agree to this... but what did you have in mind?" she asked.

"The *Interceptor* is orbiting Zuckabar and it needs a new commander. Picking the right person is the first step. Do you have anyone who would add value to the operation? Someone sufficiently aggressive might act as a catalyst. But not anyone the Navy would miss."

"Aggressive, you say..." she said. There were few officers in the Navy she could justify throwing under the aircar. She could think of at least one. "You know, I just might."

"Who?" he asked.

CHAPTER THREE

L ieutenant (SG) Jacob T. Grimm ran his hand along the Corsair's unfolded wing. He glanced at his NavPad, noticing the bird was on its third failed maintenance check.

"Chief Harding, what's going on?" he asked as he came around the stern where the maintenance chief had the engine compartment pulled open.

The brawny man with a perpetual five o'clock shadow and a grease-stained tunic shook his head. "Not sure, El-Tee. The boys downstairs dropped her off and said she was shaking on transition. This is as far as I've gotten," he said with a gesture toward the panel.

Jacob held up his NavPad, showing Chief Harding the image of the Corsair along with its history. "Look." The two men huddled around the display.

"Well, I'll be damned. Is this right?" Harding asked.

"If it isn't, I want to know why," Jacob replied.

"Are you telling me this bird has been down-voted three times in two months and no one has checked the engines?" Harding asked.

It was unusual, to say the least. Sloppy, even. Jacob checked to make sure it hadn't happened on his watch. Thankfully, all the maintenance logs were from the other four bays on Bethesda. "Looks like it. I want you to have third watch pull apart her air breathers, and if that isn't the problem—"

The chief of the deck groaned. "Then pull the gravcoil. Got it."

Jacob hit the note function and checked one more thing off his list. He'd been the Officer of the Deck for Naval Space Station Bethesda for almost a year, and he was happy to do it. After the shock of *Orion,* and the aftermath, a quiet place to rebuild his reputation was what he needed. Long hours and a never-ending workload helped him keep his nightmares at bay as well.

"Listen, I'm going to make my rounds, and if it ends up being the coil, I'll come back up and help you pull it, copy?" he asked.

Chief Harding's smile stretched wide. "I'm not sure the Navy will allow you to be an officer if you do real work, sir," Harding said.

"You have no idea how true that is," Jacob replied. He checked his NavPad; the screen flashed, letting him know he had ten minutes to get to the Wardroom. He waved goodbye to Harding and headed for the nearest lift.

He'd spent the year and a half working his butt off. His promotion to *Senior Grade* Lieutenant was already in the works when Pascal happened. However, Senior grade ranks were normally reserved for officers in transition. The rank would be made permanent contingent on his successful completion of command school. But no. Shortly after his bittersweet promotion, he received the letter revoking his command school billet due to "unforeseen consequences." They hadn't told him what those were, but he imagined having his face plastered all over the Alliance as *the Butcher of Pascal,* didn't endear him to the admiralty.

He waited a year before re-applying, adding his post-Pascal glowing FITREPs from Bethesda to his application. Technically, he had done nothing wrong, and in point of fact, had done everything *right.* It was politics that were destroying his career.

However, today was the day. His CO would have the answer for him at lunch. If he didn't get in, then his days in the Navy were numbered. He could only stay in grade another year before the promotion board would have to promote or muster him. Which meant he would be mustered.

It was a quick trip via magnetic tube to his quarters. It would not do well to show up in his work uniform, especially with it wrinkled and dirty from crawling around the boat bay all morning.

Ten minutes later, he walked into the Wardroom exactly thirty seconds early, wearing a crisp uniform and a clean shave. He even managed to smile as he sat down at the far end of the table.

Lunch was a selection of local dishes. Bethesda orbited Vishnu, the oldest settled planet in the Alliance, and they had a fantastic array of Indian food. The station never hurt for flavorful meals.

The Wardroom took the rectangular tables and pushed them all together to seat twenty-six on the sides and two at the very end. The tables were organized by section and rank. As the deck officer, his section was at the very end. He sat next to two lieutenants who wouldn't even look at him, let alone speak to him, for fear of having his stigma rub off on them.

The hatch slid open, and Captain Albrecht and Commander Anand entered, the station's CO and XO respectively. Everyone in the room rose to their feet and waited until they took their seats before sitting down themselves. Albrecht was older, with solid lines and grey hair cut recruit short. Anand was a native of Vishnu; her dark hair, eyes, and skin contrasted with her white dress uniform.

Conversation broke out as the drinks arrived. It was less a formal meal than a structured get-together. Jacob tried to enter in when the lieutenant to his left started talking about the Vishnu's chances at the Olympics, but he quickly looked away and found a different subject.

After the food, the CO ordered coffee. Jacob leaned back, first puzzled, then angry. He was careful not to react. In the time he'd served on Bethesda, they had never ordered coffee before announcing promotions and departures. Even if he wasn't getting into command school, he deserved to know. He stomped down on his feelings, though. Emotionally unstable officers weren't anyone's favorite. He remained seated, watching as officer after officer departed. None looked his way, leaving him feeling as if everyone knew something he didn't.

When it was just the three of them, Commander Anand motioned for him to move closer. Her dark features broke into a smile as he sat down.

"How are things down on the deck?" she asked to break the ice. She was far more personable than the CO, who was busy examining his coffee cup.

Confusion delayed his answer. If it was a report she wanted, she could ask him to deliver an official one at any time. He took longer than he should have before answering.

"Sorry, ma'am," he said. "We're having trouble with a Corsair. I think it's going to end up being the gravcoil, but Chief Harding is starting with the air breathers and—"

The CO waved his hand, interrupting him.

"Jacob, you've been here eleven months." His sudden interruption added to Jacob's confusion.

Calling him by his first name caught him off guard. He

wanted to correct him about how long he was aboard, but confusion held his tongue.

"Sir?" he asked.

Were they maneuvering him? After Pascal, he'd had hundreds of interviews. At first, it was all informational. What was the energy signature? The flight profile, and mass readings? Did you have any knowledge of who the ships belonged to?

Then they began to pressure him to admit knowledge he didn't have, then it turned to something far more sickening. After that, he was always on guard around people, not trusting them. He'd stuck through it, though. There were days he wished he'd gone Ensign Ping's route and resigned his commission.

The Navy was everything to him. His mother and her father had both served. After his mother's sacrifice in the last war—a sacrifice that had paid for him to go to the Academy—he just couldn't resign in disgrace. Not after all she had done for him. If he did, all anyone would remember was his nickname, and they would forget that Master Chief Melinda Grimm had saved hundreds of lives at the cost of her own.

"What the CO is saying, Jacob, is that you don't have any friends here. Do you?" she asked politely.

Now he was really confused. *Friends?* No one wanted to be friends with him. He'd heard the nickname the news networks had given him. How his real name had "leaked." He'd spent three weeks on leave before taking the assignment to Bethesda. His dad had spoken all of five words to him the entire time.

He shook his head.

"No, ma'am. I'm... focused on the Navy at the moment." He hoped they would take the hint and get to the point. This was an awkward way to inform him about the command school results.

"As far as I'm concerned," Anand said, "You're a good officer. Your crews like you and you haven't filed a single Captain's

Mast in your time here. Is that negligence, or do you command your men that well?" she asked.

Their demeanor said relaxed, but their questions felt like a trap. Regardless, though, there was only one answer for an officer to give.

"My people work hard at their jobs, ma'am. I haven't had any trouble with them," he said. Which was true. In his mind, and he felt like the Navy agreed with him; a Captain's Mast was the last resort, a failure on everyone's part to correct behavior.

"Thank you, Lieutenant," Anand said. She glanced at the CO, who gave her a slight nod in return. She turned back to Jacob, "Dismissed."

"Ma'am?" he asked with evident confusion.

She raised an eyebrow at him. Jacob coughed, snapped to attention from panic, and performed a parade-ground about-face, marching out of the Wardroom without looking back.

The nearest lift wasn't far. He walked in a bit of a daze. The events he had desperately tried to bury, crashing into him. Was this it, then? Would Pascal haunt him forever? He shook his head as his confusion followed him like an angry swarm of bees.

They hadn't said a word about command school. Not knowing was worse than the rejection he desperately fought to avoid. No one went after two rejections.

He found himself in front of his quarters with no recollection of the route he had taken. As he reached for the entry panel, his NavPad buzzed, followed by a bosun's pipe emanating from the small speaker.

It was a classic notification of official orders. He turned and leaned against the hatch, pulled the pad out of his pocket, and pressed his thumb down on the center of the screen.

Lieutenant (SG) Jacob T. Grimm, verified. You are directed to report to the planet Zuckabar Central in the Zuckabar system, with all haste. Travel itinerary will follow.

A few seconds later, his travel per diem and tickets buzzed their arrival. He opened them automatically, his awareness severely curtailed at the shock of the notification.

One hour? he asked himself, dumbfounded at the time frame.

He had an hour to pack his things and get to the next shuttle departing for ground station, then another shuttle to the spaceport and a civilian transport to Zuckabar.

The Navy never used "all haste" lightly. There was no time to ask for clarification, no time at all. He had to pack, and fast, if he wanted to make it. But what about command school? It wasn't in Zuckabar. In fact, he wasn't even aware of a Navy base there.

He barely had time to throw his spare uniform and what little clothing he had into the large blue Navy-issue duffel bag. The only non-work thing he had was his classic wooden guitar, which he hadn't played since before his career took a dive. It was still in the hard case he transported it in from his last station.

Twenty minutes later, he hastily sent a message to his roommate. Then, still in his crisp day uniform, he hustled for the lift. It carried him across the two-kilometer-long space station in less than ten minutes, depositing him on the transport deck outside the correct shuttle.

He jogged, breathing hard as the weight of the bag reminded him of his poor physical condition. He arrived with a few minutes to spare, handing his NavPad to the SP manning the gate. The SP immediately removed any sensitive information stored about his current duty station. Upon arriving at Zuckabar, it would get a similar treatment in reverse.

"Good luck, Lieutenant," the SP said with a smile, handing back his NavPad.

"Thanks," Jacob replied.

After stowing his bag and guitar in the overhead, he settled into the shuttle's acceleration seat. She was a modified Corsair, built for maximum passengers instead of the usual mix of armament and transportation. It was a thirty-minute flight to the ground station, enough time for him to figure out what transport ship he was flying on.

To his surprise, not only was it not a Navy ship taking him to Zuckabar, it wasn't even a large liner like the Navy usually used to move personnel around. Jacob double-checked his orders while he waited in the small line of passengers. At least the freighter was registered in the Systems Alliance. He still shook his head, thinking of what the next eight days would entail. Small tramp freighters weren't known for their great accommodations.

CSV *Dagger* was parked on the landing pad at the largest spaceport on Vishnu. The ship wasn't new, but it was certainly well cared for. He could tell that from the freshly painted flourish under the hull identifier. Someone cared for the ship.

The main hatch opened, rolling up into the hull as a platform extended down. Two burly men trotted out, punching each other's shoulders as they joked. Jacob didn't catch the context of their shared amusement as they clamped their mouths shut upon seeing the waiting line of passengers.

Six people, including Jacob, waited with bags and boarding passes in the late afternoon sun. Vishnu was moderately tilted, with even temperatures near year-round. On the equator, which was where they were, it never went above twenty-three degrees or below four.

Jacob still had his day uniform on, and while it wasn't warm, it wasn't the most comfortable thing to wear while rushing to catch his flight.

The two men went to the front of the line and started checking passes with a hand scanner. Jacob shifted his bag to present his NavPad with the code displayed on the screen.

"What's this?" the inspector asked when they got to him.

"Last minute, is my guess. I don't have a physical pass, but this should work," Jacob told him.

He shook his head. "Too easy to forge, squidy. Go back and get a real pass and we'll talk."

Jacob clenched his jaw. According to the ticket, the ship lifted off in less than thirty minutes. There wasn't time to go back and print out a ticket. Also, the pejorative "squidy" coming from a civilian made him want to punch the man square in the jaw.

Jacob put his bag down, leveling his shoulders and standing up to his full height. While the crewman was wide, he wasn't as tall as Jacob. He didn't like using his height as a weapon, but he would if he had to. "If you aren't authorized, or smart enough, to figure this out, go get someone who is," he said. "Because when the Navy says 'go on this ship,' I'm going on this ship. *Civvy*." He emphasized the last word to make sure the man knew exactly what Jacob thought of him.

The man glanced at his partner and then back at Jacob. "You believe the balls on this guy," he said. Jacob tensed. The man's act of looking away and talking to his partner was a distraction, meant to make Jacob take his eyes off him. He didn't fall for it.

"Seymour, cut the crap and get on the ship. You know as well as I do he's authorized," a woman said from the top of the gangplank.

The second man laughed, slapping his friend's shoulder. They turned and followed the other passengers up into the ship. Seymour gave him an evil snarl as he disappeared.

Jacob looked to his savior and forced a smile on his face to override the shot of adrenaline he'd received.

It wasn't too hard to force, though.

The woman sauntering down the gangplank was dressed in brown leather, with a hip-hugging pair of pants held up by a wide gun belt. The holster was empty, as carrying weapons at the spaceport was illegal, but it wasn't hard for him to imagine what she would look like with one. Her long, silky black hair flowed around her shoulders, a perfect accompaniment to her light brown skin.

"Captain Nadia Dagher," she said in a light alto. She held her hand out to him.

"Lieutenant Jacob T. Grimm," he said, accepting her hand. "Dagher, like the ship?" He nodded to the trading vessel. The actions of her crew were long forgotten as Jacob gazed at her deep brown eyes and soft skin.

"Something on my face?" she asked with a grin.

"No, sorry," he said, quickly looking away as he blushed. "Sorry," he said again with even more conviction.

She shrugged. "I'm teasing. Now, hotshot, let me see those orders of yours," she said, holding out her hand.

He fumbled for the NavPad, almost dropping it before handing it over. His face turned an even darker shade of red.

"Everything seems in order, big guy. You ready for the trip?" she asked, looking up at him.

"Uh, yes." He kicked himself for his sudden fit of self-doubt.

She didn't seem to mind. "Well, your cabin is all the way to the aft on deck three. Next to the coil exhaust. The crew's a bit rough around the edges, but they'll lay off if you treat them right."

"I'll do my best," he said. Turning, he picked up his bag and guitar and hefted them over his shoulder.

"You play that thing or is it just to excite freighter skippers?" she asked as he walked up the ramp.

For the first time since he saw her, he felt a little at ease and some of his confidence returned. "Can't it be for both?"

"Oh, we're going to get along just fine, cowboy," she said from behind.

CHAPTER FOUR

PLANET NIFLHEIM, THE CORRIDOR

Fadhl Fawaz moved from shadow to shadow, skipping over the puddles of fresh rainwater without disturbing them. Only the scattering of what passed for rodents on Niflheim noted his presence with their overly large eyes.

Despite the thermal protection his coat provided, the cold managed to seep into him. It was always cold, and he hated every second on the miserable ball of ice.

A beat-up ground car passed by, its dingy yellow lights illuminating the street in front of him. He froze, pressing up against the shadows until only the stars lit the street.

For Fadhl, this was the endgame. The culmination of six months of operations in the Corridor by him and the rest of the Internal Security Bureau.

The tavern he approached lay on the edge of the shantytown known as Hel. It was a dilapidated building as worn down and decrepit as the rest of the backwater colonies found in the Corridor. They weren't officially recognized, and Niflheim's colony appeared on no galactic maps of the area. In the

Caliphate, they were known as "pirate coves." Only fools and pirates would choose to live on a barely habitable planet; Fadhl was neither.

He paused one more time, glancing behind him. He held his breath, counting to ten as he'd been trained, his eyes darting back and forth for even the slightest sign someone was following him.

No one appeared. He brushed his hand against his sidearm to reassure himself, then moved out. It wasn't that he was worried, but locals were unpredictable and that made them dangerous.

Inside the tavern looked no better than the outside. The foul smell of stale tobacco and watered-down ale assaulted his nose as he stepped through. The man behind the bar grunted when Fadhl entered, but no one else in the near-empty place cared.

The bar itself ran the length of the far wall and shielded the server from any direct contact with his patrons. Fadhl slipped the Consortium currency out of his pocket as he walked over and slapped the hard, golden coin down on the whiskey-stained surface.

"Beer," he said in a perfect Consortium accent. He was given special dispensation to consume alcohol and pork for the duration of his mission. He didn't like it, but he would do his sworn duty.

The man nodded, reached under the bar, and set down a can of local brew with a sealed lid. The coin, far more than a single beer's worth of currency, vanished.

Fadhl pulled the tab, letting the foam spit and splash for a moment before taking a long pull of the acrid drink. It tasted like donkey dung, but he forced it down with the appropriate amount of pretend zeal. Once he was satisfied he'd made an impression, he turned to survey the room, leaning against the bar as he did so.

Two women hunkered down in the corner, available for whoever had the coin. They looked far too used for his taste. He recognized the look of a beaten animal when he saw one. They weren't a threat or a problem.

The three men in the far corner, though, they were both. And exactly who he was looking for.

He caught the eye of one, a tall man with a dark, bushy beard. His clothes were simple, mostly leather and wool to keep out the chill night.

Fadhl gave them a few moments to examine him before moving in their direction. A few meters from the table they shifted around. The bearded man produced a beat-up sonic screamer. Fadhl's own maser pistol had better range and a far more lethal shot, but at proximity, stunned was as good as dead.

"No closer, if you value your balls." The bearded man waved the gun to the right. Fadhl followed, holding out his coat so they could see his weapon. No fool went unarmed on Niflheim. Not bringing a weapon would have ended with his death, either from the pirates or someone else.

The third man, sitting with his back to the wall, held a small pad no bigger than his palm. Blue light flashed across his face for a moment before he put it in his pocket. "He's clean."

"Alright then, have a seat," the weapon holder ordered.

Fadhl pulled the chair out, far enough that his legs wouldn't be trapped by the table if he had to move. "Captain Duval?" he asked the bearded man. Fadhl's face was clean-shaven and his skin dyed a light blue, just the way the gene-altering-obsessed people of the Consortium favored at the moment.

A nod was his only answer.

"I'm Takumi." He smiled as his cover name slipped easily from his mouth. It was a common name in the Consortium. Combined with his perfect accent and the coin he spent, not to mention his clothes and weapon all being purchased in the Consortium, no one would suspect otherwise.

"It's a pleasure, Mr. Takumi. Now, you've gone to a lot of effort to meet with the Black Legion. Mind telling me why?"

"You've shown a... willingness... to target ships regardless of their flag. We—that is, I—would like to offer you support in doing so in the future." His slip was intentional. "You go about your business, with more backing than before of course, and when the time is right... well, I'm sure one more ship for you to raid won't make a difference, will it?"

Duval was no fool. The prissy man with the fancy accent and too new clothes didn't just fall out of the sky to hand him a boon. If he was smart, he'd walk away. And he was smart.

The problem was he also needed to eat. His crew was tight, tighter than family. His cobbled-together ship, which the crew had affectionately named *Raptor*, barely counted as a corvette. With the merchants acting smarter these days, he needed all the help he could get. The Raptor hadn't pulled a good haul in a month, and if something didn't change soon, he would lose his command.

Someone in the Corridor had been brazenly attacking the big merchant houses. The route was too long for the Consortium or the Alliance to patrol the whole way, and they were not close enough allies for either to build a base without it encroaching on what was nominally neutral territory. It was a stalemate of their own making and it made for a profit. Or at least it had...

In response, the traders had started traveling in convoys and hiring protection. He'd heard of a crew last week who boarded a merchie only to have a squad of highly-trained mercs turn the tide on them.

"Mr. Takumi, what would you be offering us that we

couldn't take from your corpse?" It was a calculated move to see how serious the man before him really was.

The man pretending to be Takumi smiled. "Captain Duval, I don't think you want to do that. I think you want to listen to what I have to offer you."

"Which is?"

Takumi leaned in conspiratorially and whispered a single word: "Frigate."

"That's a fancy word and it can mean a lot of things. Can you be more specific?" Duval asked.

Takumi glanced left and right as if he were afraid of being overheard. "Forty thousand tons of ex-Consortium combat frigate. Is that specific enough for you?"

Yes, it was.

"You have my attention. Now, where are we going?"

CHAPTER FIVE

Jacob swiped across the screen of his NavPad, reading the publicly available info on the Zuckabar system. It wasn't much.

The main industry was mining. Heavy metals were abundant in the outer asteroid belt. Those supplied the massive shipyard, *Kremlin Station,* orbiting Zuckabar Central, They built M-class freighters as well as repairing those coming through the Consortium-Alliance trade route.

Geographically, the system was interesting. Millions of years before, several planets orbited the main sequence star. That was before Zuck-Alpha became a white dwarf and Zuck-Bravo a pulsar. The only habitable planet—and according to the Navy, "habitable" was defined as any planet a human could survive on without a breathing apparatus—was Zuckabar Central. It was 20,000 kilometers wide and covered in clouds and a whopping 700 million kilometers from the two suns. The only way anyone lived on it was after three centuries of terraforming by the Guild. Jacob didn't even want to think about how much that cost.

"What a crap-hole," Nadia said from the doorway. Jacob

turned, mild amusement on his face as he took in the ship commander. She folded her arms and leaned against the hatch frame like she was waiting to catch a bus.

"Then why are you going there?" he asked.

"The galaxy may never know," she replied coyly. "Or it could be money."

"It's money," he said with a smile.

"Isn't it always," she said, followed by a sigh.

She certainly had the "mysterious trader captain" stereotype down pat. Jacob tossed the NavPad on the little bunk and pulled himself up to stand. He was too tall for the little ship and had to bend over slightly, even in his quarters.

"Is it mealtime?" he asked.

She nodded and threw him a wave.

"I thought you'd like to eat with the officers," she said.

Jacob raised an eyebrow before slipping on the black watch cap to keep his ears warm.

"You have a different mess for the bridge crew?" he asked. He'd genuinely thought the ship too small to have multiple galleys.

He wasn't in uniform, but the cap was a universal spacer adornment. Ships were almost always on the cold side, enough to be uncomfortable without warm clothes and a watch cap. If a ship was warm, something was terribly wrong.

She shook her head, sending her silky black hair cascading over her shoulders from under her own cap.

"Not exactly. Oh, and bring your guitar?" she asked. Her eyes sparkled with mischief.

"Sure," he said. It only took him a second to undo the latches and pull out the precious instrument. Part of him didn't want to. Joy lived in the guitar, and he had no joy. But he couldn't bring himself to refuse her.

He followed her as she gave him a short tour of the ship, all three levels. Deck three was all crew and passenger quarters, along with the fusion and engineering rooms. Deck two was the ship's main cargo hold and galley. The top deck held the bridge, recreation, and the captain's quarters.

Instead of taking the small lift, she climbed the stairs—a luxury on most ships. Most Navy personnel were accustomed to using ladders to move between decks, with lifts reserved for moving cargo. At least on the smaller ships. Anything bigger than a heavy cruiser was far too large to traverse on foot. Jacob had only ever seen those in passing. The largest ship he'd served on was *Orion,* and he'd busted his butt climbing those ladders.

"I love how compact your ship is," he said as they ascended the last staircase to the top deck. "The big ships are a marvel, but there's nothing quite like knowing every nook and cranny."

"Me too. She's light, fast, and agile. We don't have a huge cargo capacity, but I'm not a bulk freighter. What I move tends to be small and valuable..." she threw a look over her shoulder at him, "and well worth the wait." She turned back, not missing a beat as she continued up.

Jacob pushed down the blush in his face. It wasn't as if he'd never flirted with a woman before, but damn, she was in a class all her own. There was just something about her... He couldn't put his finger on it, but he certainly liked it.

Bulk freighters, like the huge M-Class Cargo ships Zuckabar made, could carry literally millions of tons of goods, but they were slow and cumbersome. Their mass made it virtually impossible to accelerate at anything higher than a hundred gs.

"What do you carry?" he asked.

She turned at the top of the stairs, away from the recreation room, and headed for a hatch on the far side, next to the bridge.

"Mostly people. I'm faster than the star liners and more reliable than trains on New Berlin. You'd be surprised by how often a company or agency needs a person moved quickly and discreetly," she said.

She punched a code on the panel next to the hatch. It slid sideways, revealing her cabin.

He followed her in, whistling in astonishment. Her cabin was three times as big as the one he had on Bethesda, and that was huge compared to *Orion*. Hers was stocked with luxurious adornments, including a queen-sized bed with a fluffy-comforter and overstuffed pillows. The head was on the far side, and he spotted a *water* shower in there. Off to the right was a walk-in closet. To a Navy officer, the amount of space she used was downright obscene.

He entered, leaning his guitar against the bulkhead next to the hatch. A table decorated with a pristine white cloth dominated the center of the room. Two steaming plates of noodles with white sauce were set opposite each other, framing a chilled bottle of wine and two glasses.

"Will anyone else be joining us?" he asked as he looked around.

She pulled her gun belt off and tossed it on the bed. This time, she was armed, which struck him as odd. Who walked around armed on their own ship?

"Nope. You and I are the only officers on board." She gestured to the table. "Welcome to the Wardroom." Her grin was infectious and it made him want to smile even more.

He sat down opposite her. She reached to pour him wine and he held his hand up in a stop gesture.

"You don't like wine?" she asked.

"I don't drink alcohol," he said. It was always a little tricky bringing up the subject and he wouldn't have even mentioned it had she not wanted to serve him. For most spacers, the idea of not drinking alcohol or coffee was border-line heresy.

"Curiouser and curiouser," she murmured as she poured her own glass.

Jacob waited for her to begin before picking up his fork. The food tasted as good as it smelled. He raised an eyebrow at her.

"This is delicious," he told her.

"Don't I know it. Worth every penny too," she said.

They ate in silence for a few minutes. The awkward tension of a first date built up around him. He was very good at not saying anything. He could handle silence; it gave him time to think. She, though, was every bit as good at handling it as he was. She even smiled and winked when he looked at her expectantly. It turned into a game of who could eat in silence the longest.

Main plate done, she got up and brought two cups of honest-to-goodness chocolate pudding out of her mini-fridge.

"Is this a bribe?" he asked as she handed it to him.

"More like an investment," she said as she took a spoonful in her mouth. Her eyes rolled up and her cheeks brightened. "God, that's good," she said.

He took a small bite, keenly aware that his physical fitness was far below his normal standards.

"Very," he agreed as he took a second spoonful.

"Bethesda, huh? You like being a deck officer?" she asked. She twirled her spoon like a gunfighter then went in for another helping.

"I take it you know who I am... so why not just ask?" he said. Walls of alertness came right up as he examined her in a new light. Yes, she was beautiful and alluring, but he sensed hidden dangers under her flirtatious exterior.

She shrugged. "It's not my business."

"Thank you for that. I don't get to talk to many people in the service without it coming up. Mostly they just whisper my nickname in passing. It's why I liked serving on *Bethesda*. Plenty of hard work, always a ship to maintain or cargo to move. It kept me busy," he said.

She pushed her pudding aside. "No command decisions to make..." She trailed off. Her smile assured him it wasn't meant as an insult.

He chuckled at the way she said it. An offhand remark added on to what he was really saying. "The last time I made one of those..." He shook his head. Two years was more than enough time to come to terms with the actual decision. He'd replayed it a hundred times in his head. He'd done everything right.

Everything.

But it still felt wrong. He wished to God he hadn't manned the watch that day. Of course, the alternative was too terrible to contemplate.

"Are you ready to serve aboard ship again?" she asked.

"I'm an officer in the Systems Alliance Navy, I'll do what I always do... my duty," he said.

"Mhmm. That's *The Book* talking," she murmured.

"Sometimes that's all we have," he said. He glanced longingly at the pudding, then pushed it away.

"So," she said, looking over at the guitar leaning against the wall. "*Can* you play?" Her smile was the only thing capable of enticing him to.

"Not in a long time," he said.

"Care to see if you've still got it, big guy?" she asked as she leaned forward and placed a hand on his arm.

———

Years of clandestine work had taught Nadia a thing or two about people. She was what she would call, "a good judge of character." When Admiral DeBeck had told her to probe the tall, broad-shouldered senior grade lieutenant, she'd assumed it was to see if he was a traitor or a turn risk. After spending four days with him, she knew him to be neither. He was thoughtful, considerate, and dedicated.

She didn't know what DeBeck's game was—he wasn't obligated to tell her—but she hoped Jacob Grimm made it through in one piece. She would like to see more of him. However, if Admiral DeBeck expected him to fold, he was going to be disappointed. Jacob might be hurting from what happened in Pascal, but this man's shoulders were strong enough to carry the burden, among other things, she thought with a smile.

CHAPTER SIX

Iker Bellaits hardly noticed the class filing out as the bell rang. Astrophysics 101 wasn't even his class. He loathed teaching the lower levels and couldn't wait for the day to be over. Despite this being the beginning of the semester, it was his last day teaching for the year. Which suited him just fine, since it only got in the way of his real work.

Before him on his university pad was his itinerary for the next three months, starting with a two-week trip to Zuckabar. Once there, the ship he chartered would fly his prescribed course.

That was the time-consuming part. Once there, he would need to fly along the ecliptic in ever-larger orbits, listening for the unique sound of space-time.

His calculations suggested a month, maybe two at most, and he would find the prize. However, thanks to the grants he had received, money was no longer a problem.

He'd spent last year in the Consortium system, Praetor, listening for the source. He knew what to look for; he just needed people to leave him alone long enough to find it. He had to be careful, though. All his notes and discoveries were with him on the small molecular memory chip he carried in his shoe. It was possible he was being overly cautious, but if the galaxy knew what he was after—there would be a mad rush to discover it. He wouldn't risk losing everything he'd worked his entire life for on a gamble. There would be no mistakes.

He leaned back, running his hands through his thinning hair. Even with gene therapy, his age was starting to show. He was closer to ninety than he'd like to admit, and while he still felt in his forties, time was running out. No amount of medical care would let him live forever.

The computer buzzed, letting him know it was time to go. He would make some excuse for leaving his work here at the university and pass it off to a teacher's assistant. The university would just have to get by without him. If he was right—and he *had* to be right—then what he discovered in Zuckabar would change everything. No amount of political maneuvering by the dean of science could get him fired then. He'd spend the rest of his life studying his findings as the most famous scientist in the galaxy... Maybe even in history.

An hour later, he stood dressed in his travel clothes, with a large leather backpack and his weather-beaten duffel bag—all the equipment he would need he could procure on Zuckabar Central or Kremlin Station. Besides, it was better to pack light. Everything else he owned was in the tiny house the university provided for him.

He checked the time. He had a little over two hours to catch the shuttle to High-Point, and from there, he was on his way. Nothing could stop him now!

"Professor Bellaits?" a young woman called out to him.

He turned his attention from the sky and took notice. He blinked several times as his mind caught up with him.

"Daisy?" he asked. She was one of his best students from the advanced quantum-astrophysics course he'd taught a few years before. She'd graduated and gone on to some corporate job last he heard.

Her warm smile greeted him, instantly making him feel much younger than he had a moment before. She was dressed in boots, brown cargo pants, a thick turtleneck sweater, and a hip-length black jacket with a travel bag swung over one shoulder. Her tan skin looked remarkably youthful in the morning light. She smiled, her full red lips splitting her face.

"You didn't think you could leave without me, did you?" she asked.

He had no idea what she was talking about. It took him a second, looking away from her, to pull his mind together.

Iker Bellaits was a man of science, with a laser focus on research. When people started talking money, conditions, and travel plans, his mind wandered. The near-unlimited funds his benefactors had handed him came with only one condition: he was to be accompanied by Daisy at all times.

"You know we're going to be gone for a while? Most of that time spent in deep space in cramped quarters?" he asked. For a moment, he thought maybe she would back out, but her smile grew even larger.

"I spent most of my life on freighters, sir. My parents traded between the Alliance and Consortium twice a year. My employers knew what they were doing when they hired me. I have enough knowledge of the subject to prove useful to you and I'm familiar with Zuckabar. Not to mention, I'm a friendly face. Don't worry, sir, you're in good hands. I'll take care of everything so you can focus on your research," she said with a smile.

She was certainly chipper. An optimist to keep him company wasn't a bad idea. Not to mention, nothing made an old man feel young like a beautiful girl at his side. He sighed. Those days were long past, but the reminder would be nice. Not that she would think of him that way, nor would he ever try anything. It would just be nice to have her along.

Yes, this was going to be the best year of his life.

The aircar swooped out of the sky and came to hover next to them. Iker picked up his bag and loaded it in the trunk with a smile, daydreaming about how the future of the galaxy was about to change.

CHAPTER SEVEN

J acob finished packing his things. For comfort, he'd spent the trip in civilian clothes. It was time to put them aside and don his uniform. He leaned toward wearing the white and gold dress uniform he brought with him, however, it wasn't comfortable or practical. The odds of him reaching his new assignment with it still clean were zero-to-none. A standard Navy officer's work uniform would do.

A high-collared black sweater held his rank insignia in gold on his epaulets, along with his name and service on his chest. Under that, he wore a white turtleneck, black cargo trousers, and service boots to finish it off. He stopped as he slid the pants on, the blood-red stripe on the outside of his right leg reminding him of all that he had lost—and all he hoped to earn back.

Once he was dressed, he dropped his two bags by the gangplank and headed up to the bridge. Landing on a new planet was a once in a long while opportunity he didn't want to miss.

Nadia swiveled around in her chair to look him up and down as he entered. "The prodigal son returns," she said.

Aside from several enjoyable evenings with the dark-haired

captain, he'd spent most of the past eight days in his quarters. There was a lot of reading on Zuckabar with its five-hundred-year history.

Not to mention learning about Commodore Xin's mission. While his orders hadn't specified who he would be reporting to, which in and of itself was extremely odd, there really was only one option.

Four destroyers made up Commodore Xin's picket. As a senior grade lieutenant, he could be assigned to any of them—in Ops or Engineering or maybe even astrogation.

That was unless they were opening a permanent ground station on Zuckabar Central, but he didn't think that was likely given the location and population. Technically, the Navy were guests of the local government. No permanent installations were allowed, other than a barracks and garage for visiting ships.

He did feel bad about spending most of his time alone, especially with the very pretty captain who, at the very least, didn't mind talking to him. Which was more than he could say about anyone else the last few years. It was a nice change of pace, and he found himself wishing he could stay on her ship longer.

"Permission to enter the bridge?" he asked as he stepped on.

"Denied," she said with a stern expression. He went stiff, thinking her serious. After a moment, her face split into a full-lipped smile and she waved him in.

Dagger's bridge was the opposite of *Orion*'s—or any of the other ships he'd served on. Spacious was the word that came to mind. Civilian ships didn't follow the same restrictions naval vessels did, and when they designed the little freighter, they made sure to capitalize on that freedom.

"We're approaching Zuck Central. I thought you'd like to look," she said. He came to stand next to her, admiring the wide-angle screen dominating the front of her bridge. It was a truly impressive picture. Navy ships relied on many smaller screens for important information; the main viewer was often for communications or briefings.

Zuckabar Central dominated the viewer. They approached at an angle; he could make out the blue haze of atmosphere, but that was all he saw. The planet itself was engulfed by a massive storm, which, if the papers he read were to be believed, never ended.

The *Dagger* was currently decelerating toward the planet at twenty-five gravities. A leisurely pace that would put minimal pressure on the gravcoil. The mild gravity wake spreading out behind her wasn't nearly enough to disturb traffic farther than a thousand klicks in any direction.

"You're quite the ship handler," he said as a compliment. Too many small ships blazed into orbit at max deceleration to save time, regardless of the effects on other shipping. The larger the mass of the ship, the stronger and more pervasive the gravity wake, but even a small ship like the *Dagger* could put out a seriously disruptive gravwake at close range.

"Do unto others," she said. "We're ten minutes from orbit. After that, it's a matter of waiting for Zuck Central to give us clearance to land at Moscow Harbor." She pointed at the bank of monitors showing different ships in orbit. "Looks like traffic is light."

It was a complicated affair and he didn't want to interfere with her expert handling, but there were dozens of ships out there and none of them were Navy.

"Where is the flotilla parked?" he asked. He'd looked at the helm's plot but didn't see any USN ship codes.

She turned to him, raising an eyebrow. "They're not here," she said.

He blinked a couple of times as he processed what she said.

While his orders hadn't specified an assignment, it would have to be with the flotilla of destroyers, wouldn't it?

"Then why am I here?" he asked.

"I don't know what to tell you. We passed the flotilla when we went through Novastad. They're not due to rotate back here for months," she said with a shrug.

"Skip, incoming from Zuck Central," her comms officer said. Nadia motioned to her ear and the man sent the message directly to her.

"Requesting orbital insertion vector zero-five-five," she responded to whatever they had said.

Jacob tuned her out, letting her attend to the job of running her ship. He had more pressing concerns. His orders had told him to report to Zuckabar for reassignment, and he assumed it meant with the flotilla of destroyers patrolling the Protectorate. If they weren't in Zuckabar, though, why was he?

As if on cue, his NavPad beeped as a new message arrived. He fished it out of his cargo pocket and pressed his thumb on the reader. The shrill of bosun's pipes played as his orders appeared on the little screen.

Lieutenant (SG) Jacob T. Grimm, you are directed and ordered to report to the USS Interceptor, Hull Number DD 1071 to assume command of said ship. You are frocked to Lieutenant Commander upon taking command. Commission letter will follow.
-Fleet Admiral Noelle Villanueva and NAVPERS

It took a few moments to process the words on the screen. He stood in shock, staring at the NavPad like it was a snake.

He was only a senior grade lieutenant. A destroyer command was a lieutenant commander's billet. There had to be a mistake? If he'd been promoted, surely Commander Albrecht would have informed him.

This had to be a mix-up. They meant report to the commander of *Interceptor* and somehow the wires were crossed. There was no way he was commanding a ship.

Not that he could think of a single instance where someone was given command by accident. There were too many checks and balances, from the promotion board to NAVPERS. Too many eyes had to sign off on these kinds of orders for an accident to happen.

Even if it was a mistake, he was obligated to carry out his orders as he understood them, personal feelings be damned. Fear gripped his heart—the same fear he'd felt during three days of brutal interrogation after Pascal. Was this a trick? A test? Could he command a ship knowing what might happen?

First things first, he needed to know if the ship was even here. If it was a mistake, then it was likely she wasn't.

Jacob tapped Nadia's shoulder, discreetly getting her attention.

"Nadia, can you locate the *Interceptor* in orbit?" he asked. To his ears, his voice sounded calm, unnaturally so.

She raised an eyebrow, picking up on his sudden stiffness before she nodded and pointed at the screen located on her chair.

"Pete, scan orbit for any NavyTrans and put it on my station."

The man hunched over his station and filtered through several different batches of ship codes before finally shaking his head.

"I don't see any," Pete said.

Jacob sighed inwardly with relief, careful to keep his emotions from showing. But, for a tiny moment, his relief was bracketed with regret. A part of him desperately wanted to feel the deck under his feet again and serve aboard ship. Despite the fear, he yearned for the bittersweet responsibility and authority of command.

Nadia pushed herself up and walked over to Pete's station, leaning over to fiddle with the controls.

"I'm not blind, Skip," he said, annoyed at her intrusion into *his* domain.

"I didn't think you were," she replied. "I had a hunch and wanted to see if I was right before asking you to look," she said, clipping him on the back of the head. He winced, but not from pain.

"It's not in orbit, per se," she said before sauntering back to her chair. "It's parked outside Kremlin Station. Main screen," she ordered.

Jacob's relief vanished.

The view of the planet and space behind it wavered and disappeared, replaced by the massive Kremlin Station, a spinning cylinder in space. It dwarfed *Bethesda* in size. Eight kilometers long, it was easily big enough to repair any ship in the fleet, including a battleship. Large bay doors allowed ships to enter one end of the cylinder and exit the other. The exact middle of the station had a zero-g pocket, while the spin would give those living inside an approximation of gravity.

However, it was civilian-owned and was mostly used to maintain the massive freighters that frequented the system. It also supported the infrastructure for the system's workforce, many of whom were Alliance citizens who mined the mineral-rich asteroid belts common in Zuckabar.

Kremlin Station hovered in the Lagrange point opposite the

planet, 1.5 million kilometers out, using the planet's strong magnetic field as a shield from the system's deadly binary stars.

Like a tiny pinprick of light, *Interceptor*'s transponder blinked next to the station. Nadia manipulated the controls on the arm of her chair and zoomed in until a ship filled the screen.

"What a wreck," Pete muttered. Jacob stifled a retort. He wanted to defend his Navy, especially from civilians who disparaged it. However, the man wasn't wrong. Pits and scars from a long time in service were obvious, even from this distance. The hull code was barely visible, faded from years of neglect. The ship was old enough that it took Jacob a solid thirty seconds to identify the class.

Nadia beat him to it. "Is that a Hellcat?" she asked, letting out a low whistle. "I don't think I've ever seen one."

"I didn't know any were still in service," he said. His NavPad beeped, updating him with his ship's information via a small icon on the top of his screen. He pressed it to see what he was in for.

It wasn't pretty.

The NavPad only gave him an overview of the situation. *Interceptor*'s normal compliment of a 136 crew was considerably short. Her main drive status was listed as "inoperable."

Just when he thought it couldn't get worse, he saw the dates, blinked, and made himself re-read them. He looked up at the ship, Nadia, then his pad. There was no way he was reading it right.

"Nadia," he said, showing her the screen.

She glanced at it, then up at him and cocked her head to the side, raising one eyebrow. "Unlucky," she said.

Three months. That was how long *Interceptor* had stayed parked in orbit around Kremlin, with no drive and no mission.

He groaned inwardly. Nothing good came of a ship sitting for so long. Spacing was a hard job, made harder when not on a mission or in a home port. Crew morale had to suck. What captain would allow his ship to sit stagnant for three months?

"Well," Nadia said with a grin, "she's got character." Nadia pulled his attention back to the main screen.

From what he could see, character was all she had. "That's one way to put it," he replied.

Giving a junior officer who was on the fast track to captain command of a ship wasn't unheard of. But... he wasn't on the fast track. Not even close.

Nothing about the situation made sense to him. He'd applied for command school, and while his previous CO hadn't said so, clearly they had turned him down. Otherwise, he would be there instead of in *Zuckabar*.

He shook himself and kicked his own butt in gear. No matter the situation, he had a job to do. His mom had taught him an important lesson the last time he had seen her: Duty first, feelings second.

Mentally, he started running through all the things he would have to do. Every class he'd ever attended, every paper he'd ever read about command flipped through his mind like a film.

"Can you take me right to her?" he asked.

Nadia gave him a sympathetic smile. "Sorry, we're only cleared to land at Zuck Central, the big white ball of snow you see on the main viewer. You can probably contact her from there and have your Corsair pilot come get you," she said.

The ship shook as she passed through the gravity wake of an outgoing M-class hauler accelerating at ten gravities. He reached up and took hold of the grab bar as his boots automatically sealed him to the deck.

"Okay, landing stations, everyone," Nadia said as she slipped into her chair and activated her grav-harness. "Let's see what Zuck has to offer us."

CHAPTER EIGHT

Lieutenant (SG) Kimiko Yuki sat in the center seat of *Interceptor*'s bridge. It was another day blending into one long mass of days that seemed like they were never going to end.

For three months, *Interceptor* had sat without her gravcoil. A useless hunk of iron orbiting an even larger hunk of iron. No mission, no future. Honestly, Yuki kept waiting for a barge to show up and haul the hunk of junk she "commanded" to the breakers.

Not exactly how she envisioned her first command.

Without *Interceptor*'s primary gravcoil, the best the ship could do was coast around on thrusters alone, moving at a few meters per second, barely more than a slow crawl, useful for docking but not much else. The secondary gravcoil was enough to keep the artificial gravity running and not a lot else. They were a glorified space reef at the moment. A vacuum barnacle stuck on the side of Kremlin Station.

Every time she requested an update on the repairs, the maintenance facility gave her the runaround, claiming she didn't have the authority to request the information. She suspected, but couldn't prove, they were stalling to milk the Navy for money.

It wasn't like they had to answer to a lowly lieutenant. They could wait until Commodore Xin returned and then expedite the repair, all the while billing the USN for their time and effort.

Kremlin Station was the only place she could go. Fort Kirk was the closest actual Alliance military facility, and there were four starlanes between her and them. Again, no gravcoil meant no FTL travel, no way to cross even one starlane.

It left one Lieutenant (SG) Yuki, formally the executive officer, current acting CO of the USS *Interceptor*, twiddling her thumbs while the ship's morale plummeted.

Half the crew was on extended leave on the surface of Zuckabar, doing who knew what. The place was barely better than a frontier planet, with gambling and other vices readily available.

She'd fought. Hell, she'd fought the ever-worsening morale tooth and nail... for about a week. Then she washed her hands of it.

"Lieutenant?" Ensign Hössbacher said from the comms station. He glanced between her and his comms panel with quick, jerky movements.

"Yes?" she asked, unsuccessfully hiding her annoyance with the junior officer. She couldn't even sulk in peace.

"I have an urgent message, flagged for Commander Cole's eyes only?" he informed her.

Yuki let out a sharp laugh. Leave it to the Navy to issue orders to a dead man. Commander Cole died from a heart attack right after the station techs upgraded their computers and removed the gravcoil. It was like he knew what was coming and took the only way out.

"Right, transfer it over," she said.

Without permanent orders, she was limited in what she had access to. Three months was more than enough time for the

Admiralty to receive her report and issue orders. It looked like they finally got around to it.

Pressing the authorization on the command chair, she held her thumb over the reader until the computer was satisfied. The multifunction display flashed to life.

Commander Cole, you stand relieved. Please report with all haste to Zuckabar Central. Return to Alexandria for new assignment.

-NAVPERS

"What the actual fu—" She caught herself. The Navy's new regs about officer behavior were tightly enforced. Tightly. She glanced around, making sure none of the ratings manning the other stations had heard her slip.

Could this mean they were going to depart this hell hole of a system? Excitement swelled in her. She sat up a little straighter, breathed a little harder. Back to the real Navy, no more babysitting.

"Ma'am, another message is coming in; this one's for you," Hössbacher said. The young ensign was fresh off his midship cruise and nervous as hell. She wished he would calm down.

"Did a packet arrive in-system?" she asked.

While the space-going people of the 30th century had FTL engines via gravcoil, there was no FTL communication. Packets arrived every few days, either from a courier ship or delivered via standard traffic, paid for by the Navy. Any ship could carry a packet in their comms array and transmit it upon arrival. Since radio communications powered by a fusion plant traveled at the speed of light, a packet would arrive hours before the ship that carried them.

"Not that I'm aware, ma'am. There's a lot of traffic in-system, though. If it was transmitted upon arrival, uh..." Ensign Hössbacher fumbled over the math for a moment.

Yuki tapped her fingers in annoyance. Zuckabar's primary star, a white dwarf orbiting a pulsar, made the gravitational computations tricky. Usually, ships entering a system transitioned from the starlanes well outside the limit of six billion kilometers. Some pilots liked to shave hours off their time and would run closer, but it wasn't always safe. Especially not in Zuckabar, with its funky binary stars.

"Maybe seven hours ago?" he finally said while looking at his computer.

"Maybe? Can you find out which ship transmitted it, please... *after* sending the message to my station?" she asked. She didn't bother hiding her annoyance that time. "And for the record, *Ensign,* don't ever answer a direct question with 'maybe' ever again. Got it?"

Hössbacher flushed, his ears burning red.

"A—aye, ma'am. Sorry, ma'am."

She shouldn't be so hard on the kid, but months of frustration and anger were getting the better of her. If the next message was them getting the hell out of Zuck, she would apologize to the kid.

The message appeared on the MFD attached to the right of the center seat.

Lieutenant Yuki, you are directed to welcome Lieutenant Commander (frocked) Jacob T. Grimm. He will assume command of DD 1071 as of arrival. Please show him all respect and deference due a commander of the United Systems Alliance Navy. Thank you for your service as acting commander. It will be noted in your jacket.

-Office of Fleet Admiral Villanueva and
NAVPERS

Yuki pushed back on her chair arms as if she could retreat from the message. She blinked several times, trying to sort out what it meant.

When it hit, she let out a long, silent curse.

Why in the actual hell would high-command frock some random officer when they could have just given her the authority to take command? It wasn't like they were going to do anything other than drive the ship to the nearest breaker. How hard could it be?

Then something tickled her memory. The officer's name... She switched screens and did a quick search. Two results popped up in the *Navy Times*. The most recent was from two years before.

"Ma'am, I found the ship and you're not going to like it," Hössbacher said.

Yuki glanced up from the screen and glared at the ensign. She hunched her shoulders as if to say, "Well?"

"Sorry, ma'am. It was transmitted by the CSV *Dagger*," he said as he pulled up the plot. Her screen updated and showed the ship inserting into an orbit that would lead to it landing on the planet in the next hour.

"You've got to be kidding me... They didn't transmit when they came in-system? They waited until they were here to send the message?"

Oh hell. She had to recall the crew and a dozen other things before the new *captain* came aboard.

"Comms, get me Chief Boudreaux, ASAP," she said. "Right now!"

A few seconds later, the bridge's speaker crackled to life. Yuki heard the horn-heavy music that was popular on the planet, which meant her Corsair pilot was in a club. She begged her ancestors that the woman wasn't drunk.

"Boudreaux here," said the French-accented pilot.

"Chief, I need you to get to Zuck spaceport, ASAFP," Yuki said. She gripped the arms of the chair so hard, her knuckles turned white.

"What for?" Boudreaux asked.

Yuki ignored the informality of the question. Too much time had gone by with the crew being lazy. She couldn't suddenly jump on them when she had already de facto given up her authority.

"We received orders for a new CO whose ship is angling for approach on the planet right damn now. If you hurry, you might just be there when he disembarks," she said.

"Mon Dieu. Aye, on the way. Boudreaux out." The comm crackled and died.

Yuki sank down into her chair. She was screwed. Any commander worth his salt was going to take one look at the travesty of her command and lay it all at her feet. No one was going to stick their neck out for her. No one.

"What do you want to do, ma'am?" Hössbacher asked.

Do? There wasn't anything to do. She could blame everyone else and hope the new skipper was eager to spread it around or throw herself at his mercy. Either way sounded bad to her. The officers she'd served under since she left her midship cruise hadn't instilled her with confidence. Where was the Navy her father talked about? The one that cared about *duty, honor, courage*? If it ever existed, it was ancient history.

An idea hit her, one so simple, it might just work. If only there was someone who could take the blame and not be hurt by the last three months?

Like a deceased former commander?

It would take some planning. In the meantime, she pulled up the crew screen, swiped over to the recall button, and held it down until it flashed red. Within seconds, every NavPad on every member of her crew would scream at them until they returned to the Navy barracks on-station. There was no chance of getting them back on board before the new CO arrived, but she could show him the last-minute messages and that should clear her.

She let out a breath. Until she met her new CO, there wasn't much else to do. Other than clean the ever-living crap out of every rusty surface *Interceptor* had.

CHAPTER NINE

Jacob watched the last of the other passengers disembark before him. He tarried at the top next to Nadia, not wanting to hurry.

"Time to go," she whispered. She hooked her arm in his and led him down the gangplank.

The first thing Jacob noticed upon stepping off the ship was the smell. Second was the sub-zero temperature threatening to freeze him where he stood. The heating circuits in his uniform immediately went into overdrive trying to protect him, but it was a losing battle.

The smell, though, was like eggs left out on the counter for a decade.

Nadia laughed as he crinkled his nose and tried to cover his mouth with the sleeve of his coat.

She casually lifted a scarf from around her neck to her face. It sealed to her and he caught sight of the nano-tech re-breather going to work, filtering out any harmful particulates in the air, along with keeping her face warm. She also wore a slim blue parka with a frilly fur hood with the same tech as his uniform, but hers was far more heavy duty than his.

"I don't suppose you have another one of those?" he asked, nodding at the scarf as he set his bags down. She shook her head.

"I had to special order it last time I was on Alexandria. It cost me a thousand bucks." She pointed to the starport entrance two hundred meters away. "The air inside is filtered. They don't get out all the sulfur, but a good portion of it. Not to mention they have fusion batteries to run the heaters. It's nice and cozy."

"It's in my mouth, ugh. I'm going to smell this for a week," he said.

"A week, hell, try a month." She ran a hand over the length of her scarf. "Worth every penny."

She lingered silently while he examined the horizon. The sky was white, with only a few hundred meters of visibility. In fact, everything was covered in dirty brown snow and ice, with splashes of yellow, most likely from the aforementioned sulfur.

The Navy's definition of habitable wasn't the same as his. He wouldn't live on Zuckabar for all the money in the galaxy.

He turned to the charming freighter skipper and gave her his best rakish smile.

"You coming back this way any time soon?" he asked.

He couldn't see her mouth because of the scarf, but her eyes sparkled. She shifted her weight, resting her hand on the anachronistic slug-thrower slung on her thigh.

"Ahh, Lieutenant, are you asking me out on a date?" she asked.

He coughed, bringing a hand up to run through his hair before replacing his watch cap.

"Yes, ma'am, I am." He smiled back at her, hardly noticing the cold for a moment as his heart thumped in his chest.

She inched closer to him, placing one hand on his chest.

"Well, then the good news is, I'm not going anywhere. I'm

spending the next six months in-system on a science expedition. Dinner?"

Her sudden question caught him off guard, even though he'd asked. "Yes," he said with clarity and confidence he didn't quite feel.

"Your place or mine?" she asked. Her soft brown eyes drew him in, moving him ever so closer to her.

He chuckled. "Considering the shape my new command is in, I'm thinking yours."

She reached up with one hand and slid the scarf down from her mouth.

"You never know, she might surprise you." Nadia leaned into him, and Jacob bent over slightly. She placed her lips lightly on his cheek. "See you around the galaxy, spacer."

He watched her dance up the gangplank. With a quick twist, she blew him a kiss. A second later, she disappeared behind the closing hatch.

"I can't wait," he whispered. He'd never met anyone like her, so confident, yet casually flirtatious. Aboard ship, it was hard to find someone to spend time with, since dating inside the chain of command was forbidden. Part of the life of a spacer was either marrying, then leaving her or him alone for months or even years at a time, or staying single.

Dating and women were the last thing on his mind for the last few years. Part of him had slept through it; a part that was suddenly very much awake and desired to see the beautiful space captain again. He frowned, suddenly filled with regret at not spending more time with her when he had the chance.

Jacob took a deep breath of the putrid air and let it out. With it, he sent all his emotional baggage. It was time to compartmentalize.

The spaceport was situated on a hill, overlooking what passed for a city. However, with atmospheric conditions as they were, he couldn't see much farther than the cluster of low buildings. Even with all his gear, the cold was getting to him. Not to mention the 1.1g's that made everything, including his own body, heavier.

He felt like he was hacking up a lung by the time he made it to the airlock entrance. People walked by with scarf-covered faces, clearly more prepared than he was. It took him a few minutes to hack his lungs out.

Once he could breathe again, he found one of the many public heating stations and thawed himself out.

As the heater worked its magic, he organized the tasks before him, laying them out one by one and *seeing* them in his mind. He might not have attended command school, but he was an officer of the United Systems Alliance Navy. In his time in service, he'd served on five ships: corvettes, destroyers, UnReps, a light cruiser, and a tour of duty in the backseat of a Corsair. He knew *how* command worked, and he knew what made a good commander.

Of course, *knowing* and *doing* were two entirely different things. Which was probably what command school was for.

First things first, he needed to get to the ship in order to access the crew and ship files. Normally, an incoming commander would be sent all records long before he took command. However, the Navy, in their infinite wisdom, had chosen to forgo that custom by notifying him of his command upon arrival.

What if they hadn't notified the CO? That thought terrified him. If his predecessor was well-liked, then it would make the transition with the crew even more difficult. Instead of a new CO, he would be seen as replacing a beloved commander. It was a lot for him to take in. He distracted himself by looking around.

The terminal handled more than just the spaceport. As Jacob watched, aircars came and went, along with shuttles both up to orbit and around the icy planet. There was more than one crew of miners heading off to work and coming back.

Jacob grunted, shifting the weight of his bags. He was already tiring under the increased gravity. Rationally, he knew it was only a ten percent increase, but it felt like so much more.

"Okay, Jacob, now what?" he muttered to himself. There was no "you are here" map for the terminal. He checked his NavPad, but it didn't offer any help either.

"Commander Grimm?" a lyrical accented soprano asked.

He turned around to see a petite woman with dark hair, skin, and eyes, wearing a swishy dress under a stylish pink parka. Hi-tech leggings protected her lower half, and a watch cap, not unlike his but far more stylish, covered her head and ears—though plenty of her silky black hair came out from under. She was short, only coming up to his chest.

"Not yet," he said as he walked toward her.

She threw him a lazy salute, ignoring that they were indoors and she was out of uniform.

"Chief Warrant Officer Boudreaux. I'm your Corsair aviator. It's good to see you, sir. We'd given up hope of getting a new CO."

He didn't return the salute, but instead offered his hand. She smiled and took it.

"Good to meet you, Chief. Where are we going?"

"The Mudcat is outside, this way." She pointed toward a far door and started walking.

It only took a minute to reach the exit. As they left the terminal, she pulled a scarf up around her mouth and nose. The public database on Zuckabar notably left information about the horrendous smell absent—almost like they wanted to trick people into coming, and they knew no one would if the smell was public knowledge.

She pointed at the Mudcat, though she hardly needed to.

The military vehicle was massive, with its six-wheeled independent axle, slanted armor, and tires almost as tall as him. It had room for eight personnel or six armored Marines. Regardless of the terrain—mud, snow, forest, or swamp—it would do the job. Which was great, since it constantly snowed on Zuckabar Central.

She held her hand out, activating the rear door. Jacob tossed his bags in the back and climbed into the front passenger seat. The interior was immaculate, which surprised him. Based on the exterior of the *Interceptor*, he expected a mess.

Chief Boudreaux climbed into the driver seat, which automatically adjusted until she was pressed up against the controls, looking over the steering wheel like a child driving her parent's car. The fusion battery-powered engine hummed to life. Between the battery and its own atmospheric generator, the Mudcat could operate independently for an extended period. Something Jacob was infinitely grateful for since the filtered air *didn't* smell of rotten eggs. After a few minutes of driving, the obnoxious sulfur smell was gone and the cabin was warm enough that his jacket stopped trying to cook him.

He held his hands over the heater vents, luxuriating in feeling them again. "Where are we heading, Chief?" he asked.

"The bird is parked at the barracks. We have our own landing pad on the outskirts of the city," she said without taking her eyes off the road.

The Mudcat's weight would imply it wasn't maneuverable, but no one had told Chief Boudreaux that. She tore through the city's traffic, barreling around corners with the sound of tortured wheels and controlled fishtails. The vehicle gripped the ice- and snow-covered roads like it was on rails. Jacob found himself hanging on to the grab bar.

"Pilots," he muttered.

"Aviators," she countered with a grin.

They drove in silence for a few more minutes when Jacob noticed one of several scarf vendors he had seen dotting the town. They appeared to be normal, or perhaps materially enhanced scarfs, not the kind Nadia had. He noted the vendor's location and made a mental reminder to visit her, or one like it if he was coming back.

After a few moments, he started to relax and decided to go over what little he had on his NavPad one more time. There was no such thing as too prepared.

"Chief, what's the status on the boat?" he asked.

"Dead in the water, sir," she said. "Literally. No gravcoil." She took another turn, sliding the Mudcat around a bend then back out on a familiar-looking street.

Was it him, or was the scarf vendor they were passing the same one he'd seen a few minutes before? He made sure to remember the color of her parka as they continued on.

He pretended to be engrossed in his NavPad but really kept one eye on the road.

Sure enough, Boudreaux made two left turns, a right turn, three more lefts, and then they drove right back by the woman selling scarfs. It was snowy and windy outside and she probably figured since he didn't know his way around, he wouldn't notice. She was stalling, giving her shipmates time to make things right.

"Chief?" he asked without looking up from his NavPad.

"Yes, sir?" she asked innocently.

Jacob could appreciate the esprit de corps she showed, covering for her shipmates, buying them time while driving the new captain around. It was a risk; she didn't know him, he could easily be resentful of her playing him. However, warrant officers were an odd bunch and aviators were the oddest of them all. He decided to let her off the hook.

"I appreciate what you're doing, and I even admire it. Let's just say that until I take command, I see nothing, okay?" he asked.

She grinned, turning the Mudcat hard to the right and down an alley. "Roger that, sir!"

"Feel free to spread that around. In fact, I'd appreciate it if you did," he told her.

She didn't answer but slid the Mudcat to a stop outside a squat concrete building with three stories. Flecks of blue and gold paint streaked around the building's corners, signaling that it had at one time been a color other than gray. Its windows were so scratched from the constant blowing snow and ice that they were opaque. Snow piled up around the outside and at least a foot on the roof.

The Mudcat's doors hummed as the hydraulics slid them open. He hopped out, struggling against the severe wind as his feet hit the ice-covered road.

Boudreaux reached around the back and pulled out his bag and guitar, setting them down in the snow before sliding out and triggering the computer to shut the doors. Grimm made his way around the front, using one hand as a guide on the truck and the other to shield his face from the constant gale. He retrieved his bags and hefted them over his shoulder.

"Does this wind ever die down?" he asked as he trekked across the front of the Mudcat to the nominal gate of the barracks property.

"Nope. Our science geeks argue about why, but they generally agree it has to do with the high-density core and the constant bombardment of the pulsar... or something," she said, waving her hand in the air as if it meant nothing. "Not to mention the giant terraforming fusion reactors at the poles, spewing water vapor high into the atmosphere to trap heat," she said.

"This is *with* trapped heat?" His face was already so cold, he couldn't feel his nose.

"Yes, sir. They tell me it raises anywhere from a quarter to one-half degree every year. They've been at it for three hundred years, so you can imagine how cold it used to be." She had to shout to be heard over the roaring gale.

After four meters of walking, his face felt like it was going to fall off. Even his nanite-powered uniform struggled just to keep him from freezing. He couldn't imagine it being colder.

Boudreaux led him up a set of small stairs to the front door. Her hand swiped past the sensor and the doors slid apart.

Jacob thought the smell of sulfur was bad, but the B.O. wafting out of the barracks made him want to go back out.

The main room was small, only big enough for the CQ desk and a couch. Takeout boxes, discarded clothing, and empty cans of alcohol littered the floor.

He wrinkled his nose in distaste as they passed through the barracks. The condition of the place showed a serious lack of discipline.

At the end of the long hall in front of him, a blue light blinked, letting him know the Corsair was on station.

Boudreaux gave him an apologetic smile as she led him through the piles of filth to the main hallway and toward the landing pad.

They passed one junction, and it was as if it had a force field defending the hall. There was an actual line where the cleanliness started. There were six doors and he imagined each one of those rooms was just as clean.

"Let me guess... Marine country?" he asked the chief.

"Yes, sir. They don't seem to have an 'off' switch," she said. "Are you still sure about your statement, sir?"

Was he? He had to be. If the crew worried about covering their butts, they would never give him their best.

"Yes, Chief. One hundred percent." He sounded much more confident than he felt. What the hell was the admiralty thinking, putting him in charge of a ship this bad off?

The back door led to the Corsair landing pad behind the building. The door was sturdy, with a push bar for opening.

Jacob put his back to the door and heaved. He dreaded going back out into the cold, but the sooner they were off this rock, the sooner he could never come back. The wind caught the door and slammed it open.

"The worse it is, the more it's true, Chief. Otherwise, I'll never accomplish anything," he said as they trudged out, one hand braced against the wind. "Get the Corsair ready. I want lift-off ASAP."

She grinned as she walked by him, putting a shoulder to the wind. "Aye, aye," she said.

He followed her onto the landing platform, letting out a low whistle. As the deck officer on *Bethesda*, he'd seen a number of them, all outfitted for whatever mission they were on.

Her Corsair, while covered in ice and a layer of snow, looked in great shape. Its spread wings, twin tails, and nose-mounted 10mm chain-coilgun gave it a mean look—as if it were tensing to leap in the air at any moment. They were the Navy's workhorse, but where they shined was in close air support.

Then he caught sight of the mass of bodies lined up to board.

Off to the left, standing in a line next to the wall, partially shielded by the elevated landing pad, was a good portion of the crew, all huddled together for warmth, trying to disappear in their parkas. At least fifty of them... which was half the ship's complement.

That couldn't be right? Half—no, more than half the crew huddled against the wall waiting to board. The idea of leaving so few spacers, not to mention officers and PO's, aboard a ship of war was beyond the pale.

Still, he meant what he said.

Boudreaux made it to the nose of the ship and depressed the exterior panel, lowering a ladder so she could climb up to the cockpit.

For the moment, Jacob ignored the crew. The side doors were already slowly sliding open and he half jogged to the ship and tossed his bag and instrument inside.

He was pleased with the interior shape of the small ship, nodding to himself with satisfaction. Corsairs were fast, maneuverable, and a joy to ride in. It was one of the things the Navy had done right in the last ten years. However, that wasn't what pleased him. It was clean. And that said more about Chief Boudreaux than anything else. She took care of her craft.

"Okay," he said loud enough to be heard over the wind. "Is the bosun here?"

The host of ratings shook their heads and then Jacob noticed two people standing near the front. An older man with a pronounced bald spot and a younger man with his hands deep in his pockets and his face downcast.

"Any officers, please board the Corsair. We're dusting off as soon as the chief is ready," he yelled to be heard over the roar of the rising engine noise.

The two men stepped forward heading for the Corsair. They didn't meet his eyes as they passed.

Once they were on board, he turned back to the assorted spacers. None of them were in uniform, which didn't help. He'd have to trust them for the moment.

"Who's the highest-ranking spacer here?"

A woman with long, jet-black hair and dark brown skin stepped forward. "I am, sir. Chief Petty Officer Suresh," she said.

He stepped forward and held out his hand and was pleasantly surprised when she took it.

"Chief, listen. Whatever happened before I take command doesn't matter. I don't care. Got it?" he told her.

The vaguely worried expression on her face turned immediately to a stilted uncertain grin. "Sir?" she asked as if she couldn't believe her ears.

He glanced down at his NavPad and punched in her name. Sure enough, it came back with her as the highest-ranking NCO on the ship.

"As of this moment, you're the COB, got it?" It was within the captain's purview to select a Chief of the Boat. Not all captains did. It was a tradition Jacob liked, and it represented the captain's trust in his noncoms.

"Got it," she said.

"Good. Get this place cleaned up. Once I'm on the ship, I'll send Boudreaux back with the Corsair. Don't leave anything behind—we're not coming back any time soon."

"Aye, aye, sir." Suresh snapped to attention and threw him a textbook salute.

Jacob returned the salute, turned, and climbed into the Corsair. He had to cover his ears as the air-breathing plasma engines ignited with a howl that deafened the area and immediately vaporized the accumulated snow behind and under the dropship.

Once in, he punched the acknowledgment button by the side hatch to let Boudreaux know everyone was on board.

He didn't take his seat. Instead, he held on to the grab bar, watching the COB ordering the spacers back into the barracks.

The engine noise turned to thunder, and the ship shook and lifted straight up for fifty feet, pivoting away until he could no longer see the barracks. The nose dipped forward as the engines rotated with a clunk that vibrated the ship. He thumbed the switch closing the hatch and made his way up to the cockpit.

Corsairs had many roles in the Navy. They were versatile. Capable of being outfitted with a crew of four—pilot, co-pilot, and two electronics specialists to operate the EW suits. The cockpit was elevated above the passenger compartment and could be reached by an internal ladder.

At the base of the short ladder, Jacob yelled up to Boudreaux. "Permission to take the second seat?" he asked.

"Granted," Boudreaux said with a grin. He climbed into the rear seat and strapped into the five-point safety harness. Once he was secure, he slipped on the headset so he could hear Boudreaux and any radio traffic.

"Zebra Tower, this is Charlie-One-One, permission to break orbit?" Boudreaux asked the ground station.

"Charlie-One-One, this is Zebra Tower, you have permission on departure lane seven-three. Please proceed and mind the wind. It's fierce today," the voice on the other end responded clearly.

While they ascended, Jacob pulled out his NavPad and flicked over to the screen of the *Interceptor*. He wouldn't have access to the ship's private information until he was actually in command, which, despite having his orders, he wasn't. The Navy ran a certain way, and despite the current SNAFU, he didn't expect it to affect how everything else was done.

He would have watched the ascent—it was exactly the sort of thing he loved—but Zuckabar was strictly instrument flight reckoning. There was nothing to see but white snow and hail, punctuated by the occasional sudden turbulence. The rhythmic noise of the ice pellets bouncing off the ship was almost a lullaby.

"Chief, who are the two officers who came up with us?" he asked her through the internal comms.

"The bald one is Commander Rod Beckett, our chief engineer. The other is Lieutenant Commander Stanislaw, our ship's surgeon," she said.

She had a slight tick when she said the surgeon's name. Maybe he imagined it, but she didn't seem to like him.

He searched the controls for a moment until he found the internal cameras and flipped them on. Commander Beckett was asleep, eyes closed as the ship shook him back and forth in his acceleration chair. Commander Stanislaw had a bag over his face and was heaving into it.

Not a good sign, but then again, nothing on this assignment was turning out as he expected. He was still reeling from the sudden knowledge of command.

He was going to need every officer's full support to turn things around. Commander Beckett was the senior officer on board, both with time-in-service and in grade. His help would prove invaluable except... Why was a full commander, a man with Beckett's record, serving aboard a destroyer? Was he a burnout? Maybe he liked a challenge? Jacob made a note to ask him.

"Plasma turbines to gravcoil transition coming up," came Bordeaux's voice over the headset.

Jacob focused on the horizon. While he was thinking, the chief had taken the Corsair up into space and was about to kick them all in the guts.

On a bigger ship, there was a large primary gravcoil and a smaller secondary one. They would *fight* each other to provide both propulsion and gravity for the crew. The math was far too complex for him, but it was why the crew could *feel it* when ships turned and they were forced to lean to stay upright. Like the surface navies of ancient history, everything that wasn't bolted down could be thrown across the ship.

The plasma engines worked fine in the atmosphere, all the way to the edge of space, then the gravcoil took over.

The Corsair had no secondary gravcoil to provide artificial gravity. They had to rely on much older technology to relieve the g-forces applied to the crew. Older tech that wasn't nearly as efficient or as effective as a secondary gravcoil.

"Ready, sir?" she asked.

Her hand hovered over the big red switch. Jacob leaned back, breathed in and out deeply, then gave her the go-ahead.

"Punch it," he said.

The Corsair shuddered as the plasma engines tucked into the hull along with the wings, which were only necessary in atmosphere. The twin tails folded down and presented a much sleeker little craft. There wasn't a lot of space aboard a destroyer, and every inch that could shrink did. When it was all done, even though they had the Mudcat tucked underneath the tail for transport, the Corsair would fit neatly into the rear boat bay of the *Interceptor*.

"Here we go," she said, and hit the button.

CHAPTER TEN

After the minute and a half of grunting pain, the Corsair coasted the rest of the way until turn over. Jacob had a few more minutes to read up on his ship and he took it.

USS *Interceptor's* keel was laid down in 2891 as the last Hellcat-Class Destroyer. Her completion was complicated by the Navy switching to the higher mass gravcoils that became available during the ship's first few weeks of construction. It resulted in a heavier than normal destroyer—thirty-five thousand metric tons of displacement as opposed to the twenty-seven of her sister ships.

While the rest of the Hellcats had three centimeters of nano-armor, the *Interceptor* had five. The Hellcats had a reputation for toughness, and *Interceptor* was the toughest of the batch.

Jacob glanced out the window to see the endless field of stars, punctuated by a flash of light from the pulsar every few seconds.

"It really is clockwork, isn't it?" he asked the chief.

"Aye, sir. The only reason Kremlin Station survives in far

orbit is she's in the shadow of Zuckabar. Like every installation in the system, they have to be mindful of the danger of the pulsar."

The beams from the pulsar were more than just light. They were mega-powerful flashes of gamma, x-ray, and other radiation that would fry a ship without proper shielding. Other than its pulsing light and deadly emissions, it didn't do much to illuminate the system. That was left for the second half of the binary, the white dwarf star orbiting the pulsar. It emitted a bright white light that could be seen with the bare eye for thousands of light-years in any direction. However, there was no active fusion in the star; the white light was the residual heat left over from when it went supernova millions of years before.

"How long to dock?" he asked.

"ETA ten mikes," she replied coolly. "Uh, Lieutenant?" She glanced up into the small mirror affixed on the cockpit allowing them to see each other.

Jacob met her eyes with a raised eyebrow, "Yes?"

She grinned. "You want the grand tour?"

A spike of excitement ran through Jacob. Was this real? Was he really going to be the captain of a United Systems Alliance Navy ship?

Yes. Yes, he was.

"Affirmative, Chief, give me the grand tour," he told her.

Her grin grew to a broad, full smile. "Aye, sir. I love this part."

While she focused on flying, he went back to studying everything the NavPad would let him know about the ship. Four turrets mounted topside were the ship's close-in weapons. The rapid-firing, single-barrel coilguns shot 20mm projectiles at a rate of thirty per minute. An efficient crew could load a thirty-round magazine in fifteen seconds. They were excellent at point defense and moderately effective against lightly armored enemy ships.

Four 240mm torpedo tubes fore and two aft launched MK XII torpedoes. The ship's stores carried sixty of the projectiles. If the crew was running tight, they could load and launch every thirty seconds. Of course, he doubted the crew was running tight. More like one every minute. Torpedoes were excellent against large ships at long range or for ambushes, as he well knew.

Finally, the *Interceptor*'s main gun, the Long 9. A twenty-nine-meter-long coilgun capable of launching a nine-kilo, hyperdense, carbon-tungsten arrow accelerated to thirty percent the speed of light.

It wasn't as powerful as the ones aboard *Orion,* but it packed a hell of a punch. The power requirements were immense, so firing it was a slow process; it took almost a full minute to recharge the supercapacitors.

Of course, at the speeds most ships traveled, the actual shooting part of a battle tended to last minutes, not hours.

"Lieutenant, you might want to see this," Boudreaux said softly to him.

Jacob opened his eyes and stifled a gasp. Kremlin Station was above them and it was *massive*. He imagined an entire Marine Air-Land-Sea-Orbital Carrier could fit inside and still have enough space for the rest of the battle group's ships. Maybe even a Legion class battleship.

"Watch this," she said. Her hands nudged the stick to the right, gently rolling the Corsair.

Some of his earliest memories were of watching his mom's shuttle launch into space and dreaming of the day he would command a Naval warship.

After Pascal, he thought his chances were gone. Applying to command school after a year on *Bethesda* was his way of forcing the Navy to either throw him out or promote him. As he looked out into space on his way to his first command, he thought...

Decision made.

Chief Boudreaux rolled the ship until the belly faced Kremlin and the cockpit looked out into open space... open except for *her*.

The *Interceptor*. The front of her hull was painted like a shark's head, but it was old and faded, scratched and worn.

Jacob had spent most of his life waiting for this moment, and in it, all his concerns about his past, his present, and his future faded away.

He didn't care if she looked like a beaten prizefighter with her armored hull dented and streaked from action. Or if the turrets were scratched, streaked, and patched.

Only that she was his.

Chief Boudreaux flew the ship in a spiral around *Interceptor*, letting him see every nut and bolt. Every bent plate of armor exposing the outer skin of the ship.

And he loved every inch of her.

Every. Damn. One.

"When was the last time she went under refit?" he asked as Boudreaux continued to circle the ship.

"I joined the crew eight months ago in Novastad, before they started the circuit. When we arrived here in Zuckabar, I think a local crew came on board and upgraded the computers. But a physical refit? You'd have to check with the bosun," she said.

"Is that turret open to space?" he asked as Boudreaux brought the ship up and around one last time before lining up to dock with the boat bay.

If he didn't know better, he'd think she ducked her head a little.

"I'm afraid so. Number four has given us fits forever. I would ask Lieutenant Yuki about it," Boudreaux said.

She flipped a few switches and the ship spun on its axis. Lateral thrusters sputtered on and off as she aligned with the boat bay doors.

She flipped another switch, activating the radio. "*Interceptor*, this is Charlie-One-One-Actual, requesting docking clearance."

Generally, the rear boat bay doors would already be open, the Corsair would use ventral thrusters to rise up into the bay, the doors would close beneath her, and that would be that... but the doors weren't opening.

"Problem, Chief?" he asked. Jacob suppressed a grin. He hadn't missed her emphasis on "actual" meaning the commander was on board.

"No, sir, they're just having some trouble clearing equipment from the bay doors. Just one moment," she told him innocently.

"Right, I'll just be back here minding my own business," he said with a grin.

————

Yuki waved her arms frantically for the ratings to get in formation. Fifty... *fifty*... of the ship's complement were down on Zuckabar. She had barely enough people to form a proper greeting party. They'd spent the last two hours cleaning and she had everyone on board making the tiny ship sparkle. By her ancestors, she might not be able to give him a ship that worked, but the least she could do was hand over a clean one. She'd scrubbed his quarters herself, washing the deck and making sure his rack had fresh linens.

Bosun Sandivol ran up next to her with his NavPad,

showing her the latest report. Twelve spacers and four apprentices were in dress uniforms as the welcome honor guard, along
with Midship Owusu who stood at the head of the formation
where the *COB* should have been. Not that the ship had a COB.
Commander Cole hadn't cared for NCOs having too much
authority without him.

"Okay, Bosun, good job. Be ready for anything, got it?" Yuki
said.

"Aye, ma'am," Chief Petty Officer Juan Sandivol replied,
snapping to attention.

Yuki signaled the spacer third-class operating the doors to
open them. Alarms sounded and yellow lights flashed as the
twelve-meter-wide floor split in half and the doors came apart
a millimeter at a time, revealing the stationary dropship.

Boudreaux piloted it, but an unknown man, whom she
could only imagine was her future commander, occupied the
second seat. Boudreaux deftly raised her ship, crossing the
Interceptor's Richman Field that held the atmosphere in place.
Once the Corsair cleared the doors, they closed underneath her
and the alarms silenced. Landing struts lowered and the dropship came to rest on the deck.

Yuki took a deep breath, readying herself for what was
about to happen. She'd barely had time to formulate a plan, but
she was sure she could pull off blaming everything on
Commander Cole. All she had to do was delay her new CO long
enough for the flotilla to return and then she could request a
lateral transfer and he would have no reason to say no. At
worst, she would have a mediocre rating from an officer who
had only commanded her for a few months.

"Bosun," she said.

The side hatches opened and her new CO stepped off,
hopping down onto the deck. He was tall—taller than any
man on the ship. He had to duck to exit the Corsair. His

travel uniform was a little dusty from his interlude on Zuckabar, but his black pants with their blood-red stripe up the side were neat, as was his black turtleneck sweater. He held his cover in his hands and she stiffened to see that he held two. One black, like everyone aboard wore, and one red, the color only the ship's captain was authorized to wear.

As he approached, Bosun Sandivol played the welcoming pipe. Its whistle filled the small boat bay and brought everyone's attention front and center.

He stopped before reaching her, his toes edging the yellow line on the floor designating the official entry into the ship.

He turned in a sharp about-face, saluting the ship's flag painted on the far bulkhead. After that, he turned back to her.

"Lieutenant Yuki, Lieutenant Jacob Grimm. Permission to come aboard, ma'am?" he asked formally.

She snapped to attention. The Navy loved tradition, and even though he was taking command, until he did so, this was still her ship, and he was still a lieutenant.

"Permission granted, sir," she said.

He smiled and gestured to the hatches leading to the rest of the ship. "After you, Lieutenant," he said.

———

Jacob admired the greeting party as they fell out. All the spacers were in their dress greys and the officers in blue.

"Formation, return to duty... dismissed!"

He heard just as the automated hatches closed behind him. He did note, with dissatisfaction, that the ship seemed to be wide open. Not a single hatch was dogged. Even under Condition Whiskey, the least actionable a ship could have, the hatches leading to the lower decks should be dogged. After all, accidents happened, and if one section of the ship was open to space...

He shook his head, remembering what he'd told Boudreaux. He wouldn't hold anyone, not the lowest rating nor all the way up to Lieutenant Yuki, accountable for behaviors or decisions they made when he wasn't in command.

Lieutenant Yuki led him forward only a few frames before turning to the lift and waving her hands. The ship had six lifts, each one accompanied by a ladder that could be used in an emergency. *Interceptor* only had six decks plus the O-Deck. The lifts were barely big enough for the three of them. Squeezing in beside her, he did his best to make it work. He pressed himself back against the bulkhead as the bosun entered.

Once they were in, she pressed the big top button with the word "Bridge/O-Deck" smudged next to it.

"How long have you been aboard, Bosun?" he asked the petty officer.

"Eight months, sir. I served on *Avenger* before transferring here," he said.

Jacob had heard tales of *Avenger*. It was a storied ship, with the coveted fleet "E for excellence" after winning several war games in a row. Not to mention that its anti-piracy patrols on the border with the Terran Republic were legend.

Interceptor seemed like the place good careers went to die. Or in Jacob's case, bad careers. That thought sobered him, but he managed to keep his expression neutral. He was the "Old Man" and he didn't want the crew thinking he was unhappy.

The hatch swished open, revealing the passageway leading to the bridge, only three meters away. Jacob followed Lieutenant Yuki and the bosun onto the bridge, taking a moment to savor the feeling as he stepped across the threshold.

Like most Navy ships, the bridge was small and cramped, not at all like *Dagger*'s wide-open spaces. Off to the right was the master operations position as well as comms and astroga-tion. Both stations answered to the operations officer, so it made sense for them to be right next to each other. On the left was the Tactical station, with only one seat but twice as many controls.

In the forward section, sunk into the deck and directly in front of the captain's chair, was the Pit. The life of the ship. Jacob felt bad for the poor spacer manning the helm. He seemed nervous as hell and afraid to touch anything.

Jacob resisted the urge to visit each station. What he was about to do was a time-honored tradition and he didn't want to screw it up... especially since he had never even practiced it before.

He stood next to the captain's chair and placed his thumb squarely on the reader to verify his identity. The ship's computer linked to his NavPad and the device beeped, alerting him to his new orders.

He cleared his throat for a second, then pressed the button labeled "all hands," activating every speaker on the ship. A sharp whistle filled the corridors. From ratings working main-tenance to the men and women manning the MK III Fusion Reactor, all hands turned to the screen to see their new commander as he read himself in.

He held the NavPad out to Yuki, who glanced at it before placing her thumb on the reader to verify her receipt of the orders.

Then, he began:

"From the Office of the Chief Naval Officer and the desk of the President of the United Systems Alliance,

All who bear witness, know that, reposing special trust and confidence in the patriotism, valor, fidelity and abilities of Jacob T.

Grimm, I do appoint him as master of the vessel bearing the hull number DD 1071, known as the United Systems Ship Interceptor. As such from the day these orders are read, this Officer will therefore carefully and diligently discharge the duties of the office to which appointed, by doing and performing all manner of things thereunto belonging. For the duration of his assignment, he shall be frocked as a Lieutenant Commander and treated with the respect of such rank.

And I do strictly charge and require those Officers and other personnel of lesser rank to render such obedience as is due an officer of this grade and position. And this Officer is to observe and follow such orders and directives, from time to time, as may be given by me, or the future President of the United Systems Alliance, or other Superior Officers acting in accordance with the laws of the United Systems Alliance.

This commission is to continue at the pleasure of the President of the United Systems Alliance for the time being, under the provisions of those Public Laws relating to Officers of the Armed Forces of the United Systems Alliance and the component thereof in which this appointment is made, that being the United Systems Alliance Navy.

Affirmed on the Capitol of Alexandria, this 30th day of July in the year of our Lord 2933, with power entrusted by the United Systems Alliance, Friends in Peace, Family in War.

Signed, Fleet Admiral Noelle Villanueva and President Johan Sebastian Axwell."

Jacob turned the NavPad to the screen and the same orders he read were sent to every crew member's instrument. He turned to Lieutenant Yuki and snapped to attention. She followed suit.

"Lieutenant Kimiko Yuki, I relieve you," he said with more confidence than he felt.

"Commander Grimm, I stand relieved," she replied formally.

He sat down in the captain's chair, giddiness warring with fear as he leaned over the speaker. The line was still open and the crew listened.

"I want all hands to report current status to department heads by—," he looked at the time readout on the single small MFD attached to the con. He'd been on *Dagger* time and he was disappointed to realize he'd have to add six hours to his day. "—eighteen hundred hours. Dismissed."

He pressed the close-call button and turned the chair, which squeaked as he did so. Yuki stood stiffly, still at attention next to him, along with the bosun right behind her.

"XO, I think we'll save any meetings until tomorrow when the rest of the crew can join us, don't you think?" he asked.

Her eyes narrowed, and for a moment, he recognized the expression on her face. It was one he carried so often since Pascal: fear and doubt. She was concerned he was trying to trap her and he didn't know how to belay those concerns until they got to know one another better.

"As the captain suggests, sir," she said with a flicker of anger in her dark brown eyes.

CHAPTER ELEVEN

Talmage St. John adjusted the patch on his left eye. It itched, especially when he worked late into the night. Which meant it had itched every night for the last several months.

He leaned back and rubbed his temples, trying to stave off the oncoming headache. As a senator in the United Systems Alliance Congress, a headache was always oncoming.

"Senator St. John, it's time to eat," his assistant said. The young man came in with a wrapped sandwich and canned drink. St. John looked up at him inquisitively.

"Sorry, sir. Eva was here earlier and gave me specific orders to make sure you ate if you were in the office past seven." He put the food down and turned to find a napkin.

"It's fine, Charles. Get back to work. I've got this," Talmage said.

He watched the man leave, then chuckled about his wife. She was amazing. Doing all the things she did and still managing to take care of him. Honestly, if he'd known how hard these last three years were going to be, he would have never run for office.

Talmage picked up the sandwich and went to the window overlooking the capitol. It was late, and the valley was a field of lights, like stars in the sky. He silently ate his food, admiring the engineering feat required to make the Alliance work as smoothly as it did. All eighteen systems had an equal say in running the government. Senatorial elections came every five years. Which meant he was up for re-election in two more years. After all this... strife... would he want to do it again?

There were eighteen senators, either elected or appointed, one from each of the planets. They had a free hand in deciding how they selected their senators. New Austin, his home, elected its senators. Seabring, the third largest planet in the Alliance, had a hereditary senator.

The Senate had the final say on every law, regulation, and legislation that was proposed by the House. Which, in his mind, was far less orderly. The House controlled the money and it was made up of hundreds of lawmakers, all of whom wanted more power. Each system sent representatives, all elected, with the number based on the population. One representative for every hundred million people.

Alexandria's population of seven billion gave them seventy seats. New Austin, his own home, had ten seats. followed by Seabring with seven. The rest of the planets had anywhere between one and three representatives each.

Then there was the president, elected at the beginning of each decade and serving a ten-year term. Like most governments, the Commander-in-Chief was charged with direct control of the executive branch. All in all, the Alliance did a fair job of preserving an actual republic like the one they immigrated from on Earth. But no system was perfect and the infighting and political maneuvering took their toll on both the system and the people who manned it.

The message waiting light blinked subtly in his field of

vision. He was on the appropriations committee for the Navy—which wasn't a job any senator wanted—and there was almost always a message for him, either asking for more money or demanding funding be cut further.

He was only a college student when the last war ended, but with over a hundred thousand dead Navy personnel and trillions of dollars in lost ships as its legacy, the public wanted to blame someone. The president and Congress of the time didn't want it to be them, so they did what any good politician did: they lied.

Which was a shame, because the Navy had acquitted itself well in the Caliph theater. It was only against the technologically superior forces of the Iron Legion in the Terran theater that the disaster had struck.

Activating the first message, he read through it. Nothing terribly important that he needed to deal with immediately. Discarding that message, he decided it was time to go through all of them before they piled up.

The third message was innocuous on its face, but he read deeper into it. A simple assignment change, nothing he really needed to know. Except someone had sent it to him. Why anyone would go out of their way to notify him of something as lowly as a destroyer's new commander was...

He saw the name. He read it twice, the second time saying the name out loud because he couldn't believe Fleet Admiral Villanueva would do such a thing.

He flipped his implant over to encrypted mode and made a call. He would ask her in person. After a few seconds, her young assistant picked up the call and blanched as he recognized the senator. A moment later, he was transferred to the admiral.

"Senator St. John, always a pleasure," Fleet Admiral Villanueva said. He shouldn't be surprised she was working late as well. After all, career politicians and admirals had a lot in common.

"Is your end secure?" he asked with zero formality.

Generally, encryption was handled by Alliance Intelligence, but they focused on foreign spies, and St. John had learned early on that political enemies were far more dangerous than spies from other nations.

"It is now," she said. "What can I do for you?"

"You can explain to me why you put a senior grade lieutenant in charge of a destroyer in Zuckabar," he said flatly. If she caught his intention, she showed no sign.

"I don't actually make the assignments, Senator. I can have NavPer send you over all the pertinent—"

"Cut the crap, Admiral. You and I don't really know each other, but let me assure you, I am on the Navy's side. I think my record speaks for itself. Lord knows the media has raked me over the coals for it and even my own 'side' has done a number on me. I know this is crazy forward coming from a career politician, but half the reason I have this job is that I'm the only one interested in helping the Navy. I think I've proven myself." He unconsciously reached up to touch the eye-patch, a remnant of the accident that had cost him his own naval career. "Now, if you are planning something, I want to know now, not in six months when I hear about it on the news. Let's start again. Why did you assign the *Butcher of Pascal* to the *Interceptor*?"

Her face stayed stone-still and Talmage made a note never to play any kind of betting game with this woman.

"Because I needed an officer no one would miss. He's already flushed his career down the toilet with his overly aggressive cowboy behavior—if you'll forgive the expression— in Pascal. Something is happening in Zuckabar and we want to be able to intervene if things go south. Having a 'known' loose cannon in place will allow us to move in when we need to. If

Congress complains, we can point to the *Butcher of Pascal* and say we were trying to stop an interstellar incident before it happened."

She said all of it without even flinching.

"May I call you Noelle?" he asked suddenly, sitting back and taking in her reaction.

The sudden change of his tone finally caused her to flinch. "I wish you would," she replied.

"Noelle, I wasn't sure about you. Your predecessor blocked me at every turn, and if I may be so bold, so do the CNO and the Secretary. They are playing 'The Game,' ensuring their careers survive. After the way certain members of Congress have acted, I can't say I blame them."

She raised an eyebrow at his declaration and a slight, oh so slight, grin shadowed her face.

"I have nothing but praise to heap upon my immediate superior," Noelle said formally.

Talmage laughed inwardly at how she couched her language even with the encryption running. She was a pro.

"Regardless, I think you're someone I can work with. Read me in on what you're thinking and let's see if we can make it work. Please. Take a chance. If there is even a small possibility of returning the Navy to the level of readiness we both know it needs, then we have to take it." He really was hanging himself out in the vacuum. Congress had done an excellent job of making the Navy the "bad guy" ever since the last war. He knew it was crap, Congress knew, and the Navy certainly knew, but the media ate it up. As long as the other political side had the protection of the media and control of the House, they would never, ever face a serious question about their ethics and how they treated the Navy.

If only he could push through a resolution to allow the Navy to ramp up to its pre-war levels, the Alliance would have a much stronger position and a better ability to protect her people.

Noelle visibly warred with herself, eyes narrowing, forehead crinkling. Finally, she reached a decision and spoke.

"It isn't just me. One second," she said.

The screen blanked several times before coming back with two faces in place. Admiral Wit DeBeck's visage frowned at him.

"Senator, Admiral, to what do I owe the honor of this call?" Admiral DeBeck said.

"Is your encryption on?" Talmage asked.

"I'd be a pretty poor head of Naval Intelligence if it wasn't," DeBeck said with a grin.

"He knows, Wit," Noelle said abruptly. "Or at least he knows we're up to something. And he wants to be read in."

Wit's eyes widened, then narrowed like lasers. "I don't know what you're talking about and I have more important things to deal with."

Talmage rubbed his face as he started again. Going down the list of things he had done for the Navy, and that he certainly knew there was no way Grimm's assignment to the *Interceptor* was a random act of NavPer.

Talmage looked between the two decorated admirals with more time in service than he had been alive. He had one chance to convince possibly the most paranoid man in the nation to trust him.

"I think the three of us all agree that when the next war comes, and it will, we will have given up before it even starts. Regardless of whether it's the Iron Empire or the Caliphate, where will that leave our people?" he asked.

"The fact that you even noticed means you're paying very close attention," Wit said flatly.

"I'm the head of the Senate Commission on Naval Affairs. It's literally my job. It's just that no one has done it worth a damn in so long, people have forgotten how. Now, you want to tell me what you're up to?" Talmage asked.

Thirty minutes later, Talmage closed the line with the two admirals and stared blankly at the wall, disbelief boiling up around him. It took him a solid minute to reconcile their actions in his head.

He could only draw one conclusion. They were out of their damned minds.

No, he corrected himself. They were desperate. Desperate to do the job their sense of responsibility demanded they do, even while their superiors tied their hands.

He had two options: Help them and be complicit in the death of thousands, or expose them and be responsible, at least partially, for the death of millions.

There were days he loved his job. This day wasn't one of them.

CHAPTER TWELVE

Duval spun around in his chair, admiring the shiny bridge where his crew operated. The frigate, which they had named "Chuck," was a thing of beauty. He seriously doubted it had even undergone its commissioning trials before it fell in his lap. Thanks to the fool "Takumi," a military-grade, 40,000-ton torpedo frigate was all his... well... all his crew's. Which made it his, as long as they continued to elect him captain.

Which meant he needed a prize to capture. This far out from the Minsc primary, they were in the perfect position to sit quietly and hunt, waiting for the right opportunity. With the *Raptor* "above" them a few million klicks and their sensor nets linked, they had a fantastic picture of the environment.

Any captain could come in at two billion kilometers and be happy with their transition. Some could skillfully navigate in at one, and a few would push their luck going deeper into the limit. However, ships were expensive, gravcoils even more so, and no one wanted to risk a multi-billion-dollar cargo ship by driving too deep into Minsc's red dwarf primary. Merchants would almost always err on the side of caution and come in around one and a half.

If they were in a train of ships, they might even transition at two, saving their ship the stress. After all, this close to Zuckabar was safe, wasn't it?

He would be happy to dispel the notion of safety for them.

"Skip, we got a contact, bearing three-twenty-ish..."

"Ish?" he asked.

DeShawn, his sensor man, just shrugged. "I'm still getting used to this equipment. Make that two, no, three contacts. They just came out of the starlane... 1.4 billion klicks from primary, bearing one-eight-seven. They're accelerating at fifty gravities, no—sorry, seventy-five *g*s. That's got to be close to their max."

Duval growled with satisfaction as he pulled up the contacts on his large MFD. The attached screen showed a top-down look at the solar system. Up and down were really mean-ingless in space, but the mind needed some way to orient. This way was as good as any other.

Chuck, exactly as Duval had planned, was lying doggo five-hundred million klicks behind the new contact. Every second they accelerated, they pulled away from him, but—and this was the big but—he had a military-grade gravcoil in a fully opera-tional frigate. He didn't even need to catch them, just pull within a million klicks and fire a torpedo...

He figured they'd surrender the second they knew the pirate was on them. The rear ship was the unlucky one. The other two would run for help as soon as they could, but they'd never get out of the system in time. No. Duval had them.

"Helm, pursuit, keep us in their wake. Three hundred gravi-ties," he said.

Laura Kane tapped in the course, verified it with the computer, and hit the engage button. The gravcoil wound up and the frigate shot through space, hidden inside the freighter's own wake.

"How long 'til they see us?" he asked DeShawn.

"Half an hour, tops. Once we're close enough, they'd have to be blind not to pick up our space-time signature," DeShawn said.

Duval double-checked the math. Cutting across the outer system would take close to a day before they could reach the starlane leading to Zuckabar. They would certainly take out the third freighter. However, if he had the opportunity, he would certainly go for two.

"Full acceleration. Kane, bring the forty mikes on line. We're going to blow by number three here. I'll order them to come to a complete stop, and if they don't immediately comply, blow a hole in their bow."

"You got it, boss," Kane said with glee.

Maybe he was being too ambitious, but why settle for one prize when he could have two?

———

Merchant Captain Sara Takahashi blew gently on the steaming mug of coffee. The mug, a gift from her grandchildren, said *Captain Grandma,* framed with a heart. She held it in one hand while reading the daily duty roster in the other.

"Uh, Skipper, I've got something weird..." Sato said. The blue-skinned young man was the only other person on the bridge. Ship time, it was the middle of the night. Sara never slept more than four hours anyway, which made fourth watch perfect for her.

"Let me hear it," she said as she put her coffee down. The screen on her chair blinked, then pulsed with a rhythmic wave, like the beating of a drum, but much smaller. There were several pulses per second as the computer showed them every gravitic disruption they could hear. Then Sato filtered out Minsc's primary star, which at their distance was easy. Much closer, though, and the time-space disruption would wash over everything. After that, he filtered out the two ships ahead of them, leaving only *Agamemnon*'s gravwake... or did it?

There was a beat that didn't quite match, like a resonance, an echo...

Icy dread shot through her as she ran through a million possibilities down to exactly one.

"Bring the ship to max speed, Sato, please."

"Ma'am?" Sato asked in confusion.

"We're being followed. Most likely pirates. Full acceleration and send a warning to the other two ships to do the same. Tell their captains, with my compliments, I will screen them as soon as I have more information," she ordered.

She could see her dread mirrored in Sato's face as he made the adjustment. She pushed the "all hands" button on her chair. In sixty years of merchanting, she'd only ever encountered pirates once before. She knew she had escaped with luck then, but this time, there would be no luck. While she waited for the crew to respond, she closed her eyes and prayed. She had forty-three crew members. Fifteen of them were women. It didn't take an experienced spacer to understand what would happen to them if the ship was taken.

———

"They're changing course, Duval," Kane said from her position at the helm. "Our bird just went full power and turned... thirty degrees to port."

It wasn't the best for him, but it wouldn't matter. They

would close the distance, disable the ship, and then grab the others.

"The other two are changing course— they're scattering. There's no way we're getting more than one now," Kane said.

"Dammit," Duval cursed, slamming his fist down on the control console. One ship would be a huge prize, but to have all three and lose them... "Fine. Open a channel." He waited until DeShawn signaled him. "This is Captain Duval of the *Chuck*. Zero your acceleration and prepare to be boarded. Any sign of resistance and we will perforate your hull and leave you to die then take what we want anyway. You've already pissed me off. Don't make it harder on yourself."

In the time since the pursuit had started, they'd closed the distance by two hundred and fifty million kilometers. The message flashed out at the speed of light, arriving at the *Agamemnon* fifteen minutes later.

———

"We can't outrun her, Sara," Hitoshi, *Agamemnon*'s first mate, said quietly. The rest of the crew were huddled in the mess hall while she and her first mate ran the ship from the bridge. If the pirate was serious, he wouldn't give her much time to reply. She sat back in her chair, cupping her chin while weighing the lives of her crew in her hands.

"If we surrender... you know what's going to happen," she said. Fear wasn't a feeling she was accustomed to, but she had it, nonetheless.

"We'll be alive, and where there's life, there's hope. Maybe one of the other ships will notify the Navy or maybe we'll get lucky... but when they catch up to us... They're in a *frigate*. Where they got it is beyond me, but they will turn our baby into Swiss cheese."

Captain Sara Takahashi nodded her understanding. After a few more moments, she signaled him to activate the comms.

"This is Captain Takahashi of the Consortium Trading Vessel *Agamemnon*. We will comply. There's no need for violence. You can have our cargo and move on; we won't resist."

———

"...resist."

"Ha!" Duval shouted. "Put us alongside."

It took a few more hours to match speed and come up along the freighter. In that time, the other two were almost out of the gravity well. It didn't matter. *Agamemnon* was an M-class freighter. Duval could sell her on Tarsus or even Medial for an easy ten million, regardless of what she carried.

He hoisted his 10mm pistol, waiting for the airlock to turn green. It was mostly for show. He wasn't stupid enough to go in first.

The hatches swung open and a young man stood on the other side of the lock with his hands up. Two of Duval's pirates charged through, slamming him in the gut before knocking him against the wall and kicking him until he stopped moving.

The other ten men went in after.

Once they radioed it was clear, Duval followed, holding his gun out but loosely to the side. The mess hall had forty-two people in it, all standing against the far wall. An old bat with a crisp uniform stood front and center, as if she were presenting her people for inspection.

The vast majority of the crew were Consortium, including all the women. Which was good for him. With sapphire skin, glowing tattoos, and genetically modified eyes that were twenty percent larger than regular humans', they would fetch a very fine price on the slave markets. In a way, it was their own fault, leaping wholeheartedly into genetic manipulation. He'd never met a woman from the Consortium who wasn't stunningly beautiful.

"Captain Duval? I surrender the—"

Duval raised his pistol and shot Captain Sara Takahashi in the face. The explosion from the kinetic weapon deafened the room. One of the crew wailed like a banshee, dropping to her knees and screaming.

The pirates pulled out laser cutters, supremely sharp blades, and went to work slaughtering the men. There was no resistance. When they were done, fifteen crying women were huddled together in the far corner, covered in blood and tears.

"Well?" DeShawn asked.

"I'm thinking. Kane, what's the cargo?" he asked over the comms.

"Electronics. Screens. High-end stuff. Seventy-five percent of it is Mushu-Ivar brand. Rough guess, twenty million?"

Duval smiled. *What a haul!* Including the price they could get for the ship, that was thirty million, which meant the 500k for each Consortium woman would fetch on the slave market was less an issue. He glanced over at the huddled mass. Three of them were over forty. They wouldn't get as much, but the other thirteen...

"Three for the crew, the rest in cryo for the market," he ordered.

"Then we're going to Medial?" DeShawn asked with a grin.

"Not all of us. Leave a few men here to run the ship. Take *Raptor* and escort this bucket all the way there. Sell her for what you can get. No haggling; just unload her and return ASAP."

DeShawn nodded, eyes gleaming at the possibilities. And the money. So much money.

"DeShawn, don't screw me on this, got it? You know who we're really working for. Don't for a second think you can hide from them," Duval said in a whisper so only the other man could hear him. "Or me."

That took some of the gleam out of his eyes.

"Right. I'd say you can trust me, but we're pirates. How about, you can trust my self-interest," DeShawn said with a grin.

"That I can do," Duval replied.

He turned to leave, but one of the women caught his eye. She had glowing purple eyes and long, bright green hair.

"DeShawn, four for the crew. Bring her to me," he pointed at the girl, "and the rest in cryo." Duval liked operating in round numbers. Eight women for the market. Two million and counting.

Two or three more hauls like this and he and his men could retire to any planet they wanted.

CHAPTER THIRTEEN

J acob sat on his bench-like bunk rubbing his face, focusing on the task ahead. He'd barely slept the night before and he needed to act and feel like he was fully rested.

His spartan quarters were lavish in size and features compared to the rest of the crew. He had a bunk, dresser, mirror, and his own head with a standing shower. No decorations, though, no photos, no mementos.

His bag was dumped at the end of the rack and he'd slid his guitar under the bed to keep it out of the way. He wouldn't be playing it anytime soon.

This ship felt hollow. Or was it him?

It was time to change that. He stood up and went to the head, taking a moment to splash cold water on his face. On most ships, the crew took their cue from the CO. If he wore a dress uniform, then all the officers did. Jacob hated wearing dress uniforms.

He decided on boots instead of dress shoes, the black cargo slacks with the blood-red stripe down the right leg denoting his combat experience, and the white, high-necked shirt with the black sweater on top. His red watch cap finished it off. If the officers dressed like him, they would be comfortable and warm.

He checked himself in the mirror, wanting to make sure everything was perfect on his uniform. His last name, *GRIMM*, was displayed over the right side of his chest and *NAVY* on the left. The sweater's pair of epaulets carried his rank. His right shoulder bore the *Interceptor*'s badge, a cartoon grinning shark with the words "First to Fight" on the top, and the ship's designation, DD-1071, on the bottom.

Satisfied, he exited his quarters, heading straight to the bridge. The briefing room hatch was opposite his quarters and the bridge was only a few hurried steps away.

To his surprise, a very short—barely more than one and a half meters tall—female Marine lance corporal stood at a perfect parade rest next to the open hatch leading to the bridge. She wore the standard grey and white camouflage shipboard uniform. After all, the ship *could* be boarded at any moment.

Jacob figured he should feel lucky she wasn't carrying a sidearm. Some Marine units took their duties a little too seriously. According to the nametag, her name was Jennings. Like most Marines, she wore no watch cap. Instead, her golden blonde hair was tightly bundled in a neat bun.

She snapped to attention as he walked by and shouted, "Captain on the Bridge."

He froze and glanced back at her. She was back in parade rest, not so much as a single blonde strand out of place.

The ensign and midship jumped to their feet so fast, they didn't get out of the way of their consoles and banged their knees painfully on the protruding metal. The other two stations were manned by Lieutenant (JG) Mark West, the operations officer, and Lieutenant (JG) Carter Fawkes, weapons officer, neither of whom seemed particularly motivated to stand or even look at him.

Chief Petty Officer Devi Suresh, the ship's coxswain and now COB, sat calmly in the helm, sipping a cup of hot coffee while she scrolled through passing ship traffic. Of everyone on the bridge, he could overlook her lack of reaction the most. The recessed helm, referred to as "the Pit," wasn't easy to get in or out of. She didn't need to snap to, but the rest of them had no idea what to expect and should have stood as soon as he entered, regardless of the Marine's overzealous shout.

Instead, two of his senior staff stayed at their stations with enlisted ratings next to them. The ratings were unsure if they should stand or sit, but ultimately followed the lead of their officers and didn't stand.

Only the midship and ensign were on their toes, and from the looks on their faces, it was more out of fear than a sense of duty.

It was awful discipline and Jacob made it worse by muttering a hasty "as you were" before taking the con.

"Captain has the con," Chief Suresh said without looking up from her screen as he sat down.

He was sure command school would have covered how to behave. Eight months of "what the hell to do with a crew that hasn't had a proper CO?"

He pulled up the duty log on the MFD and went over the day's calendar.

It was empty.

He went back a week, then a month, then three months before he found a logged duty roster.

It was as if when the previous CO had died, the ship died with him. No training exercises, no watch logs, nothing. He queried the computer on the current ship's complement.

Ninety-one including himself. Fifteen short of what The Book called for on a Hellcat. Undermanned for sure. Fifteen didn't sound like a lot, but even a handful of missing crew could severely impact operations. The rest of the spacers on board would need to work hard to make up the difference. Unfortunately, from what he was seeing, no one was working hard, just coasting on momentum alone.

He needed to do *something,* anything, to shake the crew up, to push them out of the malaise they were in. Even the officers. But could he? Hell, other than the orders in his NavPad, he had no clue why the Navy chose him to command the destroyer. Maybe he was just a convenient placeholder to ride herd until a real candidate could be made available? That was certainly what the crew was thinking.

A moment of doubt stifled his will, swinging him back down the path toward the awful moment where he witnessed the small corpses floating in space. How his mother's heroic sacrifice would mean nothing because of her son.

He shook his head.

If the Navy was looking for an officer to fill an empty gap, why not promote the XO? Why use him at all? Jacob thought back to the conversation with his last CO and how he walked out feeling odd about the whole thing. Was it a test? He had to believe the Navy picked him for a reason.

Duty. Honor. Courage. His mother's words rang in his ear.

Clenching his jaw, he examined the bridge crew more closely. It was first watch, which started at 0700 ship time, and they looked like they'd slept in their uniforms. They weren't even wearing the same styles. Some wore day dress, others work outfits. A few wore watch caps, but the rest were either in shore caps or nothing.

If he did nothing, then it would be taken as a sign of compliance and the behavior would continue. After that, it would be almost impossible to make a difference. He either changed things now or never.

"Lieutenant Fawkes, do you know where the XO is?" he

asked. On a normal bridge, there was a quiet reserve, but almost always a steady hum of noise from equipment or comms traffic—nothing loud enough to prevent a normal conversational tone from being heard. Which was why he was stunned when the lieutenant didn't respond.

Should he chastise the man? Repeat himself? Get up and move closer?

"Sir," Chief Suresh said, "the XO is in the mess." She glanced at him, then Fawkes, then back to Jacob and gave him the kind of look NCOs often gave lost officers.

Interceptor was too small for an officers-only Wardroom. There was only one mess, and the ratings, NCOs, and officers shared it. If the captain needed a private meal, he could use the briefing room.

"Chief, can you come with me, please? Ensign Hössbacher, take the helm. Fawkes, you have the con," Jacob said as he stood.

The ensign flushed as he stumbled across the small bridge to take the seat vacated by Suresh.

Fawkes didn't even look up as he said, "I have the con, aye."

At least Fawkes acknowledged him that time.

Jacob left the bridge and strode past Jennings straight to the ladder. He mounted it in reverse and slid down to the next deck. He cleared the way for Suresh to follow, but he stopped her from going on.

"Chief, I know this is a little weird to ask, but—" He stopped as a spacer first class named Weatherly walked by, carrying a box of something heavy toward engineering.

"Sir, I've spent the last twenty-three years in the Navy. There isn't anything you can say I haven't heard before," she said. She was shorter than him, but somehow she felt taller, bigger. Her brown eyes bore into him with a serenity and confidence he certainly didn't feel. Unlike everyone else onboard, her uniform was impeccable. Creases that could cut bread ran down her arms, her boots shined like small suns, and there wasn't a hair out of place on her head. He imagined her department was probably in the same shape, but since she was the coxswain, her department was two POs and herself.

"I haven't been to command school. Hell, I haven't been on a ship in two years. I don't know what I'm doing or what to do—"

She held up her hand to stop him. "Captain, if I may?"

"Of course," he said.

"Sir, what the crew needs, and begging the captain's pardon, what you need, is a swift kick in the ass. Begging the captain's pardon, sir."

Jacob froze, his face going slack before splitting into a grin. He put a hand on her shoulder and looked her dead in the eye.

"Chief, you're a credit to the Navy," he said.

"Remember that when it comes time to promote me," Chief Suresh said wryly.

"Oh, I'll put in a good word," he said.

She shook her head. "No, sir—*don't*. I like serving aboard ship. I certainly like flying 'em. Senior Chiefs go to big piles of pig-iron and talk about their feelings and keep an eye on the puppies. I like my tin can," she said, patting the side of the hull. "This is where I'm supposed to be."

"Got it. Would you go find the XO for me and ask her to join me on the bridge? I think it's time for that ass-kicking you were talking about," he said.

"Aye, aye, sir," she said. After she left, Jacob climbed back up the ladder, feeling better than when he'd woken up. There was a to-do list a mile long. He still didn't know where the ship's gravcoil was or when it would be back. He didn't have enough crew to properly run the ship. And worst of all, he didn't even have orders regarding what to do in Zuckabar if he could move the ship.

However, if he couldn't get the crew to respect him and see him more as their CO and not as a temporary commander, then none of it mattered.

Back on the O-Deck, he stopped next to Jennings before entering the bridge. He gave her a nod and she snapped to attention.

"Captain on deck," she bellowed. In his experience, Marines loved yelling at anyone, especially the Navy. It didn't surprise him at all to see her grin as he stepped through.

No one stood this time.

That was fine by him. What the ship lacked was discipline. Once learned, it could never be truly lost, only forgotten. Jacob would remind them what discipline was if he had to drag each and every one of them the length of the keel by their ears.

Lieutenant Commander (frocked) Jacob T. Grimm marched over to his command chair and sat down. From the way the leather was cracked and the paint scratched, it was probably the original chair from when the ship launched.

It squeaked when he turned and wasn't nearly as comfortable as the newer command chairs. It also came with only one MFD; the vast majority of the controls he needed were on the right arm. A row of shielded buttons, their labels long since faded, was in easy reach.

But for now, it had the one thing he needed. He flipped the shield up and his thumb hovered over the Big Red Button. The last time he'd pressed it, he'd taken his ship into a battle that changed his life forever. This wasn't that. He pushed his thumb down hard on the alarm. His MFD lit up and he knew the next words out of his mouth would be heard by every spacer on the tin can.

"Set Condition Zulu, action stations!"

———

Chief Suresh had just finished telling the XO the captain would like to see her. Yuki figured she had a few minutes to finish her coffee. But then why was the chief grinning like a madwoman?

"Set Condition Zulu, action stations!" the captain said over the main speaker. Yuki spit out her coffee in disbelief as red lights flared to life and the klaxon sounded. Crew members hovered in inaction until Chief Suresh bellowed,

"Get your butts moving, you useless excuse for spacers!" Her voice echoed through the room and even Yuki found herself moving in visceral response.

She went out the hatch, turned left, and ran for main damage control, her official station during any alert. DCS was three decks down and forward of the fusion reactor.

Halfway there, while dodging spacers running for their lives, she realized she'd forgotten her emergency life support suit, which was in her footlocker in the cabin she shared with Lance Corporal Jennings—on deck six at the very stern of the ship.

"Dammit," she muttered as she turned around and ran back the other way. As she passed spacers, she yelled at them to don their suits in a vain effort to minimize the screw-up. No department could count itself at one hundred percent readiness until every spacer had their ELS suit on. It was a hard fail if they didn't.

A full fifteen minutes passed as she found her suit, slid into it, and made her way back to DCS. When she arrived, Petty Officer Hanz, her primary assistant, and Spacer First Class Baker were there. However, Baker wasn't in his ELS suit.

She glared at him and he shrank in his seat. Yuki slid into the main chair. With a press of her thumb, she activated the "all-ready" signal, even though they technically weren't.

As XO, she should have been in on the alert, not Chief Suresh. This was the last thing she expected from a pencil-pushing disgraced officer sent here on temporary duty.

"Bridge, DCS. All hands ready," she said. Then she looked at Baker and scowled. He turned fifty shades of red and sank even lower into his chair.

"DCS, Captain. XO, would you join me in the briefing room? I'd like to go over the results of the alert," he said as if he were asking how the weather was.

"Aye, sir, I'll be right there," she replied.

There was no way he was staying in command, so what the hell was he up to? She would have to talk to him to find out.

———

With a satisfied grin, Jacob released the comm button. He'd shaken things up, no doubt. Now he needed to go about putting it all back together, and that was going to take a lot of time and a lot of blood, sweat, and tears.

"Lieutenant West?" he said in a normal tone.

"Yes, sir?" the man replied immediately.

"Schedule a briefing for eighteen hundred hours. Just the officers for now, and the bosun, of course. No exceptions. Understood?"

"Uh, aye, sir, 1800 hours, all officers and the bosun. No exceptions."

"You have the con, West. Set Condition Yankee," he said as he headed for the exit.

"Not X-ray, sir?" West asked. "We're not exactly mobile."

Jacob froze, turning deliberately to the lieutenant, who was half out of his chair to take the con. He marched over to him, reaching up to hold the grab bar as he towered over the younger man.

"Do you have a problem with your ears, mister?" he asked.

West paled noticeably. He looked around the bridge for help, but there was none to be found. Jacob's stunt with the alert worked exactly as he had hoped. They had no idea what to expect from him.

"No—no, sir. Condition Yankee, I have the con."

"Good man," Jacob said. He let go of the bar and walked with purpose off the bridge.

By the time he made it to the briefing room, West's voice rang out over the ship, changing it from action stations to Condition Yankee, which was Navy speak for ship underway. Which they were not. However, it was a higher alert status and required the crew to be at their posts. Until such time as he could institute a training schedule, this would have to do.

The briefing room, opposite his quarters on the O-Deck, had a sliding hatch just like the bridge, but smaller. He gripped the vertical bar and pulled. Nothing happened. Using both hands, he heaved. Still nothing.

"One step forward..." he muttered. He looked over at the Marine guarding the bridge. "Jennings," he called her over.

She raised an eyebrow and replied, "Sir?"

He pointed at the hatch. "Is there a trick to this?" he asked her.

She snapped to attention and parade-marched over next to him.

"If the captain wouldn't mind, sir?" she said, gesturing to the control panel. He placed his hand on the pad. The electronic lock whirred and the hatch jerked but remained stubbornly closed. Jennings grabbed the open bar and slid the massive hatch aside as if it were nothing.

Once it was open, she stepped back, did a perfect about-face, and marched back to the bridge hatch, where she executed another perfect about-face and snapped into parade rest.

He might mock the Marines mentally for their devotion to appearance, but it also came with an equally strong devotion to duty, something he fully understood. Jacob ducked into the briefing room and moved to the far end.

The brown table's lacquer had long since faded, and the old chairs lining it were as worn as his command chair. Nothing on the ship looked like it was installed in the last twenty years.

Just as he sat down in the far chair, Lieutenant Yuki strode in, still in her ELS suit, a scowl on her face.

"Reporting as ordered, sir," she growled.

Jacob didn't like her tone, not one bit. He got it. He was the new guy and this wasn't his ship. Maybe the Navy would recall him tomorrow, but until then, he had his orders, and by God, he would execute them faithfully if it killed him.

"Sit down, XO," he said, remaining calm. He gestured to the chair closest to him.

"All due respect, sir, sitting in these things is a pain in the aft. If this isn't urgent, I can switch out and be back in—"

"Sit. Down," he said again, this time not quite as calm.

She slid into the seat farthest from him.

"When I came on board, I told Chief Boudreaux and Chief Suresh, our new COB by the way, that I didn't care what happened before I arrived," he said. Jacob raised his hand to stop her from interrupting him. "I get it, XO. You got the crap sandwich. Your CO died, the gravcoil is out of commission, and you've been stuck here what, two months?" He nodded for her to answer.

"Just under three, sir," she replied.

"Like I said, I get it. I don't know anyone who could hold a command together under those circumstances. I meant what I said. I don't care what came before and—"

She interrupted him, leaning forward as she spoke.

"All due respect, *sir*, we're the same rank. You have me by a week and a frock, so please don't sit there and condescend like I'm some wet-behind-her-ears midship. You've been on this ship less than a day. I've done nothing wrong. I've followed every order given me. There is nothing that has happened here that will land on me in any way," she said.

The truth was, Jacob knew officers who would do exactly what she feared. They would show up and put everything on her, dump her to another command with a negative recommend. And her career would be hurt, possibly irrevocably. She was doing what she felt she had to in defending herself. He hated his Navy for having officers who would act dishonorably. It reflected poorly on everyone who served. It wasn't what he was raised to believe. Being an officer was a duty, with a heavy responsibility for the welfare of every man and woman who served under him. The fact that she had prepared this defense ahead of time told him she was familiar with exactly the kind of officer he despised.

Of course, that wasn't him. He realized that, in order to reset the situation, she needed to trust him. For that to happen, he needed her to listen to him.

Her rant sputtered to a stop when Jacob's lips split into a grin. He covered his mouth with one hand, trying not to laugh. The absurdity of it all. Here he was trying to fix everything, and she was trying to make sure she wasn't blamed.

"Kimiko, right?" he asked.

"Yes... but I prefer Kim," she said, holding her head to the side as if she were expecting an attack.

"Okay, Kim. Listen. I'm sure you read my file. You know... who I am and what I've been doing for the last two years. I literally have nothing to gain by throwing you under the keel. *Nothing.* And I most certainly have much to lose. I can't whip this heap into shape without you. I don't know why the Navy put me out here, but this is my one chance to do something good with my career before it's over. You know they'll never promote the *'Butcher of Pascal.'* I've applied for command school twice and I was turned down both times." While they hadn't officially turned him down, posting him to the *Interceptor* was essentially the same thing. "Once my time-in-service is up, they're going to muster me."

Jacob hadn't actually said those words out loud before, but they were true. He'd spent his time since Pascal as a deck officer in a quiet part of space. In six months, he turned thirty-two, and if his promotion to lieutenant commander wasn't permanent by then, he was out of the Navy.

"I'm... I'm sorry, sir. I hadn't thought of it that way. It's just, well, my last CO was pretty... underhanded, and I guess it stuck." She shifted uncomfortably in her seat.

"Bad COs are like that," Jacob replied. "Kim, let's start over. This ship is hollow and sick. It needs some serious help. Where do we start?"

She seemed to relax, looking him in the eyes, and for a moment, he thought maybe she would turn him down.

"If you're serious, sir, then I suggest we start from the top down. Let's look at—"

Jacob felt better than he had since the incident in Pascal. Like a fog had lifted. Maybe, just maybe, he'd give some clear-headedness to his XO. All it took was a butt whooping from a certain COB.

It was time for him to be a command officer again.

CHAPTER FOURTEEN

J acob pinched the bridge of his nose, trying to wrap his head around what Commander Beckett was telling him. The clock on his NavPad read nineteen thirty hours, and despite being an hour and a half into the meeting, he felt like he knew less than when he came in.

The briefing room was jammed packed with ship's officers. If he ever wanted to meet his entire senior staff, NCOs included, he'd have to do it in the mess hall.

The only non-officer in the room was the bosun, Chief Petty Officer Sandivol, who sat in the seat to Jacob's immediate right. He was older than Jacob, with more time in service than anyone on board—with the exception of the COB. His round face broke into easy smiles, and of all the people he'd met so far, the bosun seemed the most affable to him.

He would have liked Chief Suresh to be involved, but he also needed a qualified hand at the con, and she was it.

Commander Rod Beckett, his chief engineer, sat between the bosun and the XO. Rod was an older fatherly figure type who didn't seem to let anything faze him. He also didn't seem willing to give him more detailed answers than an abrupt yes or no.

Yuki sat directly across from Jacob. Her matching uniform was far more svelte on her than him. If he were an outsider looking in, he might think someone let a student in on the briefing, but one had only to be in her presence to feel her command authority.

As the second officer, Lieutenant Mark West sat to her right. Where Yuki had the dark hair and eyes of her Asian heritage, with his short blond hair and blue eyes, West looked like he stepped out of an Iron Empire recruiting poster

Unfortunately, he also seemed unwilling to accept Jacob's command. Which could be a problem down the road. As the head of Ops, West had more spacers under him than any other department. If they saw him being disrespectful, they would be.

As he looked around the room for help, he found none. No one would meet his inquisitive eyes or explain why they sat without a gravcoil for three months with virtually no attempt to have it returned.

"The gravcoil was removed from the ship by Kremlin Station's repair vessel... but they don't have it because...?" he asked.

"Because they don't actually do the repairs. They farm it out to another company," Beckett replied.

"And we don't know who that is because?" he asked. Jacob was purposefully asking leading questions to draw out the men and women in his command. He felt like he'd come to an accord of sorts with the XO, but everyone else on board had a serious case of CYA. Even the XO was still withdrawn, waiting to see if he was the real deal or not.

"Only the ship's CO of record has access to that info. Commander Cole—God rest his soul—didn't allow Lieutenant Yuki access to the command level information. After he died,

NavPer, in their infinite wisdom, didn't send the codes for the XO to take temporary command," he explained.

"SNAFU, then," Jacob said with a grin. It was the oldest story in any military. The "normal" situation was all fouled up. It would be extraordinary if it wasn't.

"As the captain says," Beckett replied. The older man cracked a small smile. "Sometimes everything goes wrong in a perfect storm of wrongness and then we get left sitting in it."

The mood lightened, or maybe it was Jacob's imagination, but they seemed less formal, less rigid.

"Well put. Okay, here is what I want," Jacob said. "I know you all think the Navy is going to recall me tomorrow, and they might, but until then, we've got a job to do. The *Interceptor* is a wreck"—he held up his hand to forestall complaint—"I'm not blaming anyone here. *No one*. Not even a little. Not the newest spacer's apprentice nor the senior officers." He said the last bit looking at Yuki then Beckett, holding each's gaze for a long second. As a commander, Beckett could have done something, but for whatever reason chose not to. However, Jacob would be true to his word. If he could get the ship back in fighting trim, this could all be easily swept under the rug.

"I'm going to start looking for the gravcoil. If I have to go over to Kremlin and search every warehouse, I will. Kim, I'd like you to run hourly battle station drills." A groan rolled through the room and he tightened his lips in an effort to keep his displeasure invisible. Hourly drills meant a lot of work on top of all the other things that needed doing. "The response time to our earlier drill was..." He glanced at Kim, who then looked at her pad, a deep crimson spreading over her face at having to recite the shameful numbers.

"Seventeen minutes fourteen seconds," she said.

He didn't need to tell them how horribly bad that time was. "I want us under two minutes," Jacob said.

"Sir, that's pretty audacious," Lieutenant West spoke out. "The fleet average for destroyers is two minutes, fifteen seconds, and—"

"And I think we can be better than *average*, Mark. Or are you saying you're not up for the challenge? I know Ops can be a tough post with a lot of responsibility..." He didn't outright say he would replace the lieutenant, but the implication was certainly there. It was normal to move officers around the ship, especially junior ones, but everyone would know it was a demotion.

Jacob even purposely glanced at Lieutenant Carter Fawkes, who ran Tactical and was also *Interceptor*'s third officer. The insinuation had the desired effect.

Lieutenant West clamped his mouth shut, leaned back, and shook his head. "No, sir. I mean, yes, sir. Ops up to the challenge."

"Good. Two minutes. God forbid we have to actually go into battle. I don't think we'll have the *quarter-hour* it took last time. Now, Rod," he turned to the chief engineer, "I noticed some loose hull plating on the port side stern when I came in. Also, am I right in thinking the number four turret is open to space?"

He hoped that by using their first names, they would warm up to him and realize he wasn't the enemy. It was a technique he had seen but never used himself. Jacob pictured the kind of ship he wanted to run in his head, and it was one based on mutual respect and the core values of the Navy.

The rest of the meeting went where he needed it to go. Step by step, each department was given a task to help return the ship to operational status along with rebuilding the morale of the crew. From cleaning and inventory lists to repairs and ammo counts, it was all laid out.

"One last thing. Lieutenant Bonds?" Jacob turned to the broad-shouldered dark-skinned Marine who stood against the bulkhead. He'd remained silent during the meeting, but Jacob felt his approving gaze on him all the same.

"Sir?" he asked in a deep bass that rumbled as he spoke.

"I appreciate that the Marines like to train groundside, but for the time being, I'd like you to remain aboard ship until we've got this situation... better in hand," Jacob said.

"Aye, sir. Can do," Bonds replied. "I'll distribute my Marines as needed to assist any department as requested."

"If there's nothing else?" Jacob said, bringing the meeting to a close. He stood and all the officers leaped up with him, then slowly filed out.

Commander Beckett lingered in the back until it was only the two of them. "Sir, if I may?" Beckett asked.

Jacob nodded. "Speak freely. I don't want you thinking I'm going to jump down your throat. What's on your mind, Rod... or do you prefer Rodney?"

The older engineer winced. "Rod, if you please, sir," he said with a bit of distaste on his face.

"Excellent. What's on your mind?" Jacob asked as he moved around the briefing room table to half sit on the surface.

"Zuckabar isn't Alliance territory, not really. Don't assume a level of law and order that doesn't actually exist," Rod said in a much quieter tone than required.

Jacob narrowed his eyes as the concept hit him. "I hadn't thought about that. Isn't there law enforcement on the station?" he asked.

"Oh sure. If you're one of the big mining consortiums or the Merchant's Guild, you'll get help, but everyone else, well, be careful. Don't go out alone if you know what I mean," Rod said.

Jacob chewed on that for a moment before thanking his engineer. "Understood. And thank you. Hopefully, I can find some answers, but in the meantime, we need the rest of the ship up and running."

"I'm on it, sir," Beckett said.

"Dismissed."

Jacob liked to think he was no fool. *Not* listening to Commander Beckett with his many years of experience would be the height of hubris... but on the other hand, what was he to do about it? They needed their gravcoil. If he kept his wits about him, he should be okay. It wasn't as if he was a wet-behind-the-ears ensign on his first cruise.

He tapped the comms button on the table next to his chair.

"Bridge, Captain. Can you patch me through to whoever controls the repair services aboard Kremlin Station?" he asked.

"Bridge, Spacer Second Class McCall. Aye, sir. Patching you in... one moment."

The background noise shifted and a series of beeps cycled through until the line clicked.

"What?" a gruff voice answered.

"This is Commander Grimm of the USS *Interceptor*. I'm calling to inquire about our gravcoil," Jacob said. He wanted to smooth talk them as best he could; yelling and screaming wouldn't move the needle. However, the man who answered seemed upset already.

Static answered him and he resisted the urge to repeat himself. A few more moments passed before the man replied. "I don't have it," the voice said.

"Yes... I know. Can you tell me who does?" Jacob asked.

"No."

The man's laconic answers were infuriating, but Jacob was getting good at holding his tongue and practicing patience. After all, he was herding cats on his own ship. What was one more person?

"Can you tell me who I can call that can answer my question?" he asked.

While he waited for the answer, he took out his NavPad and

punched in the relevant information to find the regs on civilian repair of military equipment.

"Yeah, yeah, one minute." The line clicked and music played as he held.

While he waited, he scanned the regs. Apparently, no one told Kremlin Station they were supposed to provide weekly reports for non mission-critical items. With mission-critical equipment like the gravcoil—daily.

The line clicked back on. "Longhorn Shipping and Holding is who you want," the man said. Then the line died.

Jacob stared at the comm unit for a moment. As a former deck officer, he'd dealt with his fair share of civilian maintenance crews, but this was ridiculous.

Still, he had his answer. Sort of. No number to call. It was going to require more research. He hit a few buttons on his NavPad, linking it up with Kremlin Station's directory. It was time to do some digging.

At some point, Spacer Second Class Mendez brought him a cold drink and a sandwich. He devoured the sandwich in a few minutes and downed the drink, washing away much of his frustration with the tangy, carbonated juice mixed with a mild stimulant.

Jacob buried his head back in the NavPad. So far, he'd identified three different companies that operated under the Longhorn umbrella. He figured if he just dug a little deeper, he'd hit the mark.

Chief Suresh kept one eye on the clock while she checked local traffic coming in and out of Zuckabar. It was early, ship time, and the mess hadn't brought her coffee yet. As if the kid feared for his life, he appeared a moment later with a tray of coffee mugs.

She debated jumping down his throat for his tardiness, but in the end, the enchanting smell of coffee drew her laser focus.

"Sorry, Chief," he said sheepishly. "I'm shorthanded down there and I wanted to make sure the captain's breakfast was ready before I came up here."

Raising the cup to her lips, she sipped the black go-juice and sighed.

"All's forgiven, Spacer," she said.

The largest problem the destroyer had was her complete lack of authority. As far as Zuckabar's government was concerned, they were a sovereign nation. They had their own police, customs, and laws—everything but a military. Which, in the last war, was where the Systems Alliance came in, providing ships and crew for Zuckabar and the three other single-system planetary governments between here and MacGregor's World.

It wasn't like the *Interceptor* was supposed to be patrolling the system for illicit activity. Smuggling was strictly an internal matter. Piracy, however, in all its forms, fell under Navy jurisdiction, no matter where they were, even if they were in another nation's sovereign space—unless they were given strict instructions not to interfere. However, for the last twenty years, the Alliance had become isolationist and reactionary. Policies that were set well above Chief Suresh's pay grade.

Combing through the reports of crime in a system of millions of people wasn't easy, but then again, she was a coxswain on a destroyer with no propulsion. She really didn't have much else to do during her time on watch.

Three spots on the outskirts of the system were the problem areas, all of them far enough away from the deadly radiation emitted by the pulsar. *If* the captain decided to go on patrol, those were the places she would recommend.

"Chief," Ensign Hössbacher said. "I've got an incoming distress signal. A Merchant skipper broadcasting on all stations. Sounds like pirates, Chief. Hit them in Minsc about halfway through the system."

"How many made it?" she asked.

"Two. The third one surrendered. There's video coming in. It looks like the captain of the taken ship set up a camera and recorded the whole thing, broadcasting it in real-time to the other ships in the train," Hössbacher told her with one hand on his comms panel and the other furiously typing to record the information.

Chief Petty Officer Devi Suresh liked to think she'd seen it all. Decades in service had hardened her to many things. But pirates... If it were up to her, they would all be executed in the most painful way possible.

As she watched the video, her fists balled up, knuckles turning white from the pressure. Behind her, she heard the young ensign retch into a bag as the video rolled long after the elderly captain's death.

"Bloody pirates," she muttered. "When you're done stinking up the deck, better call the captain."

———

From his command chair on the bridge, Jacob watched the same video of Captain Takahashi's last stand—along with the conversation the pirate named Duval had with his crew about the survivors. It turned his stomach the way they slaughtered the helpless crew and carted the women off to cryo... or worse. Who was he kidding, though? In that situation, both fates were worse.

"Dammit," he muttered. This was *exactly* the kind of thing the Navy was supposed to stop. It was why the Alliance existed

—freedom of the starlanes and anti-piracy. Part of Jacob would like to think there was something he could do, or could have done, to help that ship, but by the time he received the message, Takahashi's death was over thirty hours old.

At max acceleration, even if they *could* accelerate, it would take the *Interceptor* hours to reach the starlane to Minsc and then another eight hours crossing. By the time they arrived in-system, even a slow, broken-down husk of a pirate ship would be long gone.

On top of that, they were taking the remaining crew to Medial, in Caliphate territory. It was a month there through back routes and barely charted systems. He would never catch them.

No. They were long gone. All he could do was hope those poor women found some peace. They wouldn't, though, and he knew it.

"XO, log it. Load a packet and send it with the next available ship. Maybe HQ can reinforce the trade route or something. Did they manage to ID the ship?" he asked the COB.

Suresh shook her head. "The sensor data showed a large mass and some power readings. The pirates probably have a retrofitted freighter. Strap a larger gravcoil to it and they can move pretty fast. It isn't safe, or practical... but if they were either, they wouldn't be pirates."

He nodded, sitting back in his command chair fighting off the feeling of helplessness—a feeling he knew every one of his crew shared. He decided to capitalize on the moment and triggered an all-hands broadcast.

"This is the captain speaking. No doubt you've all seen, or heard, of the events in Minsc. This is exactly the kind of thing we're out here to prevent. It's why the United Systems Alliance Navy was created three hundred and forty years ago. We banded together to fight back against tyranny and piracy. The good crew of *Agamemnon* are beyond our reach. We can only hope for mercy and grace on the living and honor for the dead. Once the *Interceptor* is space-worthy, we'll go hunting and see how those pirate scum fare against a warship. Captain out."

He looked up and realized the bridge crew was staring at him. Suresh grinned like a Marine at an open bar.

"What? Too much?" he asked.

"No, sir. Just the right amount," she said.

CHAPTER FIFTEEN

I ker and Daisy walked down the ramp to officially step foot on Zuckabar Central for the first time. And it was cold. No. Water out of the tap early in the morning was cold. This was *freezing*. He huddled in his thermal jacket as they walked briskly across the open field to the main building.

"I forgot how cold this place was," Daisy said, trotting next to him. She was prepared, with gloves, boots, and a wool hat pulled down around her ears. Of course, all their clothes had self-contained heating and cooling. Even so, it couldn't overcome the penetrating frost of a planet so far away from its sun. But it was enough to keep them alive while they moved around outside for short amounts of time.

"Three hundred years may be a long time to a human, but for terraforming..." he said with a shrug. "Barely a drop in the bucket. At least Zuckabar's core is the right mix of liquid and dense solid to generate a strong magnetic field. Otherwise, the surface would be barren."

He glanced up through the dim sky, barely able to make out the white dwarf, the only one of the two stars visible. The star had spent its fuel a million years earlier, but it still glowed from the sheer amount of heat left over from when it went supernova.

They finally made it inside and he luxuriated in the heating. Even with his top-of-the-line thermal protection, the cold had seeped in and he was too old to endure it for long.

He had arranged for everything beforehand, but he still had to go to different stores to pick up the equipment. Most of what he used was right off the shelf. The ship he'd hired would need a few upgrades and he'd discussed them with the captain. It was cheaper for him to buy those upgrades on Zuckabar than lug them over a commercial flight.

"Daisy, can you arrange a car for us? Something with cargo space?"

"Sure thing, Professor, I'm on it." She took off down toward the central part of the spaceport. He needed a few minutes to warm up before he could run around and be that chipper.

He followed her down to the main hub. The spaceport was big and busy. Hundreds of people came through daily. Zuckabar Central, or Zuck as the locals called it, was more than a habitable planet in a mining system; it had a plethora of heavy metals readily available in its crust. With the consistently rising temperature, they had mined more in the last twenty-five years than the three hundred previously.

With its distance from the primary, its super-dense core, and strong magnetic field, it was a literal gold mine. And while the planet was great for everyone else, it was the uniqueness of her binary stars that interested Professor Bellaits.

Few celestial bodies disrupted space-time quite like a pulsar, let alone a pulsar with an orbiting white dwarf! If he was right, it could be the key to a bright future for the Alliance... and the key to him making an indelible mark in the history books!

CHAPTER SIXTEEN

Commander Beckett sipped his piping hot coffee while he monitored the fusion reactor's output from his station in the reactor room. It had fluctuated a few times during the night, and he didn't want to be caught unawares if they needed a new flow regulator.

At least that was what he told himself. It wasn't at all because he felt more than a little guilty about the way he had ignored the ship's situation since Commander Cole's heart attack. He could tell himself all day long it wasn't his responsibility... that *his* department had done everything they were required to do by the regs. But not once had he spoken to Lieutenant Yuki about the gravcoil repairs, nor had he offered to call Kremlin Station and use his knowledge of the situation to speed things up.

And when the new captain came on board, had he offered the man help? No.

Since the pirate attack, the crew had a new sense of purpose—at least he felt like they did. His engineering teams were working around the clock to put all the subsystems and secondaries at one hundred percent. If and when they recovered the gravcoil, he wanted the *Interceptor* ready to fly.

Every major component aboard ship was marked with a radio-isotope tag. There was no way to erase it. Unfortunately, it was a short-range signal used to track inventory. Every time a part changed hands, it was scanned, logged, and entered. The captain was trying to figure out who had the gravcoil by asking.

Which was why he had two screens open. One monitoring the fusion reactor, the other researching exactly who had the gravcoil. By researching, he meant hacking.

His eyes lit up when he pulled up the inventory of the third warehouse's computer system he had illegally, but discreetly, hacked his way into.

"Aha!" he said, startling Spacer Beech as he cleaned the main console.

"You okay, sir?" Beech asked.

"Fine, just got excited is all. Get back to your task," he said.

He downloaded a copy, marked it as urgent, and sent it to the captain's NavPad. That would make up for his prior lack of good judgment—he hoped.

———

Jacob had a strict rule about official duty before breakfast: he didn't do it. His first commander had instilled in him the importance of starting the day right. Making his rack, putting on a clean uniform, leaving his living space in an orderly fashion, and having breakfast before doing *any* paperwork.

The *Interceptor* was too small to have multiple mess decks. Instead, they had scheduled times to eat. Of course, as the captain, Jacob could eat whenever he wanted.

0900 seemed like the best time. Most of the crew had already eaten and he had the mess to himself. It was the largest single space on the ship and he enjoyed eating while going over the previous night's log on his NavPad.

The food, though, it could be better. He moved the remnants of his eggs and potatoes around the plate. Not that he was blaming the Spacer Mendez, who was one of three people making food for the entire crew. Destroyers weren't known for their vast stores, and procuring fresh food was damn near impossible in a system with limited farming.

Once he was down to just his orange-colored juice, he activated the mail function on his NavPad. The ready light flashed repeatedly as message after message came into his inbox, all of them flagged as important.

"My least favorite part of the job," he muttered to himself.

He imagined a huge section of command school was learning to deal with the unending mountain of paperwork. It would have been useful to know.

It wasn't all bad. In the week he'd been aboard, there were occasionally fun things, like promotions and awards. For instance, at some point in the next month, Chief Suresh would earn another time-in-service stripe. Each one was worth four years and she already had five of them.

Then there were the requests for administrative punishments, formally known as a Captain's Mast. The attitudes of the ratings followed their command structure. The officers had let things slide for too long. Morale and attitude wouldn't turn on a dime. There were discipline problems and the NCOs were running them up the flagpole and the officers then passed them on to him.

In turn, he was turning them all around. The officers and non-comms had to deal with their own crew issues. The crew needed to see their NCOs and officers as leadership, not just him. As long as there were no criminal offenses, he was going to continue to refuse Captain's Mast requests.

The biggest offender was Lieutenant West's Operations department. Which made sense, since Ops was the single largest group. Still... West seemed all too eager to pass things up the chain.

An email arrived from Commander Beckett, opening by itself since it was marked *urgent* from a department head. He scanned it in a hurry, his eyes going wide with surprise. He'd refrain from asking Beckett how he'd acquired the information; he was just glad the commander was engaged.

He hit the comm button on his NavPad.

"Boat bay, Captain. I need transport to Kremlin Station ASAP," he said.

"Boat bay, Hernandez. I'll let the chief know, sir."

"Good man. Thank you. Captain out."

He downed the rest of his drink and headed for his quarters. His day uniform was fine for aboard ship, but he needed something a little more practical if he was going to go running around the station.

———

For the most part, Chief Warrant Officer Boudreaux's boat bay had avoided the malaise infecting the rest of the crew. The *Interceptor* only had one Corsair, and Chief Boudreaux was one of two people on board who could fly her. The two petty officers who reported to her kept the bay running smoothly while she personally handled the vast majority of maintenance on the Corsair and Mudcat.

The 'Cat was snugly attached under the tail of the Corsair. There was just enough vertical room in the bay for the dropship with her atmospheric control surfaces folded. Everything in the place had to be locked together in a complex puzzle of machinery. If they needed the Corsair sans the 'Cat, they could detach her and secure her against the starboard bulkhead on her side. It was a sight to see, but it worked.

Chief Boudreaux jogged down from the control deck, which was a fancy name for a two-person room where the control computers were housed, on her way to warm up the dropship. The captain needed to go to Kremlin, and with any luck, that meant he'd found the gravcoil.

Her comm crackled to life and Lieutenant Bonds' baritone filled her ear.

"Chief, I need you to hold departure until I have two Marines ready to go with the captain," Bonds said.

"He's going to the maintenance station, Paul, not battle," Boudreaux replied.

She imagined him cringing as she used his first name. He hated it, but she was given a lot more leeway than anyone else on board considering her rank and specialty. Besides, she liked teasing the hulking man.

"Just stall him, Chief. Bonds out."

The comm clicked off and she shrugged. It wasn't anything to her. If the Marines wanted an excuse to parade around in fatigues and carry sidearms, who was she to argue? After all, she would take any opportunity to fly, even if it was an air tour.

———

Jacob approached the boat bay with his nose straight down at his NavPad, still trying to get ahead of the million things he needed to do, know, and be. One of the things he would like to do, which hadn't made his list, was find a source of fresh food for the mess. Crew morale would improve dramatically if the quality of the food went up.

Unfortunately, it was the least important on a list of urgent requirements. Number Four turret was still open to space, they were short on metallic hydrogen fuel for the reactor, and on and on and on.

He pulled up short when he noticed two Marines standing outside the boat bay hatch. Jennings, he knew from her bridge watch. She was short and compact, with blonde hair, bright blue eyes, and the overdeveloped shoulder and neck muscles of someone from a high-G world. She wore a Marine shore party uniform, which included a combat loadout.

Next to her was a taller young man with clearly Asian features. He held out a gun belt for Jacob, equipped with an MP-17, the official sidearm of the Navy and Marines.

"Uh, Corporal Jennings," he squinted to read the man's name tag, "PFC Naki, what's this?"

Jennings didn't miss a beat. "It's the captain's sidearm, sir. An MP-17, good for five-hundred shots. It's limited to semi-automatic... for you, sir."

He pressed his lips together and resisted the urge to roll his eyes. Marines had this way of treating everyone who wasn't a Marine, regardless of rank, as little children in need of hand-holding.

"I understand that, Corporal. Why are you giving me one?" he asked.

"Lieutenant Bonds' orders, sir. I can help you put it on if you like?" Jennings said.

Should he even bother arguing? "I take from your shore dress you're coming with me?" he asked.

"Aye, sir," she replied.

He slid the NavPad in his side cargo pocket and took the gun belt. The last time he'd worn one was for firearm training at the Academy, and it took him a moment to recall how to latch it around his waist. Seemingly satisfied with the accuracy of his memory, he finished strapping it on and then looked to Jennings for approval.

"Good enough, sir," she said. High praise indeed. Once that was settled, he proceeded to the boat bay with both Marines in lockstep behind him.

"Oh good, they're here," Chief Boudreaux said as she gestured to the Marines. "We can leave when you're ready, sir."

He nodded to her. "Let's go, Chief. The faster we get over there, the faster we get our gravcoil back."

"Aye, aye, sir!" she said with a grin.

CHAPTER SEVENTEEN

K*remlin Station* was a wonder of technology. Jacob had tried to keep his mind focused, determined to use the twenty-minute flight time to put more paperwork in the "finished" column. After the massive spinning station came into view, though, it was all over. He watched breathlessly as Chief Boudreaux flew the Corsair around to the main port.

"How old is this station?" Jacob asked over the internal comms.

"It's from the original colony ship, sir. They converted it to a station when they arrived and found the system uninhabitable," PFC Naki said.

The Marines were down below in the main compartment, strapped into the crew chairs under and behind the cockpit. Boudreaux was flying solo since she didn't need an electronics operator for a taxi mission.

"When did you become a historian, PFC?" Chief Boudreaux asked.

"No, ma'am, I just like reading. The El-Tee wasn't keen on us having much downtime. Lots of training and studying," Naki said.

"Look over there, sir," Boudreaux said as she tilted the ship. A massive freighter, large enough to swallow a hundred *Interceptor*s, emerged from the main dock, exiting the station with enough room on either side they could have fit another one alongside.

"The central axis is zero-g. They don't use gravcoils, just centripetal spin. All the population lives on the 'walls,' so when we enter, look up and you'll see where we're going," Chief Boudreaux said.

"How many people live on it, Chief?" Jacob asked.

"About two million, I think. Not much when you think of the big mega habitats at some of the older planets," Chief Boudreaux replied.

A couple of million sounded like a lot to Jacob. All packed into a spinning can. Not to mention the millions more throughout the system. On Alexandria, where he grew up, there were plenty of space stations, but nothing quite like Kremlin. He imagined having to build it from scratch, with nothing but what they came with.

"That must have been a hardy bunch who survived this," he said absently.

"Aye, sir," PFC Naki replied. "They lost half the original colonists just building the thing. Another half before the farms produced enough food to self-sustain."

Boudreaux shifted the dropship away from the station, traversing until there was nothing but black.

"I've got to line us up, sir. We're on gravcoil for final arrival, then once we're in, we switch to plasma. Ready?" she asked.

"Always," Jacob replied. He put his NavPad away, making sure the pocket was securely shut before crossing his arms over his chest and grabbing the crash webbing.

"Okay, here we go," she said. Boudreaux flipped the ship back around, pointing the nose at the docking entrance. Jacob thought he could see the shimmer of the massive Richman Field holding the atmosphere at bay, but it was impossible to be sure from so far away.

A Richman Field used a two-dimensional quantum state to create a stasis that allowed molecules of high density, like ships and people, to pass through, but held low-density molecules, like most gasses, at bay.

Boudreaux tapped the throttle and it was like a whole person sat on his chest. She decelerated for ten seconds at two gs. At the end, the ship came to rest at zero relative to Kremlin. Once she was sure they were lined up, she tapped the throttle forward, sending them into the station.

A yellow path showed her the correct flight trajectory on the heads-up-display. While she flew, he dealt with space traffic control.

"Kremlin STC, this is Charlie-One-One, we are on course for entry at fifteen thirty hours on heading of three-five-niner. How copy?" Jacob asked.

The voice that responded had a thick accent with clipped words. He spoke as if he were ordering food at a restaurant while not actually paying attention to what he ordered.

"Charlie-One-One, good copy. Proceed on course. Welcome to Kremlin Station."

Jacob keyed his mike to respond when he caught Boudreaux smiling at him from the pilot seat.

"Don't bother, sir; they aren't chatty," she said.

"Roger that, Chief," he replied.

The Corsair hit the Richman Field a few seconds later. The ship shook as she impacted with the atmosphere at two hundred kilometers an hour. Plasma engines roared to life as the wings and tail fought for control. Surfaces all over the ship expanded, giving her extra lift and more maneuverability.

"Smooth," Jacob said.

"Sorry, sir," Chief Boudreaux replied. Her cheeks burned red and she looked down to keep him from seeing her embarrassment.

"It's fine, Chief. I took a tour as a backseat on an S&R bird. I had my fair share of transition troubles," he reassured her.

As impressive as the outside of the station was, Jacob felt like it had nothing on the inside. Thousands of buildings were built on and into the walls. It looked like a giant city but inverted. The center of the station was one long line of ships under repair. They were held motionless relative to the station with a ring of restraints.

Tall spires led from the living levels, all the way up to the dry-docks. Giant built-in lifts carried workers and equipment to the ships. Jacob assumed the zero-g made it much more economical to repair and build ships, though he wondered what would happen if a tool fell from one... best not look up, he mused to himself.

Boudreaux took the scenic route, for his benefit he was sure.

"We don't have our own landing pad like we do on the planet, but the main terminal is fine," she said.

The main terminal was more like a giant parking garage for aircars, small spacecraft, and other private modes of transportation. She flew around in one large circle, banking to the left until she identified their berth.

"It's that one there, sir," she said, pointing with her off hand while the other held on to the stick.

Their airspeed was down to under a hundred as Boudreaux flipped the switch converting her to hover. The wings twisted upward, pointing the plasma turbines at a forty-five-degree angle to the ground.

She looked down through the translucent panels at her feet, flying by touch as she tilted the nose up and sat the dropship down with barely a shudder.

"Okay, that was smooth," he complimented her.

"Thank you, sir. Some days are better than others," she said.

He unbuckled, slid down the internal ladder to the main deck, and made his way back to the hatch connecting the Mudcat to the Corsair. The two Marines fell in step behind him.

"I sent the location to your NavPad, Chief," he told her over his shoulder.

"Aye, sir. I'll have us there on the bounce," she said as she came down behind him.

"Well, I just hope they have our gravcoil all repaired and ready to go," he said.

———

Merlin Nevil growled, slamming the door to his office before throwing himself into the patchwork chair. His flimsy desk shook as he banged his fists on the thin top.

"Bloody fools, that who I work with," he growled.

Merlin cursed at himself more than the idiots he employed. The job was too good to be true. He should have quit months ago.

Half the goods in the warehouse he managed were stolen or misappropriated from the various ships that rolled through Zuckabar. Combined with their operations on the other three protectorate worlds, this was turning out to be a profitable little enterprise. Similar warehouses funneled their stolen goods to him, and he, in turn, selected the right freighter to take them to his contacts in the Corridor.

That was until someone couldn't contain their greed. Eight people worked directly for him and they were all in the warehouse. One of them had violated their primary rule.

Nothing big. Nothing that would get them noticed. Their lives depended on the head of the operation, Merlin's boss, not finding out they were piggybacking stolen goods with the main merchandise. After all, what was a few hundred k to the man making millions from the Caliphate?

They had their part to play in this operation. Merlin might not have been a high and mighty officer in the Alliance Army, but he understood operational parameters well enough to know you didn't step outside of them.

A crate of grenades here, a case of MP-17s there. Heck, they'd even managed to secure a shoulder-launched plasma missile. Something the planets in the Corridor, or any planet with a rebel faction, would pay an arm and a leg for.

A few more days and their ship would depart the system as part of a freight train headed for the Consortium. All loaded with legitimate trade goods, except *Madrigal*. She would break down one jump from Niflheim. Once the train left her behind, his contacts would move in and secure the goods. It was a win-win for the outfit. Not only would Merlin be paid for the goods, but they'd also collect a percentage of the insurance from the lost freighter! Too bad about the crew, though. But those were the breaks. The ship was almost full. His crew was loading the first of the last three cargo containers, and in another few days the warehouse would be squeaky clean.

Of course, that was when it all went to hell. The Navy got their head out of their collective asses and assigned a new captain to the destroyer hanging over their heads like an executioner's ax.

Nevil let out a sigh, leaning back in his chair, rubbing the bridge of his nose. No, it wasn't the Navy's fault. It was his. His people got sloppy and greedy. He could yell at them all day long about their lack of professionalism, but they were *criminals* for a reason. Ultimately, it was his job to keep them in check or dispose of them.

The Navy just wanted a refurbished gravcoil and Nevil had

no idea where it was. One of his people had either shipped it out by mistake or on purpose and pocketed the money. Maybe it was on *Madrigal,* but he couldn't tell the Navy that, lest they go snooping around and find more than they should.

His contacts at central were keeping the *Interceptor*'s captain busy, sending him on wild goose chases and playing message tag with him. All they had to do was buy Merlin a few more days and it would be moot.

As long as they didn't know which warehouse, he was safe. However, his paranoia got the best of him, imagining nightmare scenarios where he spent the rest of his life in prison. Could the new captain raid the place? It wasn't unheard of. The Navy had their jackbooted jarheaded thugs at their disposal. Damn crayon eaters.

"Samantha!" he yelled.

His second-in-command was pretty to look at, which was nice, but she was also a psychopath. Bad for relationships, but at the moment, he could use her desire to inflict pain. No matter what, she would look out for herself first, and that was a useful personality trait for controlling murderers.

"What?" she replied, sticking her head in the door. Her straight blonde hair moved like a golden curtain.

"We need to evac all the stolen goods to site B for departure to the ship," he said. He already knew what her response would be. He felt the tension in his gut roil up.

"What? That's ten hours of work and the ship isn't even in orbit yet. What the hell's wrong with you?" Samantha asked.

Merlin rubbed a hand down his face, trying to ease the headache he knew was coming.

"What's wrong with me is that the Navy could be here any minute and demand a gravcoil we don't have because you sold it out the back door!" His voice rose as he spoke until he was yelling.

"Don't try and pin that crap on me, I never—"

He leaped up, slamming his fists down on the table. She flinched from his sudden aggression. Samantha might be a vicious killer, but he out-massed her by a hundred kilos.

"This isn't about blame, Sam; it's about going to prison. Half the stuff in here we don't have a legal registry for. If they request a site inspection, it wouldn't take a genius to figure out what was going on and—"

"Hey, Nevil," Kearne yelled from the warehouse floor. Sam moved out of the way, allowing the overweight man to squeeze into the door next to her. "Hi, Sam," he said in his pathetic way.

Merlin glared at the fat man.

"What, Kearne? I'm in the middle of something—"

"There's a big six-wheeled truck outside and a bunch of uniforms with guns getting out. What do we do?" Kearne asked.

Merlin's face flushed as his body went into fight or flight. He clenched his jaw, doing everything he could to stay calm.

"Okay, don't freak out. Maybe I can get them to go away or something," Merlin said.

He didn't sound confident, even to himself.

"And if you can't?" Sam asked.

He looked at her with pure hate in his eyes. He wanted nothing more than to kill every one of them and run. But he couldn't. Not out of some sense of loyalty, but that he knew he couldn't run from his employers.

"Okay, move everyone to the loading docks, break out those pulse rifles we got last week, and then arm everyone else with pistols," he said.

"You're gonna kill some Navy pukes?" Sam asked. The glee in her eyes seriously terrified him.

"If I have to. I'll lead 'em back by the transport parts. You can use the lifts as cover and shoot them when I'm clear," Merlin said.

She nodded, a flush on her face and a smile on her lips. He couldn't tell if she was more excited about killing the sailors or if she imagined *accidentally* shooting him in the crossfire. He needed to keep her on a leash.

An idea occurred to him that would maximize her usefulness while keeping himself safe.

"Sam, get your knife. You'll want to get in close, I imagine."

"Oh, baby, do I," she said before running off to her locker.

"Jesus, man. She's a psycho," Kearne commented. He watched her run away like a lovesick puppy.

"Let's hope so," Merlin said.

"How are you going to explain it?" Kearne asked. "It's not like it won't blow our cover."

"I won't have to. We'll leave them to rot and get the hell off station and out of the system. By the time anyone knows something is wrong, we will be long gone. You better go get your rifle and a grenade. If they leave anyone in their truck, deal with them. No witnesses."

"Understood," Kearne said. He turned to go, but then stopped. "If I kill a couple of them, you think Sam will go out with me?" he asked.

"Dude, I'm sure she would," Merlin said to goad the man into doing his very best. He also suspected Kearne wouldn't survive an encounter with the psycho.

Assuming any of them were still alive.

———

Jacob stepped out of the Mudcat, sliding down to the ceracrete ground. The area around the warehouse was surrounded by a small decorative rock wall. There were identical warehouses as far as he could see in either direction.

He pulled at the gun belt, trying to loosen it.

"Leave it alone, sir; it makes you look like an amateur you keep messing with it," Jennings said as she walked by him.

Jacob wanted to argue with her but decided against it as he remembered the last time he argued with a Marine.

He only did it once.

"Chief Boudreaux, hang tight here. We shouldn't be long," he said to the aviator.

"Aye, sir, I'll just sit and watch the sky," she said with a grin.

Other than the lack of sky, Jacob found himself thinking that Kremlin could be any planet. The buildings were indistinguishable from planetside. There were even trees scattered among the squat, nondescript brown warehouses.

The front of the one they wanted only had a palm reader next to the solid metal door. Jacob put his hand on the pad to no avail. When it didn't activate, he rapped on the door with his knuckles.

"Maybe no one's home," PFC Naki said.

"Where else would they be? It's the middle of their day," Jacob said. He rubbed his hand where he hit the door.

Day, of course, was a relative term and mostly meaningless on a space station. Most systems only had one planet, maybe a moon sometimes. The trick with time was giving everyone a common frame of reference. By tradition, that time frame belonged to whatever planet or outpost in a given system had the most people. However, it wasn't always practical to use whatever a planet considered a day. So there was also the standard twenty-four-hour clock from old Earth. It was the "universal" time, even though Earth hadn't been humanity's sole home in five hundred years.

A loud clank of metal sounded behind the door. Jacob whipped around, stood up straight, and presented his best face forward. The door opened halfway and an older man with a wrinkled face and patchy hair peered around the frame.

"No public service here. You'll need to contact corporate," he barked.

He started to close the door. Jacob stuck his booted foot in the way and smiled as innocently as he could.

"I'm Commander Grimm, USS *Interceptor*. I believe you have our gravcoil?" he asked. Jacob kept his voice firm but inquisitive.

The man looked from Grimm to the two Marines flanking him, then ever so slightly to their sidearms, and back to Jacob.

"I'd have to check the computer. I'll let you know in a day or so," he said.

"I wish it were that easy," Jacob countered. He was trying his best to be disarming. He'd certainly dealt with enough pushy types in his life that he didn't want to be one. "The problem is, my CO is going to be up my butt with a flashlight if I don't produce something—anything— about the status of our gravcoil. I just need to see it. If you're still repairing it, that's fine, I just need to put eyes on it so I can tell him what the situation is, understand?" Technically, he'd never met his CO. Commodore Xin was months from being back in Zuckabar. Who knew, maybe he was a great officer who would be okay with a ship under his command out of action. However, everyone could relate to a grumpy boss.

The man glanced again at the Marines again. His hesitation and constant fidgety movements struck Jacob as odd.

"Anything I can say that would convince you to come back tomorrow?" the man asked.

"I'm afraid not, sir. I need my ship operational or I need to be able to report why," Jacob said.

The man sighed, as if a heavy decision had befallen him. His whole demeanor could be explained away by overwork or exhaustion, or maybe he was a jerk. Jacob didn't know, but something felt off.

"Fine, give me a minute," the man said as he closed the door.

"Anything about that seem weird to you two?" Jacob asked his Marines over his shoulder.

"Everything, sir," PFC Naki answered.

"Keep your eyes peeled," Jacob said.

"Head on a swivel, sir," Private Naki replied.

The door opened again and the man gestured for them to enter. "Merlin Nevil. A pleasure to meet you," he said, holding out his hand.

Jacob took it and smiled. "Thank you for acquiescing, Mr. Nevil. I'm sure you understand what it's like to have an angry CO," he said with a smile.

Mr. Nevil returned the smile. "Of course. This way." He led them back through the office into the warehouse proper.

"I know you're all very busy and I promise I'm not here to make more work for you," Jacob said in a continuing effort to reassure the man. With each step, though, his unease grew.

The warehouse itself was massive, filled with goods and supplies of all kinds. Rows that stretched out perpendicular to their walk went on for a hundred meters at least. It looked like they were preparing a shipment, with the anti-grav lifters parked near the loading bay. The shelves were filled with metal and wooden crates, loose parts were stuffed in between, and Jacob found it hard to believe anyone could find anything in the mess.

Something bugged him about the place, though. Something subtle. As they neared the back of the warehouse, Jacob spotted several large crates lined up opposite the last stack, along with several lifts parked in a line.

"Do you handle a lot of the Navy jobs, Mr. Nevil?" Jacob asked.

He shook his head. "It's luck of the draw, really. When your ship came up damaged, the system governor's office decided who would repair it. We got lucky."

Jacob clenched his teeth together. He wanted to press the man about why it had taken so long to refit a gravcoil. Admittedly, it wasn't an easy or quick operation, but three months?

He glanced back at Jennings. She walked like she didn't have a care in the world. However, her hand rested next to her sidearm. PFC Naki was more formal, but his muscles were tensed for a fight. Jacob would have followed suit, but he couldn't figure out how to rest his hand near the butt of his pistol without looking like it was on purpose.

"We keep the gravcoil containment field in the back... right around here," Nevil said, holding his hand out to gesture around the last row of shelves.

The back of the warehouse held a collection of forklifts and maintenance vehicles parked front to back. He followed Nevil around the corner as the man increased his speed to a brisk walk. Everything about the situation was wrong. Beckett's warning came back to him.

A thought occurred to him. If he left Naki where they were, he could cover them. As he turned around to tell the PFC just that, he saw he was too late.

A blonde woman with a glowing blade sprinted toward the PFC's back.

"Naki!" he yelled.

The big man moved—just not fast enough. Three feet of monofilament blade sank into his back and out beneath his ribs. She didn't stop there, though.

She yanked her sword out of him, spilling his blood in a shower of gore. She turned to Jacob, a cold, hard smile forming on her face. Then she charged him.

He froze. For a split second, he saw death in her eyes and it was his. A blur of motion flashed by as Jennings rushed toward the danger. A shot of adrenaline crashed into Jacob. He processed what he was seeing like it was in slow motion.

Jennings dropped at the last second, using her diminutive height to her advantage. The mono-blade flashed over the Marine's head and she gathered herself and exploded upward, connecting with the woman's jaw.

Jacob heard the unmistakable sound of bones breaking as the short lance corporal's fist impacted. The murderer flew up through the air to crash down onto the hard floor, her head bouncing off the floor as she hit.

The woman was dazed but alive. Jennings yanked her sidearm, bringing it up in a perfect combat stance.

"No!" the woman screamed, raising her hand.

Jennings fired. Her MP-17 spat a hyper-accelerated silicate sliver. The round smashed into the woman's nose and blasted out the back of her head, spreading bone and blood all over the ceracrete floor.

Time sped up, as if Jennings killing the woman snapped the rest of the ambush into motion. Rifles burst to life with an ear-splitting crack in the close quarters.

Bullets slashed around Jacob like horizontal rain. Jennings dropped to one knee and returned fire. She hit a man in the shoulder, spinning him. His screams turned to sobs as he flopped to the ground, his arm severed from his body.

Jacob took a step back, turning sideways as he tried to come to terms with what was happening.

They were trying to kill his Marines.

Jennings grunted as two rounds impacted her chest, her uniform condensed and hardened, protecting her from penetration.

His instincts screamed at him to run, but his tactical mind took over.

They were out in the open, with nothing to hide behind,

and they needed cover; a firing position that would shield them until help could arrive. It wouldn't take their foes much longer to start hitting accurately after the shock of their friend's death faded. Jacob scanned the area and he had a thought. He ran toward the shelves and slammed into a wooden box on the lowest rack. It easily slid out the back.

"Jennings," he yelled as he grabbed Private Naki by the strap attached to the back of his jacket for just such events. He grunted as he pulled the Marine right up to the open space. Then he dove through, intending to turn around and pull the private the rest of the way.

Except he tripped, sliding off the other side face first into the ceracrete floor. He felt his nose break and hot blood flowed freely. He finished pulling himself through, spun around, and reached out to secure a hold on the PFC.

Jacob struggled through the pain, yanking Naki through the gap, into the relative safety of the row.

Jennings stood up. Moving with excruciating precision, she pivoted, firing her pistol in a steady stream of deadly shots, backing up until her boot hit the rack. She spun and dove through, sliding off the other side and twisting to aim back the way she came.

She made it look easy.

Jacob fumbled with his own gun, pulling it out and holding it with both hands, using the base of the shelf as cover. The words of his pistol instructor came back to him: "Slow is smooth and smooth is fast," he muttered as took aim.

He clicked the safety off, extended his arms, and squeezed the trigger. The weapon bucked. The silicate flechettes impacted the cover his attackers used.

"You hit, sir?" she said, gesturing at his face. She moved past him, putting one hand on Naki's throat, while firing her MP-17 with the other.

"No, I—it's not important. Is he alive?" He was forced to spit out blood as it continued to flow over his lips and chin.

"Yes." She hit a button on Naki's sleeve and medical nanites went into action, stabilizing him and working to stop the bleeding.

"We need out of here," Jacob said. He fired again as a scraggly man leaped up and charged at them. Silicate slivers ripped right through his neck, severing it almost in half. He gurgled as he went down.

She glanced down both aisles. They were practically in the middle.

"In about one minute, they're going to figure out to flank us and then we're dead. I'll run down that way"—she gestured down the aisle toward where they had come in—"while you run the other way. They'll focus on me and you make your escape."

A bullet shattered a small device next to his head and he ducked reflexively. "No way. I'm not leaving you or Naki."

"Sir, if you die, the El-Tee will have my hide," Jennings said.

Jacob shook his head. "No. We all go or none of us goes. I won't go back on the Corsair alone and..." He broke out into a smile.

"What?" she asked.

"I have a really good idea. Keep them busy," he ordered.

He turned and hunkered down, trying to stay small while he activated the comms to Boudreaux. "Chief," he yelled.

———

Vivienne Boudreaux had her feet up on the dash, reading a trashy romance novel she'd bought on her NavPad, waiting for the shore party to return.

Then she heard something loud and sharp. She glanced up from her book, looking around.

She put her feet down and leaned forward, cocking one ear to the side trying to figure out what she heard.

"Chief!" The captain's voice broke over the comms, causing her to jump.

"Sir?" she asked.

"We're under fire in here and—" Whatever he said was lost when her window banged. She jumped away from it and turned to see what had happened. The window spiderwebbed from a one-centimeter crater.

"Captain, someone's shooting at me!" she yelled.

"Join the club. I need you to remote fly the Corsair here and provide CAS. Can you do it?" he asked.

The Mudcat shook a second time as another round hit right next to the first. The armor held, but it cracked more.

Fly the Corsair as close air support *inside* the station?

"On it," she said. Ditching her NavPad, she scrambled over the front seats, past the next two rows of rear- and front-facing seats, until she was in the rear compartment.

The box was easy to open and the controls came to life, instantly elevating from their storage position. A holographic screen popped up, showing her exactly what the linked Corsair's forward camera saw.

She decided to forgo getting permission from ATC. Despite her situation, she found herself grinning as she fired the ship up.

Normally, it would take minutes to ready a Corsair to fly, but most of that was perfunctory pre-maintenance checks and services. She kept her bird in top shape for just such emergencies.

Overriding the standard procedures, she slapped the engine start, wrapped her hands around the HOTAS, and jammed the throttle forward. In her mind, she imagined the whine of the plasma turbines as they launched the craft into the air.

It was a twenty-second flight to the warehouse. She thumbed the "weapons hot" button then switched her visual over to Forward Looking Radio Wave. The walls vanished and she could see the people within the warehouse as white splotches against the grey outline of the building.

The Mudcat shook again, violently, throwing her to the side. The Corsair mimicked her movement, losing visual for a moment. She fought with the controls to bring the bird back around.

The Corsair screamed overhead, shaking the Mudcat with her exhaust. She threw the engines in reverse, coming to a near hover. Boudreaux blinked in astonishment.

The Mudcat was on fire. A small explosion had set the surrounding terrain ablaze as well.

She used the scanner to find her assailant. A hundred meters away, behind a low decorative wall, a man was cycling a large rifle and firing at her.

Boudreaux thumbed the safety off the multi-barrel coilgun, locked the ship in place, then switched to the gun. The crosshairs sprang to life and she placed them right over the man with the rifle and pulled the trigger. Dozens of ten-millimeter tungsten balls roared out of the barrel at fifteen hundred meters per second.

Kearne exploded, burned, and vaporized all at the same time.

———

More bullets rained around them. Jacob did his best to find targets, but after Jennings had killed another, they were moving more carefully. Any second, they would have them flanked.

"Captain, I'm here," Chief Boudreaux said over the comms.

"Danger close!" he yelled. He spotted movement and saw a man turn down the aisle toward them, a big rifle shouldered and ready to fire. Jacob dove, slamming into Jennings, shielding her with his body as the man fired.

Boudreaux's voice was lost in the thunder that erupted around them. The roof vanished and concrete exploded as the Corsair's chain gun did its deadly work.

The 10mm rounds blew fist-sized chunks of ceracrete out from the center of impact.

A sudden silence fell over the building. Jacob's ears rang and he blinked several times to clear his vision.

"Captain?" Corporal Jennings asked him from where her face was pressed up against his chest.

"Yes?" he asked.

"You can get off me now, sir," she said with a grin.

"Right!" He pushed himself up, looking around at the devastation. Half the building was just... gone. And the rest was on fire. Pulpy bits of flesh that used to be human beings were pasted over the back side of the building. He tried not to look too closely at them.

"I'll carry Naki. You cover me," he told her.

"Negative, sir," she said as she heaved Naki up and over to rest on both her shoulders. "Switch your pistol to carbine and cover me."

"Corporal, you're going to have to tell me about your home-world some time," he said in amazement.

He fiddled with the pistol for a moment until he found the right setting. Once activated, nanites used reservoirs of matter to enlarge the pistol until it was a small rifle.

He shouldered it then led her toward the missing wall. He made sure to look behind him, even though he knew the sight would haunt him for a long time to come.

———

Merlin Nevil had never run so damn fast in his life. He was shaking from fear and swore he would hear those guns in his ears until the end of his days.

He was half a block away when he turned and looked back at the burning ruins of his life. Just one more score and he would have been set. Now he'd have to call the whole thing off. He'd managed to run off with the plasma launcher and... What if?

He turned, shouldering the weapon. Sure, he could sell it, but if he took out the Corsair, then maybe he could recover the situation. Go back in, kill the people on the ground, and—

———

Threat warning on the Corsair flared to life and Chief Boudreaux reacted without hesitation. The chain gun burped one last time and Merlin Nevil ceased to exist.

CHAPTER EIGHTEEN

P etty Officer First Class Prisca Desper stood ready behind the large yellow and black striped line that marked the bay doors. She had two ratings with her, carrying an anti-grav stretcher. Hanging off her shoulder, she had everything she thought she would need in an easy-to-search-through bag. From what Jennings had said, there were knife and gunshot wounds. Her boss, Commander Stanislav, was down in sickbay getting the surgery suite ready.

Amber lights flashed. The hatches cracked open for the floating Corsair waiting to rise up into the bay. It lifted up, revealing the Mudcat. Desper gasped. When they said they were attacked, she assumed muggers; the Mudcat's exterior was blackened and one of the windows looked almost shattered.

Spacer Apprentice Whips let out a long whistle. Spacer Second Class Eggers straight swore.

"Eggers, secure that," Desper said sharply. The young man stiffened and shut his mouth. She certainly couldn't blame him. The Mudcat looked as if it had been downrange of a live-fire exercise that turned into a bonfire.

She squeezed her fist together, anger flooding through her at anyone who would attack her shipmates. Then she took a breath and let it all out. There was no time for feelings. She needed to be the cold machine in order to do what she must to save lives.

The bay doors swung shut and the Corsair rested on the floor as the amber warning lights shut off. Barely a second passed before the side hatch was thrown open and the captain, covered in blood, leaped out and pointed back inside.

"Move it," she shouted, running forward. She leaped past the captain and into the Corsair. Private Naki was sprawled out and part of his lower torso was... missing. Something had carved him up like a turkey.

Whips dropped to his knees and vomited upon seeing the wound. Desper didn't have time. "On three," she said to Eggers. He grabbed Naki's feet and she his shoulders. She counted, and they slid the wounded private onto the AG stretcher.

Jacob watched them leave the boat bay with Naki hooked up to machines to help him breathe and stay alive. Jennings ran after them, leaving him and Chief Boudreaux in the Corsair.

"You good, Chief?" he asked.

"Me, Skipper, I'm not the one covered in blood," Boudreaux said.

He glanced down at himself and realized he'd bled quite a lot. As the adrenaline wore off, his face began to ache in earnest.

"Ow," he muttered. "Chief? I want the Corsair ready to go back down ASAP. Call whoever you need to call, do what you need to do, but in fifteen minutes you launch. Got it?"

"Aye, sir," she said. Within seconds, she was shouting at her boat crew to turn her around.

Jacob marched to the hatch and slapped one of the easily accessible comm panels.

"Comms, McCall here," the rating on the bridge replied.

"McCall, this is the captain," Jacob said. Eventually, everyone on the ship would recognize his voice, but until then, he needed to remind them who they were speaking with. "Can you transfer me to Lieutenant Bonds?"

"Aye, sir. One second," McCall said.

Static on the line clicked twice before the Marine's voice came back. "Go for Bonds."

"Lieutenant, this is the captain. I want you and your Marines loaded out in combat gear and I want it yesterday."

"Yes, sir. Where are we going?" he asked with a hint of eagerness.

"Kremlin Station. Someone just tried to kill us, and I want to know why. Chief Boudreaux knows the exact location," Jacob said. He ran through what just happened as fast as he could for the Marine.

"Aye, sir. We'll assemble in the boat bay in... eight minutes. Bonds out."

Jacob trusted the Marine to do the job. The boat bay was about to get extremely busy.

He headed for the nearest ladder, crew hustling out of his way as he stormed down the hatchway. Deck three to deck one, then doubling back to the stern and up the ladder to the O-Deck. The exercise and time let the adrenaline fade from his system and allow him some clarity of thought.

"Make a hole," someone shouted as he passed by. He climbed up, re-energized by anger as the situation became clearer. They'd stolen his gravcoil and either wouldn't or couldn't give it back. Instead, they decided to murder his shore party and disappear. Probably on a freighter leaving system soon.

"Captain on the bridge," a Marine whose name he didn't catch shouted as he walked by. Everyone jumped to their feet immediately.

It pleased him that he had their attention. It was good enough, for the moment.

"As you were," he said. "And from now on, only the Officer of the Watch needs to acknowledge my entrance, understood?" he asked.

A chorus of "aye, aye"s followed. Lieutenant West had the con and he vacated the seat and moved aside before he saw Jacob's face.

"Holy crap, sir. Are you okay?" West said in shock as his eyes went wide.

Jacob ignored him and turned to the comms station. "McCall?"

A kid in a uniform that looked entirely too big for him turned from the comms station.

"Sir?" he asked.

"Who's in charge of Kremlin Station?" he asked.

McCall blinked a couple of times before turning back to his computer and punching in a command. "Sergei Rasputin, sir."

The name tickled Jacob's brain and he glanced at West.

"Uh, he's the governor of Zuckabar, sir. His official seat is in the station, but he runs the whole system," West replied.

"Got it. McCall, I want to speak to him right now," Jacob ordered.

"Aye, sir. Calling the station," McCall said.

Not ten seconds later, the boat bay signaled. "Corsair is on departure, Captain," Boudreaux said over the comm.

"Acknowledged." He glanced around the room, then down at himself. Exhaustion was setting in, but he wouldn't, couldn't leave the bridge, nor did he want to. "Mark, can you have the mess send up some of that energy drink they call OJ?" he asked. He softened his visage and tone enough that the crew wouldn't think he was mad at them.

"Aye, sir." The Ops officer turned and went to his station,

leaned over the rating who was currently manning it, and called the mess.

Jacob leaned back in the con, pinching the bridge of his nose to help ease the pain while he pondered his next move.

———

Once again, Chief Boudreaux flew the Corsair toward the gigantic space station. Her adrenaline spike from earlier had left her feeling a little worn, which she fixed by downing a cup of coffee before taking off.

"Chief," Lieutenant Bonds called over the internal comms.

"Yes?" she replied.

"The captain seemed insistent we hurry. Take us right to the scene, no stopping, understood?" he asked.

She glanced down at her instruments for a moment before edging the ship a few degrees to port. "You want a combat drop?"

"A-ffirmative," he said.

"Roger that. One combat drop coming up," Boudreaux said with surprise. Combat drops meant no asking for permission or waiting in lines to enter.

"Kremlin Station, this is Charlie-One-One requesting cleared approach vector into the station," she said.

When they didn't immediately respond, she felt like something was up. This close, radio transmissions were instantaneous.

However, the Marines wanted a combat drop, which meant she didn't stop for anything or anyone. Was it really serious enough to warrant violating civilian rules of transport? It didn't matter: she had her orders.

Boudreaux blocked out the horrible visual of the people

who literally disintegrated under her cannon fire. Yes, it warranted a combat drop.

Kremlin ATC needed to respond soon with her flight path. The entrance flew by off to starboard and she turned the Corsair, bringing the gravcoil around to decelerate and then slammed it hard. The Marines would feel like hell, but she turned the ship on a dime.

She hit relative zero then shot forward for several seconds, heading right toward the opening. The square entrance grew larger by the second until the inside of the station dominated her field of view.

Her radio crackled to life. "Charlie-One-One, you are denied clearance. Turn off your vector immediately," a harried voice said.

"Negative, Kremlin Tower; Charlie-One-One is on official Navy business. Please clear approach vector... one-eight-seven. I will *not* be stopping," she informed them.

Just in case they decided to get cute, she tapped the active ECM button, flooding space with gigawatts of static to prevent radar-guided weapons from targeting her.

She rolled the ship, lining up with her destination as she approached the Richman Field. With one hand, she flipped open the safety on the plasma turbines, waiting for the moment when the Corsair crossed the border.

Electromagnetic energy sparkled off the hull as the ship hit the field.

Chief Boudreaux flipped the switch then punched the button dropping the wings to variable control. The ship shuddered then *thunked* as everything moved into place.

The transition from space to air shook them violently as it suddenly slammed into the atmosphere, slowing down dramatically as the ship now had to contend with the thick air. Plasma turbines screamed to life as she slammed the throttle forward.

She deftly maneuvered her around until the nose was pointed where she wanted to go.

Kremlin Station's ATC operator swore at her before cutting the line. She was ready to pull her headset off anyway. The kind of flying she was doing, dodging other air vehicles, required concentration, and he was a distraction she didn't need.

Once past the opening, she dropped to the deck, shaking the buildings as she flew by them. When they drove the Mudcat, the trip had taken nearly thirty minutes; in the Corsair, it took less than three seconds.

She rolled the ship at the last second and flipped the vertical wings to point the thrusters down. The Corsair went from 500 KPH to a stop in three seconds. The air screamed around the wings as she came to a hover. The Mudcat detached, dropping two meters to the ground, bouncing on its massive suspension.

Boudreaux smashed the throttle forward, burning through the station's sky to orbit five hundred meters out where she could provide fire support for the Marines at a moment's notice.

———

Lieutenant Paul Bonds braced as the Mudcat dropped. They were in soft armor for the deployment. Donning their space armor or Raptor-powered armor wouldn't have fit the captain's timetable. Bonds admired the man for his decisive action. He wasn't sure there was a captain in the fleet who would have given the order Grimm did.

Private Cole slammed the throttle and all six wheels spun, lunging the big armored vehicle down the lane where Boudreaux had dropped them. There was a crowd forming along the street leading to the burned-out building. Three air cars hovered over the scene, with red and blue lights flashing in the station's afternoon light.

None of that mattered to Bonds. Navy personnel and *his* Marines had come under fire. One of them fought for his life onboard the *Interceptor*. If he couldn't be there for Naki, he'd damn well make sure the right people paid for the damage.

Cole slammed the brakes, locking the tires up and skidding to a halt. Four hatches opened at once and the Marines bounded out, two-by-two, dropping into cover and clearing their fields of fire before advancing on the building.

Bonds noticed the uniformed officers on scene at what used to be the entrance of the building before Chief Boudreaux shot the hell out of it.

"Clear," Gunny Hicks yelled. Most of this was for show. Bonds wanted no resistance from the locals. This was his crime scene, and his Marines and the Navy were going to investigate it.

He slipped out of the 'Cat, his MP-17 holstered on his hip and the larger rifle version slung over his back. He knew how intimidating the Marines looked in full kit; black and gray camouflage with armored plates over vital areas and their harnesses loaded down with extra ammo and grenades. He walked toward the gathered police officers, boots crunching on rubble as he did so.

"The lady certainly knows how to party," Gunny Hicks said over the team comm.

Someone let out a low whistle in agreement. From the ground, Bonds picked out at least two dead Tangos... or what was left of them. The coilgun on the front of the Corsair didn't leave a lot of anything.

"Who are you supposed to be?" a greasy bearded officer asked. The officer's uniform was wrinkled and there was a yellow stain on his sleeve. Bonds immediately didn't like the man.

"The man in charge. Lieutenant Paul Bonds, Alliance

Marine Corps. Thank you for securing the scene, but your presence is no longer permissible. This is a military matter," he informed them. His voice rumbled like rocks falling.

Bonds might as well have told the man to eat his gun for the incredulous look the officer gave him.

"Perimeter secure," the gunny said, appearing next to Bonds.

"Let the swabbies in the back know it's safe to come out," Bonds ordered.

The Marines had dragged two of Beckett's engineers down with them. How the hell would a Marine know what a gravcoil looked like outside the ship? Or if it was usable? The swabbies could figure it out, though.

"Now listen here, *Marine*." Greasy Beard used the word as a pejorative. "This is a Kremlin Station police matter. You can just take your fancy show and your men and get the hell off my station," he said.

Paul looked back at the Mudcat, making sure the Navy ratings were getting out before turning back to Greasy Beard. He narrowed his eyes at the man, bringing out his inner drill instructor as he spoke.

"Marines—*my Marines*—were assaulted on these premises while trying to recover sensitive Navy equipment. When military personnel are attacked while on duty, regardless of where they are, it becomes a military matter. Period. End of discussion. If you don't want you and your men embarrassed by being mag-cuffed and left on the street, I suggest you pull back and re-assess your authority." His tone brooked no debate.

"Now one damn second—" Greasy Beard took one step forward and reached for his pistol. Apparently, the man with him had far more intelligence and grabbed his arm.

"Dammit, Pasha, they're Alliance Marines. You want to

throw down with them? Get your head out of your ass and just call the governor."

Pasha wasn't happy about having to leave, but the other man convinced him it was in his best interest. Which it absolutely was. Pasha hadn't seen PFC Owens standing four feet behind them with a stun stick in one hand and mag-cuffs in the other.

———

"I've got the governor on the line, sir," McCall said from comms.

"On my screen," Jacob replied. As the image came to life, he heard footsteps and glanced over to see Yuki enter the bridge, her eyes going wide when she saw the blood on him. He turned back to the screen to see a red-faced man with a bushy, black, beard glaring daggers at him.

"Captain Grimm, I don't even know where to begin with all the laws you've broken. I demand you immediately withdraw all military personnel from the planet and the station and turn yourself in to my law enforcement for prosecution!"

Jacob's blood boiled, but he managed to keep a lid on his temper. He had the moral and legal authority here. He didn't need to ruin it by getting angry.

"Governor Rasputin, perhaps you're not aware of the situation, but I was attacked, one of my crew was wounded, perhaps fatally... in a warehouse *on your station*. My ship is missing its gravcoil, and when we tried to retrieve it, we were nearly killed. I don't think that's a coincidence."

"What you *believe* has nothing to do with it. This is my system and my station. You will turn yourself over for prosecution—"

Jacob leaned back and really looked at the governor. He was awfully dismissive of the attack, even with the blood on Jacob's shirt. The governor went on for a minute ranting about laws and treaties and how no mere commander had the authority to do what he did.

"Governor. You don't seem to understand the magnitude of the situation. As far as I'm concerned, everyone who had access to our gravcoil is complicit in this crime. That includes the ship that removed it, the shipyard, the transport drivers, the people in the warehouse, and anyone who did business with them. Under the Treaty of Protection, we can seize everything and investigate. Or you can get off your high horse and assist us." Jacob was done caring. Maybe it was the exhaustion, or maybe it was the pain, he didn't know. But he wasn't going to let this go on another second. And he certainly wasn't to go back down. If he did, his crew would never trust him.

The governor paused, mouth open. He looked off screen for a moment then narrowed his eyes at Jacob and sat back in his expensive chair, assessing the commander from a new light. Clearly, he had a lawyer who had actually read the treaty. Just as Jacob had on his eight-day flight to Zuckabar.

"My Prosecutor General tells me the treaty does in fact grant you this authority." He glanced to the side again. "Mark my words, *Commander*, you will regret this."

The screen filled with static for a moment before shutting off. No one on the bridge moved. The tension from the confrontation lay thick in the air.

"I think you ruffled some feathers, Skipper," the XO said.

Had he heard her right? He turned, shocked, and she gave a small nod. Trust earned. She'd called him Skipper.

There were many ways to address officers in uniform. With the lower ranks, the more formal the daily address, the less respect they were shown. Skipper was the ultimate honorific for the same reason Jennings called Lieutenant Bonds "El-Tee." She respected him.

Yuki had said it out loud, in front of the rest of the crew. He realized he was staring and then smiled at her with a slight nod.

"I'm sure the governor and I will be the best of friends. In the meantime," he said, standing shakily to his feet, "XO, you have the con. I'll be in sickbay if you need me."

"Aye, Skipper," Yuki said. "I have the con."

CHAPTER NINETEEN

Professor Bellaits had outfitted the CSV *Dagger* with the advanced gravitic sensors he would need as they circumnavigated the system listening for space-time disruption. Zuckabar was a trade hub; the constant shipping activity slightly complicated his job, but no more so than the Praetor system in the Consortium where he'd spent most of last year doing the same thing. The two systems were the key.

"Professor?" Daisy asked him from the door.

"Yes?" he replied without looking up from his field journal. It was a pocket-sized computer with every measurement, map, and note he'd made about his theories on gravity for the past fifty years.

"The, uh, captain?" She stumbled over the word. "She said we're ready to lift whenever you are."

"Excellent, I'll eat in my cabin," he said absently. He missed the look of concern Daisy gave him.

"No, sir, lift-off. We're taking off, not eating," she said.

He shook his head, laughing as he stood. "Right. Yes. Let's do that." Daisy turned, leading him up three flights to the bridge deck.

As they entered the bridge, Daisy peeled off to speak with one of the ship's crew. Professor Bellaits, though, wanted the best seat in the house. He went directly to the captain's chair and stood next to Nadia Dagher.

Bellaits wasn't a navy man—at all—but he could see efficiency in the way Captain Dagher ran her ship. The crew were well dressed, clean, and orderly. The bridge itself had plenty of lighting, and the metallic surfaces were free from dirt. He noticed the carpet could use replacing, but other than that, he found no fault with the way she kept her ship.

"Professor, thank you for joining us." The dark-haired captain pointed at the main screen. "We're going to make one stop on Kremlin; overnight, I'm afraid," Nadia told him.

"I was under the impression we were starting immediately?" he asked. He pulled his field journal up to eye level, holding it out to read the dates.

"*Dagger*'s material reserves are low and if we want to stay out for more than a month before returning... Well, we don't want to run out of the basics," Nadia said with a grin.

"Yes, yes. Of course. You're the captain after all. As long as we are..." he checked the calculations on his journal, "...on an orbital plane at more than one billion kilometers from the primaries in the next four days."

"That's rather specific," she said with a raised eyebrow.

"There's no room for error, none at all. It has to be one billion."

He missed the worry flashing across her face. "Professor, you came highly recommended, and your money is as good as anyone's, but is there a danger to my ship I should be aware of?" she asked in a whisper.

Unfortunately, Professor Bellaits lacked the social awareness to answer in kind.

"Danger? No danger, none at all," he said louder than

before. The only danger was someone discovering the prize before him. They had no time to lose.

———

When Nadia had received the message from an old contact, informing her about the job and, more importantly, the large amount of money for doing practically nothing, she'd cheered. Despite what she had told the good-looking commander during the trip here, jobs had dried up of late. While she nominally owned *Dagger,* the crew still had to be paid and expendables purchased.

She wondered, though, was it chance she just happened to see the job while they were parked on Alexandria? She wouldn't put it past Admiral DeBeck to set something like this up for her. The old man had shepherded her career, of sorts. Always giving her the choice assignments... until the last one.

He always had an ulterior motive, though. Like how he sent Jacob her way so she could probe him for information. What could he have gained from giving her a semi-senile old man looking for space ghosts?

Of course, she admitted, she was *very* good at her former job. Spying was second nature to her and she'd enjoyed it immensely. Enough that sometimes, late at night, she regretted leaving.

She shook her head free of the regretful thoughts and focused on the job at hand.

Two billion klicks out would put them about even with the outermost asteroid belt. Though calling it a *belt* was generous. There would be no danger of collision, but pirates...? Maybe.

Everyone in the system had heard about the pirate attack on *Agamemnon.* That was Minsc, though, and a large freighter. She could pull acceleration much higher than an M-class. She also had a gun or two the authorities didn't know about.

Which was good, because Zuckabar's in-system patrol craft weren't enough to defend her against a foreign aggressor. And since the Alliance wasn't interested in expanding the borders or patrolling the route beyond the Protectorate, well, something had to give.

And it wouldn't be the pirates. If the attack recently broadcasted was any indication, they were just getting bolder. Lucky for her, the *Dagger* wasn't a viable target.

"Take her up, Barnes," she said to her helmsman. The *Dagger* rumbled as she lifted off the ice-covered planet. She imagined what it would look like in a few hundred more years. Maybe less white? The snow was bad today and visibility was zero. It was all instrument reckoning from the moment they lifted off.

Gravcoils were great for propulsion in a vacuum, but deep in a planet's gravity well, they simply didn't work. The ship shook as it rotated on its lateral thrusters, and they were all pushed back as the plasma turbines shot her up into space. Her hand shot out and grabbed the professor to hold him in place until he reached up and secured his hold on the grab bar.

"Sorry," he muttered.

Endless white was quickly replaced by the blackness of space as the *Dagger* shot out of the atmosphere.

"Well done, Barnes," she said. He beamed at the compliment. She always liked to make sure her crew knew when they'd done a good job.

"Captain?" Pete said from the comm station.

"Yes?"

"There's a lot of elevated chatter over at Kremlin. We're twenty minutes out, but it sounds like they're closing the station for a few hours." He glanced at her, sharing a look of shock. They *never* closed the station.

"What? Closing the station?" she repeated, despite having heard him clearly.

"Right? There was an incident and... Oh wow." Pete stopped cold, cocking his head to the side. His eyes went wide with shock. "You got to see this."

He hit a button and the giant forward view screen lit up with a video from inside the Kremlin. From what she could tell, the view was just one of a thousand cameras Kremlin used to keep the peace. There was a series of buildings, warehouses from the looks of it, a decorative rock wall and... an Alliance-issue Mudcat parked in front of one. The image was in perfect clarity, even though the camera itself was probably a few hundred meters away.

"Is this live?" Bellaits asked. She was so engrossed in the footage, she'd forgotten he was there.

Just as she opened her mouth to answer, a Corsair screamed into view. The camera shook from its passage. A moment later, the audio cut out as the chain gun on her nose went to work, obliterating a rock wall and a person hiding behind it. Then it turned its ferocious cannon on the building.

"Mother of God," someone whispered.

Nadia was no stranger to combat. She'd spent the better part of her career as a special agent with the Office of Naval Intelligence. It had all been small and personal. The level of violence the Corsair brought to the field was unlike anything she'd experienced. It was awe-inspiring.

"That was twenty minutes ago," Pete said, transfixed by the scene.

"Did the military go insane? How could they do that to those people?" the professor's assistant cried out.

Nadia examined the bottom of the feed closer. Only half the Mudcat was visible, but from what she could tell, it was on fire.

Someone had attacked them and the man she'd agreed to have dinner with had unleashed hell in response. He certainly wasn't holding back.

She didn't know if that excited or scared her... Maybe both?

CHAPTER TWENTY

Lieutenant Bonds eyed Gunny Hicks, Lance Corporal Jennings, and the rest of the platoon—minus PFC Naki —as they made their final equipment checks while snug in the belly of the Corsair.

Each Marine was greenlit by another. They wore what they affectionately called "space armor." It was the Marine variant of the ELS suits, armored for combat and equipped with a full comm and sensor package. Once fully donned, they looked more like medieval robots than Marines, with metal plates over the vitals and sleek, angled visors designed to deflect attacks.

Space armor was worn whenever boarding a potentially hostile ship—or when repelling borders in the rare cases where it happened. The Alliance Marines learned long before not to trust anyone on a suspect ship; it was too easy for a guilty party to blow an airlock or trap a person in a section of the ship and dump toxic fumes into the ventilation system. In their armor, they were immune to any environmental hazard and could even maneuver in space with limited thrusters.

After spending forty-eight hours straight studying the ruined computers they had recovered from the warehouse, the XO had found what they were looking for. The Terran Republic freighter *Madrigal* was the end destination for all the illicit goods Merlin Nevil and his deceased crew were shipping out of the system. It was just in the nick of time too. *Madrigal* was scheduled to depart in less than twenty-four hours.

Since the captain's last attempt to go looking for the gravcoil had resulted in a small battle, he decided to leave it to Lieutenant Paul Bonds and his Marines to ask any further questions.

Something Bonds was more than happy to do.

"Marines, who are we?" Gunny Hicks yelled as they lined up in the main section of the Corsair.

"Killers," they shouted back as one.

"Damn straight. El-Tee, we're ready," the gunny said.

Bonds nodded, checking the readout on his heads-up display. "Chief, time?"

Boudreaux's voice crackled back in his ear as if she stood next to him. "Thirty seconds."

"Have they seen us?" he asked.

"Who do you think is flying this ship? A monkey? We're running silent, *Paul*," she said.

Lieutenant Bonds cringed as she used his first name. The damn woman liked to get under his skin at any given opportunity.

"Fair enough, Viv," he said before cutting the connection. Using *her* first name was the only thing he could think of to get back at her.

He imagined her shocked face and it brought a smile to his own. Then he cleared his mind for the task at hand.

"Gunny, stack up," he bellowed.

"You heard the man, eyeholes and elbows, stack up!" Gunny Hicks didn't quite yell, but he had a way of talking like a drill instructor at all times.

The Marines lined up on the airlock, each one placing their left hand on the shoulder of the Marine in front of them.

The Corsair was designed for a variety of roles and could connect to virtually any airlock. For boarding in combat situations, though, they used the airlock built into the belly, it allowed the Corsair's weapon systems and ECM to cover them while they entered.

Bonds pulled up an external camera, eying their progress. The freighter was massive but the crew area was fairly small, maybe twice the size of the *Interceptor*. His Marines would be on top of any hostiles in a heartbeat. Then they would have their ship's gravcoil back, and if they were lucky, some answers.

The captain was taking a huge chance on this. Boarding a foreign-flagged vessel wasn't quite like raiding an embassy, but it could have ramifications. All of which were well above Bonds' paygrade. His was but to do or die, not to question why.

Of course, he knew the reason the captain was being so bold... What did the man have to lose? In more than one way, it was refreshing to have a commander who gave a damn; in another way, a bit nerve-racking. But whatever the captain did and wherever he went, after the way he risked his life to pull PFC Naki out of the fire and lit those bastards up with the Corsair, the Marines of Third Platoon Company B would follow.

"Contact," Chief Boudreaux said over the open channel. The ship *thunked* as it sealed to the freighter.

"Oorah, Marines," Bonds said.

The Marines shouted their ancient battle cry back at him.

"Owens, burn it," the gunny ordered.

The Corsair hatch slid sideways to reveal the emergency airlock located on *Madrigal*'s stern compartment. PFC Owens, the platoon's electronics expert, dropped to one knee and hooked a cable to the external computer on the hull of the ship. "Ten seconds," he said.

Bonds flexed his fingers, taking deep breaths to relax his mind and let his training take over. Despite his rank and experience, he'd never actually done what they were about to do in a live-fire capacity. In fact, he didn't think any of the Marines under his command had. They'd trained for close-quarters combat, of course, day in and day out since they joined the Corps. This was why they trained as if it were real; so when it *was* real, their training would kick in. He was ready. *They* were ready.

The airlock slid open. Hicks yelled, "Go! Go! Go!"

Jennings leaped in first. Gravity on the Corsair was at odds with the *Madrigal*, leaving Jennings looking as if she went down a slide, leaping into the hole then sliding out the other side on her back with her MP-17 stretched out in front of her in carbine mode. She remained in position, covering the corridor while the rest of the Marines came in behind her.

Once the platoon was inside, Owens shut the hatch and encrypted the computer, preventing anyone but the Marines from opening it again.

"Alpha team, bridge. Bravo, engineering," Bonds said. It was more of a reflex than anything else. His people knew their assignments.

He took Jennings and Owens with him to the bridge while the gunny took the rest of the team to the engine room. Once they had control of the ship and the crew was accounted for, they could then search her top to bottom.

Like most freighters, the halls were a tight fit, just enough room for a single person in armor. One of the many advantages of the highly configurable MP-17 was its ability, at the touch of a button, to change from pistol, SMG, carbine, rifle, or sniper rifle in a few seconds. In these tight quarters, SMGs or carbines worked best,

"What the fu—" a man said as he came out of a stateroom

right by Jennings. She punched him in the stomach, instantly dropping him to his knees. Jennings slammed his face into the deck and proceeded to mag-cuff him and toss him back in the room. Bonds winced at the impact and the red smear on the deck.

"Clear," she said.

Bonds didn't envy that man. Having sparred with Jennings, he knew she hit like a hammer wielded by a gorilla.

They resumed their progress to the bridge, checking each intersection as they went. The time on his HUD updated to 0405—the perfect time to raid a ship in port. The crew would be deep into the last watch, half asleep, and they would never expect what was coming.

Once they were at the bridge level, Bonds signaled them to hold back. He flipped the selector switch on his MP-17 to non-lethal ten-millimeter rounds that stung like hell and hit hard enough to leave fist-sized bruises.

He ducked his head in, taking in the scene. The bridge was located at the top of the ship, with a large viewscreen over-looking the topside hull. Unlike a Navy ship with its circular bridge design, the freighter had three rows of stations, with the captain's chair position against the stern bulkhead.

Three crew members occupied the bridge. Two of them were sitting with their feet up on the front row consoles, watching a movie on the screen. The third, a woman with short-cropped brown hair, was at least nominally on duty, glancing at her workstation every once in a while before resuming watching the movie with the other two.

Bonds turned to his Marines and raised three fingers. He would go in first, moving hard left. Owens was second, taking the middle, and Jennings would go hard starboard. They would pie the room, take out their sectors, and converge on the middle.

Bonds shook his shoulders to loosen them up before inching up to the bridge hatch. Owens put a hand on his shoulder, letting him know they were ready.

He charged in, going far left, leaving Owens and Jennings to take the closer targets. He made it halfway across the bridge before the first person noticed. She turned her head, saw them, and opened her mouth to shout when Jennings fired. The 10mm stun round bounced off her shoulder, tipping her backward over her chair.

The two other crew started moving and Owens and Bonds fired. Their dead-center shots brought the men down with groans of pain.

Seconds after entering the bridge, they controlled the ship.

"Owens, lock down comms and computers. Jennings, secure the hostiles."

One of the crew partially recovered and started swearing at them. Jennings slapped him across the face, turned him over, and cuffed his hands behind his back.

———

The atmosphere on *Interceptor*'s bridge felt thick and full of tension. Or more likely, Jacob's muscles were tense.

It was one thing to command his crew while they were on the ship, another entirely to send them where he couldn't help. Even if he wanted to assist, they could only move the *Interceptor* on thrusters. It would take hours at that speed to reach RTV *Madrigal*.

Instead, he swiveled slightly back and forth in his command chair, drumming his fingers silently on the armrest. It was third watch, and he could tell the crew was a little nervous to have him on duty. He wouldn't normally be up this early, but there was no way he could sleep while his people were in danger.

Not for the first time, he hovered his finger over the call button, determined to find out what was going on. He knew better, though, and put his hand down. They would report when there was something to report. Instead, he rubbed his palms down his uniform pants to relieve his stress.

He heard footsteps behind him and glanced over his shoulder; Lieutenant Yuki entered the bridge holding two cups with steam wafting off them.

"Kim, what are you doing up?" he asked as she joined him at the chair. She handed him a cup. He thought it was coffee at first, but no, it was mint tea. *How* had she figured out he didn't drink coffee? It wasn't something spacers advertised, since coffee was the true lifeblood of the Navy.

"We're having trouble with the number four turret again. It keeps freezing while traversing, but not every time, making it annoying to troubleshoot. I was down there with an engineering crew taking it apart to see if we could figure out how to make the damn thing work," she said.

He raised his cup to her and smiled. Crew morale was climbing steadily. It had taken time, and oh so many drills, and he was generous with his praise when the crew did well. At first, he worried it would be months, but discipline was an old friend and it was far easier to re-instill than create. He was quite shocked at how fast things were improving.

"Any luck?" he asked.

Before she could answer, Spacer Second Class Gouger interrupted from comms, "Sir, Lieutenant Bonds for you."

"On my panel. Kim, you should hear this too," Jacob said.

The XO nodded, leaning in so the pickup would show her on the screen.

Bonds' helmet was in the process of retracting when the screen went live. He had a bead of sweat on his brow but otherwise looked unperturbed.

"Skipper, we have control of the *Madrigal*. There wasn't much resistance. If the whole crew is hardened criminals, I'll eat my bars," he said.

"No casualties, then?" Jacob asked.

Bonds shook his head. "None, sir. Maybe some wounded pride at how easily we took them down. PFC Owens is in their computers. He's ready to link to *Interceptor* and let the XO handle it from there. She'll know what to do with it."

Jacob turned to Yuki. "Can you get with Ensign Hössbacher and go over the logs?"

"Aye, sir. On it." She turned and left the bridge, calling the ensign to wake him up as she did so.

"The XO will have our end set up shortly. Do you need any assistance going over the actual cargo?" he asked.

"Not right now, sir. Corporal Jennings is down there opening every crate, nook, and cranny and... One second, sir," he said, holding his finger to the screen. He turned his head, listening to whatever information was coming in. His face hardened, lips going thin as he tensed.

Jacob had to fight the urge to press him on the details.

"Uh, Captain, I think you're going to want to see this in person... and bring the doc," he said. Jacob didn't know Lieutenant Bonds well, but from the way he looked and sounded, something serious had happened.

"Send the Corsair back. I'm on my way," Jacob said, already standing up.

An hour later, the Corsair approached the *Madrigal* for the second time. Having control of the freighter meant they could use the standard commercial airlock, keeping the Corsair in line with the *Madrigal*'s gravity. Once the ship locked on, the light next to the hatch turned green.

Jacob stopped Commander Stanislaw from opening the hatch right away. Instead, he waited the requisite few seconds after the light turned green to make sure the seal was in place. As good as their tech was, this was the military after all. Seals didn't fail often, but when they did, people died.

"All clear," Boudreaux said over the comms.

Jacob hit the button cycling the lock, and the heavy hatch rolled aside. He stepped into the *Madrigal*'s gravity, his stomach doing a momentary flip-flop as he passed from one gravity field to another.

This time, he hadn't needed the Marines to tell him to come armed. The regs required it and he knew them up and down. His MP-17 was buckled on and holstered, along with an extra mag in his field jacket. Just in case.

Commander Stanislaw and Chief Petty Officer Pierre followed behind him at a comfortable distance. They wore the white uniforms with the silver cross on the chest denoting medical personnel.

Lance Corporal Jennings greeted them at the end of the corridor. She looked relaxed, as if she were out on a stroll, her rifle resting easy on her chest, with the barrel pointed down and both hands on the stock. After Kremlin, though, Jacob knew it was a façade. With her cat-like reflexes and razor-sharp combat skills, the woman was always ready to fight.

"This way, sir. We're going to the main hold. You won't effing believe this," she said. Jacob appreciated the innovative way the Marines managed to get around the Navy's "no swearing" policy.

He followed her along the metal halls then down two flights of stairs. It was cold in the ship, even colder than the *Interceptor*, which made him glad for his watch cap and field jacket fighting to keep him warm.

At the bottom of the second flight, the room opened and there was a long hallway large enough to drive a cargo lift through. The rails on the ceiling confirmed that it was indeed the main hold. Meter thick pressure hatches were wide open and Jacob paused for a second when he saw what the Marines were doing.

The crew of the *Madrigal* were on their knees, hands behind their heads, with their fingers interlaced and ankles crossed. Two Marines had their MP-17s out and pointed at the prisoners.

"El-Tee," Jacob greeted Bonds once inside. He'd heard the other Marines call the lieutenant by the nickname and wanted to impress upon them and Bonds that he was the kind of captain who didn't need every interaction to be strictly formal. "What's going on?" A feeling of confusion and dread nagged at him. Bonds and the rest of the Marines had their helmets retracted, showing their confidence in their control of the ship. Yet the way he'd told him to hurry over had him worried.

"The good news first, sir. Owens?" he shouted.

A Marine with bright red hair cut high and tight poked his head out from behind a stack of equipment on the far wall. "I've got it. One refurbished military-grade gravcoil. It's ours, sir. We can get the *Interceptor* back up and running in no time."

Jacob let out a sigh of relief. This was the best news he'd heard all week. "Well done, Paul. You and your Marines are a credit—"

Bonds shook his head in a sharp movement. "That was the good news, sir. Now for the bad." He motioned for the doctor to follow.

Jacob worried about the doctor. Stanislaw hadn't spoken on the twenty-minute flight over from the destroyer. According to his FITREPs, he was good at his job but extremely introverted.

Jacob followed the Marines past the first row of secured cargo. All of it sealed with Alliance branded customs tape and set to be delivered. "Where was this ship heading?" he asked.

"Praetor most likely, since it's the closest to the Caliphate."

Jacob cocked his head at the Marine, wondering why he'd brought that up.

They led him toward the first of many rows of white, oblong boxes with Alliance customs taped around them. A large sticker on each box indicated they were individually powered.

Two of the containers were open. Mist crawled out and over the sides, falling to the deck before disappearing. Lieutenant Bonds stopped next to one and waved for Jacob to look.

His heart sank as he approached, his subconscious putting the puzzle together before he saw the lock of golden blonde hair on the woman's head. She was lying in the fetal position, stark naked, hooked into the cryo-pod.

"What the—" Jacob reflexively took a step back, a low growl sounding in his throat. "Commander Stanislaw," he said, pointing at the woman.

Stanislaw and Chief Pierre rushed to the cryo-pod. To their credit, they moved swiftly and professionally, not missing a beat as they went to work.

Rage built in Jacob, a visceral primal tidal wave of fury wrapped him in heat and he did everything he could not to draw his sidearm and start shooting the crew.

"Have you touched anything?" Commander Stanislaw asked the Marine while scanning the woman.

"No, sir. We opened a second one to see if it was a fluke. We didn't try to wake them," he said. Jacob noticed Bonds' thick voice. The large man was visibly angry, but was making every attempt to stay calm.

"The manifest says these are perishable goods of an assorted edible variety," Jennings added as they went to work.

"Is she alive?" Jacob asked. Cryo-pod travel wasn't used anymore. With the advent of the gravcoil and the discovery of starlanes centuries before, there was no need. Even if a ship planned to sail out to the nearest edge of the galaxy, they could go and be back in a couple of years.

Before the gravcoil, colonies were established using sleeper ships on four-hundred-year journeys to stars relatively close to Earth. Only a few of those ever made it to their intended world.

Once the gravcoil was invented and the starlanes were discovered, faster-than-light travel made cryo pods largely unnecessary. Most sleeper ships arrived at their destination with colonies already built—if they arrived at all. Cryo-pod tech was safe, but there was just no need to use it anymore. Except for people who were gravely ill and needed more time to reach a hospital or... if the shipper needed to move people undetected.

"She's alive," Commander Stanislaw said from the second crate with a relieved sigh. "And in good health. No major illness or disease."

"This one too, sir," Chief Pierre added. "Vitals are strong. She's probably fine to wake, but..." He glanced around at the assorted boxes.

"How many?" Jacob asked.

"Two hundred and forty," Bonds said in his deep voice. "So far."

"Two hundred and forty?" he repeated helplessly.

"So far," Bonds said again.

They didn't have the medical supplies or facilities to wake them properly. Even if he did, the life support needed for so many people on board a ship was enormous. Neither of the ships he had access to would work.

"There are eight more cargo decks in the main hold and four more auxiliary holds. It's hard to say how many in total," Bonds informed him.

"Are you serious, Paul? There are more than these here?" Jacob asked, waving his arm to encompass what he could see.

Bonds nodded. "Yes, sir. We've eyeballed the other decks; they all have rows and rows of these... pods... in them."

What were the odds the *Interceptor* would stumble across the only ship like this? Zero to none. There had to be more. How many more was what he didn't know.

"Sir?" Chief Pierre asked from where he knelt next to the first pod.

"Yes?" Jacob replied.

"Whoever she is, she's not an Alliance citizen. Which means she's spent a while in this cryo-pod. Based on the level of toxicity I'm reading... I'd say Terran Republic, maybe even Earth."

"It's worse than just this, Captain," Bonds said. "We don't have the details yet, but, on a hunch, the gunny opened a few of the non-cryo pods and they were mislabeled as well."

"Which means black market," Jacob said. This was getting worse by the second.

The new captain of the *Interceptor* pondered what to do next. Despite his brave front with the governor, at the end of the day, he was just a lieutenant commander, and not even a real one at that! A frocking was a fragile thing. Granted for a need to fill a role, it could be taken away just as quickly.

He turned and walked away from them. Bonds started to follow, but Jacob held his hand out for him to stay back. He needed a moment. He tapped the comm unit in his ear.

"Chief Boudreaux, put me through to the ship," he said.

The Corsair had a tight-beam laser pointed at the *Interceptor*. All communications went through the secure line and it took a few seconds for her to transfer him.

There was a moment of static, then he heard the comms watch officer answer. "I need to speak to the XO," he told the young man. A few seconds later, Yuki's voice filled his ear.

"Yes, sir?"

"Kim, we have a problem and I need you to look up the regs

for me." He glanced up and made sure no one was in earshot of him. Despite that, he pitched his voice low. "Can you get to a computer?" He could use his Nav-Pad, but it wasn't really about knowing the regs—he knew them. It was about his XO confirming his interpretation. When the review board asked, he wanted to make sure he didn't act unilaterally.

"Yes, sir. One mike," Yuki said.

He heard her rustle around for a second and then she was ready.

"What is the penalty for a civilian caught smuggling involuntary human cargo and what do I do with the ship?" he asked. Involuntary human cargo was such a clinical description for a fate as old as humanity. They were slaves.

He'd never even heard of a slave ring in Alliance space before. Oh, there were always rumors of human trafficking, but… he'd never seen it firsthand. Almost every nation, even the Iron Empire, was against slavery. The only exception was the Caliphate of Hamid.

Ships were searched regularly during customs inspections. For this ship to have arrived here with these people on board seemed unlikely. But it seemed just as unlikely that they were transferred from another ship. Any such transfer would have to be inspected, wouldn't it? Ships whose end destinations were in or near Caliphate space were searched even more thoroughly.

Kim's voice came back real quiet. "Are you sure, sir?"

"Yes. No question. I'll have Bonds send you the details," he said, voice barely above a whisper.

She sighed heavily into the mic. "Sir, uh, I don't know. I don't want to be the only voice here. Maybe we should contact Kremlin Station and—"

"Kim, what do the regs say?" he asked again, making it clear he was ordering her.

"They're to be arrested and sent to Alexandria for trial.

Where, if they are found guilty, they will be shot. As for the ship, we seize it and all the cargo and send it back to HQ," she said.

Shot. There was no doubt they were guilty, of that he was sure. Would the Alliance risk an altercation with the Terran Republic to punish slavers?

In his heart, he fervently wished so. He wished the Navy he dreamed of as a boy, the Navy his mother had sacrificed her life for, would act as honorably as possible.

In his head, he knew the crew would probably go free and return to Republic space, where the likelihood of them receiving punishment was slim. It wasn't that the Republic was corrupt, or more precisely, not *only* corrupt. They were the oldest nation, almost eight hundred years old, and they had laws stacked on laws. From what he'd read at the Academy, there was always a loophole.

"How many hands you think we'd need to operate the ship?" he asked.

She tapped away on her end for a minute. "We don't exactly have crew to spare, sir," Yuki said. He could hear the frown in her voice.

"I know, but how many?" In his own mind, he thought fifteen, but there was no way they could send that many over.

"Ten, at least. I know a couple of ratings with civilian experience who could do it, but we'll have to send one officer, maybe two... not to mention enough to guard the crew round the clock. Say, eighteen."

No matter how he added it up, it would leave the *Interceptor* critically, dangerously, shorthanded, and he couldn't do it. Even if every department donated a crew member, it would leave them unable to operate the destroyer in anything but a severely diminished capacity.

Nor could he send it back to Alexandria with a skeleton crew. It was a big, slow ship, and the chance of her making the journey back to Alliance space without intervention was slim. Someone was going to miss their "cargo" and come looking for it. Of course, if it stayed here, the picket would return and he could let Commodore Xin escort it back, which might be the prudent thing to do.

"Kim? Have West come over with the three newest apprentices. Enough for a watch each. We might not be able to send *Madrigal* back to Alliance space, but we can man her in case of emergency. We'll also detach the Marine platoon here to act as security." Spacer's apprentices were the lowest rank in the Navy. Brand new from boot camp, with very little training, they were apprenticing on the job. Once they were competent, they would be promoted to spacer second class. The *Interceptor* could afford to do without them.

"Aye, sir, I'm on it," Yuki said.

He terminated the call and motioned for Bonds to join him. The lieutenant was probably the only person on board who was as tall as Jacob; he was sure he could share a drink with the man and trade stories about bumping into bulkheads.

"Paul, move your Marines, and all the supplies you will need, to the *Madrigal*. Full combat kit. We don't have the crew to send her back like the regs require, but we can keep her secure until Commodore Xin returns with the picket," he said.

"PFC Naki is still in sickbay, sir. But other than him, that will leave the *Interceptor* with no Marines and I'm not a fan of that, sir," Bonds said.

Jacob nodded, placing a hand on the man's shoulder. "Me either. However, with this much at stake, we can't risk the *Madrigal*'s crew trying something." Jacob glanced at the line of crew still on their knees. "No comms, right? No one knows we've seized the ship?" he asked.

"Yes, sir. No one knows. Begging the captain's pardon, but why the secrecy? This is a big win for us. We saved a lot of lives here, not to mention the recovery of stolen property. What's going on?"

"I agree, and I would like to keep them saved. There's at least five hundred million Alliance dollars' worth of slaves back there... and counting. If word got out they were on the ship, what exactly could we do to stop every pirate with a gunboat from seizing this rig? Or the people who were expecting it on the other end? Or Kremlin Station?"

"We're not in Alliance space..." Commander Beckett's warning came back to him about how dangerous Zuckabar could be. "Bottom line, until the Commodore returns or I can get a secure message to the fleet, we're on babysitting duty. On top of the fact," he grimaced as he realized what he was going to say, "that once the gravcoil is reinstalled, I'm going to *have* to take the *Interceptor* out on regular patrols or it will be a dead giveaway what has happened."

Bonds' eyes widened. He hadn't thought about the possibility of a counterattack. Or that their only real protection was secrecy.

"Get all your Marines and find a very, *very* secure place for the prisoners. They cannot, under any circumstances, be allowed access to comms. Then lock this ship down, understood?" Jacob asked.

"Semper fi, sir," Bonds replied.

"Jennings," Jacob called the Marine. She trotted over as if her combat gear weighed nothing.

"Sir?" she asked.

"I want you to go out into the passageway. I'm thinking at least two of the crew had to be involved. It's too big for a one-man job, and three would be too much of a risk. Whoever tries to leave are the ones we want. Stop them, don't kill them," he said.

"Hall. Stop. Don't kill. Aye, sir." She ran to the immense

pressure hatches and acted like she was leaving for the upper decks, but there were plenty of places to hide in the cargo delivery hatchway.

Bonds started bellowing out orders to his Marines. Jacob left the man to his job. He had a less enviable task ahead of him. How to interrogate the prisoners... They didn't know, not for sure anyway, that the Alliance wouldn't execute them. Maybe he could use it against them?

He was glad for the interval since his initial realization of what was going on. It had given him time to let his fury boil down to something more manageable.

He walked slowly, giving himself time to observe *Madrigal*'s crew as he made his way to them. He stopped, obviously examining the kneeling merchants, meeting each pair of eyes, daring them to look away.

They were frightened and tired. A few were indignant. The captain, though, she had a poker face. He already knew her name, but he asked anyway, to distance her from any importance she might feel.

"Which one of you sorry lot is the captain?" he asked.

"Captain Winston, Commander of the *Terran Republic* Trading Vessel *Madrigal*. I might add... and since you have allowed me to speak, I protest this illegal invasion, this act of piracy, you and your *Marines* have committed against my ship," she snarled. The way she said "Marines" dripped with contempt. It bothered him, but he let it go.

Jacob glanced back at the white containers with the human cargo. She could easily see they had opened them, but not what was in them, which meant she was either the best actor in the galaxy or she didn't know.

It was time to find out.

"Captain, as of this moment, your ship is seized and you and your entire crew are under arrest for human trafficking, which, in the Alliance, carries a penalty of death. So I would be a little more forthcoming and a little less belligerent," he said. He looked up and down at the crew as he spoke.

Her eyes went wide and then she blinked several times and her hands lowered from her head as if she couldn't believe what he had told her. All the anger and indignance vanished in an instant.

A woman on the far end with a bruise on her face broke into sobs and collapsed.

"What...?" Winston asked. "What do you think we're doing?" Her voice wavered with disbelief.

Jacob was waiting for what happened next. After all, if the penalty was death, what did they have to lose? Two men leaped up and ran for the hatch. The Marines on guard lifted their weapons to fire, a warning on their lips, when Jacob held up his hand to stop them.

Jennings stepped out from behind the pressure hatch and stiff-armed one before shoulder-checking the other up against the bulkhead.

They dropped like stones.

He couldn't help but smile. High-g people weren't just stronger, they were also heavier and denser. In hand-to-hand, mass and skill ruled the day. She had both.

"Jennings, find a place to interrogate those two and find out what they know," he ordered.

"Aye, sir."

"And, Jennings?" he called.

"Sir?" she asked, looking over her shoulder. She had a leg in each hand as she dragged them away.

"Don't kill them," he said.

She grinned in reply.

It was for show and they both knew it. But the *Madrigal* crew wouldn't.

Jacob turned back to the rest of the freighter's crew.

"If you are one hundred percent forthcoming and honestly answer every question put to you, and if you're completely cooperative, I'll recommend lenience. I can't guarantee you won't still be executed, but it's your best chance. If you really didn't know about the two hundred and forty plus souls in cryo pods, or all the stolen goods inside your ship, then cooperating is your only chance of living through this... Do you understand?"

Captain Winston nodded in stunned disbelief, but she understood.

CHAPTER TWENTY-ONE

"Are you sure, Dimitri?" Governor Rasputin asked his right-hand man and head of internal security.

Dimitri Kasparov nodded. "Yes, sir, I even double-checked. Captain Winston declared an orbital emergency. According to her report, the aft gravcoil ring has a hairline fracture. The *Interceptor* responded immediately and is now parked next to the *Madrigal*, rendering assistance."

Governor Rasputin looked out from his office on Kremlin Station. His home was a marvel of technology, a wonder built during a previous age of technological expansion. His ancestors had settled Zuckabar hundreds of years earlier, converting their colony ships into one massive space station. Of course, they'd made a drastic miscalculation. While Zuckabar Central had all the signs of a habitable planet, they hadn't known until they'd arrived it was anything but.

However, his people were nothing if not resourceful. The station he now resided on was built by such resourcefulness. The landing craft his ancestors had arrived with were converted to ore processing stations. The shuttles meant to carry them to the surface were sent out on yearlong mining operations. It took a hundred years and many lives before they had a station capable of acting as a habitat for the entire colony, before the real work began.

And then help finally arrived. Help they didn't need, in his opinion, but was forced upon them. The Terraforming Guild had practically enslaved the colony to pay for the giant fusion reactors on each pole. Over the last three hundred years, they had formed a thicker atmosphere, raised the temperature, and made the planet minimally viable. All for a hefty cut of their system's gross domestic product. A cut so steep, Rasputin could no longer pay and continue to prosper.

He wanted no part of the Alliance, or the Guild's extortion. His system, his people would be free.

Governor Rasputin, knew, though, in his heart of hearts, that his people wouldn't have endured without outside interference.

Twenty-five years ago, he was ready to enact his plan, then the war happened. He couldn't free himself from the Guild, only to let his system fall into the barbaric hands of the Caliphate.

So he signed a treaty with the Alliance, adding one more master to the bill.

It had taken him every day since the war ended twenty years before, but he was ready again. Everything was in motion.

At least it *was*... The *Interceptor* might be only a destroyer, but she was more powerful than all his small craft combined. And she broke down on his doorstep.

Then her commander died, so it wouldn't matter if the ship had a working gravcoil. His agents in the Alliance assured him he needn't worry. A salvage tug was bound for Zuckabar and would tow the ship away. But they either lied to him or were misled themselves because no tug ever arrived.

What did he get instead? A mere lieutenant commander with delusions of grandeur.

If they discovered what was on board *Madrigal*, they would send her back to Alliance space and there was precious little he could do about it.

However, if the tiny insignificant destroyer and her idiot captain were dead or missing and the *Madrigal* gone, then he could say whatever he wanted about it, regardless of any report the *Interceptor* filed.

Maybe it wouldn't buy the time he wanted, but it might buy the time he needed.

"Dimitri, take a ship to Minsc and see if you can contact Duval. If he's not there, go to Niflheim and leave him a message. Tell him it's time to pay his debt," Rasputin said.

"Sir, you want him to come here?" Dimitri asked.

"Why not? We might lose some shipping in the short term, but this is the only viable system to depart from and people have short memories. Besides, what better way to rid ourselves of the Alliance. After all, if they can't even protect us from pirates, why should we allow them in the system?" he asked.

"Da. It will be done," Dimitri said.

"And, Dimitri, we also need to deal with *Madrigal*."

"*Madrigal*, sir? I thought they were just delayed?" he asked.

Rasputin shook his head. "No, not delayed. They know. They know what's on board and are stalling for time."

"Then why not leave the system with her? Surely the *Interceptor* could escort the ship back safely."

Rasputin chuckled. "Because the man we're dealing with, Dimitri, is cautious. Against a serious threat, he knows his ship is a defense in name only. Oh sure," he waved his hand dismissively, "she could certainly take out one pirate ship. Maybe even two, but three or more could easily bring her down. He must know whoever owns that cargo is going to come looking for it. He wants to keep it here, where he thinks it's safe."

Dimitri nodded and headed for the door.

"And, Dimitri?"

"Yes, sir?"

"Make sure no one on *Madrigal* is left to tell the tale," Rasputin said.

"Not even our people?" Dimitri asked.

Rasputin nodded in reply.

"Da," Dimitri said.

If they destroyed the *Interceptor* and recovered *Madrigal*, then they could resume business as usual. However, it would have to be soon. They could only tolerate another month, maybe a little more. He needed to act. Once he had the money from the cargo—and his cut from Duval's success—he could buy the warships needed to defend his home. They would throw the Guild out of the system and dissolve the treaty with the Alliance.

After that... who knew. There were three other star systems between him and the Alliance; he could have them all.

He stared out his large window for a long time, imagining what his family could accomplish with the freedom he was about to grant them.

———

Dimitri wasn't a large man, but no one would think he wasn't intimidating. He wasn't the head of internal security for his charming personality—he had fought his way up, and looked like a man on the edge of violence.

He loved his home system with all his heart. He knew—not believed, *knew*—Governor Rasputin was the man to bring the kind of freedom and prosperity his people craved. Far too long had they chafed under the Terraforming Guild's extortion. Once they were gone and the Alliance dismissed like the pesky dogs they were, Rasputin would become a new Czar, leading his people to a bright future.

Kremlin Station's day-night cycle was hitting twilight when he parked his hover-bike outside of *Kamchatka*. It wasn't the most reputable place to find help on the station, but it was the place to go if a person needed something on the quiet side. Most of the bars were either filled with regulars who worked the yards, or gathering spots for the younger crowd. What he needed were the undesirables. There were a lot of them in *Kamchatka* and it didn't take long to find what he was looking for. Instead of his usual crew, he needed expendable but reliable mercs.

CHAPTER TWENTY-TWO

Chief Minister Halim fervently wished he were still asleep instead of going over endless traffic reports his spies in the Zuckabar system relayed to him. Sometimes he missed his younger days, exploring, fighting, conquering, all for the honor of his Caliph.

Then he got old. However, there were perks to age. As he progressed in rank with the Internal Security Bureau, he went from risking his life as a spy to infiltrating enemy star systems the Caliphate considered vulnerable. The rewards were plenty, both in this life and the next.

He and his men were hiding in a secret base on the rim of the third asteroid belt, far outside the usual shipping lanes. Massive passive sensor dishes, disguised as asteroids, orbited the rock they were on, giving them a complete picture of the traffic coming into and out of Zuckabar from both Minsc and Praxis.

The asteroid was equidistant between the two starlanes, and far south of the ecliptic. The odds of anyone stumbling upon them were so low as to not be calculable. Even if they did, they weren't without their defenses. A squad of elite Immortals were stationed with them, along with a Dhib-class assault ship. They saw everything in the system, and nothing could see or hurt them.

Systems like Zuckabar had everything they wanted and needed. Compared to a Caliph run system, it was near lawless —despite the Alliance naval presence. Piracy was rampant in the Corridor and neither the Alliance nor the fools in the Consortium were willing, or able, to do anything about it.

He should know. After all, it was his agent who provided the pirates with a stolen Consortium frigate.

Once their spy reported on Professor Bellaits' findings, then they would know if it was worth the expenditure. Then all they had to worry about was the Alliance Navy.

Halim had been a young man in the last war and had served on the admiral's ship, the pride of the Caliph Navy. He had witnessed the one and only engagement between his people's forces and the Alliance. The Alliance had defeated them soundly. It was an affront on the Caliph's honor they would never forget, and they would not make that mistake again.

They had learned, in the last twenty years, that there were other ways to hurt their enemy.

The ISB was well aware of, and had even helped foster, the anti-Navy rhetoric in the Alliance systems, weakening them from the inside. They were certain that if Zuckabar was taken, the Alliance would be unable to respond before they had it fortified past the point of a bloodless battle. Which could only happen if Professor Bellaits found what he was looking for.

The Alliance wouldn't commit the forces and the Caliphate would have a foothold on their doorstep. When the next war broke out, and it would, first the Consortium would fall, then the Alliance. They would leave the Iron Empire and Terran Republic to settle their own squabbles as the Caliphate conquered the rest of the galaxy. When the time was right, the Empire would fall too, and then all would be as it should.

Including the Alliance ship. But its presence did complicate things. It had to leave or be dealt with for the operation to proceed to its final conclusion. If it had to be destroyed, then it had to be destroyed on schedule, and as part of the plan. Too early, and the Alliance would send ships to reinforce the area. Too late, and it would do them no good.

And while the Caliphate of Hamid fully intended to return to the war and destroy or enslave the infidels, they also weren't suicidal. They needed more time to prepare their final solution. In the meantime, they were happy to pay pirates to destabilize the borders of the nations they so hated and to broadcast propaganda to the populations, garnering sympathy from fools who thought they could curry favor... like dogs begging for treats.

"Minister Halim?" His second-in-command called his name.

"Yes, Shareef?" he asked. Something about the man was different. He had a smile on his face, and Shareef rarely smiled.

"We're receiving a burst transmission. Call sign *Kafir*."

Halim straightened right up. That was the call sign for their spy on the civilian ship. She had spent the last decade infiltrating the Alliance and would have spent the next two decades working her way into their government had she not relayed the professor's plans to her superiors. Her discovery was what made the entire mission possible.

"Play it," he ordered.

The man hit a button and the speaker burst to life.

"Mission commenced. Route enclosed. *Kafir* out," the voice said.

"Did we get the route?" he asked.

"Yes, sir," his comms officer answered. "On screen."

The screen lit up, showing the system and a bright blue dot where their own base was. Opposite the system, a red line appeared, spiraling out and then back in to cross near the blue dot.

"Excellent. This is it, brothers, the time we've waited for so patiently. Tell the Immortals to gear up; they may have to go on a moment's notice. When *Kafir* signals, we strike!"

Halim was excited for the operation to conclude, but he was even more excited at the thought of returning home.

CHAPTER TWENTY-THREE

With the *Interceptor* parked in orbit next to *Madrigal*, it was a relative cinch for the crew to unspool the gravcoil into space and maneuver it to the stern of the destroyer. The entire engineering department, including Commander Rod Beckett, floated in space. Rod's right-hand-man, Chief Petty Officer Redfern, and his right-hand-man, Spacer Beech, were in exo-suits.

The suits' technical designation, EXO-141 Suit, Maintenance, was a mouthful. Like virtually every military since the dawn of time, they had their own name for the ungainly primate-looking exoskeletons, *Gorilla suits.*

Once in them, with their long arms and curved heads, they kind of resembled the simians of Earth's past. The suits were equipped with everything the engineering department would need to repair damaged external systems on the ship.

Or, in this case, to install the gravcoil.

After Rod spent the better part of two days examining the coil to make sure the molecular structure was intact, he started the lengthy and arduous process of moving the mass-intensive gravcoil from the freighter to the *Interceptor*.

Rod hovered outside the stern of the ship in his thruster-pack-equipped ELS suit. Since it was impossible to spot the twenty-millimeter-wide gravcoil with the naked eye, the progress of the coil as it snaked its way to them was highlighted on his HUD.

Madrigal was one hundred meters off the port and dwarfed the *Interceptor* like a mountain, blocking all light from the white planet beneath. Chief Suresh had done a great job of parking the ship relative to the freighter and in the perfect alignment to transfer the gravcoil.

It was a simple matter to depressurize the cargo hold and power down the secondary gravcoil, allowing them to unspool the coil into space.

Powerful thrusters were required to move the gravcoil. Normally, a Navy repair ship would do the job, but they didn't have access to one, so they had to figure out how to do it without. Something the captain insisted had to be possible and that had taken Rod's entire engineering department a solid day to solve before they could proceed.

Rod grinned in the starlight of space. A single day to turn the impossible, possible. His captain didn't ask much.

When Beech had come up with the idea of using the "Gorilla suits" to move the unbelievably heavy gravcoil, Rod thought it was madness. And it was, under regular gravity. But with *Madrigal*'s gravity off, it was a matter of getting the thing moving then carefully guiding it across, centimeter by centimeter.

"Coming up on entry point. Move it three millimeters on this heading," Rod said over the comms. He had a "top" down look of the coil on half of his HUD, along with a three-dimensional sphere showing where it lined up with the ship.

"You know how hard this is to move, right, sir?" Beech replied.

"If you hit the ship, you could damage the coil. Stop it if you need to, but do not miss," he ordered.

"Damage the coil?" Chief Redfern broke in. "You'll punch a hole in the ship."

———

Beech's palms sweated inside the climate-controlled suit. He knew their plan would work—at least he hoped it would. He was young and lacked the decades in uniform that the two men he worked with had. However, he'd grown up on freighters, repairing anything and everything. He knew his stuff.

He put every gram of thrust into moving the gravcoil's leading end three millimeters as instructed.

It hurtled toward the waiting receptacle at one meter per second, leaving him less than twenty seconds to change its heading. He overrode the suit's safety systems and put the thrusters on full reverse. The suit shook with strain and alarms screamed as heat built dangerously high. Sweat welled on him as the heat overrode the suit's ability to keep him cool.

But the gravcoil moved. Slowly. When it was ten centimeters from impact, the line turned green. He reversed thrust to keep from going too far, and just as it would have missed alignment, it slid into the waiting slot.

"Contact!" Beech shouted. "We have mating. The gravcoil is in."

"Stand clear," Beckett said over the comms.

"Clear," Beech replied as he thrust away from the gravcoil.

———

Commander Beckett immediately keyed the remote systems on *Interceptor* and the engine powered up at one-half of one percent. The coil housing surged with power, pulling the grav-coil through the loops like a kid sucking up spaghetti.

"Skipper," he said over the comm line to the bridge. "We have a gravcoil."

———

On the bridge, Jacob breathed a sigh of relief. Once the gravcoil was operational, he'd have an actual command.

"Well done, Rod. Give my compliments to your crew. You pulled off a miracle here," he said.

"Aye, sir," the engineer replied. "Remember that when it comes time to buy the drinks."

"First round's on me," Jacob replied.

———

Kim scrolled through the endless reports on traffic through the system. She silently swiveled back and forth in her office chair, staring at her screen in the otherwise dark room.

She found the small room near the main computer housing more comfortable than her own quarters, not to mention she liked having the place to herself. No one came down to the computer core.

Chief Suresh had done a good job of tracking traffic while the rest of the crew had screwed around. A slash of shame went through Yuki as she thought of her own complicity in how the ship had been run. What had she been thinking? She could hear her father's voice in her internal reproach.

The truth was, she hadn't been thinking. Commander Cole's death had shaken her. With the loss of the gravcoil and the Navy not sending follow-up orders on top of his death, she had lost herself in the moment, existing rather than taking the initiative the way she was taught. And when a helping hand had reached out to her, she pushed it away and tried to make sure none of the blame would land on her.

Then along came Commander Grimm. Any other officer would have taken command and proceeded to lay down blame. Either because he was on his way out of the Navy or because he was a good man—she couldn't tell—Grimm gave everyone aboard ship a second chance.

The Navy wasn't all bad, she admitted to herself. She certainly enjoyed her time more than she disliked it. However, the constant attitude of the civilian government blaming the Navy for the failures in the last war (one that was a distant memory of her childhood) grated on the Navy's morale. It was as if the whole Navy was in CYA mode.

The rest of the Navy needed their own personal Commander Grimm to kick them in the ass and get them moving.

No more, she swore to herself. She would put the petty jealousy of Grimm's promotion in a box and chuck it out the airlock. She had a duty to do, and she would do it. If, after what happened to him, he could still do his duty, then she could certainly do hers.

Now, if they could just find out when *Madrigal* came in-system and when the cargo was transferred to her, then maybe they could start sorting this mess out.

———

"Bridge, engine room, we're as ready as we're gonna be, Captain," Commander Beckett said over the comm station.

Despite the late hour, Jacob had his primary watch officers on duty. If something went wrong, he wanted the most experienced personnel to handle it.

The only person missing was Lieutenant West, who was back on *Madrigal*. Regs required one officer, lieutenant or higher, to man any seized ships.

So far, all the checks across the board had come back green. It was now or never.

"Astro," Jacob said to Midship Owusu, "plot us a course out-system. Minsc starlane."

"Aye, sir, course to Minsc starlane," Owusu replied.

Owusu's screen was duplicated on Jacob's MFD and he watched as the officer-in-training plotted the course. He didn't like to ride herd on officers, but midships were a little different. He wouldn't make any corrections, though, unless the course was egregious.

Not to mention, plotting courses was one of his favorite tasks on a starship. The sheer joy of looking at the universe and seeing all the possible places one could go in a lifetime. The Alliance was near the end of the Orion Spur, six thousand light-years from Earth. There were still thousands of star systems farther east—not that east was exactly the right word, but it was the only real way to conceptualize the vastness of the Milky Way galaxy.

Finding new starlanes was the job of scouts, often one- or two-person ships with over-powered computers and space-time sensors allowing them to find the smallest trace of a starlane.

The Navy used to buy that information and send out specialized destroyers to explore the newly found star systems, cataloging what they had to offer. All that came to an end at the beginning of the last war and never started up again. It was as if everyone in the Galaxy was on uneven footing, unsure of what to do next.

"Course plotted, sir. Bearing zero-niner-four mark three-five at two-five gravities for six-zero minutes then change to three-zero-zero gravities with turnover in three-point-five hours," Owusu said, reading from his screen.

Jacob double-checked the numbers. It was a solid course. What Jacob especially liked was the renewed sense of vigor Owusu showed. The entire ship, really.

"Coxswain, bring us about," he ordered.

Chief Suresh grinned and rubbed her palms together eagerly before making a big show of cracking every single one of her knuckles. It was slightly unprofessional, but other than using the *Interceptor*'s thrusters to move her painfully slowly over to *Madrigal*, the chief hadn't exactly stretched her ship-handling skills. Jacob was more than happy to give her leeway.

"Aye, aye, sir. Zero-niner-four mark three-five at two-five gravities for six-zero minutes. Course laid in on your order, sir," she said.

Technically, he already had given the order, but he appreciated the gravity of the moment and what she was offering him.

"Helm... execute," he said.

The *Interceptor* rolled to starboard on her thrusters, the nose lining up with the bearing as the gravcoil powered the ship forward. She instantly accelerated to twenty-five *g*s, shooting through space.

For a speedy little tin can like *Interceptor*, twenty-five *g*s was a drop in the bucket compared to her maximum of five hundred and sixty *g*s, her theoretical maximum. Navy regs never allowed a ship, or any vehicle, to exceed eighty percent max to keep wear and tear to a minimum. If they were in combat, or there was some sort of emergency, then they could justify maximum acceleration. Until then, they would travel at "full speed," which was Navy lingo for eighty percent of their true maximum.

"Skipper," Ensign Hössbacher said from the comms station. "Call from *Madrigal*."

Jacob pointed at his MFD and the ensign nodded, transferring the call over. Lieutenant Bonds' angular face filled the pickup.

"We've got the *Madrigal* secure, sir. The crew, minus the two troublemakers, are giving us their full cooperation. We're opening every box on the tug and it isn't pretty." Bonds' expression showed Jacob exactly how painful the El-Tee found it.

"How many so far?" Jacob asked. He didn't need to refer to the item in particular. They were keeping the human cargo on a need-to-know basis. The Marines all knew. Dr. Stanislaw, Chief Pierre, and the XO were the only others. Since Chief Pierre remained behind as medic to tend to the prisoners, that end was secure.

"Two thousand, so far. We're only about halfway through the manifest," Bonds said.

Jacob's face froze as he tried not to register the horrific scale of the operation. He was no expert on human trafficking or the open slave markets of the Caliph, but he knew that the cargo was inching toward *billions* of dollars.

"Well done, El-Tee. Let us know if you need anything. We'll be no more than six hours away at any given time. Not to mention we'll stay inside the starlanes. We should be able to beat any ship back if need be, but it's about time people in this system saw a Navy destroyer doing her job," Jacob said.

"Understood, sir, we'll be fine. We'll stay busy inventorying the cargo. We can't trust the computer or the crew, which means we're opening every box by hand. Bravo-two-five out."

They were in a painful Catch-22. On one hand, the *Madrigal* needed to be protected. On the other, they had to test the grav-coil and patrol the system. Ultimately, they decided secrecy was the best protection for the freighter. As long as no one knew the Navy had seized her, there would be no reason to investigate her downed gravcoil.

If *Interceptor* had her gravcoil and stayed parked next to the freighter, it would be a dead giveaway something was up. Jacob was prepared to put up a hell of a fight for the lives on the ship. However, a lone destroyer wasn't much of a defense against a concentrated effort. The plan they came up with was the best compromise they could think of. The Marines could more than handle any attempted boarding action and the *Interceptor* could, well... intercept any suspicious ships passing through the system.

It was great that the *Madrigal*'s crew was cooperating, but he didn't trust them for a second. They were facing some hefty charges and had only his word that they wouldn't be executed. He didn't think they were the bad sort, but returning to their home in the Republic would be infinitely preferable to standing trial in the Alliance. And they understood the situation as well as he did; they knew his Marines were the only thing keeping them from being slaughtered.

"Comms, prepare a packet, priority alpha. Send it to the next ship heading for Praxis," he ordered. "Program the final destination for Fort Kirk."

"Aye, sir, one packet. Ready."

Jacob keyed in his log to the packet, along with a priority request for backup and what they found on *Madrigal*.

"Send it," he ordered.

"Sending... CTF *Kurosawa* has confirmed receipt of packet. They will deliver post-haste," Ensign Hössbacher said.

"Give the captain of the *Kurosawa* my compliments," Jacob said.

Without FTL communications, the only real way to send information back and forth was through relay ships and packets. "Packet" was a holdover term from a bygone era. Mostly, it meant a packet of information uploaded to a friendly ship's computers and set to relay to the first Alliance ship or station.

From there, it would bounce around until it made its destination. Fort Kirk would know what to do with it once it arrived.

Kurosawa was a big, slow freighter, not unlike *Madrigal*. However, once she drove down the starlane to Praxis, she would use her radio to transmit the data to the first ship that could take it to the next system, and so on and so forth.

If the rest of the destroyers were in-system, this would be a breeze. One destroyer could be overwhelmed, but four? It would take more than any pirate could throw. Unfortunately, he didn't have four destroyers, just the one.

And one was going to have to be enough.

CHAPTER TWENTY-FOUR

Nadia couldn't remember the last time she was bored flying her ship. Perhaps there really was a first time for everything. It was bad enough that she was feeling restless, but worse, her crew was bored.

Professor Bellaits had them running around the fringes of Zuckabar, listening for space-time echoes in all the wrong places, according to everything modern astrophysics told her.

At least his assistant was interesting to talk with. Nadia was quickly approaching thirty and she had only her crew for company most days. It was nice to talk to another woman, even if she was a bit on the young and naïve side.

Compared to her adventures with ONI, her time on Dagher was downright geriatric.

"Coming up on another course correction, Nadia," Barnes said from the helm. She nodded, waving her fingers nonchalantly in his direction. Days and days of course corrections. They were chugging around the system at a measly twenty-five gravities, allowed to go no faster than three thousand kilometers per second, using the massive gravity of the binary stars as a guide to swing around the ecliptic. They corrected the course, accelerated in the right direction, then shut the gravcoil down while the professor listened to his equipment. He wouldn't say what he was looking for, other than it was space-time related.

The crew had a pool going. The leading bet was a new star-lane... but to where? It made no sense to her. Zuckabar was a fringe system, but starlanes were loud and relatively easy to find. If there was another one of any use, someone would have found it already.

"Skipper," Barnes said as he crossed from his station to kneel next to her.

"Yes?" she asked, raising an eyebrow at him. Barnes had worked for her for over a year now. He was a fine pilot and astrogator and had probably saved her thousands of dollars on each run with how close he was able to ride the rail of a starlane.

"I don't want to tell you your business, but whatever this *professor* is looking for, it isn't out here."

She nodded for him to go on.

"We're too close to the suns for a new starlane, plain and simple. Gravity on a pulsar is a monster. Add in the white dwarf and there's no way, none, that he's going to find a new starlane this close. I don't care what fancy equipment he bought. If he wanted a new starlane heading out of Zuck, we would need to find it out in the six billion klick range and then follow it back in. Not here."

His opinion confirmed what she already knew. There were two reasons to listen for the drumbeat gravity did on space-time. The most common was listening for other ships in close proximity. The other was finding starlanes. But, as Barnes pointed out, they were far too close to the primaries to hear anything as muffled as a starlane... which, even if he was trying to find one, again, where could it possibly lead? The only places worth going already had strong lanes.

"That's interesting, Barnes, and I'm not saying I don't agree with you, but his money spends as good as anyone's," she said.

Her astrogator nodded, his hand reflexively coming up to massage his short brown goatee. "Yeah, but, Nadia, what if it isn't a starlane he's looking for? What if it's something..." he glanced around the bridge, making sure no one else was listening, "...more sinister," he said in a whisper.

Nadia adjusted in her seat, her leathers creaking as she moved slightly closer to him.

"What are you thinking?" No one on the ship knew of her past with ONI. When she was in the Navy, she was a "foreign office clerk," assigned to ambassadors and admirals who served in embassies around the galaxy. Her duty, while interesting to her, was more tedious than most people would believe. No late-night rendezvous, code names, or secret call signs. It was all about observing while being unobserved. Despite her athletic build, natural good looks, and silky black hair, she could disappear in a crowd, loiter on the outskirts of a dinner party, or move among guests at a dance, all the while listening for the one phrase, the one statement, that led to crucial intelligence on an enemy, and sometimes friends.

She'd tired of the dance, though. Especially after what happened on *Malia*. Spending her nights listening to strangers try to cover up their sins wasn't for her. She was appreciative of ONI and the training it provided, but it wasn't what she wanted to spend her life doing. She'd enlisted when she was eighteen, and when it came time to re-up, she didn't. After ten years of service, she was a private citizen again.

The admiral hadn't wanted her to leave and tried to offer everything under the sun to get her to stay. In the end, it just wasn't what she was meant to do.

Luckily for her, or perhaps simply good planning, she'd saved nearly every penny. Most of her time in the Navy was spent in Temporary Additional Duty (TAD), light-years from home. She never paid rent, bought food, or even clothes, since ONI always wanted her to look the part... whatever part they required. And while she was a Chief Petty Officer when she left, not a commissioned officer, she still made good money. Which she saved and invested with a whip-smart young man on Alexandria.

Enough so that when she stepped out of ONI's shadow, she could afford the down payment on *Dagger* and do something real with her life... or at least that was the plan. As it turned out, the life of a freighter captain was about as boring as dinner parties with the Terran Republic's geriatric legislators.

She shook her head, realizing Barnes was speaking even as her mind wandered to the past. What she wouldn't give for a good mystery.

"—he's clearly hiding something, Skipper. What if he isn't who he says he is? What if he's working for a..." Barnes leaned in even closer, as if the two other people on the bridge were enemy agents. "... foreign government," he said almost inaudibly.

She leaned in even closer, eyes narrowing, "Or he could be a crackpot professor of astrophysics who's nearing the end of his life and desperate to have a legacy beyond 'crackpot professor'... maybe?" she said with a shrug.

Barnes's grin told her he took it the way she meant, with humor. He stood up and smiled at her. "Thanks for hearing me out, Skip. I'm probably just bored. These course corrections aren't exactly taxing my ability." He turned and reseated himself in his chair off to her side.

"Maybe you can use the course corrections as a game. Try and figure out what he'll have us do next?" she asked.

"Could be fun," he said.

She smiled back at him then turned to her own MFD,

tapping a few keys to open a secure comm channel. It would take probably a week at least to get any information from Alexandria to her here in Zuckabar, but... she pulled open a channel no one outside of ONI knew existed and tapped away at her request.

The admiral would be surprised to receive a message from her, no doubt, but maybe Barnes was onto something. She didn't for one second think the professor was some kind of foreign operative... but maybe... maybe there was more to him than met the eye.

————

Daisy went about her duty on the little freighter. Mostly it consisted of preparing the professor's meals, making sure he had clean clothes to work in, and generally looking after his health. To her, he was an important man. A brilliant astrophysicist for sure. But also, the stereotypical absent-minded professor.

She went about cleaning his cabin, annoyed at his inability to pick up his dirty clothes. If it weren't for her, he'd wear the same outfit day in and day out, no matter how bad it smelled.

Once the room was de-cluttered, she laid out his clothes for the next day. He was in the cargo hold, glued to his gear. He wouldn't return here until exhaustion forced him to. Then she would slip in and take his dirty clothes, forcing him to change.

Her alarm beeped, letting her know it was time to bring him lunch. She finished up and left the cabin, turned into the small hall, and found her way to the ship's mess. In the few weeks they had spent on board, she'd done her best to endear herself to the crew. It paid off in smiles and a first-in-line spot for the hot food.

"Daisy, nice to see you this morning," said Porter, the broad-shouldered older man who ran the mess hall.

"Nice to see you, Dave," she replied, using his first name. He smiled, thrilled she'd remembered. While in school, Daisy had done her best to fit in, not be noticed, or look out of place. But once she was out of school, her whole approach changed. She was young, pretty, and had charisma to spare, and she wielded it like a sword. The right smile or twinkle of an eye in the right place opened doors for her.

She left the mess, pausing at the hatch for just a moment as if considering looking back, then turned and walked out. She knew the effect it would have on Dave Porter. He was an older man, almost forty, and that made it even easier for her to manipulate him.

The ship wasn't big enough to have a transit system. One could walk from bow to stern in less than a minute if need be. Taking the stairs while carrying food complicated the trip, but she was as agile as she was pretty. She approached the cargo bay, shifting the hot food to one hand while she keyed the door open with the other.

Professor Bellaits was where she'd left him, cross-legged on a small mat, pressed up against his equipment, one hand on the large headphones he wore and the other on the digital readout, adjusting it on the fly.

The tray of food she'd brought him last night was sitting next to him, cold and untouched.

"Professor," she said with a mixture of irritation and humor, "you need to eat, sir. It won't do any of us good if you drop from starvation," she said as she moved the tray and put the fresh one down.

"Yes, yes, I'll use the bathroom here in a minute," he said without looking at her.

She glanced at the readouts. The "sound" he was listening

for would be no more than a flutter among drumbeats, and as far as she could tell, only the beating drum of the binaries appeared on screen. The other screen showed background gamma radiation. He would adjust the space-time detectors then the radiation settings. Back and forth endlessly.

"Professor," she said again, pressing the pause button on the equipment. That got his attention. He blinked several times before looking up at her as if just realizing she stood next to him.

"Oh, Daisy, yes?" he said as he glanced between her and the space-time listening sensors.

"You need to eat," she said, pointing at the food. "Now."

"Right, quite right. One must keep up one's strength." He reached for the sandwich with one hand and the machine with the other. She blocked the machine with her hand.

"Professor," she grumbled. "Food first."

Like an errant child, he pouted for a moment then proceeded to wolf down the meal as fast as humanly possible. It wasn't until he ate the first bite that he realized how hungry he'd become. After a few moments, the sandwich, salad, and crackers were gone. He downed the tall glass of milk before picking up the coffee and sipping it.

"Satisfied?" he asked her with a mischievous grin.

"For now." She took both trays; before she was out of the hold, he was back on the machine listening for the faintest cry of gravity or spike of gamma rays she hoped he would find.

She dumped the trays in the recycle and headed for the cabin she called home. Where the professor had gotten a two-bunk birth with a private bathroom, she practically had a closet, with a single bunk and a locker to stow her gear. She used the communal bathroom in the hall with the rest of the crew.

She sat on the edge of her bunk, unzipping her tunic and

reaching inside to pull out two items. One, a small handgun, designed for last-ditch defense. It wouldn't penetrate armor of any kind, but it would easily kill an unarmored person. The other was a tiny black box barely larger than a business card, with a red square for her thumb.

From her kit, she placed a rug gently on the deck facing the systems suns. Satisfied the time was correct, she knelt and said her prayers to Allah.

CHAPTER TWENTY-FIVE

Jacob woke with a start, covered in sweat, with the terrible images of dead children floating in his vision. Children he'd killed when he ordered *Orion* to fire.

He rubbed his eyes for a good thirty seconds, clearing the morbid images and wrestling himself awake before sitting up and dropping his feet to the deck.

There was no going back to the rack for him as he reached for the button to turn on the lights.

Nothing happened.

He hit it again.

Then a third time.

He pushed the comm button. "Officer of the Watch, Fawkes," came the voice from the speaker.

"Carter, the lights in my cabin aren't coming on. Can you send someone from engineering when they have a second?"

"Uh, sir, I was just about to comm *you*. No one's lights are coming on. The main passageways are using emergency lighting, along with all critical compartments," Fawkes said.

Jacob rubbed his face awake as the news washed over him. Emergency lighting was self-contained, triggered by alert conditions or loss of power. Generally, only a power loss would precipitate a loss of lighting... but the comms worked.

"I'll be there in a minute," he said before closing the circuit. He hastily pulled on his uniform and watch cap before heading for the hatch...

...which didn't open.

"Bridge," he said as he slapped the comm button. "Are the hatches on fail-secure?"

"Sorry, sir, give me a moment. We're having—" Fawkes voice died with the comm.

Jacob looked at the button next to the hatch and pressed it again. The light had flickered and died. When he pressed it again, he got nothing, not even static.

"Okay, this is damn peculiar," he muttered.

The lighting going out could be an accident or a malfunction. Lord knew, his ship was forty-plus years old and had seen combat more than once. The outer hull alone needed a full yard to repair, but one thing going wrong versus multiple, and unrelated, systems failing? They'd used the gravcoil without failure, putting the ship through trials even the builder would find adequate. Emergency course corrections, spurts at full power— all had performed flawlessly. Along with the ship, the crew's morale had improved in leaps and bounds but... all these systems failing at once? His gut churned its familiar warning.

The hatches would only fail-secure if there was a hull breach in the area. He would have to gamble the corridor was safe. If there was a hull breach on this level, the bridge would know without a doubt.

Rubbing his hands together for a moment to stave off the increasing cold, he opened the panel next to the hatch with the lever for manual release. He pulled on it to bring it all the way down and he heard the soft *click* as the lock released.

With one foot braced against the wall, he used both hands

to pull with all his might. The hatch groaned and screeched as the metal slid against metal without the magnetic assistance power provided. When it was a quarter way open, he squeezed out.

The comforting presence of the Marine sentry was absent as he passed the main bridge hatch into a red-lit room of confusion. It would have been unfair to the small platoon of Marines to ask them to guard so many prisoners without their full complement. Aboard ship, they did provide many useful functions—like damage control and search and rescue—but no technical function that was required for the operation of the ship.

"Talk to me, Carter," Jacob said as he walked onto the bridge. They had already opened the hatch.

Lieutenant Fawkes looked up as the captain used his first name.

"Sir, power's down across the board. No lights, life support, or propulsion," the young man said.

Jacob frowned. He was glad Carter had been upfront about it. Another sign the ship's crew were turning around was their lack of CYA, even among the officers. Carter was barely four years younger than he was, but it felt like a much larger gulf than a mere handful of years. Some officers might resent the small age difference, but good ones didn't.

"Astro, where are we?" he asked.

Petty Officer Second Class Oliv turned in her chair. She was his most experienced astrogator, and with West on detached duty, she was also instructing Midship Owusu on his studies.

"We're still on our previous course, sir. Zero-niner-four, for the last two hours, at an acceleration of three-zero-zero *gs*. Our last velocity update was two-seven-four-niner KPS," she said in her lightly accented voice. "Obviously, we're no longer accelerating," she added.

"Well, at least we're not heading for a planet. Okay, let's work the problem, people. First things first... Carter, what is our priority?" he asked. One of the things his first CO had done was always turn a crisis into an educational opportunity to teach the junior officers and ratings what to do in a calm, rational manner.

"Sir, you, uh, don't know?" Carter replied hesitantly.

Jacob cracked a grin as he sat down in the command chair. He didn't take it personally that the lieutenant would assume the worst. Of course, it was bad form for him to say it out loud.

"Carter, I do know. And Petty Officer Oliv knows." He glanced over at the astrogator and she nodded back. "What I want to do is show you what to do in a way you will remember."

"Aye, sir. Understood. What would the captain suggest we do?" Fawkes asked.

"It's not that easy, Carter. Take a moment. I know you're stressed. Think through the problem. What is our most pressing need?"

Carter glanced around at the other five people crammed onto the small bridge. Ops, Astro, Helm, Comms, and Tactical, along with their CO.

"We need to restore life support first, right? Sir?" he asked, his voice tentative.

Jacob shook his head. "It's good thinking. After all, we need life support to stay alive on the tin can. But no. We're not engineering. We couldn't restore life support with a wrench and an illustrated guide," Jacob said.

That got a chuckle out of them. Staying calm and working the problem logically would almost always win the day. It was a tough skill to teach, since it was almost impossible to predict who would panic until the emergency was already upon them. Which was why they drilled so often. Sure, a spacer might still panic, but they would have their training to fall back on. Like muscle memory.

"We need to speak to engineering... We need comms, sir," Fawkes said.

"Excellent. Gouger, what's our internal comms status?" he asked the young spacer second class manning the communications console.

Gouger gulped and stuttered. This was third watch, the middle of the ship's "night." A lowly spacer, especially one who had only served for two years in the Navy to begin with, rarely had to speak to the captain directly. It took him a second to spit out the words.

"No comms, uh, Captain, sir," Gouger said.

"'Sir' is fine, Gouger. It's okay, son, no one is going to get on you here. I take it the panel has no power?" Jacob asked.

"Aye, sir, the system is offline. I can't even run diagnostics," Gouger said as he gained a little confidence.

"Okay then, Carter, how do we talk to engineering? If all the hatches between us and them are failed secure, what do we do?" Jacob asked. He glanced at PO Oliv, who gave him a "steady" motion with her hand. The POs knew the officers better than anyone, and if she thought he could do it, he would rely on her judgment.

Carter thought about it for a second before responding. "We manually open the hatches?"

"We could, but it could take an hour to open that many. And... what if there was a micrometeorite impact? Somehow it got through both the particle shielding and the gravwake? We could have decompressed areas and not know it if we blindly opened hatches..." Jacob trailed off, letting them imagine how badly that could go.

Carter nodded somberly. Being blown out into space was on the top of every spacer's list of "how not to die."

"ELS..." Carter muttered. "The short-range systems built into the ELS suit? We could use one of those to talk to Commander Beckett!"

"Now you're thinking." Jacob turned to Gouger. "Can you run to my cabin and fetch mine, Spacer?"

"Aye, sir, on it." Gouger leaped up and hustled down the corridor to the captain's quarters.

———

Commander Beckett grumbled as he made his way through the small maintenance tunnel that ran the length of the ship. He had entered from his quarters, just aft of the rec room on frame twenty, and crawled all the way to frame sixty-five, which was under the currently empty Marine country. Once there, he used the emergency ladder to make his way up to deck five. From there, it was a short leg using the narrow crawlspace existing between each deck.

His elbows and knees were raw from crawling, but at least he was making progress. If there were actual decompression, the crawl space hatches would have closed as well. They were on a separate system from the main hatches. Still, he was getting too old to be crawling about in the dark through the bowels of a ship.

Briefly, he regretted turning down a tour on a battleship for his final cruise. At least if this had happened on one of the kilometer-long monsters, the maintenance tubes were big enough to walk through.

He slid himself painfully over one last intersection before coming to the hatch he needed. In Rod Beckett's long career, it had never occurred to him to leave his tools behind at the end of his watch. The same way Marines carried a weapon at all times, Rod always had his tools, on or off duty.

The panel next to the hatch opened with the touch of his control wand and he went to work hot-wiring the system. After thirty seconds, the hatch slid aside, bathing him in the bright red light of the reactor room. He blinked several times as his eyes adjusted.

"PO Stas?" he bellowed as he pulled himself out on his larger-than-regulation belly.

"Commander Beckett? How did you..." Petty Officer Third Class Stas was taken aback by the chief engineer's sudden appearance.

"You spend enough time on tin cans, son, and you learn a few tricks. It's pretty cold in here. Is life support down?" Rod asked.

"Yes, sir. Everything is. I've got Spacer Alderman and Diagnostics Trevors working on the main hatch. It failed secure as soon as the power went down."

"What about the ELS storage?" he asked.

"Sir I... I hadn't thought of that," he said sheepishly.

"Next time you will. Help an old man up," he said, holding out his hand. PO Stas took it in a firm grip and hefted the engineer to his feet. "Go get in a suit, comm the bridge, and give them a head's up that this isn't a malfunction."

"Sir?" PO Stas blinked in stunned disbelief. "What else could it be?"

Rod glanced at the reactor. "Does that look like it doesn't have any power?"

"How long, Stas?" Jacob asked.

"At our current rate of consumption, a little over an hour. But less in some compartments," he replied.

An hour didn't give them much time to get life support back online, but it was all they had. "Tell Commander Beckett to get life support up and running, whatever it takes. Keep me in the loop, though. Understood?" Jacob asked.

"Aye, sir," the garbled voice of the petty officer replied.

Jacob pulled the helmet off and looked around the bridge. He was pleased to see they were calm and focused on their jobs. Non-combat emergency situations were far more common than combat ones, but usually, they were in the form of natural disasters or other ships in distress... other ships than the one they were serving on.

He didn't need Commander Beckett to spell it out for him. Too many disparate systems had failed at the same time for it to be a coincidence. All that was left was to tell the crew what he suspected before they figured it out for themselves.

"Okay, people, listen up. It's the opinion of Commander Beckett that this wasn't a malfunction or accident." Jacob let that sink in for a moment. "Regardless, we have a lot of work ahead of us. Oliv, take Gouger with you and see if you can get the hatches open between here and the mess deck."

"Aye, sir, hatches open to the mess deck," she said. She pointed at Gouger, and with a jerk of her thumb, marched off the bridge. The young man leaped up, almost forgetting to leave his comms gear at the station. He had to stop and detach himself and then he was out the hatch right behind her.

"Carter, take this," Grimm handed his helmet to the tactical officer, "and see if you can get a hold of anyone else, especially the XO. Make sure to let them know to stay calm and try and make their way to the mess, roger?"

"Aye, aye, sir." Carter slipped the helmet on.

That left PO 1st Class Collins manning the helm and the only other person on the bridge. Grimm walked over and knelt next to her. "Collins, stay here. If power comes back, I want us full stop before we hit something we can't see."

"Aye, sir. Full stop," the petite brown-haired woman said.

CHAPTER TWENTY-SIX

Main engineering was a mess of open panels and exposed circuits as the engineering watch crew, who were trapped there, attempted to track down the reason none of their systems would respond.

"This is ridiculous," Beckett muttered as he scrolled through lines of code. The ship's computer systems were hard-wired, which meant they were nearly impossible to alter. Everything was firmware loaded from a backup. The optical cables were in hardened nano steel tubes as an extra layer of protection, and the ship had four individual runs connecting everything. It wasn't rocket science to protect a ship's computer from an unauthorized breach. It literally couldn't happen.

Yet, as impossible as sabotage was, *something* was wrong and Commander Rod Beckett would be damned if he knew what. Systems that were separated by compartmentalization were having failures at the same time. Another technical impossibility.

A few hundred years ago, cyber-attacks on ships were as common as space battles—until the Navy wised up and switched to their current system that couldn't be accessed externally and only minimally changed internally. Only a handful of people aboard ship even had the expertise to write the complex code running the ship, but no one—not him, not the captain, nobody—could change it.

"It's a good thing we didn't jump to Minsc," Stas said from above.

Beckett leaned back and looked up to where his assistant was going over the main panel on the upper engineering deck. It wasn't really an upper deck, more like a scaffolding to allow ease of access to the fusion reactor's control system.

"Why is that?" Beckett asked, curious as to what the petty officer was thinking.

"Because, based on when everything shut down, we would have made it halfway across the system and then... poof," Stas said. He made the explosion with his hands.

"What did you say?" Rod asked.

"Minsc. If we had jumped to Minsc, we would be floating dead in space. Or any other system, really. The Navy would have had to send a repair ship if they sent anything at all."

Beckett jerked upright as a stark realization hit him. He picked up the ELS helmet and pulled it over his head.

"This is Commander Beckett; is anyone near the main computer room?" He prayed someone was. The main computer was housed in three nodes for maximum redundancy. However, the largest of the three was tucked into the bow above the grav-coil. The other two were backups, but it had to be the number one computer node.

"XO here, go ahead?" Lieutenant Yuki replied.

"Pull the gravcoil connections on the server then reset it," Rod said.

"How copy? Pull the gravcoil connections?" she asked.

"Yes. Immediately, XO. As fast as you can," Rod said.

Lieutenant Yuki pulled the ELS helmet off her head and sat it on the desk she was using to study. She glanced down at the schematic for the number four turret, still struggling to find the problem. She was staying up late and waking up early in an effort to make up lost ground. The turret would have to wait, though.

She unlatched the deck plating and pulled it aside. Once she made sure it was all clear, she jumped down into the crawl-space. The gravcoil connectors were bright red, where the rest of the systems were yellow, green, and white. Each color had a code meaning one of many things, but right now, she wanted only the red ones.

The connectors she needed to unplug ran underneath the two cooling towers and then into the server interface. They were easy to detach, if she shut the computer off, drained the cooling towers, and removed the port tower. All in all, a process that would take twelve hours, by The Book.

Based on Commander Beckett's urgency, they didn't have twelve hours.

Angling herself sideways, she reached as far as she could go without touching one of the towers. Her fingertips brushed the cable connector.

She needed another ten centimeters. To unplug the magnetic cables, she had to exert ten kilos of force. It wasn't much, but not something she could just do with them pinched between her fingers.

She took a deep breath of stale air and tried again. Her finger brushed against them, but she couldn't quite grasp them.

Her uniform touched the cooling tower to her right and cold air like the depth of space spread over her skin. She bit back a grimace and pushed herself until she couldn't take it anymore and sat back.

Her breath came in gasps. She turned to the side, pulling her skin and looking back as far as she could to see the damage. Her cracked and broken uniform exposed a piece of bright red skin. She hadn't even touched the housing.

She took a deep breath, steadying herself. What she was about to do was going to hurt like hell, but she couldn't see another option.

Steeling herself, she lunged forward. Her shoulder and back pushed against the cooling tower and she let out a primal scream. Fire like a torch burned her back, and just as it was too much, her fingers wrapped around the cord.

Kim fell back and the cables came with her, ripped from their housing by her weight. She writhed in agony, trying to move her arm so she could roll over, but the right side of her torso wouldn't respond.

With every second, the pain grew more and more intense. Crying, she pushed herself up on her good arm and crawled to the controls for the main computer.

She crawled to the node, each meter an exercise in agony. Tears obscured her vision, but she managed to slap her hand on the security screen.

"Authorization Granted, Lieutenant Yuki," the automated voice replied.

There were four shielded red buttons—each one had to be pushed in order. She pulled up the first shield and pressed the reset. She slid along the node to the second one. The pain grew with every second. By the time she reached the third button, she trembled in shock and her body was numb. She used her good hand like a club, shoving the shield up and then pressing the button flat with her elbow.

The first server hummed then died.

Her vision dimmed. Stumbling, she fell and hit the deck face first. Remarkably, the pain from the fall cleared her head for a moment. Reaching with all her strength, she slid her fingers under the shield and pushed the last button.

———

Beckett and his engineering team erupted in cheers as the lights came back on and fresh air flowed from the vents.

"Way to go, XO!" he yelled over the suit's comm, then pushed the comm switch on his desk. "Engineering to the captain."

"Go for CO," Jacob replied.

"Sir, the XO fixed the problem and... wait one." He turned the volume up on his helmet since he thought he heard a faint sound.

Sure enough, it repeated. "Help," the XO whispered.

"Medical emergency in the main computer room!" Beckett shouted, praying he wasn't too late.

———

"...and that's the gist of it, sir," Commander Beckett finished his report. The briefing room was packed for Beckett's rundown on what had gone wrong. A holographic representation of the ship floated above the large table. The gravcoil and connectors were outlined in red and the ones connecting the main computer node were highlighted.

Jacob drummed his fingers on the table before responding, using the action to collect his thoughts. When the admiralty assigned him to command the *Interceptor*, he hadn't known what to expect, but human trafficking rings, black market ships, and sabotage weren't on any of his lists.

"First of all, excellent work, all of you," he said, looking around at each and every one of them. While Beckett and Yuki had played a key role in returning power to the ship, the rest of the crew had performed remarkably. "Please pass along my accolades to the non-comms and ratings." Heads nodded around the table. "XO, how are you feeling?"

Yuki's pale face and her arm in a sling were at odds with her chipper tone and smile. "Like I went three rounds with a mad gorilla, sir. Commander Stanislaw says I'll be okay in a few days, just need to give the regen-nanites time to do their job." The modern medical miracles they were able to pull off always left Jacob in awe. Private Naki was still down in sickbay, but he was almost one hundred percent better thanks to the nanites injected into his system, rebuilding his damaged cells from the inside out. Jacob had broken his nose when he landed face first on the concrete floor while trying to find cover. After a few days, he couldn't even tell anything had ever been wrong.

"I'm grateful you made it out in one piece. Now, PO Stas had some interesting insight and I'd like Commander Beckett to address it. Rod?"

The older man stood up and cleared his throat. "Stas did the math on how far we traveled when the ship shut down. Turns out, if we'd gone through a starlane, we would be in another system with our ship disabled. We'd all be dead, and the ship salvaged by pirates or recovered by the Navy."

"Was the gravcoil modified in some way?" Jacob asked. They'd confiscated the one they found on *Madrigal*. It matched *Interceptor*'s invoice and it was the right size.

Rod shook his head. "No. As far as I can tell, someone tampered with the code in the computers."

"Uh, Commander," Lieutenant Fawkes said, "that's not possible."

Yuki, Jacob, and Rod all smiled a knowing grin.

"In theory, Lieutenant, you are correct. I'm not sure how they did it, but I know how the code infiltrated the system after we installed the coil. Once the coil was installed, the computer nodes were all connected to it. The bad code used the coil pathways and that's why so many unconnected systems were impacted."

"Then how are we alive?" Ensign Hössbacher asked. Jacob's lips twitched into a little smile. If the lowest ranking officer was willing to speak up in a meeting, then things really were coming together.

"Good question. Rod?" Jacob nodded for the older man to continue.

"Because our ship is old. Not every system is tied into the central computer. If they could have, I'm sure they would have opened all the airlocks. However, while the computer monitors the locks, she can't control them. They have to be opened by hand. We got lucky, no doubt, sir," Rod said.

Jacob nodded at the seriousness of the statement. They knew piracy was a huge problem in this sector of space. It appeared the pirates were in league with someone in Zuckabar, or at least had intelligence resources in the small system. Unfortunately, unless they came into Zuckabar, his hands were tied. What pirate would? It would be suicide. No pirate ship ever flown could stand up to a real warship in a fight. No. Best case, they would back off their activities until after the *Interceptor* was gone, then it would be business as usual. Still, it bothered him that they had stumbled upon so much illicit activity in the relatively short time he'd commanded the ship. If this was what they found so far, what would they find next?

Jacob noticed his XO glancing down at her NavPad. Her face crinkling up like she was looking at something distasteful. He gave her a moment to work through her thoughts, allowing the silence in the room to flourish. He often found people were uncomfortable in silence and would volunteer information. However, once they were used to long silences in meetings, it gave the participants time to ponder questions and formulate their own.

"XO, you have some insight?" he asked.

She glanced back and forth among the officers. She bit her lip, debating what to say before she squared her shoulders and spoke.

"Yes, sir, I do. I'm afraid I'm responsible for this mess," she said.

The gathered officers became deathly still.

"I don't see how, Kim," Jacob said quietly. "You nearly killed yourself fixing it."

She gave him a small smile. "Thank you for that, sir. But it's true." Pressing the holo-button on her NavPad, she slid it across the table into the middle. Work orders popped up, showing the computer refit the ship had undergone some months ago. Jacob vaguely recalled Chief Boudreaux mentioning it when he first came aboard.

"Just after we lost our gravcoil, a crew from Kremlin came on board to refit and upgrade the main computer. It was also around the time Commander Cole passed away." She took a deep breath and lifted her head, looking him dead in the eye. "I didn't double-check their work."

Jacob nodded, thinking for a moment. It was brave of her to come forward. Even though he had worked hard to foster trust with them, something like this could damage her career. The XO's primary function was the running of the crew and over-seeing exactly this kind of situation.

"Don't beat yourself up, Kim," Commander Beckett said from the other side of the table. "They messed with the guts of my ship. I should have looked at their work as well."

Jacob reached across the table and turned the NavPad

toward him. He keyed in the file on Cole's death. The commander was average across the board, according to his FITREPs. Which was why, at forty-seven, he was still a commander. Unlike lieutenants, the Navy invested heavily for a person to reach full commander. They wouldn't kick him out for not advancing in rank.

Which was why Jacob needed this promotion to stick. Otherwise, they *would* throw him out.

He cleared his mind of those dark thoughts, the ones that kept him up at night and taunted him with staining his mother's legacy.

Refocusing, he scrolled to the date of death. A sudden, massive coronary had killed Commander Cole.

"Dominique?" Jacob asked without looking up.

The gathered officers glanced around, trying to figure out who the captain was speaking to.

Commander Stanislaw cleared his throat. "Uh, I prefer Commander, sir. Or Doctor, if you like."

Hopefully, the commander would move past his extreme introverted state one day, but right then, Jacob needed his skills as a medical professional.

"Noted. When Commander Cole came on board, did you give him a physical?" he asked.

"It's regulation, sir. Within the first three months of coming aboard, all officers must be evaluated for their fitness. I, uh, still need to do yours."

Jacob nodded. It was Navy regs, but assuming they were followed would get him into trouble.

"Were there any indications of a problem with his heart?" he asked.

Commander Stanislaw shook his head. "No sir. He was healthy. Had I gotten to him a few minutes sooner, I could have saved him, but he died so suddenly and traumatically, there was nothing to be done."

"Thank you, Commander," Jacob said. He glanced up at the man and nodded. The doctor looked away, as if he realized he'd spoken and was trying to hide.

"Skip?" Yuki said. "You want to share with the rest of us where you're going with this?"

"Three days," he murmured. "Three days," he said louder for the crew. "The computer refit left the ship, and three days later, Commander Cole died. Of a heart attack of all things. It's not exactly a common occurrence, not with our medical technology. Does that strike anyone here as a coincidence?"

"Excuse me, sir?" Yuki asked.

He looked up and noticed all the officers and the bosun were looking at him inquisitively, waiting for an explanation. His mind raced to connect the dots. His forming theory lacked a connection, though. The ship was parked next to Kremlin. Of course, if there was a Navy refit, they would be the ones to do it. After all, they had the contracts.

"Rod, can you check the computer and see who did the work?" he asked his engineer.

"Sure, one sec." The older man pulled up his own NavPad and tapped away on the keys. "You might be onto something, Skipper," he said with a sober expression.

"Let me guess," Jacob said. "Longhorn?"

"Got it in one," Beckett replied.

Jacob turned back to the invoices. Scanning the list, he found the name of the manager who oversaw the computer repair.

Merlin Nevil.

He'd only met the man once, right before Chief Boudreaux turned him into a splash on the wall.

"I wish we had something more to go on. This seems awful

flimsy... but right now, I don't see how Commander Cole's death and the sabotage aren't related. Thoughts?" Jacob asked. "There's no wrong answer here. If you have an idea, let us know." He looked at each officer in turn.

"I think we can safely say," Commander Beckett said, "that we all concur."

"Thank you, all of you. When Commodore Xin returns, I'd like to give him everything we have on this. Kim, compile a report of everything we know. Append Beckett's and Stanislaw's testimony and any proof you can find to support these." He waved at the holographic documents.

Kim reached over and took her NavPad back. "Sir, about the commodore. I have the schedule, and they must be running behind, because they haven't sent us a packet update since before you came on board," Yuki said.

"I'm sure the commodore is exercising prudence. He'll be here and we will have the ships to escort *Madrigal* to safety." He put as much confidence in his voice as she could. It was the only thing they could do.

"Now, here is what I would like to do," Jacob said. "I want a FOD check of the entire ship. Top to bottom. Followed by a level one diagnostics of every system." He held his hand up to forestall any complaints. "I know I'm asking for seventy hours of work, but this has to be done. If they hadn't played it cute, they could have set the gravcoil to accelerate beyond our ability to compensate and killed us all. Or put a bomb on the fusion reactor, or any of a hundred things. I want a hundred percent confidence in every system, understood?"

A chorus of nods and "Yes, sirs," came back.

Jacob smiled. "Okay, people. You've got your orders, now execute them."

CHAPTER TWENTY-SEVEN

Nadia woke with her heart pumping and her brain half convinced she was still on *Malia*, fighting insurgents who were far better armed than any rebel group had a right to be. The fighting had gotten bloody, and before the battle was over, Nadia killed more than her fair share while protecting the ambassador on the way to his shuttle off-planet.

She shook her head, trying to clear the nightmares that came with such action. Really, if she were being honest with herself, it was then she decided she was done with ONI and spy life.

Her sweat-soaked tank top was an uncomfortable reminder of the cold ship. She padded across the cabin to her walk-in closet, the memories of her terrible dream fading as she did so.

She pulled out her work clothes, slipping them on and fastening the belts and buckles. She liked shiny things and tended to wear outfits with an excess of buckles, straps, and buttons. It made her feel more like the rogue space captain she played.

A few moments later, she strolled onto the bridge. Her third watch crewman, Pete, lounged in the captain's chair, watching adult films on the big viewer dominating the forward hull.

"So this is what you do in the middle of the night?" she said with a small grin.

"Crap," Pete muttered. He fumbled to turn it off and managed to only pause it in the worst place possible. When he finally did shut it off, he was bright red with embarrassment.

"I know the late shift can be boring, but save that for your quarters or the VR machines, understood?" she asked.

"Roger, Skip. Sorry," he said hurriedly.

"Forget about it. Anything on sensors?" she asked by way of changing the subject.

He shook his head and tapped the plot on the command chair. "Nothing but rocks, asteroids, and empty space. Whatever he's looking for isn't out here."

The ship was spiraling out of the system at intervals of five million klicks, each spiral taking them farther and farther away. With each passing day, she wondered if maybe Barnes was onto something. What could the professor possibly be looking for?

An impulse hit her and she waved for Pete to retake the center seat as she turned and left the bridge. She took the stairs down to deck two, where the main hold was located. The professor hadn't only paid for her transportation, he'd bought out all the cabins and the hold, guaranteeing him privacy.

She knew it was a weakness, but whenever anyone tried to keep a secret from her, she had the urge to root it out. Probably why she made a good spy. Not great for interpersonal relationships, though.

Of course, she wasn't spying, per se, only curious as to what the professor was up to. After all, curiosity of the unknown was a virtue. She was also an excellent liar. Even to herself.

She keyed open the passenger access and stepped through.

Her normal cargo of luxury goods and medical supplies fit neatly in *Dagger*'s hold. The ten-meter by eight-meter space could be stacked to the rafters with the small but expensive goods she hauled. However, today, the large room sat empty.

The professor used the far corner as his own personal habitat. Apparently, he'd tired of making the trek to his bunk every night and was sleeping on a camping cot next to his equipment. Even asleep, he wore the space-time detecting headphones. She shook her head at his dedication. He was the epitome of the absent-minded professor. Either he really was one, or he put on a hell of an act.

She knelt and examined his space-time gravity and radiation detection equipment. It was off the rack, with a few extra upgrades like nearly unlimited memory for later playback. He could probably record millions of hours of sensor data on it.

How long did he expect to be out here? She had other jobs booked for later that year.

She pressed a button, transferring the sound from his headphones to the external speakers. Behind the static, she heard the steady beat of Zuckabar's binary stars. Despite all they knew about gravity and propulsion, there was still so much they *didn't* know. However, it was one of, if not the most studied phenomena in the galaxy. There was big money in finding new starlanes; even ones that shaved only a few hours off a course were worth finding. For the large trading consortiums and corporations, an hour off a cargo run would result in millions of dollars saved over the lifetime of a ship.

On the screen, lines jumped up and down, showing the current gamma-ray exposure. From what she could tell, it was space normal. At least for a system with a pulsar in it.

Professor Bellaits didn't strike her as a man who was concerned about worldly matters. He wouldn't be doing whatever he was doing for money. He wore clothes off the rack and lived on campus. Hell, he probably only had a few hundred dollars in the bank. He would've had to use grant money to bankroll this trip. Why all the secrecy then? He could've used the money to hire a science cruiser to come out here.

Something triggered her instinct. She might have left her life as a spy behind, but the life hadn't left her. A sixth sense, a warning of danger, flared to life within her gut.

She listened for a few more moments before switching it back to his headphones. He didn't stir the slightest. Standing up, she turned and froze. Daisy stood right behind her. "What are you doing?" she demanded in a loud whisper.

Nadia slipped right into her persona, not even fazed by the girl sneaking up on her, something very few people could do.

"I was just curious about what he was listening to," she said.

Something dangerous flashed in Daisy's eyes, so quickly, Nadia thought she might have imagined it. She'd spent more than a little time with the woman and enjoyed her company, but here was something she hadn't seen before—or even suspected. Nadia smiled, pointing at the machine as she continued on.

"I thought maybe it was playing music, but all I heard were drumbeats," she said with a goofy grin. "Is it music?" As a spy, she could go places and do things no one else could because of her ability to affect a non-threatening persona. Sure, she could be stealthy, even invisible if the conditions were right, but more importantly, she made people believe she was unimportant, no threat at all. She felt herself easily gliding into the role of the air-headed but lucky captain.

Daisy relaxed as if the threat of violence in her eyes had never existed. "No, silly, it's not music. Aren't you a captain? Don't you know what space-time sounds like?"

Nadia's eyes went wide, feigning ignorance as she stepped

aside and let Daisy by so the girl could adjust something on the machine.

"No, actually. I'm no astrogator. To be completely honest, I was really a glorified assistant to an admiral most of the time I was in the Navy," Nadia lied. "I spent most my days running to the cafeteria and fetching coffee."

Daisy finished making her adjustment, pulled the blanket up to the professor's chin, then made a shooing motion for them to leave.

In the corridor, the younger woman turned to Nadia, "I don't believe you were *just* an assistant. Look at this marvelous ship!"

Nadia laughed, her alto booming around the halls as they walked toward the mess. "Well, I spent most of my time aboard the flagship as we traveled from system to system. After ten years in service, I had plenty of money saved up. When Daddy died, he left me even more. I suppose I could have moved to the capitol and lived a comfortable life looking for the right man, but... well, I like adventure and seeing new places. I bought the *Dagger*, hired others to run her for me, and I get to *play* captain while having tons of fun."

They walked into the mess side-by-side, laughing and chatting away. Nadia let herself go on autopilot playing her role. She sensed that Daisy was doing the same. For a moment so short she could've imagined it, she had seen the real Daisy—and she was no college student. She was no more the professor's assistant than Nadia had been an admiral's. There was something else going on, something dangerous, and her ship was in the middle of it.

———

Daisy laughed innocently over the embarrassing college story she told her friend. It was a calculated move to garner trust. Nadia smiled at all the right moments, cringed when was necessary, and oohed and ahed as she finished. Yet all the while, Daisy was also detached. She knew the game was being played. Her network had supplied her with intelligence on the ship and her captain, but they had missed something. Captain Nadia Dagher was no mere admiral's assistant. For a split second back in the hold, she'd seen the real woman behind those clever brown eyes, and she was as deadly as she was capable. Everything following that moment was an act.

Could Daisy be one hundred percent sure? No. But she was a spy, and a good one, trained by the best. And she trusted her instincts. Everything about the captain was wrong. How had ISB missed something so crucial? It could destroy all their plans.

She laughed as Nadia said something mildly humorous, interrupting her conspiratorial thoughts. No, the woman before her was dangerous, and a threat to them all. But how could she deal with her? Perhaps the professor would achieve his goals before it became a problem, but that was wishful thinking. An accident, maybe? Life aboard any ship was dangerous. People died in accidents all the time.

No, if Nadia died, her crew would certainly insist on returning to their home port. She couldn't risk any interruption to their plans. The timetables were too strict.

Or maybe... she glanced at the door as two of the ship's maintenance crew walked in. She only had ten crew under her. Maybe... maybe she could reach out sooner than planned and guide the ship toward its final destination.

They were on the wrong side of the solar system, but in a few more days, perhaps a week, they would be in the right place. She just needed to guide the professor there, then they could replace the crew of the *Dagger* with her own people. If she did it right, the professor wouldn't even know what happened.

CHAPTER TWENTY-EIGHT

B arnes had his feet up on the console while he "watched" the bridge. It was the wee hours of the morning, ship time, and he had the place to himself. It wasn't like the ship was doing anything dangerous, and they were far enough away from the starlanes there was almost no chance of them running into another ship.

He punched a few commands into the console, bringing up the various sensor capabilities. The only thing even remotely close was a cluster of asteroids, which *Dagger* would pass by on her port side at two million klicks—practically spitting distance in stellar cartography.

Once he was sure the immediate space was clear, he went back to his pet project. Barnes considered himself the smartest person in the room, no matter who was in the room. He knew trivia and scientific facts like the back of his hand. He spent most of his personal time reading. Of course, he didn't have any degrees to back him up, but what he did have was an eagerness to learn and a clever mind.

Which was why the professor vexed him so! What could the man possibly be after? Even if there was another starlane connected to Zuckabar, it would need to lead somewhere useful. They were on the farthest "southern" edge of the Orion Spur, and while there were star systems to the "east" of their position, the really good ones were farther "north." Not down here on the edge of the Corridor. Directions like north, east, west, and south were relative in space, but if Alexandria was the center of the compass, it was as good a way of looking at things as any other system of directions.

What was the professor looking for?

He'd spent the last few weeks reading the man's papers and trying to digest their meaning. The minutia of stellar mechanics and quantum singularities were far less interesting than the abstract theory. Most of his papers dealt with gravity interaction in binary star systems. However, there were a lot of binary star systems easier to study than Zuckabar. Alpha Centauri would be cheaper, and far less difficult to investigate, since it was the largest colony of the Terran Republic.

Then, ten years ago, he stopped publishing. Withdrawing from conferences, refusing to speak, and turning down interviews, he held on to his teaching job, but only barely. He started chartering ships and visiting binary systems for months at a time. What was he looking for?

If one of the foremost experts on stellar cartography and astrophysics was here looking, then there had to be something worth finding. Something to do with binary star systems *and* pulsars. Barnes' ego would just not let it go.

He shook his head as he ran through all the different things it could be, and still none of it made sense. It wasn't a starlane and it couldn't be a black hole. In fact, Barnes couldn't think of a single possibility. Populated systems were as explored as his bedroom. Every inch was charted in detail. Humans had lived on this end of the Spur for five hundred years. There just wasn't anything to find here.

If there was some new phenomenon, it was going to be found outside the Orion Spur. Maybe if they were deep in the Corridor, maybe he would concede there was something new there... but here? In Zuckabar? It was a trash system. The only thing even marginally unique was...

Barnes dropped his feet to the deck and began typing like mad on the ship's computer. Data storage being what it was, any ship could have virtually every piece of possible information ever collected throughout the known galaxy, updated whenever in port. Sharing and collecting information was a good policy for any nation. Especially since they didn't have faster-than-light communications.

Barnes transferred his search to the main screen as he typed. His ability to do advanced calculations in his head was what made him a skilled astrogator. Now he put it to use figuring out the puzzle before him.

What if the professor was here *because* Zuckabar wasn't unique. Binary star systems, while a low percentage of total stars, were still common. But, as he constantly reminded himself, statistics and pure numbers were two *vastly different* things.

When one considered the number of stars, over two and a half *billion,* it was statistically small. Something like one pulsar for every 12,500 stars.

The absolute number of pulsars in the galaxy was huge—over two hundred thousand.

However, again by absolute numbers, that precluded Zuckabar from being unique, which was why he dismissed it on first pass.

"Bam!" he said out loud as the results came back. "Suck it!" He leaped out of the chair in excitement. He'd figured it out. He knew what the professor was looking for, and it was insane. It would change every—

Just as Barnes was about to call the captain, a loud, sharp crack filled the air followed by a piercing pain in his chest. He looked down, hand pressing against the red splotch forming on his tunic, and for the life of him, he couldn't figure out what had hit him.

Then he collapsed to the deck and died as the hole in his heart bled his life away.

Daisy slid the compact pistol back into her pocket and raced over to the dead man's panel, activating it with a wave of her hand. She held her breath as she checked the ship's comm log. No outgoing communications. If he had told anyone of his discovery, the entire operation would be for naught.

She went through the computer, using Barnes' access, and locked down everything and activated the engines. The gravcoil beneath the ship sprang to life, pushing three hundred gs. In a few minutes, they would be at a complete stop.

Nadia stirred awake with the nagging feeling something was wrong. She rolled over in her bed, throwing the thick, white down comforter aside, and sat up. She pressed her hands against her eyes to help clear the fog. The deck beneath her feet vibrated with energy, far more than the twenty-five gs of acceleration they were limited to.

She was instantly alert. Years of space travel in the Navy kicked her instincts in high gear, and she shed her clothes as she crossed to her closet then pulled on her ridiculously expensive ELS suit. The suit had everything the Navy model did, but with extended life support, limited thrusters for EVA, and padding on vital areas, as well as the most advanced nano-med tech she could afford.

Once her suit was sealed, she triggered the comm by her bed.

"Barnes, what's going on?" she asked.

She turned it off, then back on again, and repeated her inquiry.

No response.

"Any hands, respond," she said.

Nothing.

If the gravcoil was at max acceleration, then there was an emergency. Why the hell had no one called her? Why weren't they responding?

They were meandering along at a few thousand KPS. Hardly fast compared to what the ship could do at her full three hundred gravities. Could it be pirates? At their velocity, they would be easy to overtake. Zuckabar had a Navy destroyer in-system and, theoretically, that should scare off any pirates. Theoretically.

Whatever was going on wasn't good. Not at all.

She held out hope a malfunction caused the problem, but her gut told her to grab her pistol. She wrapped her gun belt around her hips and pulled it tight, then grabbed her armored jacket and slipped it over her shoulders as she ran out the door.

She zipped up her jacket as she passed the mess hall storage room. Porter stuck his head out the door. "Did we just go to full acceleration?" His eyes went wide as he realized she was wearing her combat gear, something he'd never seen outside of the occasional drills.

"Round up the crew. Comms are out and I don't know what's going on, but I want everyone at action stations."

"Roger, Skip," the older man said with a nod.

She could see the hatch leading to the bridge the instant she passed the storeroom. It was sealed shut. The panel next to the door read nominal, no hull breaches, and it still had life support. Why was it closed, then?

When she punched the button to open the door, an angry tone beeped at her. She hit it again. "Dammit," she muttered. "Barnes," she yelled through the door, pounding her first against the hard metal.

The *Dagger* had a crew of ten. She had made sure each one of them could fly the ship by themselves. In fact, everyone could do any job as needed. She might not be in the Navy anymore, but she still took precautions and ran a tight ship—which meant someone on her crew was always on the other side of that door.

"Nadia," Porter said from the galley. "Suit comms are up."

"All hands check," she said over the suit's mic. Nine voices came back in reply. "Pete, get to the hold and check on the professor and his assistant."

"Rog, Skip," Pete replied.

She paced back and forth, resisting the urge to pound on the door again. Instead, she balled up her fists in frustration.

———

Sub-Lieutenant Masud Tahan of the Fifth Immortal Guard rechecked his weapons loadout as their ship approached the infidel freighter. He relished any opportunity to see action, but it was also tempered by nerves. He had served and seen action in the second invasion of Vassid six months before. Albeit, not intense action. The rebel faction had fought bravely, for cowards, but in the end, they surrendered.

Masud closed his eyes, trying to banish the memories of what followed the surrender. Those who died fighting were the lucky ones. He didn't like that part of his duty, the massacre the rebel's actions necessitated. But his Caliph demanded no mercy for infidels or traitors. At least they were allowed to let the women and children live, sold into slavery, but alive.

The Dhib pilot's voice came over their comms. "Contact in thirty seconds."

"Is the ECM active?" he asked the pilot.

"Yes. There will be no calls for help. Allah be with you," the pilot said.

"And with you," he automatically replied.

He triggered his men's comms. "We are Immortals, and in service of our Caliph, we will never truly die." His men repeated it verbatim as they had every time before a mission.

For ten agonizing seconds, the Dhib was in full deceleration, slamming them against their harnesses with painful pressure. For the assault craft, this was the most harrowing part. Deceleration of any kind made a ship a target. Then it stopped and a loud clang reverberated through the hull.

"Contact!" the pilot yelled.

Masud hit the release button on his harness, shouldered his electrostatic rifle, marched to the front of the assault craft, and hit the button next to the emergency dock. The hatch slid open and then the one from the ship they were boarding opened as well. He charged through, knowing that the greatest potential danger was in that moment, and also knowing he would inspire his men with such a display.

"Clear," he said as he took a knee and covered the small corridor. Behind him, his squad of nine piled in, wearing full armor. It wasn't as bulky as some nations' battle armor, but it did the job and allowed them a greater degree of flexibility.

"Tell Skip I'm checking it out," a man said from around the corner up ahead. He turned the corner and froze in shock as he saw the hallway full of Caliphate Guard.

Masud looked at the images of Professor Bellaits and Kafir

on his HUD. This man was neither. He centered the rifle and squeezed the firing stud just as the man opened his mouth to shout. The rifle discharged a one-centimeter-radius line of plasma that burned through the target's chest, instantly killing him.

Masud waved his men forward and they charged. The element of surprise was still on their side, but not for long.

―――――

Nadia heard the discharge of the weapon before she heard the scream of agony that followed it. She whipped her pistol out and leaped down the stairs. With boarders below, any attempt to retake the bridge was futile.

"Skip, we got company. Caliph regulars just came through the emergency hatch and burned Porter, Jackson, and Rob down like dogs!" Pete yelled frantically over the radio.

"Are you armed?" she asked.

"What? No. No. I barely had my ELS on. I'm heading for the weapons locker now."

Dagger wasn't a large ship—only three decks. The lowest of the three, right above the gravcoil, was where the emergency lock was located. The weapons locker was in the rec room. If they wanted to take the ship, they had to come up. She went to the top of the stairs, took a knee, and aimed her gun right where a head would appear.

Pete huffed up the stairs, his helmet open for more air. He saw her gun before he saw her, and threw his hands up. She scowled at him and jerked her head for him to go by.

"Grab a weapon and watch my back," she said.

"But they're all downstairs?" he countered.

"They have the bridge. Anyone else make it?" she asked.

He shrugged. "I think most of the crew were still in their quarters suiting up," he said.

"Go weapon up," she ordered.

Then she heard another discharge, followed by a thud of flesh against the deck. They weren't taking prisoners, just murdering her crew. Her friends.

Rage rolled over her and pushed her to act, but the small part of her mind that had seen and heard such horrors before remained in control. She wanted nothing more than to run down the stairs, guns blazing, but she knew that would only get her killed. That same small part of her mind knew she was already dead, that there was no saving her. Nowhere to run.

Her mother had fled Caliphate control when she was a baby. Through the war, and the time after, she studied and wondered about her people. The horrors they committed against civilians were no secret. She would be damned if she allowed those things to happen on her ship. Maybe she had no hope of stopping them, but she would take as many of the bastards with her as possible.

Three more discharges, this time with no accompanying screams. Then silence. She pushed the sorrow to the back of her mind, saving it for later. The cold killer part of her took over completely, her body falling into trained reflexes she'd spent the better part of a decade honing.

She heard boots on the stairs, slowly moving up, attempting to be stealthy. They were well-trained professional soldiers.

She steadied her pistol and took a deep breath, letting it out slowly as she counted in her mind. Just as an armored head rounded the corner, she reached zero, and the pistol fired with a crack.

The 5.7mm round blasted through the man's armored face-plate, smashing through the bridge of his nose and killing him instantly.

Generally, armor-piercing rounds were a bad idea aboard ship, for obvious reasons. Even if it was unlikely to penetrate the hull, there were plenty of systems that could easily be destroyed by errant gunfire. However, she had never envisioned fighting aboard her ship. The sidearm was for the less savory places she visited, which was why she loaded AP rounds—an excellent choice against most armored foes. Including Caliphate soldiers.

Her target fell backward down the stairs with a clang as he rolled to the bottom. Scuffling noises from the deck below told her they were pulling the body out of the way.

Pete returned with a compact rifle shouldered and he knelt beside her. "Skip, we need to get the word out. Caliph regulars in Zuck can only mean one thing..." He let it hang.

"They have the bridge," she said. The solid silicate barrel of an electrostatic rifle poked out from below and fired. They ducked as the plasma beam flashed by their heads and slagged part of the wall behind them.

"Backup array in recreation. Even if they control the bridge, your codes should give you access. You just need to pull the panel from behind the pinball machine," he said.

She shook her head. "You go, I'll cover you and—"

"It has to be you, Nadia. Biometrics," he said with a helpless shrug.

It was her ship. Any attempt to override the main systems had to come from her.

"Aim for the head. Even if you don't penetrate, it will knock them around," she said. Placing her hand on the man's shoulder, she squeezed, knowing it would be the last they ever saw each other. He nodded.

"Give 'em hell, Pete," she said, then took off for recreation. It was five meters past the stairs and through a pressure door. The controls for the door were active and she hit the emergency close, then keyed in her override. As far as the computer was concerned, the door was preventing an atmospheric breach.

As rec rooms went, *Dagger*'s wasn't too shabby. A massive holographic display for watching movies and concerts from an extremely comfortable couch was on one end. Two total immersion VRs for more private entertainment were opposite. And then there was Black Hole Sun, the sorriest excuse for a pinball machine she could find. If she had to be aboard ship for months at a time, she wanted a pinball machine she could never beat.

Holstering her pistol, she disconnected the four nylon straps holding the game in place. Even with artificial gravity, the gravcoil still pushed things around; leaving a big, heavy machine loose could hurt it... or someone else. Once it was free, she pulled from the front, dragging it away from the wall with a grunt. Damn thing was *heavy*.

The panel came off easily enough and she held her hand against the flat screen as the computer confirmed her ID.

Captain Nadia Dagher, proceed.

She pulled up the menu just as a loud explosion boomed through the ship, blasting a huge hole in the pressure door and sending metal shards through the couch, ripping it to shreds. Nadia was out of time. She found the SOS and pushed down until it glowed red.

Two men rushed through the hole, rifles shouldered, and she recognized the armor as Caliph.

Crouching behind the machine, she drew her weapon, aimed carefully for the one on the right, and fired two rounds before switching to the second target. She fired once before he spotted her and blind-fired his weapon. The first man slumped against the wall before crashing to the floor.

The world slowed down as the plasma trail sliced through the air right at her. She willed herself to move faster, but it wasn't enough. It touched her arm and the electrical charge that followed blasted her against the wall then face first on the deck with a crunch.

She would have screamed if it wasn't for the convulsions racking her, forcing her every muscle to clench uncontrollably. They hadn't hit her with a plasma gun, but a stunner.

She took grim satisfaction in the dead soldier she had shot. Two more men entered the room, followed by Daisy.

She wanted to shout a curse at the woman. Instead, all she managed was a gurgle as spittle flew from her clenched mouth.

Another soldier came in, this one an officer by the decoration on his uniform. He carried a circlet in one hand and Nadia would have screamed anew if she could. Daisy pointed at her and the man walked over, triggering his helmet to retreat as he knelt next to her.

"Kafir tells me you are the captain?" he said in his heavily accented voice. With his free hand, he picked up her sidearm and gave it a tight smile. "You fought well, for a woman. But I'm afraid that is all over now. Your signal did not go out. My ship is jamming your communications. I'm very sorry."

The effects of the stun gun were still rolling over her and she couldn't move, couldn't even shake her head as he reached down and placed the slim silver collar around her throat. It sealed itself with a hum and her mind shut down.

CHAPTER TWENTY-NINE

Chuck was a stupid name for a ship. Especially one as fancy and deadly as the former Consortium frigate. But his people had a long history of naming ships by popular vote, and occasionally, absurdity won.

Still, Duval had a comfortable chair, his people were exceedingly happy, and they were departing Niflheim with a score of fresh recruits. It would take another week to arrive in Minsc, but he was certain *Raptor* was already there keeping an eye on things.

The cold planet they called home vanished from the screen as they accelerated to where they could enter the starlane. The only downside was the presence of their benefactor. No one had been more surprised than Duval to find "Mr. Takumi" eagerly awaiting them, insisting he be allowed to come along, and if need be, direct them to a specific target. Duval had assumed that when Takumi suggested targets, it would be through dispatch, not him riding along like some kind of pirate admiral.

The prissy man strode around Duval's ship like he owned the place. It angered him. Normally, he'd just shoot the bastard and throw him out the lock.

Normally.

However, his shiny new frigate was both an asset and a liability. Until he had the money from their previous engagement, he couldn't afford to rearm her. Even then, the torpedo launchers needed the latest in weapons technology. Without Takumi to provide them with the contacts to rearm, once they were out of weapons, they were out, and *Chuck* would be a glorified, albeit fast, passenger ship.

Everything about the man screamed fake. From his blue skin to the way his clothes fit. Someone, and logically it could be only one group, wanted him to believe the man was from the Consortium. Of course, Duval was no fool. He knew an ISB agent when he met one. He hadn't spent twenty years in the Iron Navy learning nothing. The part of him that still longed for those days shrank in shame for allowing himself to be used by the Caliphate's dreaded Internal Security Bureau.

It was a small part and easily ignored. The rewards, like the woman wearing his obedience collar back on Niflheim, made it worth the inconvenience. This was the life he was always supposed to have.

"Kane, E.T.A. to Minsc?" he asked.

"If I can run the rail close, seven days."

He nodded. "Let's not keep *Raptor* waiting. After all, I'm sure there's another merchant we need to relieve of their livelihood!" The crew cheered, even the ones who hadn't served on the last run. The pirate community was small, and word about their haul spread fast, making it easy to recruit new people.

Yes. This was going to be his year. He knew it. He just needed to return to Minsc, meet up with *Raptor*, head to Zuck to do whatever his two masters wanted, then they would be free to raid merchants to their heart's content.

———

DeShawn yawned as the *Raptor* hurtled through the starlane toward NG-495, which was directly galactic south of Minsc by Alliance reckoning. The week they'd spent on Medial was a blur of drunken debauchery that brought a smile to his face. That, along with the millions of dollars sitting in the hold. While they were there, they even had the *Raptor* undergo a software update for the tactical systems.

Not that *Raptor* would ever be anything other than a heavily armed gunboat. Pirates didn't get involved in ship-to-ship battles. Any battle at all was a loss for a pirate. It was why they spent so much time lying doggo in-system, waiting for the right mark. Least amount of effort wasn't just a motto, it was a life's ambition!

Minsc was the perfect system for such ambushes. The red dwarf primary made for a long trek across normal space, so they could sit at the twelve billion-klick line, wait for ships to pop up, and plan from there. Just like they took *Agamemnon*.

He knew Duval would have never tried for such a large target if not for the frigate he commanded. *Chuck* had an acceleration advantage that dwarfed even *Raptor*. While the little gunboat could pull north of three hundred *g*s, *Chuck* could do almost five hundred, maybe more with its military-grade gravcoil.

Sure, they wouldn't get every ship they tried for. While the starlanes were small on a galactic scale, they were still thousands of kilometers in diameter. And then there was lane drift. Even the best astrogator couldn't prevent that. Ships drifted away from their entry point and could appear on the other side anywhere within millions of square miles of the starlane.

Which got him thinking.

Maybe *Raptor* should be his ship? Duval certainly would have reinforced *Chuck* since they proved its capabilities. Pirates would be throwing themselves to sign up for a share of the bounty. Hell, he'd gotten way more for the women and cargo than Kane had estimated and he had nearly thirty million Alliance dollars on pallets sitting in the hold

What if he were to do it again? This time, though, just him and the crew of the *Raptor*? Then he could keep all of the booty. Of course, he'd need to do it on the sly. No point in angering their benefactor… or Duval.

He checked the clock. They were going to arrive in NG-495 within a few minutes… It wasn't a good place to lie doggo in, since it was only one of three systems that led to Minsc. Not to mention, the system primary was so small that freighters could skate in at the six-billion-klick mark and be across the system in a few hours… unlike Minsc, where it could take them a whole day to make the journey.

"Coming out of the starlane," Nikko said from the helm. The *Raptor* bucked and jerked as she made her transition to normal space. Velocity bled off her through the transition, and when she finally returned to normal space, she puttered along at a few hundred KPS.

It took a minute to shake the effects. DeShawn hated every second of it. "Set a course for Minsc, two-hundred gravities," he said.

The helmsman punched it in and the ship took off. It wasn't the smoothest of rides, but *Raptor* had seen them through a lot of action and DeShawn daydreamed of the day it could be his.

CHAPTER THIRTY

I nterceptor cruised through space like the shark painted on her bow sliced through water. The hum of the gravcoil was a steady, healthy thrum in Jacob's feet as he walked around the small destroyer.

One of the things he enjoyed the most, or had before Pascal, was wandering through the decks of his ship and exploring every nook and cranny. Schematics could tell him where things were, but they couldn't give him the flavor of the boat. She was special, Jacob decided, in a way he didn't think the Navy appreciated anymore.

As the last Hellcat-Class Destroyer built, she was more than forty years old, with several refits under her belt, and it showed in the crammed panels on the bridge. While technology was ever-evolving, a ship tended to stay static for years without upgrades. It wasn't worth the time and money to upgrade hardware with each new advance, which left *Interceptor* with a mix of advanced holographic displays, old touch screens, and even older manual controls.

Some things, though, would remain mechanical no matter what. Like the pressure hatches placed at regular intervals. The computer could open and close them, but there was still manual control over each one. The same for the turrets, torpedo rooms, engines—every major system.

When he was in the Academy, he had read all the books, all the manuals, everything he could get his hands on about the ships used in the Alliance Navy.

He looked back on his time in the Academy fondly, slightly embarrassed remembering the first year, where young Cadet Grimm was just sure the Navy needed a serious tech upgrade. It wasn't until he faced the realities of operations in space that he realized why the Navy had both centralized and decentralized systems in their ships.

"Captain, what brings you down to the torpedo room?" Bosun Sandivol said from his position above the tube where the four-meter-long torpedoes were fitted.

"Just walking the decks, Bosun, just walking the decks. As you were," he said with a wave of his hand.

The bosun nodded and the four ratings went back to work, performing systems checks on the equipment. *Interceptor* had four tubes forward and two aft, each one manned by a PO and four ratings.

The same mix of crew manned each of the coilgun turrets on the top deck. The other weapon, a single hypervelocity coilgun, fired a nine-kilogram payload of nano-condensed, magnetized, tungsten at thirty percent the speed of light. The twenty-nine-meter-long tube ran along the centerline of the bow. It was the most powerful weapon in their arsenal.

However, the energy required to fire the Long 9 was many thousands of times the turret guns. It took time for the capacitors to charge, and the ship was capable of no more than one round a minute.

"Captain, XO," Yuki's voice came over the comms.

He reached up and tapped a nearby comm panel. "Go for Captain."

"Sir, I think you better get to the bridge. We have a ship in trouble. She came through the Minsc starlane and, well, you should see it."

"On my way," he replied.

Jacob trotted through the passageway to the closest ladder. His spirit soared as he moved through *his* ship. She was clean, the crew was working hard, and morale was high.

"Make a hole," a spacer yelled as he approached the mess. A dozen spacers gathered outside, mostly ratings and a few POs waiting for lunch to start. They all pressed themselves up against the walls as he trotted by. A chorus of "Skipper," "Sir," and "Captain" followed him through. He returned each one with a nod.

He reached the ladder for the bridge and hauled himself up. He could take the lift, but he preferred walking through his ship the way the crew did. The lifts were used for moving supplies, cargo, and wounded personnel, not as a shortcut; officers who didn't walk the decks missed the little things that made a ship a home, and a crew a family. On the huge ships—anything larger than a heavy cruiser—you had to use lifts to get from one side to the other, but on a destroyer, it was almost sacrilegious.

His face split into a wide grin as he approached the bridge. PFC Naki stood watch on the hatch. Jacob couldn't tell he was ever even wounded.

"Akolo!" he called, using the PFC's first name. He'd looked it up after the incident on the station. There was something about almost dying together that bonded people. Naki and Jennings were excellent Marines and he would watch their careers with interest.

"Sir!" Naki replied, snapping to attention.

"Feeling better?"

"Yes, sir," he answered sharply.

"Good to hear." Jacob patted him on the arm as he walked by.

"And, sir?" Naki asked as he dropped into parade rest.

Jacob looked over his shoulder at the young man.

"Thank you for pulling my hoop out of the fire, Skipper."

Jacob gave the Marine a smile and a nod. "I expect you to return the favor."

"Yes, sir."

Jacob couldn't stop grinning as he entered the bridge. He paused for a moment to take in who was on watch. Yuki waved him over to astrogation, where PO2 Oliv sat hunched over her console. It wasn't a large bridge and it took only a few steps to reach them. He grabbed the bar above his head and leaned over to examine her display, since it was clearly what they were looking at.

"Sitrep?" he asked.

"The ATV *Bonaventure* came out of the Minsc starlane three-point-five hours ago. She's broadcasting a distress call and is accelerating out of control, heading perpendicular to Zuck Central." As she spoke, she pointed at a faint dot on the system map, showing the location of the disabled freighter.

For any ship, there were two universal speed limits they hit well before the speed of light—which was impossible to achieve in real space. One was the ship's gravcoil strength. The other was the relative strength of the coil at the front of the ship versus the stern. Theoretically, *Interceptor* could accelerate all the way to .06c before they had to put on the brakes. Most freighters maxed out at .03c before shearing forces broke them in half. For smaller ships, this wasn't a problem—there simply wasn't enough distance from the bow to the stern for those forces to come into play. However, with the much larger freighters like *Madrigal*, even a small gravitic imbalance from the bow would be multiplied a hundredfold by the forces at the stern, leading, eventually, to the ship cracking in half like a piece of dry wood.

"How long does she have?" he asked. He frowned, looking at the display.

Oliv pointed to their current location as a yellow dot flared to life. "If we leave in the next five minutes, we can make it to her with a little over thirty mikes to spare, sir. We can use this course." She pushed another button and a dotted yellow line formed from their current position, heading out to merge with the runaway ship. Jacob beamed with pride that the PO had already worked out the course, guessing he would greenlight the rescue.

"Good job, Oliv. Plot it and send it over to helm." Jacob gave his XO a nod to follow him as he moved to the center seat. "Let's run a battle station drill on our way there. I want the full Monty, hull depressurization and all."

"Understood. I'll set up a department head meeting for 1800 in the mess hall if that is acceptable?" she asked.

"Sounds like a plan. I'll leave the timing of the alert drill up to you, XO. I want everyone surprised," he said. "Myself included."

Yuki beamed with pride. When the captain left the running of the ship to the XO, things were working as planned. Up until this point, Jacob had a firm hand in everything. But this showed he believed in her and he knew she wouldn't let him down.

"Can do, Skipper," Yuki said.

Once she left the bridge and the helm had the course ready, Jacob leaned back. Despite the hardships they'd endured, the crew and the ship were coming together nicely.

"Chief Suresh... execute," Jacob ordered.

Power surged up from beneath, vibrating the decks as the ship shot forward. Since the ship was nowhere near another vessel, it accelerated at its max non-emergency speed of four-hundred and forty-eight gravities. For the briefest of seconds, gravity pushed the crew lightly back in their chairs as the two gravity fields fought for control.

———

ATV *Bonaventure* screamed along, continuing to accelerate at one-half kilometer per second squared as she passed ten-thousand kilometers per second velocity—dangerously fast for a freighter. For however much they accelerated, they would have to decelerate, and one-half KPS squared was her maximum power, leaving no room for errors.

Interceptor closed the distance from within the freighter's gravwake. Crossing the wake would take split-second timing, and Jacob wanted to leave the most difficult maneuver for last, allowing them to catch up as quickly as possible. They couldn't afford even a few minutes. PO Oliv had a countdown running, showing they had exactly thirty-three minutes and twenty seconds until the freighter broke apart. They had that much time to match velocity, send over the Corsair, rescue anyone on board, and get clear of the area.

As much as he would like to, there was no saving the ship. Whatever the malfunction was, if her own crew couldn't repair it, then he couldn't risk his people.

"Helm, bring us starboard, bearing zero-five-zero relative. Reduce acceleration to three-five-zero gravities," PO Oliv said from her position. Her eyes were glued to the screen as she spoke. Midship Owusu stood quietly behind her, watching everything she did. The PO's astrogation skills were second to none, almost matched by her ability to teach.

"Aye, aye. Bearing zero-five-zero relative, new acceleration set to three-five-zero," Chief Suresh said calmly from the Pit.

For the longest time, nothing was visible on the forward viewer. As they closed the distance and the gravwake narrowed, a pinpoint of blue light appeared, growing brighter as they approached.

"Twenty seconds to gravwake," Chief Suresh said.

"XO," Jacob said with a nod.

Lieutenant Yuki stood next to him, one hand holding the grab bar on the ceiling while her boots sealed her to the deck. She grabbed the mic with her free hand and keyed the shipwide.

"All hands, brace for crossing. All hands, brace for crossing," the XO's voice echoed around the ship.

Crossing another ship's wake could range from routine to outright risky. The maneuver they were attempting to pull off leaned toward the risky end. While the *Interceptor* had a more powerful gravcoil, the *Bonaventure* had more mass by a factor of a million.

This meant that while the Venture was slow and ponderous, her dense gravwake posed a greater danger. The closer they were to the ship when they crossed, the more condensed the wake was. Things were about to become interesting.

"Five seconds," Chief Suresh said as she took manual control. The computer still controlled the speed and relative closing distance, but when it came to wakes or tricky maneuvers, experience and instinct were still best.

As *Interceptor*'s bow gravwake slammed into *Bonaventure*'s, the entire ship shook, vibrating as the two conflicting gravity fields interfered with each other.

Jacob's stomach flopped as competing gravitational forces converged on the little ship.

"Five seconds to crest," PO Oliv said to the bridge. The ship jerked to the side violently for a heartbeat and then she was through. Internal gravity warred with the sudden loss of counterforce and it left the crew with a sinking feeling in their stomach as they crested an invisible hill and dropped rapidly down the other side.

Yuki grinned at her CO. "I know why they have the gravity set the way they do, but just once, I'd like to feel nothing."

"I couldn't agree more, Chief. Bring us alongside." Jacob glanced at the timer. Only twenty-five minutes to go. It took them three more minutes to line up next to *Bonaventure* and match velocity before the chief brought their distance down to one kilometer.

Bosun Sandivol let out a low whistle from the Ops station.

The *Bonaventure* was wrecked. Mangled, blackened metal was all that remained of her bridge. Several large streaks of burned hull drifted aft.

"What kind of weapon did that?" Midship Owusu muttered.

Jacob looked over at the bosun. "Juan, you or Devi ever see anything like that?" he asked the two most experienced spacers on board.

Juan shook his head slowly. "No, sir. Not ever."

"I have," Chief Suresh said with a scowl. "It's a Caliphate plasma cannon, sir."

"Oh," Jacob said in a whisper.

"I'd bet a month's pay they took the hit as they jumped into the starlane," Chief Suresh added.

Yuki spoke up. "That would explain why their acceleration remained constant since they exited. The computer is running the show and it's just following its last orders," she explained. Unlocking her boots, she walked over to astrogation, where the ship's scope was. "Oliv, radar map their hull. At this distance, we should see every nook and cranny."

"Aye, ma'am, radar map in three... two..." Oliv pressed the execute button. *Interceptor*'s lateral radar array swiveled and scanned *Bonaventure* from less than a klick. Radar waves designed for a million-klick range peeled the paint off of *Bonaventure*.

"Anything?" Yuki asked.

"Negative, ma'am. No reply, no signs of life. If you look here," Oliv pinpointed the spot on the screen where the *Bonaventure*'s lifeboats hung on the sides of the hull. "They didn't get off, ma'am. If they're alive, they're still there."

Jacob shook his head. They could guess all day long, but until he had boots on the deck, they wouldn't know.

"Boat bay, Captain."

"Boat bay, PO Kennedy, sir."

"Let Chief Boudreaux know she's clear to launch. They have," he glanced up at the countdown, "fifteen minutes. I want them off the ship with time to spare."

"Aye, sir. Fifteen minutes."

CHAPTER THIRTY-ONE

I f *Interceptor* resembled a shark with her concave bow and painted logo, then the Corsair dropping out of her boat bay looked like a remora detaching from the predator.

Her relative speed stayed the same as Boudreaux deftly engaged thrusters. Even though the Corsair had a gravcoil, her proximity to the two ships made it impractical and unnecessary. At full power, Chief Boudreaux had the ship across in less than a minute. As she approached, she rolled the dropship and connected with the *Bonaventure*'s emergency airlock.

"Contact in three... two... impact," Boudreaux said over the internal comms as the little ship shook.

As they connected with the freighter, the ship vibrated with the impact. In the crew compartment, PO Desper and Kirkland, along with six ratings, watched intently as the indicator light flickered from red to green. Kirkland held his hand up, causing them to wait a few more seconds before he gave the OK.

Spacer Rawlins leaped to it, bypassing the airlock in less than ten seconds flat. The young man gave Desper a cocky grin, showing just how fresh he was.

Bonaventure's hatchways were pitch black, and Desper's suit temperature gauge registered fifteen below, but there was atmosphere. Not an atmo anyone could breathe for more than a few seconds, though. Her suit computer registered almost thirty percent carbon dioxide. The ship's scrubbers were surely down, and if there were anyone left on the ship, they would be unconscious or dead.

"Team 1, medbay. Team 2, mess hall. Move your butts, people," Desper shouted into her comms. If there were survivors—and she doubted there were—they would be in one of those locations.

She led the team to the mess hall, which was the likely location of the most survivors. Her HUD displayed the ship's interior map, allowing her team to move directly to their target. Kirkland took his three ratings and ran for the medbay.

With each passing second, her hope of finding survivors diminished. Every compartment they passed had secure hatches. They simply didn't have the time to burn through a hatch, not with the clock ticking.

"Desper, this is Kirkland." His voice echoed in her ear, cutting in and out from interference. "All the airtight compartment hatches are sealed. We can't get into medical without burning them or bypassing, and I don't think we have the time."

She rounded the corner to the mess as he spoke and found the same thing. The airtight hatch to the mess hall was closed and locked.

"PO," Egger said as he came up beside her. He showed her the thermal readings on the scanner he carried. Sure enough, it counted eighteen people, likely unconscious, on the other side of the hatch.

"Kirkland," she said over the radio. "Does your thermal scanner pick up anything?"

"One mike," he replied. Time wasn't something they had a lot of and she willed him to hurry.

"Affirmative. Fifteen tentative life signs. Dammit," he said.

She heard the anger in his voice and felt it in her bones. They were trained to save lives, and these were lives they were meant to save. She couldn't just abandon them. She keyed the radio and changed frequency to the Corsair. "Chief, patch me to the skipper."

———

Jacob nodded solemnly as PO Desper explained the situation. They would need at least half an hour to burn the hatches. That was twenty minutes more than he could give them.

"Desper, I copy. Wait one," he said in the pickup. He looked over at Yuki. "Options?" he asked.

"I don't think we have any, Skipper. We can't stop her from here. Their bridge is slagged, along with half their control runs, and the engine is accelerating out of control. We need to get our people back before they add to the death toll."

Jacob railed against the idea of leaving thirty-three people to die. It was unfair. *Interceptor* had made it here, proving she was fast and reliable. To fail now would be a bitter pill to swallow.

At the same time, he couldn't let his own people down. Doors didn't burn fast. There was no way to do it in the ten, no, *eight* minutes until the ship ripped herself apart. As it was, they were barely going to have time to beat feet back to the Corsair.

He sucked in a mournful breath and was about to give the order to fall back when he noticed Fawkes playing with targeting solutions on his screen.

"Carter?" he asked. "Do you have an idea?"

The junior lieutenant blushed furiously and turned his

screen off. He fidgeted for a moment before speaking. "It's a silly idea, sir. I don't think it's worth mentioning."

"It was worth thinking about. Lay it on me," Jacob said. "Consider it an order."

"Well, uh, it's easier to show you, sir," he said.

He pushed a few buttons and the main viewer mirrored his screen. It showed a top-down view of both ships. Since it was to scale, *Interceptor* was hardly more than a dot next to the M-class freighter.

"*Bonaventure* is accelerating at fifty gs, which means her gravcoil is on low power. Normally, the only time our gravcoil is running that low would be in proximity to traffic lanes or in harbor. The gravity wake is dangerous, but the bubble around the ship from the prow, not so much. Sure, it's enough to send particles and debris to the side, but it couldn't stop one of our coilguns."

"Are you suggesting we shoot *her?*" Yuki asked. The way her face screwed up showed the deep incredulity she had for the idea.

"Like I said, not worth mentioning," he said, turning away to bury his head in his station.

Jacob's first reaction was like his XO's. The thought of opening fire on a freighter was ludicrous. A stray shot would punch all the way through her unarmored hull. The look on Carter Fawkes' face told a different story, and Jacob decided to see the idea through.

"Finish your theory, Carter," he prompted.

The young lieutenant looked at the captain, then, with a deep breath, continued.

"Right. If we accelerated for five seconds at thirty gs and then lined up right in front of her, I *think* we could disable the gravcoil with a single shot from turret three. At this range and with a low relative velocity, it should be a piece of cake."

Called shots in combat were a rare prospect. Usually, ships were flying away from or toward the enemy. Broadside engagements were rare and short. The best shot for taking a ship out was at close range, from the front or rear. If one were lucky enough to be directly behind a ship inside her wake, then it was an almost certain kill shot. Same thing with the front. Of course, no one in their right mind would travel in a straight line long enough to take fire from an enemy.

However, the *Bonaventure* wasn't the enemy.

"Chief Suresh, can you do it?" Jacob asked.

The woman flying the ship looked into the small mirror reflecting her face to the captain. She deliberately raised one eyebrow as if questioning his fitness for command.

Jacob made an apologetic grimace before turning to his weapon's officer.

"Carter, give the chief the targeting coordinates. Devi, execute when you're ready."

Yuki moved to stand next to his chair, locking her boots in place and grabbing the bar above. "Sir," she whispered to make sure no one heard her but him. "If this works, we'll save the crew, but if it doesn't..."

"I'm well aware we're outside the regs on this one," he said. A flare of annoyance flashed in him. Was she still worried about her career? Did she think since he had nothing to lose, he would risk everyone else's future?

"That's not what I mean, Skipper," she said softly. "I think we should recall the boarding party to the Corsair. If it works, they can get back aboard her. If it doesn't... There's no need to risk their lives."

His annoyance was instantly replaced by guilt. She was doing her job and doing it well. He'd laser-focused on saving the lives of the freighter crew, and in his eagerness to make it happen, had almost endangered the boarding party.

"Good call, Kim, and... thank you," Jacob said.

"It's my job. Someone's got to keep the captain out of trouble," she said with a grin.

"Make it happen," he replied.

"Aye, aye." She pushed the comm button next to the grab bar. "Desper, this is the XO. We've got a plan. However, it's high-risk. Get your people back to the Corsair and stand off five hundred meters. If this works, you'll re-board her in a minute."

———

"...in a minute," the XO said over the comms.

Desper cocked her head to the side, confusion sweeping over her for a heartbeat. Re-board her? The ship was going to be scrap in a few minutes. "Roger, ma'am. We're falling back." She switched her radio to the boarding party frequency. "All hands, fall back to the Corsair. Double time!"

"We just going to leave them, PO?" Eggers asked.

"What choice do we have. Now, go!" She pushed him along the corridor to get him moving.

Once they were back on the Corsair, Desper made her way to the ladder leading up to the cockpit. "Permission to come up, Chief?" she asked.

"Granted," Boudreaux said without looking down.

Desper climbed up and took the second seat, pulling the straps on and cinching them tight. Once everyone was buckled in, Boudreaux guided the little craft, no more than a flyspeck in comparison to the *Bonaventure,* away from the freighter. As she did, they both watched *Interceptor* surge forward then roll to port, lining up with *Bonaventure*'s gravcoil.

"Is the captain going to fire on the freighter?" Desper asked.

"No... he wouldn't... would he?" Chief Boudreaux responded.

Jacob watched the two ships line up. Carter had the main screen split horizontally. The top half showed the view from coilgun turret number three; the bottom half was a wireframe layout of both ships. A single line went from *Interceptor* to *Bonaventure*. Once the line connected vertically, the wireframe moved in three dimensions to show a three-quarters view, allowing Chief Suresh the angles she needed to move the ship so they were on target.

"One minute," Oliv whispered from her station. The entire bridge held their breath as the coxswain expertly guided the tin can into position. Looking back at the huge freighter, Jacob couldn't help but feel like a minnow being chased by a whale.

"Carter?" he asked.

"Just a few more seconds, sir," he said. One hand hovered over the fire control and the other pressed on the console to keep himself steady. To keep it simple, the number three turret was locked in line with the ship's keel. In essence, wherever the ship was pointed, the turret would fire in the opposite direction.

Coilgun turrets excelled at close-range engagements and space defense. In this case, though, they didn't need their ability to rapid fire and traverse quickly; they simply needed one round fired at a precise angle.

"Twenty seconds," Oliv said, keeping them up to date.

"Lieutenant Fawkes," the XO said, "this close, is our gravwake going to interfere?"

Carter answered without taking his eyes off the targeting screen. "No, ma'am, we don't have the mass to impact her course."

Lieutenant Yuki seemed satisfied with his answer.

Jacob let out his breath, silently praying it would work. He wanted—no, *needed*—to save those people. He willed it to succeed with every fiber of his being.

Commander Beckett signaled from engineering. His face appeared on Jacob's MFD. "My scans are showing tolerance. She won't last much longer, Skipper."

"Carter?" Jacob asked.

"Almost there..." Fawkes whispered. The indicator on his screen flashed as the crosshair lined up all three axes.

Lieutenant Fawkes slammed his hand down on the button. *Interceptor* shuddered as the single-barrel coilgun fired its 20mm payload.

Bonaventure's gravcoil was already under tremendous pressure from the constant acceleration. Stress on the coils brought them to their breaking point. The 20mm round slammed into the keel of the forward-most ring, shattering it like ice on a pond. Computers aboard the freighter went into automatic shutdown, killing the power to the entire coil array. Residual energy from the drive kicked the freighter into a slow spin to port as the ship trailed debris.

Jacob held his breath and realized the crew held theirs with him. Ten seconds passed, then twenty, thirty—

"Well done, Carter!" Jacob shouted as he jumped to his feet. If the ship held for thirty seconds, then it would hold.

"Thank you, sir." Lieutenant Fawkes stumbled over the words, not sure how to accept praise from his CO.

"Chief Suresh, that was the finest flying I've ever even heard about," Jacob said to the coxswain.

"Thank you, sir," she said through a yawn. He didn't know if her lack of nerves was an act or real, but either way, it truly was an amazing display of skill.

Jacob turned to Kim. "XO, get the Corsair back over there and let's save some lives."

"Aye, aye, Skipper," Kimiko Yuki said.

CHAPTER THIRTY-TWO

In any other time or any other Navy, Fleet Admiral Noelle Villeneuve would have absolute authority over matters involving the deployment and distribution of the fleet. Because it would be her fleet. One she was responsible for, and for whom the buck stopped.

She rubbed the tension out of her face and gazed out over Anchorage Bay. The light gleamed off the blue-green waters as the sun dipped below the horizon, casting long shadows.

"I take it they said no?" Admiral DeBeck said from behind her.

Noelle leaped, knocking her chair sideways as her adrenaline spiked. "What the—? How did you get in here?" she asked. She looked past him, trying to figure out how he had entered her office.

Wit held his hands out to the side. "I'm the Chief Spy of the Navy, Noelle," was his only explanation.

It took a moment, but her heart settled. She grabbed her chair and flipped it around before dropping into it with a sigh.

"Yes," she answered him, "they most certainly said no. Not only did they say no, but they also emphatically expressed their desire for me not to address the subject again."

She'd spent the last three hours in front of the House's Naval Appropriations Committee as they went through the budget bit by bit and trimmed it down further than it already was. Further. As if the bare minimum operations they were already at could be reduced.

"They want me to decommission the *Alexander* battle group, Wit. I knew things were bad, but..." She let her hands fall to her side. "This is a disaster. We only have four battle groups. Three won't be enough to patrol the systems under our protection, let alone defend us from aggression. I can't understand why they want to leave us vulnerable like this."

"I can," he said. Her head perked up until she saw the disappointed look on his face. "Several key members of the House have met with the ambassador from the Caliphate of Hamid. I think they're trying to appease them. My sources tell me the ambassador has expressed his Caliph's concern that the Alliance Navy poses a threat to the peace."

"My God," she said. Noelle collapsed into her chair; equal parts of disbelief and anger surged through her. "Don't they know that won't work? You can't beat a bully by giving in to them. If they want to appease someone, why not the Iron Empire? At least we have some common ground with them."

He nodded. "I agree. Unfortunately, we aren't in the position to do anything about it. The CNO is firmly in the camp of the opposition. He's trying to save his retirement."

"Short-sighted morons. I swear, I don't know why the president gave me this job. There's nothing I can do without—" Her computer interrupted her with an urgent signal. "One second, Wit," she said.

She pulled the screen closer and thumbed her acceptance of the packet of information labeled—*URGENT*.

"It's from *Interceptor*. You know, I was really hoping your plan would work, but—" She froze mid-sentence, unable to believe what she was reading.

"What?" Wit asked.

"I think I made the right call for the wrong reasons," she said in a whisper. Could she have been so wrong about Lieutenant Grimm?

"Noelle, you want to share the information with me?" Wit asked. He leaned over the table, resting his palms flat against it.

"Yes. I need you to call in every favor you have. I'll do the same. This is it, Wit, this is our chance. But if we don't hurry, it will be all for naught," Noelle said. She hated how excited she sounded, but this was beyond her expectations.

She turned the monitor for him to see, and Admiral Wit DeBeck, the professional spy, clenched his jaw at what he read. At what Congress had allowed to take place.

"I can get us in to see the president in fifteen minutes," he said.

"Really?" she asked.

"St. John will do the heavy lifting—he's already set it up. We just need to pull the trigger. The man would've made a hell of a spy," Wit was already headed for the door.

———

President Johan Sebastian Axwell ran his hand over his bald head, trying to reconcile all the meetings and reports he had to handle in the time he had left. His chief of staff had awakened him at 0500 for a security briefing and his day had deteriorated from there.

While all of his "paperwork" was done electronically, it didn't seem to speed the process up any. A hundred documents a day were brought for him to digitally sign.

The ancient grandfather clock carried here by the original settlers clicked over to 1900 hours with a subdued gong. There was a lot to do before he had dinner with the First Lady. At least he had that to look forward to.

"Sir," his assistant's voice came over the intercom.

"Yes," he replied without looking up.

"Fleet Admiral Villeneuve and Admiral DeBeck are here to see you, along with Senator St. John," his assistant said.

Johan frowned. He was familiar with his schedule and they weren't on it. His computer beeped, upgrading his schedule to show a one-hour meeting with the three very important people. How did they manage an hour when he couldn't even have five minutes to himself?

"Show them in, Martin," he said with a heavy sigh. He pulled his tie straight and cleaned up the wrinkles in his jacket before the door opened.

The two admirals strode into the office and stopped in front of his desk. Senator St. John came in behind them, taking a seat on one of the two luxurious leather couches to the side.

"Noelle, Wit, Talmage," the president said with a nod. "You want to tell me how you maneuvered this meeting with me—without my chief of staff present, I might add?"

"I'm afraid that was my doing, Mr. President," the senator from New Austin said in his drawl. "Your chief of staff doesn't know about this meeting."

"Then how?" President Axwell asked. He was a little stunned they could alter the schedule without Leilani Kahale knowing about it. She was far too organized and efficient to let something like this slip by her.

St. John had the decency to look embarrassed as he explained. "My wife is friends with the head of the IT dept, Mr. President. She persuaded them to add us to the schedule. I would appreciate it if this wouldn't fall back on him. There is gravity to what we're about to tell you and we couldn't risk anyone stopping us from informing you."

"You honestly think people would stop you from seeing me?" Johan asked.

Talmage glanced at the two admirals then back at the president. "No, sir. But, if they were to learn of the urgency, delaying us until our opportunity had passed would be possible."

I see," President Axwell said. He leaned back in his chair, put his hands on the desk, and nodded for them to go on. He was a little stunned. Talmage sounded like he was referring to a conspiracy.

"Sir," Admiral DeBeck started, "for the last three years, I've had agents imbedded in the Protectorate, along with a number of freelancers who report to me their findings."

Johan let out a sharp laugh. "You *are* the head of ONI. I expect you to keep a hand on what's going on. However, doesn't that clash with the Department of National Intelligence's mandate?" the president asked. "The Protectorate is their bailiwick, so to speak."

Wit shook his head. "No, sir. For years now, the governments of the Protectorate have bribed, extorted, and stolen from the Navy. My agents were investigating those specific matters. Not matters of state."

Axwell chuckled. "Okay, Wit. If that's the line you want to draw. Go ahead. I'll leave it up to Director Nizhoni and you to work out."

"Yes, sir. My job is all about lines and boxes. If everyone thinks I'm just Naval Intelligence, they leave me alone. It also allows me to gather information the others miss. Like what I'm about to show you."

Wit put his NavPad on the president's desk. It wasn't standard-issue, but an advanced prototype with as much encryption and physical security as technologically possible. The projector sprang to life showing red dots moving toward the Consortium system of Praetor.

"My counter-part in the Consortium shared this with me. For the last six months, the Caliphate has moved ships into a system three lanes from Praetor. They insist it's a training exercise. I think they're massing for a second invasion," Wit said.

The president nodded for him to continue.

"On top of that, the pirate activity in the Corridor has escalated to previously unseen levels. Trillions in cargo and ships have fallen into black market hands, not to mention the thousands of lives lost or sold into slavery in the meat markets of Medial and other planets along the Caliphate border," Wit said.

President Axwell clenched his jaw. He *hated* knowing that people from his nation were slaves in another country, but he literally could do nothing about it. The Alliance, while wealthy and relatively powerful, didn't have the Naval resources to push back. Even if they did, they were thousands of light-years away. It would take ships more than a month to reach the closest Caliphate planet to the Consortium.

Johan felt his chest tighten as Wit laid out what he knew. His stomach churned and he dreaded what came next.

"Why haven't I heard about this Caliphate fleet before?" Johan asked.

Wit pressed his lips together in a thin line. "Mr. President, I..."

St. John broke in. "What the admiral doesn't want to say is there are people in our government—Congress and bureaucrats —who want us to do nothing about the Caliphate threat. Who actually believe an alliance with them is possible and that we should do nothing to provoke them. Sorry, Admiral, I didn't mean to step on your toes, but I don't wear a uniform and I can make accusations without losing my position."

Admiral Wit turned with a smile and nodded to the senator. "Thank you, Senator."

"Are you both serious? Those are some heavy accusations," the president said. A Caliphate fleet as close as one month from Alliance space was news his military advisors should have brought to his attention. The ramifications—that they were hiding something—cast doubt on his entire government.

"Not really, sir," Wit said with a shrug. "Wanting to foster peace with another nation isn't treasonous. Even withholding information from you could be seen as 'opinion based.' After all, your daily briefings don't normally include the goings-on of the Iron Empire."

President Axwell ran one hand over his head to the back of his neck and squeezed. He had a headache coming on, he knew it. Johan opened his second drawer and pulled out the bottle of antacid he kept there. Unscrewing it, he took a swig before speaking.

"Wit, either this is serious—and I gather from your presence it is—or it's not solid enough for my own people to have brought it to me."

Why did he find the idea of Wit telling the truth so easy to believe? Did he secretly distrust his own cabinet?

If he didn't, he wouldn't have moved Noelle to Fleet Admiral and made sure Wit stayed on as the head of ONI. He had to give Congress something, so he allowed them to recommend the CNO and the Secretary. Who were firmly in the anti-Navy crowd. He figured that was enough to push Noelle through as Fleet Admiral.

"I'm sorry to interrupt, sir," Noelle spoke for the first time. "But what the admiral and senator have shared with you so far is only the backstory of what is going on *right now*."

The way she said *now* sent warning alarms off in his head. "Please continue," Johan said,

"This is why we needed an hour, sir. It's going to take some time to catch you up..." Noelle said.

She did. She told him everything.

He took it all in. The worst of it was the massive human trafficking ring *Interceptor* had uncovered. After all, it was his duty, first and foremost, to protect the citizens of the Alliance. It was what the government existed for, and they were doing a piss-poor job.

"Are you telling me you sent a fall guy to Zuckabar, but now he's doing the job we all wished we could be doing?" Johan asked.

"Yes, sir," Wit answered.

Noelle covered her mouth for a moment. "I'm afraid so, sir. Not only that, but he's in the possession of a valuable ship that people will kill for. Him, his crew, and anyone else who gets in their way," Noelle said.

"I'm going to assume Commodore..." He grasped for the name of the man assigned to the picket.

"Xin, sir," Noelle added.

"Right, Commodore Xin received this information first and is already on his way to Zuckabar?"

Noelle glanced at Wit, and the two of them looked back at the president.

Why was it Johan suspected they were testing the waters every time he asked them a question?

"No, sir," Noelle stated. "I gave the commodore standing orders to stay in Novastad until otherwise ordered."

"That's a bold move," President Axwell said. "Leaving one destroyer to handle pirates, corruption, and who knew what else was going on."

Noelle placed her NavPad next to Wit's. With the touch of a

button, a holographic image of Lieutenant Grimm appeared. "It's why I chose Lieutenant Grimm, sir. If anything went wrong, we could lay the blame on his shoulders—because of Pascal. However, I'm afraid I made the right choice for the wrong reason and I would, with your permission, desperately like to fix my mistake."

Axwell looked up and examined the admiral for a long moment. He'd known Noelle for the better part of twenty years. She was a solid, practical person who wasn't given to admitting fault, mostly because she rarely was at fault.

"Care to explain?" he asked.

"Yes, sir. Under the circumstances, Jacob Grimm has done an outstanding job as *Interceptor*'s CO. Before the incident at Pascal, he was set to go to command school and was on the fast track to captain. He had glowing FITREPs from all his commanders and those who served with him.

"However, due to the PR fall out of Pascal, his career was torpedoed. Since it is unlikely any promotion board will vote to promote him, he's due to muster out soon. His current rank is frocked, and only exists while he is physically in command of the *Interceptor*."

President Axwell nodded. The media had caused a firestorm around young Lieutenant Grimm's actions in Pascal, using him as a lightning rod to tell everyone what was wrong with the Alliance Navy. The media was fond of not letting facts get in the way of their agenda. There were days he hated his job.

"Well, he needs backup now, Noelle, regardless. What do you propose?" Johan asked.

"USS *Alexander* is in orbit along with her battle group. I suggest we form a task force, which I'm able to do at my discretion, and set sail for Zuckabar with all haste, which I can't do at my discretion," Noelle said.

"Wit, Talmage, you agree with this?" he asked.

Wit nodded.

"Agree, Mr. President? I think we should do more. This is a travesty. Clearly, the systems governors of the Protectorate were in on this nightmare. They are either conspiring to commit murder, piracy, and human trafficking at the very least, or at the most, they plan to break our long-standing treaty and attack us. I see no choice but to annex the four systems immediately, dissolve their governments, and allow new elections."

Axwell shook his head. "That would require both bodies of Congress to approve it, and we would never have the votes necessary to pull it off. I've done all I can just trying to minimize their sweeping reductions in our military."

Talmage smiled, a gleam in his eyes. "I understand, Mr. President. What I'm suggesting is that we send the admiral's task force on a training exercise. I think I can swing delaying any kind of response from the media by also proposing the annexation of the Protectorate in the Senate today at our late-night session. Once the vote is on the rolls, I can join the admirals and see the situation for myself."

The two admirals turned to stare in disbelief at the senator. President Axwell smiled at seeing Wit DeBeck taken by surprise.

"It's a nice thought, Talmage, but it will end your career," Johan said.

"For one, Mr. President, I would then be allowed to spend more time with my wife and I would be all in favor of that. However, it really won't. What it will do is embarrass those who vote against it. Humiliate them, really. When Admiral Villanueva's 'training exercise' turns up the largest human trafficking ring in our history, and whatever else she can find while out there, they will have no choice but to immediately call for a vote on annexation just to undo the damage of voting *against* it a few weeks earlier."

Johan Sebastian Axwell smiled genuinely for the first time

since he took office. "This could work," he whispered. "No one outside this room can know. No one. I'll prepare a speech, the best of my career. Noelle," he pointed at her, "the moment you verify this, send your fastest ship. No packets. I want complete operational security. As soon as it arrives in-system, I will go live and give the speech. By the time all the systems of the Alliance have heard it, Congress will have no choice but to acquiesce." He turned his chair around to look out at the south lawn and beyond it to the city rising up in the distance. "You have your authorization, Noelle. Form your task force and move out."

"Aye, sir," she said, snapping to attention. "I serve at the pleasure of the president," she added formally.

Johan hoped this worked, because if it didn't, the most he could hope for was serving out his term.

After they left his office, he bowed his head and prayed for the spacers on board the *Interceptor*. It couldn't hurt.

CHAPTER THIRTY-THREE

Yuki stepped into the packed sickbay and waved at Commander Stanislaw. He gave her the "wait one" signal as he spoke with a patient. In all, they had rescued thirty-three people from certain death. A worthy accomplishment for any ship, more especially for the *Interceptor*. Until the captain had come along, they hadn't exactly been shining examples of naval tradition.

"Yes, XO?" Commander Stanislaw said as he walked toward her.

"The skipper asked me to interview the crew. I was hoping they were up for it?" she asked.

The surgeon frowned. "Ideally, I would like them to have a few days rest before you interrogate them, but if you must... do so with caution. They've been through a very traumatic event."

"Doc, I'm not going to interrogate them. We need all the info we can get if we're going to stop these pirates," Yuki said.

Stanislaw smirked. "Indeed. My dear, you haven't served long enough in the Navy to realize we don't stop anything." He moved past her, leaving the XO stunned with his comments. She hadn't really known Commander Stanislaw that well but having him react so was surprising, even though doctors had a long history of acting like they knew better than everyone else. She shrugged, chalking it up to exhaustion.

They'd managed to download a crew list from the public database and she was surprised at how few were missing. With the damage *Bonaventure* had sustained, she would have expected two-thirds of them to have died in the initial attack.

"Is Captain Morrison here?" she asked in her officer's voice. A short man, bald and plump around the middle, raised his hand. He pushed his glasses up with the other as they seemed determined to slide off his round nose.

"Sir, I'm very sorry for your loss," Yuki said as she held out her hand. Captain Morrison shook her offered hand with a sad smile on his face.

"Thank you, ahh, Lieutenant Yuki?" Morrison said her name as a question. Yuki reflexively looked down at her space black sweater where her name tag and service were. "That's what it says on my checks, sir."

"Quite right, I guess I'm still a little shaken up," Morrison said.

Yuki offered him a sympathetic smile. "Captain Grimm has asked that I make a full inquiry to shed some light on the pirates who did this. Would you follow me?" she asked.

"Of course," Morrison said. "And again, thank you for your, uh, timely help."

"It's our duty, sir, and our honor. Please, this way?" The mess hall where she'd set up the interview space was several decks above sickbay. To make the journey easy on the older man, she guided him to the nearest lift. They rode in silence.

Once they were seated and Mendez had provided refreshments, she began.

"We weren't able to save your ship's computer, unfortunately; otherwise, we would have more info on the pirates. Is there anything you can tell us about the ship that attacked you?" Yuki asked in a pleasant yet firm voice. She was used to questioning spacers and midships who were misbehaving, not civilians. In fact, she couldn't remember the last time she had done an after-action investigation that involved civilians.

He glanced around nervously, pushing his glasses back then taking a sip of the orange-flavored juice, wincing as the taste hit him.

Yuki laughed lightly. "I know, Navy food isn't exactly a delicacy. But the juice has all the vitamins and minerals you need, plus a little—" she snapped her fingers "—pick me up. When was the first time you realized something was wrong?"

He put the juice down and looked to the side, hand pressed to his face as he thought. His face stayed strangely neutral as he spoke.

"About three minutes before we entered the starlane. We had just come to a complete stop when they appeared, four hundred thousand klicks behind us and closing fast. She was hiding in our wake the whole time and I never suspected a thing." He looked away, as if seeing the whole thing again but with a still detached expression.

"They're pirates, Captain Morrison, they do this for a living. There's no way you could have known. Did you get any readings on their ship that you remember?" she asked.

He nodded. "She was small, a corvette, no more. I don't know what guns she had, but at least a plasma turret. It slagged forward control and the bridge. It was a miracle I wasn't there... or a curse. I'm not sure," he whispered.

A knot formed in her stomach at his confession. She noted it on her pad for a follow-up. Respecting his moment, she pulled up the specs for every classification of "corvette" they had in the computer.

Ship designations varied wildly from nation to nation. In

the Alliance, a corvette was any ship with a crew smaller than twenty, whose primary duty was in-system escort and patrol. They were used mostly for S&R and customs inspections.

She was familiar with the Alliance version; back home on Rōnin, they had a couple dozen corvettes armed with state-of-the-art weapons systems. Pirates were rare, but Rōnin existed on the northern fringe of the territory and it could take the Navy weeks to reach them if there was trouble.

"A few thousand tons, you think?" she asked to clarify. Not even remotely a match for *Interceptor*'s thirty-k-ton displacement.

Again, he looked to the side. He was starting to trigger her alarms with his refusal to look at her while answering questions. Some small part of her felt like he was dodging the questions or trying to answer them in a way that shed him in a good light.

"That sounds about right," he said.

She jotted it down, along with a note about how he looked when he spoke and how he didn't stop pressing his hands together. Yuki was no body language expert, although, like all officers, she dealt with a lot of people who lied. Her instincts warred with her politeness as she truly felt sorry for this man and his ship... but he was hiding something and it was her job to figure out what.

"Did they warn you before they fired?" she asked.

He shook his head.

It was a kind of trick question. He had already stated he wasn't on the bridge, so how would he know if they had warned them or not?

"Before I ask this, let me assure you, this is for informational purposes and I am in no way judging you, but... why weren't you on the bridge?" she asked.

Shame flooded his face as his cheeks burned a deep crimson. "I was busy when the call came in and I couldn't get to the bridge in time," he whispered. He turned his body away from her, as if he could hide his dishonor from her.

Freighters were massive, but the actual crew areas weren't. Heck, she could walk from the mess hall to the bridge in maybe one minute. What could he have been doing that took more than three minutes?

"The bridge called you with the description of the pursuing ship?" she asked.

"Yes," he said, sinking down farther.

"And that was while you were searching for the starlane to Zuckabar?" she asked. She used a technique they'd taught her in the Academy. Instead of staring him down, she looked down at her NavPad and pretended to be more interested in taking notes than in what he was saying.

She'd allotted two hours for interviewing the crew, but with each answer the captain gave, she was sure she would need longer.

———

Twelve hours later, with only two small breaks, Yuki dismissed the last crewman from *Bonaventure*. Her eyes hurt and her back ached from staring down at her NavPad while the crew of the freighter answered the same questions in the same way. If they weren't lying, they'd at least practiced their stories to make sure they were all on the same page.

Their facts all lined up. Three minutes from the original contact to starlane jump and the explosion on the bridge. Two of the crew even knew about the corvette, backing up what the captain had said. No one, not one of the thirty-three people, could explain why the captain wasn't on the bridge at such a critical juncture. Anyone who did know was dead—or lying to her.

It was the latter she worried about. If Morrison was derelict in his duty, then he picked the worst time to do it. But maybe... What if he were complicit? It would explain why he knew when not to be on the bridge. Of course, if he knew there was an attack coming, he would've worn his ELS suit.

No, it didn't make sense. There had to be something else going on, but damned if she knew what.

A horrible thought occurred to her and she leaped up, rushing to her cabin. She secured the hatch behind her and dropped into the seat at the small desk. Flicking the terminal on, she pulled up all the ships that had come and gone while *Interceptor* had sat parked at Kremlin.

Her time spent searching for *Madrigal* had proven fruitless, but the *Bonaventure* tickled a memory in her brain. It was a two-month roundtrip to the Consortium's nearest planet. One of the reasons the trade route was so popular was the north-south positions of the stars. Neither direction was slowed by galactic spin, which meant transit times were as consistent as interstellar traffic could be. Consistent traffic meant consistent profit.

The names of the ships scrolled past her screen, along with their previous destinations.

She keyed the pickup. "Find *Bonaventure*."

Sure enough, one row highlighted, and *Bonaventure* was on it. Along with its route. "Compare route with *Madrigal*," she said.

The screen split in two and the routes showed up. They were identical. Starting in the Iron Empire, snaking their way through Terran space, then Alliance, and then their final destination in Consortium space.

"Show manifest for both ships," she said.

The computer spit back an error. *No manifest available.*

"Hot damn," Yuki said out loud. "That's why he's hiding something. He's a damn slaver."

Her elation was quickly trumped by the knowledge of *Bonaventure*'s route. She had already delivered her cargo. Thousands of people were headed to the slave markets of the Caliphate.

People, she realized, who would be free if she had done her damn job.

———

"XO," Jacob said, trying to snap her out of the funk she was in. "Kim?"

"Yes, sir?" she asked, her head snapping up.

"Are you sure about this?" he asked.

She shook her head. "Can I prove they are guilty in a court of law? No. However, as you can see, they started their routes in the same system, had the same ports of call, and both their manifests were missing. Any one of those things on their own would be coincidental at best and ignored as such. All three, though?" She shrugged, leaning back in her chair and tapping her fingers lightly on the table.

He nodded. She was right, of course. The ships having the same course could be accounted for by the popularity of the trade route. As for the protected cargo, companies paid to have their cargo certified so they didn't have to list valuables on the manifest.

"You're right. It suggests a correlation, but that isn't causation. I need something more before I accuse the captain of an Alliance freighter of smuggling slaves. Not to mention, you have one huge flaw in your theory," Jacob said.

"Sir? What is that?" she asked.

"*Madrigal* is a Terran Republic flagged ship and *Bonaventure* is one of ours," Jacob pointed out.

Yuki's lips turned up into a grin. "I was saving the best piece of evidence for last, Skipper." She pressed a button on her NavPad and a series of charts sprang to life over the table. "I had to get Commander Beckett's help with this part. He's pretty handy with a computer in a less legal way than I am."

Beckett was proving to be a real asset. Jacob didn't know why the man was on a little tin can. Any damn fool could see he belonged on a battleship.

"What am I looking at?" He stared confusedly at the hundreds of org charts floating over the table.

"Since they are both registered in different ports, in two different nations, it's safe to assume they are owned by different companies, right?" Yuki asked.

"Right. As close an ally as the Consortium is, we can't own businesses in their space. And vice versa," Jacob said. He focused on the charts, trying to make heads or tails of them.

"Correct," she said like he just won the spelling bee. "Buuu-uut..." She waved her hand through the hundreds of org charts until both lanes vanished and only one appeared.

"Are you saying that if you go back far enough, they're owned by the same company?" he asked. It was hard to hide his incredulity. The Alliance had law enforcement for this sort of thing after all. There were checks and balances to prevent this very situation from occurring.

"Yes, sir, I am, and you're never going to believe who the majority shareholder is." Yuki's tone turned grim.

She waved her hand again and the org chart vanished, replaced by the picture of a man Jacob had spoken to but never met in person.

Governor Rasputin of Zuckabar.

"Oh damn," Jacob muttered.

Pirates were one thing. They were broken, discarded people, fleeing from a society where they didn't fit. He didn't think they were crazy, per se, just unwilling or unable to control their barbaric nature inside a civilization with rules and laws. All they desired was money and power.

When he was on *Orion,* they had taken out a pirate haven on the northern side of the Alliance. From the outside, it looked like any other small town. It wasn't until they were on the ground that the rot showed through. And here he was again, seeing the rot close up.

"I think this is the last piece of the puzzle, Kim. Well done," he whispered.

"Yes, sir, and... thank you, sir," she said with genuine pride.

———

The COB and bosun stood before Jacob in their official dress uniforms. The two veteran non-comms wouldn't have looked out of place at a parade—except for the gun belts they wore, complete with loaded MP-17s configured as handguns.

Jacob wore his dress whites, peaked hat and all. He'd had the bosun fabricate the outfit for him since he hadn't brought a set.

All of this pomp and circumstance was to impress upon Captain Bernard Morrison the seriousness of his situation. In the meantime, Jacob had ordered the rest of the *Bonaventure* crew locked in the boat bay and under guard until their guilt or innocence could be determined.

The way the crew had reacted, confusion followed by anger, told him they probably didn't know what they were carrying on their way to the Consortium. Once the XO had pieced it all together, and that was a damn fine piece of investigatory work, it was easy to ask about the white boxes in the hold. They had freely confirmed they were carrying food stuffs and other perishables. When shown a picture from *Madrigal*'s hold, they even agreed it was the same thing.

Captain Morrison looked like a beaten man standing in front of Jacob in his borrowed clothing. He held his glasses, forever polishing them as he tried to abate his nerves.

"Captain Grimm, I don't know why I'm being detained," Morrison said.

Jacob held up his hand to stop the man. "Mr. Morrison, since I don't think you're a captain anymore, or ever again, for that matter, do not insult my intelligence. You have two options: confess and hope for the best for you and *your crew*," Jacob emphasized the last part since any authority would have a hard time buying the captain was in it alone, "or deny everything and be found guilty. Followed by a summary execution."

Jacob couldn't abide slavers. He would prefer to see the man live, though. In prison for the rest of his life, but alive.

After a long minute of silence, Mr. Morrison spoke, "I... I want a lawyer."

"You've confused me with the police, sir. I am not. I'm the commander of the USS *Interceptor*. Since we are the only Alliance naval vessel in the system, indeed within ten days in any direction, I am all the law you have. Under my authority, I can have Chief Suresh," he nodded to the chief, "march you from here to the airlock and space you like the trash you are."

The man blanched, his lips pressing tight as he tried to keep from breaking down.

"I have all the evidence. I know you were carrying slaves to Consortium space. What you did after you arrived in Praetor, I don't know. I know the reason you didn't hurry to the bridge when they told you of the pirates. You knew who they were and what they would likely do. Why they attacked you, I do not know.

However, it doesn't change any of the facts. If you say nothing, I will have you summarily executed for human trafficking. Without your testimony to prove otherwise, your crew will likely spend the rest of their days in prison. Or you can cooperate. Your crew will go free and you will spend a long, long time behind bars. The choice is yours. You have fifteen seconds to decide."

Jacob leaned back, staring the man directly in the eyes, daring him to look away... and he did. After fifteen seconds, the man still said nothing, which truly surprised Jacob. Still, the odds were he would change his mind.

"Very well, Mr. Morrison. Are you prepared to hear your judgment?" Jacob asked in as professional and non-passionate manner as possible.

The man didn't move. Chief Suresh clapped her hand on his shoulder and forced him to look at her. "The prisoner will answer the question," she said.

"I... no. No, it wasn't supposed to be like this. Those damn pirates screwed up everything. I don't want to die, Captain, but I didn't have a choice. By the time I found out what we were carrying, it was already too late. I was in it up to my neck. They threatened me, you see? I had no choice, no choice at all," Captain Morrison sputtered.

A few minutes later, Bosun Sandivol marched the shaking, sobbing man out of the briefing room where the ad-hoc trial had taken place, leaving Chief Suresh with the captain.

"Do you believe him, sir?" she asked.

"It fits with everything Kim found," he replied, pressing the comms button. "XO."

"Go for XO," she replied.

"How's it going with the rest of the crew?" Jacob asked.

"I don't think anyone else is involved, sir. Or if they were, they were on the bridge when it was hit," she replied.

"Roger that. Keep it up, and make sure you put in your recommendation with the file, understood?" Jacob asked.

"Yes, sir," Yuki said before the line disconnected.

The investigating officer's recommendation carried a lot of weight with the brass. It was a poor JAG office who overturned one. Plus, it would seal her name on the entire affair and give her the credit for breaking it wide open, which she deserved. It wasn't as if it would benefit his career.

It did leave him with a huge mess, but it was a mess with his name on it, and no one else's. He hadn't lied when he told Morrison he was the ranking naval officer in the system. It was his responsibility to follow, and enforce, the law. He couldn't ignore the evidence before him.

"Devi, can you arrange for a guard rotation on Mr. Morrison and his former crew? They will be with us until we can deliver them to the Alliance," he said.

"Aye, aye, sir." Suresh snapped to attention, did a perfect about-face, and marched out.

His COB seemed to enjoy showing him exactly how squared away she was at all times. It made Jacob feel a little less put-together than he would like. Which meant he needed to do more to be on her level.

He activated the holo feature on his NavPad and looked at the evidence one more time. Morrison's testimony put the nail in the coffin. Now Jacob would need to return to Kremlin Station and arrest Governor Rasputin. He dropped his head into his hands and pressed them against his aching temples. He was an acting lieutenant commander and he was about to stir a whole bucket of trouble.

He collected everything in one file, then compressed and encoded it for Commodore Xin. Even if the commodore was already on the way, and Jacob fervently hoped he was, his duty wouldn't allow for him to wait.

Once done, he loaded the packet into the queue. "Comms, this is the captain," he said while pressing down the stud. The ship's onboard computer routed him to the comms console.

"Comms, McCall, what can I do for you, Skipper?"

"I loaded a priority packet. I need you to send it with all haste, copy?" Jacob asked.

There was a brief pause while McCall checked to make sure the packet was loaded. "Aye, sir, all haste."

"Good man," Jacob said. He disconnected the call before pulling up a map of Zuckabar. He did have one ally in the system. If he could talk to Nadia, maybe she could give him her opinion of the situation. After all, she had served in the Navy and had spent a lot more time in Zuckabar than himself. If he was going to move on the governor, he had to be damn sure.

CHAPTER THIRTY-FOUR

L ance Corporal Jennings grunted through the pain as she pushed the workout equipment to the very limits of what she could do. The compressor was set to a hundred and seventy kilograms, almost twice her actual body weight. However, with her high *g*, high pressure background, and Marine training, it was a hard but doable workout. Sweat beaded off her brow as she finished the last rep.

"Stop," she said to the compressor. It would be nice to have actual weights, but the best she could do was find a lift arm for cargo and set it to the weight she wanted.

For most of her workout, it was set to a hundred kilograms. It was the last rep, designed for maximum fatigue, where she pushed it as high she could go. The compact blonde sat up, pulling the towel down around her neck. Once it became clear *Interceptor* wouldn't be back for a while, she had started working out in her free time to keep herself sharp.

The Marines did PT in the morning with the gunny, but she always felt like it was more of a primer than a way to increase her fitness. Though there were limits, even for her. Many people mistook her hundred and fifty-two centimeters, blonde hair, and feminine figure as a sign of weakness. Sure, she could put on lipstick, a dab of blush, and black eyeliner for a night out. However, her home world was a tough place to grow up, and not just because the gravity was stronger. Anyone with half a brain could tell her neck and shoulders were far too developed to be ordinary.

On MacGregor's World, where she was from, she was nothing special. In 1.4 gs and 4 atmospheres, she was slightly above average. In 1 g and 1 atmosphere, she was exceptional. She liked being exceptional. It was the promise of that exceptionalism that led her to the Alliance Marine recruiting station. That and running away from her family.

A quick sonic shower and one pressed-to-perfection uniform later, she strode onto the bridge for her watch. It was 0400 ship time and she relieved PFC Owens.

"You stand relieved," she said formally.

"I stand relieved," he said with a yawn. "See you at chow." He gave her a friendly wave as he left the bridge. They were stretched too thin to stand watch with more than one person. There were prisoners to guard, plus they had to patrol the ship. It was a lot for one Navy officer, a Marine squad, and a handful of ratings.

She pulled the watch-board off the bulkhead and went down the checklist, making sure everything was good to go. It was. Placing it back, she sat down in the helm position. Sitting in the captain's chair felt... wrong.

An hour passed as she watched the traffic move back and forth on the screen. For a system with a large mining operation in the outer belts, they had a ton of transient travelers. A few ships would jump in from the Minsc starlane and immediately set for Praxis. Most, though, would accelerate toward Kremlin Station. The station did a lot of trading since they mined a good deal of heavy metal used in all sorts of construction.

Madrigal was parked in orbit around Zuckabar Central, the one "habitable" planet in the system. Jennings used that word with a lot of caveats. If it wasn't so incredibly large, easily ten times the size of any other planet, with its unusual mix of heavy metals and strong magnetic field, it would just be another rock in space. The way she understood it, the binary pair went nova millions of years before, and all the planets closer to the star were destroyed. Zuck Central, though, survived just enough that when the Alliance caught up to the original settlers, they were able to help.

Now the planet was terraformed, or at least that was what she was told. With an average temperature that no human could survive, it didn't really match her idea of what a terraformed planet looked like.

Ohana was her idea of successful terraforming. Sandy beaches, warm weather, and exquisite oceans. Of course, she'd been under the auspices of the Terraforming Guild for five-hundred years and she was pretty good to begin with.

Maybe in another four hundred years, Zuck Central would be like Ohana? She laughed at her own joke, the sound of her voice startling her in the silence of the bridge.

To give herself something to do, she looked at the ships nearest to *Madrigal*. There weren't many. Most vessels docked inside Kremlin Station or were orbiting the massive structure. The only reason anyone would be in orbit around Zuck was if they were too large to land or were parked awaiting repairs, like *Madrigal*.

Then a ship caught her eye. She put her feet down, leaning closer to the display as she took the controls and zoomed in. The ship was small, maybe a third the size of *Interceptor*, with the kind of lean look dropships usually had, retractable wings and tail included. It wasn't necessarily wrong, but she couldn't imagine why a dropship would be parked in orbit.

There was nothing amiss with it, nothing obvious, but something within Jennings stirred. She had a head for danger—it was the same sense she felt in the warehouse before the bloodthirsty psycho attacked them. The finely-honed sense of knowing when things didn't belong.

She manipulated the controls, magnifying the image until she could see the ship on the viewer. Passive sensors picked up her emissions, and their lower power radar sweep brushed against her hull every five minutes. But nothing beat actually seeing a ship to figure out what it was about.

And this ship was up to no good. She reached up to her collar and pressed the comm button there. "El-Tee, this is Jennings on the bridge. I need you and Gunny up here, ASAP," she said.

"Corporal?" El-Tee came back. "Give me the short version while I dress."

"Yes, sir. We're going to have company. I don't think we want the fine china out for this one."

Two minutes later, Lieutenant Bonds and Gunny Hicks marched onto the bridge. "Alright, Corporal, let's have it," Bonds ordered. If it were anyone other than Jennings, he'd tear them a new one for waking up both him and the gunny over a "feeling," but he'd served with Jennings for months and he would be damned if he ignored her. Whenever she was OPFOR in the wargames, her team won. He trusted her implicitly. The fact that Gunny Hicks did as well was another point in her favor.

"Sir, I saw this small vessel in orbit and decided to keep an eye on it," she said as she manipulated the controls to show the ship.

Bonds cocked his head sideways, looking at the funny-shaped freighter. "What class of—"

"It's a dropship, sir. Cleverly painted to look like a garbage hauler on its way to dump trash, but it's a dropship."

The gunny messed with the controls, bringing up time-lapse. Sure enough, the ship had launched from Kremlin the day before, then landed on Zuck, then back up to orbit where she drifted closer and closer to *Madrigal*.

"And you think she's on her way here?" Bonds asked.

Jennings nodded. "Yes, sir, I do."

As much as Bonds was willing to take Jennings at her word, if he were to defend himself in an after-action report, he would need to prove she was right.

"Prove it to me," he said.

"Sir," she replied. She touched the camera controls. Once it focused on the port airlock, the gunny let out a low whistle.

"Well, you asked," the gunny said with a sharp laugh.

"Yes, I did," Lieutenant Bonds replied.

The airlock connection ring was lined with shape charges pointing out. It was a cheap way to force a boarding, not relying on computers or burning the airlock. Just blow in the hatch. Of course, if everyone on board was killed, what did they care? Might even be better for them.

First Lieutenant Paul Bonds of Third Platoon, Company B, wasn't about to let that happen. "Options?" he asked.

"Move the ship?" the gunny suggested.

"We can't do anything overt without tipping our hand. Once they know we know, pretense will fly out the window. How far out is *Interceptor*?" Bonds asked.

Jennings touched the controls, bringing up the map of the system with a blinking dot representing *Interceptor*. Clearly, she'd already thought of this. He would hate to lose her, but her initiative showed she was ready to be a sergeant. He would have to put in for her when they got back to the ship.

Jennings pointed at the blinking icon that was *Interceptor*. "Even if we sent a message right now, it would take two hours to reach her. I had Owens do the math while I waited for you. Then, if she came back full throttle, another six hours. I don't think we have that much time. Maybe three hours, tops," Jennings said.

Bonds nodded in agreement, the same thoughts flying through his head. "If we sent a message, there would be no way of contacting *Interceptor* covertly. Whoever this is would just up their time table and tell *Interceptor* whatever they wanted. Worst case, they would blow the station keeping thrusters and let *Madrigal* burn up in orbit with her cargo."

"Destroy the evidence," the gunny added. "Smart move, especially if there was something onboard pointing the finger back to Kremlin Station."

"Like a whole bunch of slaves in cryo-sleep," Jennings said with a growl.

The idea that whoever was waiting for the cargo would rather kill everyone on board than risk being found out turned his stomach. Bonds had dealt with a lot of lowlifes, but these monsters took the cake.

"Okay, Jennings, good work," Bonds said.

"Thank you, sir," she replied smartly.

"Gunny," he continued, "I want you to round up the crew and find a compartment that can be isolated from the rest of the ship."

"Aye, sir," the gunny replied.

"When that's done, tell everyone to suit up. I want them with their own air to breathe. As soon as the Tango's final approach is verified, we will vent the atmo from everywhere but where the crew is and the lock the Tango's coming in on. We need to draw up some contingency plans as well. Make sure everyone is fully armed and accounted for."

The gunny and the corporal nodded. "Yes, sir," they said in unison.

"Okay, people, we have a plan. Execute it."

Jennings couldn't help but notice the El-Tee sounded like the captain. She approved.

———

Lieutenant Bonds hustled down the passageway, wanting to set the right example for his Marines. When he showed up to brief them on the OP, he would be wearing his full space armor.

It was a funny thing, the situation they were in. When the captain left them to look after *Madrigal,* he figured someone might try to take her. Even up to a full-on assault, which looked exactly like what was coming their way.

He'd spent the last nine years as an active-duty Marine officer and four before that in the Marine Officer Academy. It was all he ever wanted to do. Serve his nation, protect his people. The Alliance certainly made mistakes now and again, but they also did a lot of good.

That was why he trained his Marines, pushed them, and himself, hard. Hard enough to break and reforge them as the elite combat force he knew they could be.

It had paid off in spades. His people's drills were in the top twenty percent of fleet averages. It was time for them to prove their mettle.

As his mentor always told him, "Hope for the best, prepare for the worst." He needed to decide the best way to deploy them using his biggest advantage: surprise.

CHAPTER THIRTY-FIVE

From her position on the hull, Corporal Jennings monitored the incoming dropship's progress.

Space armor wasn't comfortable, but life as a Marine was one of voluntary discomfort in exchange for discipline, experience, and service.

PFC Owens had set up a repeater on her HUD, giving her access to the telemetry on the enemy as they approached. In a way, the Tangos were too cute. If they had hauled balls to the *Madrigal,* they would have caught the Marines without giving them time to prepare. But since they were doing their damnedest to appear normal, the platoon had more than enough time.

Unfortunately, she didn't have a heavy weapon with her. Either a shoulder-fired coilgun or a savage multi-barrel mass driver, like the ones their Raptor suits mounted back on *Interceptor*, could take the ship out from a distance of two klicks. The Rules of Engagement might have prevented them from opening fire, though, since there was a small chance the ship was legit or off course or had some other reason for flying toward *Madrigal.*

Jennings doubted they were, but she wasn't the one giving the orders.

However, with the time the enemy had given them, the El-Tee had run them through a number of boarding drills. The one they were using was a variation of a pincer the Marines favored when defending a fixed position. The enemy would come in thinking they had the advantage, until Jennings and Owens showed up on their hull, burning their way through to flank them.

It was a good plan. The only problem was, she was stuck in her armor for three hours and her nose desperately needed a scratch. *Madrigal*'s crew was stashed in the mess hall with the hatches sealed and wearing their civilian ELS suits—except for the two who were complicit in the trafficking ring. They were bound and gagged in the most secure supply closet she could find. The rest of the ship was decompressed.

The boarders would be in for a helluva surprise if they weren't wearing suits. With a grin that was every bit as ferocious as it was savage, she decided it didn't matter what they were wearing.

———

Lieutenant Bonds checked their positioning one last time. He had Gunny Hicks and his fire team positioned at the far end of the hold, forming the horizontal part of the "L" ambush. Bonds and his three had spent the better part of the last hour positioning cargo crates along the bulkhead to form a crude embrasure. If the boarders wanted to move behind them, they would have to traverse all fifty meters of the hold to do so, under fire the entire time.

Bonds had set up the cargo hold as a kill box, literally. When the last boarder came through, the reinforced hatches would close behind them and Third Platoon would light them up. He shuddered to think what would've happened if Jennings hadn't seen them coming. He doubted the Marines would have lost, but certainly many of the civilians they were protecting would have died in the process.

He opened his mouth, holding it still for the three seconds required for the water dispenser to squirt a drink. The space armor wasn't as good as the powered stuff, but they could survive for days in it all the same.

"Hicks, status," he asked over the comms.

"We're a go," the gunny replied.

"Corporal Jennings?" Bonds asked. The computer automatically switched to her channel to send the message. Each fire team had their own, and Bonds had access to all of them. In a firefight, it was better to have them access only their team, to avoid confusion. If anyone of them needed to speak to him, saying his name to start would put it through automatically.

"Five minutes to dock, sir," Jennings said.

"Do you have confirmation on the target?" he asked her.

"Confirmed. I can see the hard points where weapon mounts were removed. Owens took a few hi-res images of the explosives and he's identified them as military-grade breaching charges," Jennings said.

"Roger," Bonds replied.

There was no point in asking her if she was ready. They were. The two of them made up the backbone of his combat force. Heartbreakers and life-takers.

After he filled in the gunny, there was nothing to do but wait. Something every Marine was used to doing.

———

From his position by the airlock, Zabbo grinned cruelly. Their prey was in for a surprise. Zabbo's crew had taken down their fair share of ships using the same tactic. Sure, they were little better than pirates, but the "little" was in pay. No attacking random ships. They did a job, they got paid.

And he liked the paid part.

Nineteen of the meanest, nastiest mercs he had ever served with made up his crew. Each one carried their own weapons and equipment, from small automatics to large plasma repeaters.

Normally, a freighter wouldn't require firepower of that magnitude, but his contact had made it clear there were Alliance Marines on board and they were not to be trifled with. No games. No prisoners. No witnesses. Kill everyone on board and transport the ship to Minsc where a crew would be waiting to take her from them. Return to Zuck and receive the other half of a huge payday.

Simple. And Zabbo liked simple. Simple kept him alive and food in his belly.

"Thirty seconds," his pilot called from the front.

———

Jennings watched the camouflaged dropship approach the lower emergency lock.

"Lock A-3, deck 12," she said over comms.

"Roger," Owens replied. The expert electronics tech tapped away at the console built into his suit's arm. Inside the ship, which was already depressurized, hatches sealed shut, lifts locked down, and a path was created from the lock to the cargo hold, leading the invaders right to the ambush.

Jennings's lips twitched with anticipation. She didn't crave fighting, but she did enjoy it. Her favorite part of the Marine

Corps—well, other than being a Marine—was the combat training. Small arms, gunnery, hand-to-hand, knife fighting; she threw herself into her work like an artist.

Vibrations spread through the hull as the dropship attached. Since she and Owens were hiding in an alcove seven decks above, they momentarily lost visual on the ship. She keyed her mic. "Owens, give them five minutes to clear, then we move."

"Roger," he replied.

———

"Helmets down," Zabbo ordered. Those who didn't have their faceplates secured did so then. The rest of them were already sealed. Not a lot of people liked to breathe canned air for too long. It was suffocating.

He pointed at the lock. "Blow it." His demolitions expert shot him a thumbs-up before triggering the breaching charges. The ship shook as they detonated. He held on to one of the many grab bars above while the shuddering died down.

"Move," he ordered. His men weren't as disciplined as some fancy Marine squad, but they were mean. And in his experience, pure spite drove a man harder than some mythical sense of duty ever would.

"Stay off the comms, call out targets, and kill every living thing," he ordered.

"Even the women?" someone asked.

"Everyone. No witnesses."

A few grumbled, but they lined up, weapons at the ready.

He signaled the man in front, who opened the hatch. It opened up to reveal a jagged hole the breaching charges had created. No smoke or debris, as it was sucked out into space in the seconds after the charges went off.

He frowned looking at the corridors. They were small. Wide enough for one man at a time, but still, with their weapons, it shouldn't matter.

Zabbo, of course, went last to make sure all the men exited the dropship. Only the pilots stayed behind. They weren't part of his regular crew—he'd picked them up after his contact hired him.

"You better be here when we're done," he said over the private channel to the pilot.

"You better have our pay," the pilot replied.

It was good to know where he stood with them. They were like him, in it for the money. As long as he held it, they would stay.

He followed his men into the ship, heading toward the central hold where they would gain access to the rest of the vessel. From there, they would split up, clearing the ship.

———

Jennings watched the clock countdown to zero. "Go," she said. She and Owens leaped into action, magnetic boots sticking them to the hull of the deck. Pushing her foot down activated the magnets, contracting her calf muscle released them. She peeked over the side as the oblong dropship came into view. It was right where she thought it would be.

According to the built-in range finder, it was twenty-five meters from her position to the dropship. Of course, up and down were relative. She edged over the side, followed by Owens, and the boots did the rest, readjusting her attitude as she walked down the side.

"Weapons hot," she ordered. As she spoke, she reached over her shoulder and grasped the handle of her MP-17. It immediately sprang to life, extending until it was a full-sized battle rifle. Her space armor interfaced with it through her grip and showed her exactly where the weapon was pointed at all times, allowing for a high degree of accuracy.

She loved her MP-17. The reason the Marine Corps fought to keep them over the more advanced particle guns or directed energy weapons was one of practicality. While powerful, with their nanite steel construction, they were also durable, strong, and adaptable.

She hustled toward the ship, then unlocked her boots and leaped the last ten meters. The suit's computer adjusted her attitude, pushing her slightly toward her intended target and then slowing her dramatically as to not make a thump when she landed.

"Contact," she said.

Owens landed without vibration next to her. He shot her a grin, holding up a small box with a control panel in one hand and a scanner with a blinking screen in the other. While she covered him, he walked forward, slipping over the side until the scanner signaled the ideal place to secure the charge.

He carefully attached the box to the hull then pressed the button on top. It grew, expanding until it was in the shape of a disk big enough for an armored Marine to drop through.

Jennings moved until she was "above" it, crouched and ready. She gave Owens the signal.

He depressed the control stick and the explosive detonated with a silent flash. There was no way the crew didn't feel it. She ducked through, and as soon as she was in, the dropship's grav-coil took hold and pulled her down. Combined with her momentum, she was sliding along the floor, rifle pointed at the cockpit. The co-pilot was already half out of his seat when she fired, hitting him dead-center in the chest. He bounced against the controls, going limp and floating, held down by his partially released harness.

The pilot was obviously smarter, throwing his hands up immediately.

"Clear," she said. Owens moved in, securing the pilot's hands and disabling his suit's comms.

The two Marines left the dropship through the same lock the mercs had. The pilot was hogtied in the head and would go nowhere.

Back in *Madrigal,* they moved down the passageway toward the main cargo deck, to come up behind the boarders and cut them off from retreat.

It wasn't hard to follow the mercs undetected. Overconfidence was a deadly sin, one that got people killed. The mercs had left hatches open after searching them, and smashed items when they found nothing of value. While there was no atmo in the ship, there was gravity, and the pirates left a trail of debris.

Before long, they were two turns behind the mercs, eagerly awaiting their retreat.

———

Zabbo growled over the comms. So far, they hadn't seen a single body. Not one. If the ship was truly taken by surprise, then explosive decompression should have killed *someone.* He was left with a nagging feeling, like the one he had when his platoon had fallen to ambush on Burgess. The event that left him a merc instead of a soldier in the Terran Republic.

The cavernous cargo hold loomed before them and Zabbo's spirits lifted. The hold was full of goods. There were millions there. Maybe they could take the ship and head for Caliph space directly, sell the goods, and retire obscenely wealthy.

Only dim emergency lighting illuminated the massive hold. Zabbo couldn't hope to secure it, but then, he didn't have to. On the other side was the cargo lift, which ran vertically and horizontally through the entire ship. Once there, they could move to engineering and the bridge, and it would only be a matter of time before they hunted down the few survivors. Most of them were likely dead on the bridge anyway.

He stepped into the cargo hold, hesitating for a moment, the nagging feeling returning. He motioned with his gun for the men to pass him as he scanned the hold. A wall of cargo was stacked in front of them, forcing them to go left. Another bulkhead cut off most of the hold, but they didn't need to go there. The lift was on the right, just past the far bulkhead.

His last man stepped in and he went to follow, hesitating as that feeling turned to outright panic.

———

Lieutenant Bonds watched the mercs cluster together as they moved into the hold, not even bothering to search the "walls" as they headed toward the lift.

All but the leader.

The man who had entered the hold first and then ordered the others to go forward held back, looking over his shoulder as he did. Bonds' eyes narrowed at the man. He had the bearing of a soldier, one who hadn't practiced in a long time, but there was always something about a veteran. The way they walked, held themselves, he could tell. The hodge-podge ELS suit had a half-moon clear mask, letting the Marine see the man's scraggly hair and mottled skin.

Bonds shook his head. Whenever he saw a vet so far gone, a part of him cringed. Was he one bad tour away from a pirate's life? Or had these fallen men never truly belonged to begin with? It wasn't like everyone he'd met in the Corps was an honest, stand-up Marine. But it was his Corps and he liked to think of them that way.

Regardless, they were in the kill box. The L-shaped ambush was probably the oldest small unit tactic used. One could not improve on perfection.

"Fire," Bonds whispered. MP-17s were quiet weapons; without any atmosphere, they were dead silent. Electromagnetic forces flung silicate shards as Gunny Hicks and his two privates fired and Lieutenant Bonds and the two Marines with him opened up as well.

Shards of hardened silicate sliced through the room at high velocity, shredding ELS suits, clothing, flesh, and organs in a spray of blood and silent screams. The Marines painted the opposite bulkhead red with the blood of their enemies.

The mercs died silently, their suits offering no protection against the weapons. Within seconds, the only person left alive was the dark-skinned veteran Bonds had identified. His mouth was agape at the carnage. Before Bonds could call for his surrender, the man turned and ran.

He could have put one in his back—he had the angle—but regardless of what he was forced to do to defend his charges, he wouldn't shoot a fleeing man in the back.

Not when he had other options.

"Check One Foxtrot," he said over the radio.

———

Zabbo reeled at the slaughter he'd witnessed. He didn't care one whit for the men who died. His fear was fueled by how they died. Alive one second, sliced to pieces the next. They had no chance. None. Who fought like that? Terror powered his legs.

He had to run, flee back to the ship. Anything was better than having his flesh cut to ribbons by unseen weapons.

His mind was far afield, thinking only of escape when he turned the corner and Lance Corporal Jennings' buttstock hit him in the chest like a sledgehammer. He coughed, legs continuing forward while the rest of him slammed into the deck. His gun, kicked out of his hands, skittered across the deck and a great weight settled into his chest as he looked up at one of those brutal rifles and the brushed metallic faceplate behind it.

"I surrender," he yelled. "I surrender!"

CHAPTER THIRTY-SIX

Professor Bellaits held the specialized headphones close to his ears but listened for the faint trace of his quarry with only part of his mind.

Bellaits rarely left the hold and only contacted the bridge through the comms on the wall when he needed them to change course. The last time he had done this was when he noticed the difference. He might act the fool from time to time, playing up the absent-minded professor—or maybe he really was one—but he wasn't an idiot. He was the foremost expert on stellar cartography and astrophysics in the Alliance, maybe even in the galaxy. Though he would never say that last part in polite company. Over the last twenty years, his reputation had declined due to the "mad theories" he espoused.

For the rest of the university community, he was the "once great" Professor Bellaits, a social stigma he intended to rectify with his discovery. All his "betters" and contemporaries were under the delusion that all worth discovering had been. Bellaits knew that not to be true.

When he was a child, the idea of traveling faster than 300c

in a starlane was ludicrous until Dr. Von Stromberg invented the condensed gravcoil ring.

No, there were, and always would be, new discoveries. Dr. Von Stromberg's name would live forever in the annals of science. If he could live long enough to find the other end of the wormhole he *knew* was in Zuckabar, his name would too.

It had taken the majority of his family fortune and the last twenty years of his life, but he was so close. It was the binary stars! Oh, how he'd howled with glee when he'd made the discovery. Space-time sank like a rock around a pulsar/white-dwarf binary. Nine hundred light-years (and change) south of Zuckabar, there was another star system which matched, the two stars connected by a line of gravity so faint, no one had ever heard it before. They were too busy listening for starlanes or to the stars themselves. It never occurred to anyone that a wormhole could be a natural phenomenon. The key was the gamma-ray burst. The right frequency of gravity combined with gamma-rays and that led him to the wormhole.

He'd honestly thought someone else had figured it out. It was so obvious in hindsight. Praetor was a binary star system with a pulsar and white dwarf, as was Zuckabar. At some point beyond eight billion kilometers from the binary's bisect was one side of a hole in space. He'd found the other end in Praetor the previous summer. It had taken him the next winter and summer to figure out the math for the approximate location of the reciprocal end.

He'd known from the first moment he listened to Zuckabar's binary stars that it was out here, somewhere. He'd narrowed it down to the south side of the star system and had the captain change course. Unfortunately, it was before he realized the *Dagger* was no longer under the delightfully flirtatious captain's command.

The man who answered for the bridge had hidden his

accent well, but Iker had spent an entire year in the Caliphate some fifty years earlier, before their current ruler went on his bloodthirsty rampage.

Oh, he remembered those times fondly, and the dark-skinned Isabella... the long days and even longer nights he'd spent with her. He dismissed the thoughts of his long-passed wife before they could turn maudlin.

Regardless, he shook his head, trying to focus. Either through accident or coincidence, Caliphate forces controlled the ship, and he couldn't, wouldn't, let his discovery fall into their hands.

And as painful as it was to admit, the only person who could have told them what he was looking for was Daisy.

Then he heard it. The boom of the drum as gravity smashed into space-time and flowed down a hole like water rushing down a drain. It really wasn't a "noise," conventionally speaking, but with the right equipment, it was translated into one. Every ship was outfitted with space-time detectors, but the one he had was far more sensitive.

His eyes flashed to the gamma-ray detector, willing it to show the spike... lights flashed as gamma rays hit the ship in a burst.

Relief rushed through him. The realization of a dream he had sacrificed twenty years of his life for, delivered in one magnificent cosmic drum solo!

Inwardly, he sang with glee. Outwardly, he controlled his emotions since his invisible captors were almost certainly watching him.

In his log, he noted the exact coordinates of the ping. He had to find a way to notify the authorities of his predicament on the ship while making sure, no matter what happened, that the Alliance knew who made the momentous discovery. Of course, he also wouldn't allow the Caliphate to steal his research. Which all sounded easier than it actually was.

The door opened and Daisy walked in, wearing a translucent silk wrap around her hips and a long sleeve shirt that came down to her waist. It was far more provocative than her usual dress.

She was on schedule, but her dress made him think something was happening. Had he given away his discovery after all?

"Hello, Iker, how are you today?" she said, placing the tray of food down and picking up the one he had barely touched.

"Good, good, my dear. I think we may be in the wrong sector, though. Can you have the captain change to the following course?" He handed her a slip of paper on which he had written down the inverse of the coordinates, which would push the ship far, far away from his discovery.

She frowned while reading them, her pert lips pushing together. "Iker, this is the other side of the system. I thought you said it would be on the southern side?"

Iker scrambled to make up an excuse. "I did, didn't I? Well, I may have been wrong. At the very least, I can rule another place out."

———

He turned back to his equipment, missing the glare she gave him once his attention was off her. She stormed out, tossing the tray in the trash receptacle as soon as the hold door closed behind her.

Daisy fumed for a moment, hand on hip, while she ran through the calculations. She was no Ph.D. in astrophysics, but she was more than educated enough. A week ago, he was closing in on the point, and now he suddenly wanted to cross the system? She turned and looked at the hold for a few minutes. Was he playing her?

It wasn't like she could demand he tell her the truth. If he bothered to come out of the hold, he would know something was up. Even though the remaining six Immortals wore civilian clothes and did their best to hide their accents, he would know. Especially once he went into the rec room. Daisy shuddered at Nadia's fate. All she could think, though, was better her than Daisy.

What could he do, even if he did know? He was one old man. Any of the soldiers on board could take him in a fight. She could herself. He couldn't possibly know, though, right?

The real question was, had he found the other side of the wormhole? Unconsciously, she rubbed her neck. She'd scrubbed her entire mission for this old fool's theories. If he managed to keep the Caliphate from finding the wormhole, then it would be her neck on the chopping block. Worse, actually. Her superiors in the ISB would likely slap an obedience collar on her and sell her to the first merchant.

———

Iker finished transferring the data to the molecular storage chip. Everything he had researched in the last twenty years, including the probable location of the wormhole leading to Praetor, was stored in its molecular structure. Technically, the chips could store infinite data and last forever—as long as they weren't intentionally destroyed.

Next, he performed a factory reset on his listening equipment and personal datapad. It all had to go. As much as it pained him to do so, he would rather the data be destroyed than fall into the hands of the Caliphate. If they were after his wormhole, it could only mean they knew where the other side was.

How had he been so blind? He shook his head. There was no time for recrimination. No time at all. It was obvious Daisy hadn't bought his line about ruling out the area. She might not be as educated as him, but once someone knew what to listen and look for, the wormholes would be relatively easy to find.

No one believed they existed. How could they? Seven hundred years of galactic exploration and humanity had never discovered one. It was exponentially easier to find a starlane, and those still took months, sometimes years, to locate.

Once humanity knew what a starlane sounded like, though, it became easier and easier. The same would be true for his wormholes, and it would change *everything*.

"Iker Bellaits, the man who changed the future," he whispered to himself. He would've liked to have seen that future.

With a sharp breath for courage, he stood, checking to make sure he had the chip gripped tightly in his palm, and headed for the hatch.

If they were watching him, he wouldn't have long. As the door closed behind him, the equipment smoked and melted as the self-destruct device he'd activated went to work.

CHAPTER THIRTY-SEVEN

"Say again, Oliv?" Jacob asked.

Petty Officer Oliv punched a new command into her console, displaying the IFF codes of every ship in the system. There were hundreds. Of course, the information was hours old, depending on where the ships were. Radar wasn't particularly effective beyond ten light-seconds. And with the heavy interference from the binary, listening for the gravitic disruption of space-time was only effective within ten light-minutes of another ship.

So far, they had identified hundreds of ships in the outer system, from large freighters to the small mining vehicles that dotted Zuckabar's many asteroids.

The only ship they *couldn't* find was *Dagger*.

"Maybe they left the system?" Kim asked from her position next to the captain's chair.

"It's possible," Jacob replied half-heartedly. "She told me they were going to be here for a while, though. Something about a science experiment she was chartered to babysit." Jacob leaned back, replaying the last conversation he'd had with her. Once they had departed Kremlin, real-time communication was out the window, but she'd sent him a couple of messages since then. They were both captains and it was a lonely job and it was nice to have someone outside the ship to talk with. The last message he'd received was a week before. She'd let him know they were swinging around to galactic south in search of whatever the scientist was looking for.

After they rescued the *Bonaventure,* he had headed the *Interceptor* in the same direction. If he couldn't find her, he would have to return to Kremlin and arrest the governor. If it were at all possible, though, he wanted to ask her opinion. With her knowledge of the system, he really didn't want to miss the opportunity to consult with her about the current situation.

"Oliv, can you replay the ship's tracking for the last week, up until the last time the computer picked up her IFF?" he asked the PO.

"On it," she said. The screen displayed the tracking info in reverse at a speed of one second per hour. Ships shot around the systems and *Dagger* flashed to life, practically crawling along the ecliptic, far out on the southern plane.

"Stop," he ordered.

She hit the button, halting the movement.

"Move it forward slowly and there..." One minute, *Dagger* was on screen, and the next she wasn't. No deceleration, no SOS, nothing. Her transponder just vanished. Even if the ship were destroyed, the transponder would continue. There were few situations he could think of that would cause it to vanish. None of which were good.

"Chief Suresh, set a course for her last known location. Put us on the same heading," he said. "Full power."

Chief Suresh tapped in the course lining up the *Interceptor*'s trajectory on her computer. They were going to have to come to a full stop, reverse course, then accelerate for almost four hours before they were in the right vicinity.

"Course laid in, sir," she said.

Jacob leaned forward, worry haunting him as a myriad of terrible possibilities played before his eyes. It was probably a transponder failure, he told himself. That had to be it.

"Execute," he ordered.

Deep down, he knew he was wrong.

———

Iker Bellaits stumbled his way through the unfamiliar ship, silently cursing himself for not having taken the time to learn the layout before. It was such a small ship compared to the cruise liners he'd spent time on, he figured it wouldn't be at all hard to find the captain's quarters, but it was.

He went down the rear stairs as quietly as he knew how, while at the same time pretending to be unaware of his surroundings in case he was spotted. If they caught him, he could play the bumbling professor—he hoped.

As he stepped off the stairs onto the deck, he froze. A splash of blood painted the far wall. He had no idea if it was fresh or not. He did his best to put it out of his mind and went into the first quarters he could find. It was empty and the bed was disheveled.

Then the next, and the next. They were all empty. As he approached the end of the hall, streaks of blood formed a trail around the far corner. He followed them until he found the emergency airlock, sealed tight. The blood, though, led right to it.

When he first suspected something was wrong, part of him hoped he was mistaken—that the thick accent of the bridge crew was a coincidence. But it wasn't.

He carefully made his way toward the lock and looked through the window, then nearly puked. He held his hand over his mouth as he turned his back to the door. It was full of bloody, beaten, and quite dead, crew.

For the first time, the realization of what was going to happen hit him, and fear struck him stiff. He leaned against the wall in an effort to stay on his feet. Sweat beaded on his brow, and for several long heartbeats, he was afraid. Afraid for his life, for his legacy, for the people who hadn't yet died but would.

He wiped his face, closing his eyes hard, focusing through the fear. This was the end for him. Even if he turned over the data to the Caliphate, they would kill him. His only hope for his legacy was to find the comms panel and send out the data as a packet. Once it was out there, the galaxy would forever know that he was the man who discovered the first wormhole.

With new resolve, knowing he faced certain death, his fear faded and his muscles relaxed. The worry wasn't gone entirely, but at least he knew what he had to do.

He retraced his steps to the stairs, bypassed the second deck where the hold was, and went up to the bridge level. There was no way he could overpower the people who had taken over the ship, but maybe he could make an excuse to use one of the computers.

By the time he made it to the bridge deck, he was winded, trying hard not to breathe loud. He paused outside the open rec room hatch to catch his breath. The deck had four hatches: the bridge, the captain's quarters, a closed unmarked hatch, and the rec room. He took one step forward then froze when he heard the grunts, groans, and slaps coming from the open hatch.

Where could he go? The bridge hatches were closed. The room beside the rec had no label; it could be anything. All that remained was the lone cabin. If he was quiet and careful, he could make it. First, he needed to make sure no one was looking out the hatch from within the rec room since they would see him immediately if they were.

Taking a breath for courage, he darted his head around the frame. Immediately, he jerked it back and wished to God he had never looked.

Three men were abusing the black-haired captain. The only thing she wore was a silver collar and she looked exhausted and beaten. There were many things he disliked about aging; this was the worst. Without a weapon, there was nothing he could do for her.

At least he was now sure they were Caliphate soldiers. Pirates wouldn't be as fit, and no other Navy would do something so horrible.

He waited a few more seconds, as the noises grew. Once he was sure no one was looking, he darted across the hall as fast as his legs would carry him. Freezing, he waited for a scream, or curse, that would be a prelude to his capture. When only the noises remained, he slid his way along the wall to the cabin labeled: *Captain Nadia Dagher.*

The hatch slid open, thankfully unlocked, and he ducked inside. The room was a disaster, with the drawers opened, the bed mussed, and clothes littered the floor. It looked like a hurricane had hit the place.

He headed for the closet off to one side. It was the logical place to search. She wore a gun when off the ship; therefore, she had to have one in her cabin.

He was behind a row of dresses when the cabin door swooshed open behind him. Iker flattened himself the recess of the closet and behind her clothes.

He caught a glimpse of bare flesh as one of the soldiers from the rec room walked by, presumably on his way to use the shower in the back of the quarters.

Iker's hand brushed against hard leather as he held himself

as still as humanly possible. The water turned on and once he was sure the noise would cover him, he explored what he had found.

Her gun belt was discarded on the floor, along with torn clothes that looked like hers as well. Iker pulled the sleek pistol from the holster and examined it for a moment. He wasn't really into guns, had never served in the military, but he'd certainly seen his share of movies. He brought it to his nose and the acrid scent of gunpowder burned in the air around the weapon. It took a few minutes of playing around with it, but he felt that he had the basics down.

The slide came back and he saw the round in the chamber. It was small, smaller than he would have thought a bullet needed to be. The safety was obvious—red was a universal warning. He clicked the lever up until the red was visible, then pulled the hammer back.

It never occurred to him why the captain would have a simple weapon, but at least it wasn't a computer-controlled firearm keyed only to her.

With the gun out in front of him, he inched out of the closet toward the shower. His hand shook, requiring him to grasp it with the other. Could he kill someone? Regardless of who they were or what they had done, life itself was precious.

Life was precious, which was exactly why he would kill this man. He thought about all the people who would die if the Caliphate invaded, and that strengthened his resolve.

The man stepped in front of him, coming out of the still running shower to grab a towel. He was large, with muscles developed from a hard regime of exercise. Neither man moved. They held each other's gaze for a moment and then the soldier lunged forward, reaching for the gun.

Iker hadn't meant to fire. He fell backward, instinctively retreating when the gun barked. The small bullet ripped through the man's hand and then his chest. His lifeless body fell to the deck, a pool of blood forming as his punctured heart spewed his life on the cold metal.

Iker stumbled back farther until he hit the opposite wall, the gun in his hand weighing far more than a moment before. He looked down at the weapon and then back at the dead man.

In his whole life, not once had he ever thought of killing another human. When he was younger and less wise to the ways of the galaxy, he'd even protested the Navy for "making war" on the Caliphate. The shock and reality of the situation hit him hard and his knees buckled.

"No," he whispered to himself. "Now is not the time, Iker." He thought of the poor abused woman in the next room, of the many people the Caliphate would enslave and kill. Of his own legacy.

He went back to her closet and grabbed the first pair of pants and shirt he could find.

When he was sure the way was clear, he moved out. There was nowhere to hide. The hall from the bridge to the rec room had no place to go other than the stairs down to the next deck. Iker walked with as much purpose as he could until he stood next to the rec room door. The horrible noises had subsided and Iker could hear nothing from the room.

Had they killed her? He hoped not. He needed her to access the comms. He prayed for courage and stepped around the hatch, the gun leading the way. He froze, bile building in his throat from the smell of sweat and bodily fluids.

Then he saw her, standing in the middle of the room, naked, with bruises, cuts, and welts marring her light brown skin. Her hair was matted from sweat and other things. The length was hacked off, unevenly cut.

Her eyes followed him as he entered. He could see the fear in them. She didn't move, didn't flinch, and Iker couldn't imagine why she wasn't running—Iker let out a low growl, surprising even himself. He had only heard of the obedience collars. Many of the more educated people in the Alliance didn't believe they existed. After all, what kind of monster would create a device that shut off a human's higher brain functions, turning them into nothing more than living automatons? To add insult to injury, the person inside was fully aware of their actions and the pain they suffered, unable to resist.

Slavery was a thing he only read about in ancient history, not something he had witnessed before. The collar was the perfect solution for a society that used slaves for tasks. Whether it be labor or debauchery.

He shook his head. They didn't have much time. Whoever he had killed would be missed soon. The first thing he would need to do was examine the diabolical device. The collar looked simple enough, and there would be no logical reason to booby trap it if the person wearing it had no desire to take it off.

He went behind her and examined it carefully. It was a silver band an inch wide, and it appeared to adhere to her skin. Not a true collar, more like a fabric choker. It was cool to the touch and had a single gold ring on the back. He saw no controls or other mechanisms. They would need to keep it simple, he thought. The ring was pressed flat to the collar, and he used the pads on his fingers to pry it up. It clicked into place loud enough to startle him.

Her muscles quaked with either fear or exhaustion and only then did he realize the sadistic bastards had left her standing on the balls of her feet.

Gripping the coin-sized ring, he turned it clockwise. The device clicked again, and the collar sprang open. He tossed the device away as if it were acid.

Nadia fell, collapsing to the deck with a groan. Using her

coat like a blanket, he spread it over her before sitting on the couch next to where she collapsed.

Her eyes fluttered open, and reality crashed down on her.

The sheer horror he saw in her eyes told him she was aware of everything that had happened to her. Then something else happened. Her eyes went cold, her face slack as if emotions were for other people, not her. The way she looked scared him more than the Caliph soldiers.

"Water," she whispered. Iker ran to retrieve a bottle from the dispenser, uncapping it before handing it over. The first mouthful she swished around and spit out. The rest, she drank. He turned around to give her privacy as she slowly pulled on her coat and pants, each movement eliciting a groan of pain.

"Gun," she said. He handed it to her. She pulled the slide back far enough to make sure a round was in the chamber, then ejected the magazine and counted what was available there.

"How many?" she asked.

"Uh, I don't know. I killed one in your cabin"—her delicate eyebrows shot up in surprise at his declaration— "and there were three in here with... you," he said the last part reverently. "I'm very sorry about that."

She shook her head. "Not your fault," she said with a clipped voice. "Let's get to the bridge. If I must blow up the ship to kill them, I will, but they are all dead. Especially that bitch Daisy." Her voice sounded entirely too calm, unnaturally so.

"Captain, there is something I have to tell you," he said as they moved to stand beside the door. She peeked out. Her legs wobbled from the strain, but she managed.

"What?" she said in her cold tone.

"The reason they took your ship. I've discovered a worm-hole between here and Praetor. I fear they've known about the other end and were waiting for me to find this end before attacking. I'm very sorry," he said again. He could barely look at her, the shame and guilt in his heart weighing on him like an anvil. Unjust as they were, he couldn't help them.

Nadia stared at him blankly for a few seconds before speaking. "Stay close to me," she said. "I need to lean against you." He moved up to her, letting her borrow what little strength he had as the two of them moved toward the bridge door. He didn't know what her plan was, but he was sure it would be certain death for the Caliphate crew... and possibly him.

CHAPTER THIRTY-EIGHT

Second watch was half over and Jacob had stayed through, freeing up Kim to oversee their continued efforts to make sure the ship was operating at one hundred percent. Honestly, Jacob could go to his cabin or briefing room and leave one of the bridge crew in charge, but... then he would have to do paperwork.

The amount of said work that piled up had him sure there was something wrong with the ship's mail system. No captain, especially not one of a ship with less than a hundred people on board, should have that much paperwork every day. Then again, if the Navy had bothered to send him to command school, that might have explained it. Until such time as they did, he relegated the administrative work to an hour after breakfast and no more.

They were six hours into their search for the elusive ship, and it was wearing on him. He liked Nadia. She was exactly his type. Navy life didn't leave a lot of room for relationships, but he could see having something with the vivacious woman whose eyes always twinkled with a sarcastic glint. Of course, his attraction to her was secondary to the reason they were looking. The Navy's primary mission was protection of Alliance citizen and freedom of the space ways. A missing ship, even one that hadn't been reported missing, was a priority.

"Found her, sir," Midship Owusu said with a jump of excitement.

"Show me," Jacob replied. Owusu put the space-time detector on the main screen. Jacob leaned forward to examine the image.

"Right here. She wasn't accelerating, which was why we didn't see her sooner. Then she changed course to a heading of two-four-zero, mark three-one-one relative, accelerating at two-hundred gs."

"Can we intercept her at this angle?" They were going the wrong direction, but their relative velocity was low enough they might be able to pull it off.

In the Pit, Petty Officer Collins tapped away, comparing angles, courses, and acceleration, trying to find the least-time approach where they could match velocity with the ship and parallel her.

"I have it, sir. If we go flank speed for three-five minutes at a course of one-eight-zero relative, we can match her in two-zero hours and four-three minutes."

Flank speed? Generally, it was reserved for wartime only. Could he justify it if he had to? Who knew? Did he care? No. What were they going to do, throw him out?

"Lay it in," he said.

"Course laid in," PO Collins replied.

Jacob pressed the switch on his chair to open comms. "Engineering," he called.

"Engineering, PO Stas," came the reply.

"Stas, we're about to push her to flank. Is our girl ready?" he asked.

"Wait one, sir," he replied.

Jacob imagined the engineer sweating as he ran through every check in The Book to make sure he could tell his captain the ship was ready. No one wanted to be the poor unfortunate soul to tell the captain he couldn't do what he wanted.

"Skipper," Commander Beckett's voice cut in, "she's ready, sir. *Interceptor* won't let us down."

"Good man." He cut the line. "Ready, Collins?"

"Ready, sir," Collins said.

"Execute," he ordered. The ship hummed as the gravcoil surged to flank speed.

Interceptor spun on her axis, facing the new direction her captain had ordered, and the gravcoil pulsed to life, pulling the ship through space at an astonishing rate of five hundred and sixty *gs*. After five minutes, her velocity reached zero and she started the trek in the direction her helm wanted.

————

Nadia grunted through the pain. The damned obedience collar might have circumvented her higher brain function to turn her into a living sex doll, but it had done nothing to dull the pain or keep her from remembering the experiences they inflicted upon her. It took all her considerable will to suppress those in the back of her mind, pushing them down into a box and wrapping a metric ton of all-purpose adhesive on them. If not for her training with ONI, she doubted she could.

The professor did his best to help her as they made their way up the stairs to the bridge. When Daisy had taken the ship, she'd closed the hatch and reprogrammed it. However, it was impractical to keep the bridge hatch locked shut. Nadia hated relying on hope, but this one time, she prayed it would work in her favor.

Her legs shook from the strain, and she was breathing hard by the time they reached the panel.

"I don't know how many are in there, but before I open this door, I want you on the deck," she told him.

"On the floor?"

She gave him a screwball look. "Of course, on the floor. If I catch them by surprise, I can probably get three or four. If they shoot back, I don't want you getting hit. What you know, what you've found, it's going to change everything. I don't want these bastards getting you," Nadia said.

He complied, lying down and pressing himself flat. With her gun in hand, she pressed opened the hatch. As the hatch hummed to open, Nadia brought her free hand back to hold the pistol in a classic two-handed grip.

The hatch slid open, revealing three men she recognized from the rec room, manning the controls. None of them even looked back as the bridge door moved aside.

Stomping on the visceral anger flaring up in her, she lined up her sights on the far-left man. The pistol cracked and the man's head jerked forward as a line of blood and gore sprayed the console in front of him. She switched targets and fired again. The one in her chair was standing up and she caught him in the throat. He gurgled as blood from his carotid artery sprayed about him. The third man was moving, leaping out of his chair, and drawing his own sidearm. She fired a third, then fourth time. The third round missed, but the fourth one caught him in the leg. He went down behind the navigation console with a sharp scream of pain.

"Whatever," she muttered. Pushing herself off the wall she lurched forward, with the gun steadily pointing his way. He raised his own gun over the console and fired. Thin lines of plasma streamed out. One hit the ceiling above her, exploding the light panels and melting wiring. The second burned through a control conduit next to the hatch. The third hit her left arm. Searing pain exploded in her and she dropped to one knee as the pistol in her hand became unbearably heavy.

A distant part of her mind told her it was heavy because she only had one hand to hold it. Nadia blinked away the searing agony, pushing herself to focus. Ignoring her severed arm, she growled, digging deep, and holding her pistol steady.

He raised his hand to fire, but she fired first, hitting the pistol dead on. Her armor-piercing rounds ruptured the plasma chamber and the gun exploded like a popped water balloon, dumping searing hot plasma on its wielder. He didn't even have time to scream as his body, the navigation control, and the floor underneath him, melted.

The plasma cooled seconds after it exploded, but not in time to prevent severe damage to her ship.

Nadia sank and her remaining hand hit the deck, sending the pistol bouncing away.

The professor was there, hovering, his face pale from shock. "What... what do I do?" he asked.

She tried to lift her arm, but it wouldn't budge. Instead, she nodded toward the hatch. "Push the red button, then input three-five-seven-nine on the keypad next to it," she said with a hoarse croak.

He ran over and pushed the red button, then waited as the door crawled to a close. When the hatch finally shut, Professor Bellaits inputted the code. The pad turned red and beeped at him.

Someone screamed from behind the door. Nadia smiled as she recognized the voice of that bitch Daisy, but Nadia no longer cared. She was holding off unconsciousness and death by sheer will. She couldn't bring herself to look at her severed arm. It would be too much.

"Now what?" Bellaits asked her as he knelt back down beside her.

"Comms," she said, slipping toward the darkness. "*Interceptor*," she managed before blessed blackness claimed her.

————

"Sir, we're receiving a broadband SOS from *Dagger*, but it's in the blind," McCall said from his station.

"In the blind? They don't know we're here?" he asked.

"Doesn't appear so, sir," Spacer McCall replied. "I doubt we would even pick it up if we weren't so close."

Jacob made a hand motion, pointing at his panel. McCall hit a button and the call transferred to his screen. An older man he didn't recognize appeared... which set his alarms off. He'd spent eight days on *Dagger*, and he was sure he'd met all the crew.

"*Dagger*, this is *Interceptor*, go ahead," Jacob said. They were currently three light-seconds behind their target.

"Uh, hi. We need help. The ship's crew are dead and Caliphate soldiers are on board. We managed to retake the bridge, but... we need help," he repeated.

Jacob leaned into the comm pickup. "Say again? Caliphate soldiers?" Jacob asked, his body instantly snapping alert.

He could've heard a pin drop on the bridge as the crew went deathly silent. Caliphate soldiers in Alliance space, even the Protectorate, was an act of war. There was no way they would send troops here unless there was about to be an invasion. He *had* to have misheard.

"Uh, yes. They took the ship... I don't know when. More than a day ago, and they killed the crew—"

Shock froze Grimm with his mouth half open. Nadia was dead?

"—Well, all except the captain." The man's face frowned, and his eyes flickered off screen.

Jacob sighed inwardly with relief, though it warred with his sense of grief over her dead crew. "What's the situation now?" Jacob asked.

"We managed to take the bridge back and lock it out, but there are still soldiers on board. I don't know how many. And my assistant..." He trailed off.

"Sir," Jacob said, trying to get the man to focus. "We're actually only a few minutes away from you. Can you kill the acceleration?"

"I don't know how," he said.

"We can walk you through it. Once we're parallel, we can board and retake the ship. We'll take care not to hurt your assistant."

He shook his head. "No, you don't understand. She's a Caliphate spy. I'm sure she's why they knew to take the ship now. She told them about my work. If there is anyone on board who knows where their base is, it will be her."

Caliphate soldiers? Spies? Jacob shook his head at the wonder of what he had stumbled into as the only USN command officer in the system.

"Understood, sir. I'm going to give you over to my helm, Petty Officer Collins, one of the best. She'll walk you through what you have to do," he said as he transferred the screen to the Pit.

He tuned out what she said and focused on his own priorities.

The situation was bigger than he'd expected. The governor was likely corrupt, but... in league with the Caliphate? Or maybe just the pirates? He shook those thoughts away. He would have to save those connections for later; right now, he needed to focus on saving *Dagger*... and Nadia.

Jacob pointed at McCall and snapped his fingers. "Set Condition Zulu, action stations."

McCall gulped in response. "Aye, sir, Condition Zulu, action stations."

As the call rang out and the ship's crew ran to their places, he punched up the XO.

"Kim, I need you to put together a boarding party. Your arm's still in a sling, so don't put your name in it. Make sure you include Chief Suresh and PFC Naki. "In fact," he thought better of it for a moment, "have the COB lead it."

"Aye, sir. Boarding party. On it." She cut the line.

A moment later, the gravitic acceleration on *Dagger* shut off. Collins maneuvered the ship around the dissipating wake, coming up on her starboard side to match speed.

"Good job, Collins," Jacob said. He changed channels to the boat bay. "Chief, we have another boarding action for you."

"Aye, sir. Corsair is ready on your go," Chief Boudreaux replied.

————

The Corsair could pack in Marines and spacers, but there were only so many hands aboard ship who had the necessary training with firearms and small unit tactics. Chief Suresh, PO Kirkland, and Kennedy, as well as PFC Naki, and PO Desper for medical. Along with Trevors and Alderman for any repairs the ship might need.

The boarding party were armed with MP-17s configured as semi-automatic pistols. They wore Navy ELS suits with the bulky soft armor pulled over their torso. Naki had his Marine space armor, and though others would gladly go through the hatch first, he insisted on the forlorn hope.

"Contact," Boudreaux called from above.

Naki configured his MP-17 in carbine mode. Longer than the SMG but shorter than a full rifle, the carbine offered him the most flexibility between mobility and accuracy. He waited the requisite extra seconds before nodding to Chief Suresh. She hit the button.

He stormed through, letting the COB worry about keeping his six clear. He'd performed this drill a hundred times, but it was weird having de facto command as the only Marine on board. Relentless hours of drill prepared him for the moment, and he wouldn't fail his crew or the captain.

"Clear," COB said from behind him. Chief Suresh looked like she could go toe-to-toe with an apex lion. He didn't question her judgment.

He came to the first intersection and slipped his head around the side. Two men with electrostatic plasma rifles but in civilian clothes were behind makeshift barricades at the far end.

Naki noted their position and ducked his head back behind the corner. It wasn't likely they were manning the position regularly. They must be on alert since friendlies had taken the bridge.

He waved the boarding party back and reached down to his side, grabbing the deceptively heavy stun grenade from his hip. "Proximity detonation, maximum power," he said, activating the weapon. He knelt, not wanting to reappear in the same place, and counted to three. On three, he lunged out on his side, heaving the grenade as hard as he could. It bounced off the ceiling, arcing right between the two defenders. When the grenade sensed the two men in range, it detonated.

A concussive shockwave, strong enough to blow out unprotected eardrums and turn soft tissue to a mass of broken blood vessels and bruises, exploded between them.

They were hurled aside, slamming into the walls and

sinking to the floor. Naki leaped up, charging toward them and kicking their rifles away.

"Search the rooms," he said, pointing at the quarters on the level.

"Trevors," Suresh called to the engineering rating. "Take Alderman and go to their engineering room and secure it."

"Aye, aye," the young man said. He tapped Alderman, who looked entirely too wide-eyed to be in a boarding action, and they ran for engineering.

Desper worked to save the men's lives while Kirkland and Kennedy covered her. Naki headed up the stairs, carbine pointing to where an enemy might appear on the next level.

CHAPTER THIRTY-NINE

"Sir?" Midship Owusu said. Jacob was impressed with the young man's confidence. When he'd first come on board, the midship, barely out of the Academy, couldn't even look at him without shaking.

"Yes, Owusu?" he asked.

"Sir, I'm picking up a ping from astern. Two million klicks on... one-eight-seven mark zero-five-zero, relative. It's—" He interrupted himself, holding up his hand to the headset that translated space-time distortions into sound. "It's very small, but... I'm sure it's a ship."

"Understood. Helm, thrusters only, put us forward of *Dagger*. Oliv, drop the towed array." Jacob pressed the all-hands button on his con. "Rig for silent running." All over the ship, vents closed, non-essential machinery shut down, and anything else producing heat or radiation was secure. External radiators retracted into the ship and all electromagnetic emissions were curbed.

His crew responded, repeating his orders back and falling into the smooth, practiced discipline he had worked so hard for them to regain.

The towed array allowed them to "see" in their own gravwake, or in this case, behind them when a ship was in the way. With a ship closing on them, he wanted to remain hidden if possible. If he activated the gravcoil, then there would be no chance of hiding.

PO Collins did her job well, putting the *Interceptor* forward and ten meters off-center from the *Dagger* so the towed array would fall back behind the other ship.

"Passive only, Owusu," Jacob said.

"Aye, sir. Passive only," Midship Owusu confirmed.

Tense moments passed as the Tango, designated Hotel One, moved closer. Owusu listened hard, trying to get a solid read on its power curve.

"It's not a warship, sir. I think it's a dropship, possibly a Dhib-class if we're talking about the Caliphate," Owusu said.

"Reinforcements?" Jacob said to the screen on his chair. The XO stared back up at him from her position in DCS.

"Possibly. Whatever it is, it's a short-range craft. How did —" She looked off screen, hesitating.

"What?" he asked.

"Nothing, sir. I was going to ask how they got it here." Kim let her voice trail off.

Jacob gave her a sympathetic smile. "Water under the bridge, XO. The failures in the Protectorate started long before you were even in the Navy."

She was right, though. This was unthinkable. A Caliphate forward base in the Protectorate? Decades of mismanagement was how. The politics of the Navy and the last war were above his pay grade, but, since he was the highest-ranking officer in the system, he could deal with it as he saw fit. Besides, they were already planning on kicking him out. What else could they do to him?

What mattered the most was saving his mother's legacy

and doing something he could be proud of. For him to leave the Navy with his honor restored.

"Weapons hot, safeties off," he ordered. Live-fire exercises were a regular part of training at every level. Simulations were crucial in familiarizing spacers with the operations of the equipment, but there were some things only firing the actual weapon at a live target could teach.

For the turrets to have the best chance of striking their target, they would need the ship to be within ten thousand klicks. That way, there would be no chance for the ship to evade.

"Safeties off, weapons hot, sir," Lieutenant Fawkes replied.

"Carter, I know it's asking a lot on a small target, but if you can disable it without blowing it up, that would be great," Jacob asked.

Carter wiped his sleeve across his forehead, sweating despite the cool air. "I'll do my best, sir," he said.

The bridge crew watched in eerie silence as the small dot grew closer and closer.

———

PFC Naki rounded the second deck, weapon in front and ready. He wanted to go directly to the bridge, but he couldn't leave an area unsecured behind him.

"Desper, status," he whispered. The space armor completely hid any noise he made, but habits were habits and it was better to err on the side of caution.

"Sorry, Naki. I tried. They popped their capsules and I couldn't neutralize the poison fast enough," PO Desper replied over the crackling comm.

One of the frustrating things about fighting the Caliphate, at least from the history the El-Tee made him read, was their willingness to die rather than be captured. At least the low-level soldiers and officers. The high-ranking ones didn't seem to have a problem surrendering.

The PFC shook his head in disappointment. Hopefully, they could take at least one of them alive and find out where their base was.

Level two was the main hold. He saw the entrance from the top of the staircase, but the passageway went left and right; if he stepped out, he would expose himself to attackers he couldn't see on either side of him.

"Heartbeat sensors," he whispered. The suit's HUD blinked and picked up a number of acoustic noises. The first few seconds was a cacophony, but then the computer tuned out the Navy personnel behind him, leaving four, two on either side of the passageway in front of him.

Those electrostatic-charged plasma rifles they carried were a mean weapon, capable of burning a hole through a target from a hundred meters. He wasn't sure his armor could take even one hit from them, and he had no desire to be wounded... again.

He thumbed his remaining stun grenade. "Time detonation, maximum power," he said. The weapon beeped as it set. "Five seconds." His HUD displayed the countdown, holding at five. "Activate." The five vanished, replaced by a four, then a three...

On two, he side-armed the grenade to the right, clearing the corner. When it detonated, he leaped out to land on his side, aiming left.

Two men in civilian clothes, but armed with Caliph weapons, staggered back as the burst of light, noise, and pressure forced them to avert their eyes. He fired twice, once in each of their chests, then four more times to make sure they were dead. "Tango down," he shouted as he rolled over to cover the remaining. Suresh charged in behind him.

One of the Tangos had managed to shield himself from the worst of the blast, but he was still shaken and recovering when Suresh landed a solid dropkick in his chest, sending him flying. She was back on her feet in an instant and on top of the downed man, bashing him in the head with her pistol in an effort to knock him senseless.

The other guy bit down on his suicide pill and convulsed, frothing at the mouth.

At least they were only killing themselves, Naki thought darkly.

He was immediately back on his feet. Moving out, they circled the small deck, snaking their way through the empty hold. Nothing.

Any remaining boarders were either on the bridge deck or clear.

————

Masud Tahan wasn't happy with his soldiers. They weren't responding to his hail. The *Dagger* had cut acceleration and was drifting toward her next destination. He knew he shouldn't have left them to report directly to the ISB Minister, but he had no choice. The man didn't like comm lag, and since they were a light-minute from their asteroid base, he had to fly there personally and report, leaving his second-in-command and several soldiers alone on the ship.

He hovered over the pilot as they approached the ship from the stern. They were too far to see it with the naked eye, but he knew where it should be.

"What do you think?" he asked the pilot flying the small Dhib.

"They're dead in space, for sure. But the energy on the reactor is stable," the pilot said.

"Which means?" he asked.

"Probably not a malfunction," the pilot clarified.

Not a malfunction, which meant what? They shut their engines down? Perhaps the professor found his wormhole after all?

———

Daisy crouched, hidden behind a crate of supplies on the bulkhead side of the mess hall. She was still in shock from seeing the professor's sensitive and expensive equipment turned to slag. She was so sure, without a shadow of a doubt, that her act as the "sexy assistant" had left the already befuddled man in the dark about her true intentions.

Months of gene therapy and painful cosmetic surgeries had turned her from a dark-haired, dark-eyed Caliphate woman into what ISB analysts believed was the most desirable woman in the Alliance. She'd gone through it all to ultimately bring the Alliance infidels to their knees.

With all her work, her flawless accent, and her powerful charisma, he'd seen through her deception in a way she had not managed with him. There was no other way to explain his foresight in planning to destroy his equipment.

If only she had planned so well. Alliance Marines were storming the ship and killing her countrymen, and she couldn't fight back. The simple hold-out pistol she carried was more than enough to deal with an unarmored opponent like the one she had killed on the bridge... but against armor of any kind, it was a child's toy.

She pondered turning it on herself, fearing what wrath the Caliph would strike her with for failing in her duty. Her future, once bright, was now down to three options.

Kill herself.

Allow the Alliance to kill her.

Return to the Caliph and spend her days wearing the same collar she condemned Nadia to wear.

None of the options appealed to her. Perhaps dying while trying to kill the enemy would earn her place in the harem of the Caliphs of heaven. At least then she would rejoice in luxury in her afterlife.

For the first time in her young life, Daisy questioned her faith. When all went as planned, when her machinations proved fruitful, it was easy to believe, but now, in the end, with death looming... she doubted.

Her hand tightened on the little pistol as she heard the hatch to the mess hall open. Heavy booted footsteps echoed in the large chamber.

She counted in her mind, taking courage with each number and recanting the mantra to herself...

Three.

Allahu akbar.

Two.

Allahu akbar.

One.

She burst from behind cover, screaming as she charged the surprised Marine. "Allahu akbar!"

The pistol barked in her hand, deafening in the enclosed space. The round impacted the Marine's chest in a puff of deflected fragments.

To her surprise, he slapped the weapon out of her hand as she fired a second time, then punched her straight in the face, sending her flying to land on her butt. Then a dark-skinned she-devil slammed her to the deck, her eyes shining with glee as she repeatedly pistol-whipped Daisy until she welcomed the darkness.

"Something is wrong," Masud said. They were eleven thousand klicks aft of the ship. This close, even their handheld comms unit would receive his calls.

"If..." he spoke aloud, "if there was another ship out here, we would see it, yes?" he asked the pilot.

The man nodded. "Anything within a hundred thousand klicks would be impossible to hide. Gravcoils are too loud."

He glanced over at the scope. Two men flew the ship—pilot and co-pilot. A third operated the comms and EW systems, including passive sensors. It was extremely difficult to hide a large ship under power. Not impossible, but almost so. Not only did the gravcoil disrupt space-time with its gravitic wake, but ships put off heat and other emissions that were clearly visible in space. There was nothing to hide behind in the vastness of the universe. Even asteroid belts were relatively sparse. The only way to hide a ship was to—

Masud looked up in horror, the order to turn forming on his lips...

He was too late.

———

DD-1071 USS *Interceptor* glided effortlessly from *Dagger*'s shadow. Collins had worked her butt off, handling the ship with pure skill and intuition, maneuvering to keep *Dagger* directly between them while Owusu read off course adjustments to her. She dripped sweat as the captain gave the order. The hands-on-throttle-and-stick setup the Pit used had many advantages, the most obvious being all the many configurable controls. Both the flight stick and the throttle came with adjustable hat switches she could easily control with her thumb. With the throttle locked down, she slaved the ship's omnidirectional reaction thrusters to the hat switch. Using her thumb, she gently guided *Interceptor* out of *Dagger*'s shadow, lining the destroyer up directly on target.

"Fire," Jacob ordered.

"On the way," Carter replied as he mashed the fire button. The turret made a minuscule adjustment and delivered its payload—20mm of tungsten-reinforced nano-hardened steel at ten-thousand KPS. The gun turret shook as the barrel recoiled, absorbing some of the energy of the shot.

———

The Dhib's pilot barely had time to comprehend the Alliance destroyer appearing as if by magic. Thin, lean, and armed to the teeth, it out-massed the dropship in every aspect. Even if he'd had time to dodge, he had no real base velocity to do it from. At the moment of firing, *Interceptor* was ninety four hundred klicks away. A twenty-millimeter armor-piercing round reached out and hit in less than a second. Not even enough time for the barrel to finish recoiling.

The slug ripped through the Dhib's nose, shattering her frame as a fraction of its energy transferred. Worse, the round missed the engines and passed through the passenger compartment, igniting the atmosphere for a fleeting second and burning the men alive before the ship exploded.

———

"Good hit," Carter said looking at his screen.

Jacob sighed. He'd hoped for prisoners. However, he wouldn't disregard Carter's skill in making the shot. "Well done," he congratulated the young man. For a fleeting instant, the memories of the first time he ordered a ship to fire passed through him. It felt like such a long time ago. It wasn't nearly as painful as it used to be and was gone just as quickly.

He felt decidedly more prepared for the outcome than last time. At least with the enemy ship, there was no question what they were doing. Their very presence could be seen as an act of war.

"Astrogation, see if you can back plot their trip. Maybe we can find out where they came from," Jacob ordered.

CHAPTER FORTY

"Dimitri, surely you jest," Duval said to the man on the screen.

"No. He says you must come. The Alliance can be stopped, our plans can work, but not if the destroyer survives, or the..." Dimitri stopped, his eyes wandering to the blue-skinned man at Duval's right. Dammit all to Hades, he'd forgotten the "Consortium" man.

"Who is he?" Dimitri asked.

"No one of consequence," Duval replied with a slip of annoyance. Who was Dimitri to ask about his crew? First it was the damned ISB holding him by the balls, and now this pissant thought he could speak to the leader of the Black Legion like he was a common thug?

Even with *Raptor*'s failure to bring down the freighter, they were still swimming in money. Enough to refit his new frigate without Takumi's help. *Maybe.*

"Fine, be that way. You can explain to Rasputin who he is. For now, come to Zuckabar, destroy the *Interceptor,* and you will be well rewarded. By now, *Madrigal* is in our hands—"

Duval scowled. *Madrigal* was on the list of ships given to him by Takumi. Another huge score that belonged to him.

Dimitri saw his expression. "You can have her and the cargo; just come now."

Duval thought it over for a moment. The last M-class he'd taken sold for a bundle. *Madrigal* and her cargo... He could retire somewhere in the Terran Republic... a beach house maybe... with one or two privately held obedience-collar-enhanced companions.

Duval spotted his way out of the mess he'd built for himself. A way that didn't involve him dying.

All he had to do was take out a forty-year-old destroyer. He looked around the bridge; they were greedy for this. Hungered for it. *Chuck* was a state-of-the-art frigate, manufactured by the most technologically advanced nation in the galaxy. Twelve plasma torpedo batteries, rail guns, maser turrets for anti-torpedo fire, and of course, the main gun, a giant gamma-ray laser capable of reducing a destroyer like *Interceptor* to slag with a single hit.

Not to mention the most advanced EW suite he'd ever even heard of.

This would be no battle, it would be a slaughter.

And then he would be done.

"Okay, we'll do it." He cut the line. "Signal *Raptor* to follow us. Before we jump, I want all the cargo transferred to her. She can follow behind us and support. No need to risk her or our goods with a lucky hit."

Decision made, the crew were quick to respond, setting course for Zuckabar. One way or another, and he knew there really was only one way this would all be over soon.

CHAPTER FORTY-ONE

Fleet Admiral Noelle Villanueva paced the flag deck of the Legion class battleship USS *Alexander* BB64, the flagship of the Alliance Navy. Officially, they were designated TF-118, and were currently on a training exercise simulating an incursion in the Corridor. The idea was to find out exactly how fast they could move a sizable force from the capitol to the farthest planet in their territory. Zuckabar was nominally theirs, as part of the agreement between the Protectorate and the Alliance.

However, Congress, and, if she were being honest, the president as well, happily allowed chaos to reign in what otherwise could be the most important system in all of Alliance space. All in order to be seen as "peaceful, non-expansionists."

She let out a bark of a laugh. The crew stationed on the flag deck ignored their admiral's habit of pacing and whispering to herself.

The foolishness of the idea never ceased to amuse her. In the entire history of the Alliance, they hadn't once been the aggressor in a war. With the way Congress was operating, they were playing into their enemies' hands and would eventually lead the Alliance into another conflict they were trying to avoid.

One she feared they wouldn't win. Border skirmishes and contested planets were one thing, but the Great War of 2915 was something else. It had been on a scale the galaxy had never seen before, and she hoped would never see again.

At least President Axwell had come around. Without his sponsorship, none of this would be possible. Combined with Senator St. John's masterful deception, the four of them might... *might*... be able to change the course of history.

The young man she'd sent to command the *Interceptor* had done exactly what Admiral DeBeck had wanted, if not in the way they had both anticipated. She stymied the stab of guilt for sending an officer, and a crew, into a situation they weren't aware of. But if she hadn't, then the massive human trafficking ring wouldn't have been uncovered.

How had she so badly misjudged Grimm? She knew what it was. Despite her fervent desire to see her Navy great again, she had *believed* the media lies and political rhetoric. How could she not? Inundated with them day in and day out.

"Initiating starlane in three...two... one..."

The ship lurched for a second and she had the falling feeling in her stomach. It lasted long enough for her to believe that she was falling, then they were traveling hundreds of times the speed of light.

"How long?" she asked her astrogation station.

"Five hours, forty-three minutes, then another seven hours to reach Kremlin Station," he replied.

"Hang in there, Commander Grimm; we're coming," she whispered.

CHAPTER FORTY-TWO

J acob took Lieutenant Bonds' report like an automaton. He no longer had a choice. There was no longer any possibility of backing down. They had a witness—one of the mercs who had tried to take *Madrigal* was talking. Wouldn't shut up, according to Gunny Hicks. He had been hired by Dimitri, the governor's right-hand man. They had done it discreetly, no names were exchanged, but he'd seen the man before and knew exactly who he was.

Maybe... *maybe*... the governor could plead innocent and claim his advisor was acting of his own accord. *No,* he thought with a shake of his head. He couldn't. There was too much evidence now. Longhorn, sabotage, Commander Cole's death—and now the *Dagger* and Caliphate soldiers?

Jacob shook his head, unable to believe the events swallowing his command and the system with it.

If anyone was going to arrest the governor, it had to be him. He was the only one who could take the blame and not have it hurt his career if anything went wrong.

It needed to be done. It was the right thing to do, and it was his duty as the highest-ranking naval officer in the system. He was the only person who could do it, both legally and physically. No force the station could muster would have even a chance of stopping his Marines.

He grimaced, thinking of the shape Nadia was in when she had arrived on his ship. Limping, haggard, and missing an arm. Commander Stanislaw immediately administered a nanite induced coma for the protection of her body as well as her mind. What she had endured—what the Caliphate soldiers had done to her—was inhuman.

Jacob's knuckles were white from the strain of gripping the table. For all that, though, he knew what would hurt her worse: the loss of her entire crew, murdered and stuffed in an airlock for later disposal. At least they'd recovered the bodies for a proper burial.

Jacob reached into his tunic and fingered the small, service-authorized silver cross he wore around his neck. His mother, when she was still alive, had a devout faith that would make a priest question his own. She never doubted the existence of God. He had to admit that when things like this happened, he did.

How could the kind, just God his mother worshiped allow this to happen? A smile played at the corner of his lips. His mother's voice came to him, *Because, son, we're here to prove ourselves, to be the good people He knows we can be. If He forced us to behave, then what would that show?*

His mother's voice was a constant echo in his head, imparting the wisdom of a lifetime of service to him.

What if... what if the Caliphate had posts like this all through Alliance space? What if when ships went missing and pirates were blamed or natural disasters, it was really them? Stealing his people and selling them into bondage to fuel Caliphate expansionist dreams?

It was possible. Unfortunately, he was a lieutenant

commander, frocked, on temporary assignment before he was mustered out of service. This conundrum was the very definition of "above my pay grade."

He checked his NavPad for an update on *Dagger*'s repairs. At least another eight hours before they could be underway. Then he would have to go to Kremlin Station and arrest the leader of a sovereign system.

"Oh boy," he said with a sigh. He rubbed the sides of his head, hoping he could massage out the tension.

The briefing room hatch screeched as it was pulled open. Lieutenant Yuki poked her head in.

"You really need to get one of Beckett's boys up here with some lubricant to fix this," Kim said as she stepped the rest of the way through. "Thank you, Corporal," she said to the Marine sentry who opened it for her.

Kim gingerly walked to her chair opposite Jacob, wincing as she accidentally bumped her immobilized arm into the seat.

She worked tirelessly for the ship, often staying up later than Jacob and rising early—as if she were trying to prove to him, and the crew, she was worthy.

Jacob grimaced in feigned pain as she sat down. "There are about one million things on this ship in need of one of Beckett's boys. I'll add it to the list." He leaned over and pressed the comm button. "Galley, Captain's briefing room."

"Spacer Second Class Mendez, sir. How may I help you?"

"Send up some coffee for the XO, please."

"Aye, sir," Mendez said.

Jacob motioned for her to have a seat. "What's on your mind, XO?"

She drummed her free hand against the table, as if she were thinking about what to say next. Instead, she ran over a few crew reports with him, the after-action on the *Dagger, a*s well as the many stores they were running low on.

She looked around, hesitant for a few moments, then she bit her lip before finally deciding to just say it.

"Sir, I think we all know where this is going—" She stopped herself.

The hatch opened and Mendez came in pushing a cart, white cook's uniform marred by the morning's breakfast.

Jacob blinked, glancing down at the NavPad. He hadn't even realized breakfast had happened. They'd started their hunt for *Dagger* the day before, and, he realized, he hadn't slept a wink.

Mendez set the carafe of black coffee down in front of the XO and turned back to his cart. Jacob lifted his hand, about to ask the spacer if he had any of the orange drink he preferred, when Mendez turned with a second carafe of the stimulant-and-vitamin-laden sludge.

"Good man," Jacob said with a grin.

"It's our job, Skipper," he said. Mendez froze, fear etched in his face at how casually he'd addressed his captain.

Jacob laughed. "You're fine, Josh. Informally, I'm happy to have you call me Skipper. Otherwise, don't forget to throw a 'sir' after it."

"Yes, sir," he said before ducking sheepishly out of the room, beaming with pride that the captain knew his first name.

Kim raised one dark eyebrow at Jacob. "Most captains don't allow that kind of... informality with the ratings," she said. "Officers are one thing, but..."

"I'm sure it's something they learned in command school. Unfortunately, the Navy didn't see fit to send me. Besides, I always liked it when the skipper showed a human side. Not too much, just enough to engender loyalty." He sipped his orange drink, instantly feeling refreshed as the stimulant hit him.

———

Lieutenant Kimiko Yuki gazed at her captain in awe. Every action Grimm had taken since he came aboard upset the balance of everything Kim knew about the Navy. From doggedly pursuing the gravcoil, to doing his duty for the *Madrigal*, *Bonaventure*, and finally the *Dagger*. For whatever reason, the Navy had thrown one of their finest officers out the airlock.

She had grown to dislike the Navy over the last few months, blaming the *Interceptor* and the poor situation she found herself in. She'd fallen into a trap of self pity. Then along came the skipper. He showed her what the Navy could be. What an officer could be.

Shaking her head and smiling, she took another sip of her coffee. Maybe it wasn't the admiralty that made up her perception of "the Navy," but the men and women she served with? In which case, she was going to do her damnedest to lead like Commander Grimm.

"We've gotten lucky so far," he said, filling the silence of the room. Ships were either eerily quiet or unbearably loud, depending on the time and where on the ship a person was. In the briefing room, only the sound of air blowing from the vents filled the gaps.

"Luck is a big part of any spacer's life, you know that. Sometimes we get the carrot, and sometimes we get the stick," she said with a grin.

"Regardless, I hope the brass agrees with me. I don't think anyone expected what we found on *Madrigal*, or guessed how extensive this network is. Rasputin's involvement and the Caliphate of all things. This is just a mess." Jacob ran a hand over his face, trying to push away the exhaustion they all felt.

Kim sipped her coffee again, thinking about the events they had endured.

"You know, I'm not a woman of faith. My family were dirt-owners on Rōnin, the first to come over from Earth some five hundred years ago. Nominally, we're Shinto, but I think it's more of a tradition at this point," she said.

Jacob arched an eyebrow at her, confusion on his face. He trolled his mind for anything he knew about the most isolationist part of the Alliance. "That's interesting. I thought most of the original settlers were Buddhist?"

She let out a soft laugh. "Most of them were, but my ancestors were part of a group of settlers who weren't. While Rōnin's infrastructure and culture certainly reflect the Buddhist ideals, Shintoism expressed itself in our architecture and art. My mother... she's a painter and didn't really want her only daughter joining the Navy. Painting, though, it never did it for me. I liked the idea of seeing other planets, meeting new people—"

"And blowing them up?" Jacob asked with a grin. It was an old Navy joke and they both chuckled.

"Not yet, sir. I... Most of us haven't seen combat. I know there are a few old salts on board, but... We Shinto, we pray at shrines, leaving offerings for our ancestors to watch and protect us. I have a small one my mother gave me, but otherwise, we don't pray. However, I'm starting to feel like I should," she said.

The mood grew dark for a moment and she could see the struggle on his face. His mouth opened to respond then closed.

"It's just training, Kimiko," he whispered, as if the memories of what he'd gone through haunted him. "I wish there was more to it, but there isn't. The Marines say, 'Train like you fight and fight like you train.' I think that's as true a thing as I've ever heard." He paused, sipping his drink. "On *Orion,* when the matter in Pascal happened, I really thought I was a hero. I stopped the ships that killed hundreds of my fellow spacers, and I saved lives. Then I saw the video of who was on those ships. I suppose I could've told myself it was a setup to make us look bad, more propaganda warfare by the Caliphate, and it was, but..." Jacob shrugged. He absently drew circles on the conference table while he relived the painful events.

She held her coffee with both hands, enjoying the warmth flowing into her fingers and the comfort of having something to do with her hands. Despite what the vids would have people believe, spacers didn't go around bragging about all the ships they had destroyed.

Jacob reached whatever place he searched for and continued. "At the end of the day, I was the one who gave the order to fire. My TAC officer, she ended up resigning. I tried to talk to her before she left, but she checked into a hospital the same day. Her parents told me it was too much for her. I did pray, a lot, after that. Then I stopped, as is the way of things. When my situation didn't improve, I gave up. Only now I think I'm starting to see what my mom talked about as a kid. At least a little."

"Why didn't you quit? I heard the rumors, the pressure they put on you and the lies they told about the action," Kim whispered just loud enough for him to hear.

He shrugged. "There were a couple of times I almost did what the civilian authorities wanted, admitted to making a mistake, or to knowing there were children on board. You think to yourself you would never crack and admit a lie, but after days of interrogation, they almost had me believing I was guilty... almost."

Kimiko couldn't imagine a situation like that. She understood it could and did happen, but imagine it? "What got you through?" she asked softly.

A smile played on his lips, small with a hint of sadness. "Faith. Faith that it would work out in the end. Faith that I had made the right call, that I'd saved lives. Faith in the Navy my mother loved so much."

"I didn't mean to pry, sir. Sorry," she said quietly.

Jacob cut his hand through the air like it was nothing, shaking the melancholy that had temporarily seized him. Within a second, he was back to business.

"Ever forward, XO, and always do better than yesterday. It's all any of us can do," he said as he straightened his shoulders and looked her directly in the eyes.

Silence grew between them for a long second before she shook her head slightly, her captain's lessons sinking in. "I think so too, Skipper. Having said that," she continued much louder, "the FITREPs on the crew are looking much better. Section chiefs across the board are—"

———

Jacob listened intently as his XO went over the ship's crew, where they needed more training and who was ready for promotion or, at least, more responsibility. For him, it was crazy how natural it all seemed. From running a repair deck on a station for over a year, to commanding a destroyer. After Pascal, he was sure his career was done. It galled him, but what could he do about it? Another six months and the promotion board would deny him, then he would be out, too old to be a senior grade lieutenant. The Navy wasn't interested in career lieutenants. Since he didn't make it easy for them by resigning, it was how they would be rid of him.

That was before, though. Before he found himself on *Interceptor*, waking up feeling alive and excited to see what came next. Had he really felt that way before? He had. First up, last to bed. When he wasn't on duty, he was reading. History, tactics, everything. He loved it all. Then Pascal put him so far into the black that he became a robot, operating on "survive" mode and nothing else.

He never wanted to let go of the feeling again. He was alive and the *Interceptor* was where he belonged. Whatever he had to do to stay in the Navy, he would do it.

CHAPTER FORTY-THREE

Transition—the moment a ship exited the starlane and returned to normal space—had many names, but whatever name it went by, it mostly just sucked. Going into the starlane was uncomfortable, like suddenly falling. Coming out was the reverse, like a line yanked upward, sending you high into the air in a heartbeat.

A few puked outright, some dry heaved, and everyone coughed and grimaced their way through it. Duval had lost count of the number of times he'd transitioned. All he knew was it never felt better. Every time was a struggle for self-control.

"Status," he growled through a cough.

His man, Pablo, a short man from Caliph territory with dark skin and darker eyes, was on passive sensors. He shook his head violently then put on the headphones, allowing him to hear the drumbeat of space-time. He started to speak, then coughed for a few seconds, his whole body shaking.

Duval waited, drumming his fingers on the command chair. Even the "blue man" was having trouble, fallen to one knee and holding his stomach like he would vomit at any second.

"That was a bad one," Kane said.

"I didn't feel like it was worse than normal," Duval replied.

Kane shook her head. "It's the twin star. Their gravity is much higher than a single pair. The couple of times I've transitioned in closer, it felt even worse."

Duval nodded. Coming out of a starlane early was expensive. The longer a merchant spent in sub-light, the more time it took and the more money it cost. Something his employer didn't have. If the data Dimitri gave them was to be believed, the Navy destroyer would be somewhere in the out-system in the vicinity of the Minsc starlane. He needed the destroyer killed and *Madrigal* taken. No mean feat for a regular pirate, but one with a shiny new Consortium frigate? Piece of cake.

"Found him. Running three-five-seven true, three hundred gs, no velocity readings yet," Pablo said. "She has an escort, or she's escorting a ship. Low power signature, probably a small freighter," he added, his voice raw from coughing.

"Kane, set a course, maximum acceleration. Let's close and kill before they even know they're under attack!"

———

"Captain, Astrogation. Sir, we have a tail," Midship Owusu's voice crackled over the radio in the dark cabin. Jacob groaned as he rolled over, struggling to find the button in his half-asleep state.

"Tell me about it," he said, eyes still closed as he wished more than anything to go back to sleep. He'd stayed up all the previous night and the following morning. He couldn't have slept more than a couple of hours when Owusu woke him up.

"*Dagger* is on our port flank allowing us to see to the stern with the towed array. I was speaking with the professor about listening for anomalies when I picked up two contacts entering the system. Shortly after arriving, they fell in line, accelerating at four hundred and fifty *g*s—"

An adrenaline spike shot Jacob's eyes wide open. Only an emergency would instigate such acceleration and no freighter could pull four hundred and fifty *g*s. Not even close.

"—right for us. I didn't get a reading on the smaller ship, but the lead ship's power curve is definitely military, sir."

"Time to intercept?" he asked. He didn't bother asking if Owusu was sure. If the midship said it was military, it was.

"Assuming consistent velocity and approach, three-point-three-four hours," Owusu replied.

"Have the XO round up *Bonaventure*'s captain and meet me on the bridge. Captain out."

All thoughts of sleep were long gone as he turned on the light. It was time to go to work.

Despite his brief sleep, he was alert and ready to go. The spike of adrenaline certainly helped. An unknown military ship heading their way could only mean one thing, but they had plenty of time and there was no need to rush. Jacob put on a crisp uniform, positioning his watch cap just right so the *Interceptor*'s shark nose lined up directly with his.

Once he was done, he walked out of his cabin as if he was in no hurry. He didn't need to run to the bridge; it was practically outside his hatch.

"Captain on deck," Naki said sharply as Jacob walked by. He nodded to the Marine and smiled.

The tension on the bridge slapped him in the face. The crew peered a little harder at their screens, their hands gripped the consoles tighter. Jacob could feel it as he walked in.

Huddled over the EW console were Kim and the *Bonaventure*'s defeated ex-captain, Morrison. He looked haggard beyond belief, as if the entire weight of his whole life had come crashing down on him in one fell swoop.

Jacob made his way directly to them. "Mr. Morrison, thank you for joining us."

"I—didn't think—you're welcome," he said.

"I know your information is limited, but would you look at the power curve of these ships and tell me if you recognize them?"

Morrison pondered the screen for a long moment. Jacob couldn't decide if he was scheming or genuinely thinking through the issue.

"The little one, maybe. I can't be sure, though. I'm sorry." His head hung down even lower as he dejectedly realized he couldn't be of help.

"Thank you for trying." Jacob turned over his shoulder and signaled for the armed rating to return him to his quarters. When he was gone, Jacob moved to his chair and examined the course information.

"You think they're following us?" Kim asked as she looked down at the same data.

"Possibly. Chief?" he asked, looking at Suresh's face through the tiny mirror.

"Skip?" she replied, meeting his eyes.

"You studied the sensor data from the attack on *Agamemnon,* correct?" he asked.

"Aye, sir. What little there was," Suresh said.

"Do you see any similarity?"

Chief Suresh tapped a finger against the stick. Jacob had noticed she did that when working through a problem, as if the flight control stick was a comfort to her.

"Could be the same ship. I don't have any definitive proof, but my gut tells me it is, Skip," she said.

"Kim?" he asked. He turned his head to the XO. She was barely six inches from him and he took a long second to look directly into her brown eyes.

"I concur, Skipper," she said.

"As do I. Roy," he said to Ensign Hössbacher, "make a note in the ship's log. I believe the two ships that have recently arrived in Zuckabar are of pirate origin. Please capture all the data we have on them and ready a packet. Let me know when it's sent."

"Aye, sir. Record data, send packet. Will do," Ensign Hössbacher replied.

He had it. His well-oiled machine operating with efficiency and discipline. Jacob took a moment to appreciate the hard work from everyone involved to come so far. From the drunken disorderly crew with a broken ship, to the finely tuned naval war machine he now commanded.

"Packet loaded, sir," Hössbacher informed him.

"Send it," Jacob ordered.

Jacob watched his own screen as the data shot out at the speed of light, reaching toward a freighter heading in the opposite direction, five light-minutes out.

"Now what?" Kim asked.

"Now we see if they're really following us," Jacob said.

———

"I've got an ID on the other ship, Duval. Looks like a tramp freighter, CSV *Dagger*," Pablo said from the sensor station.

"*Dagger*? Are you sure?" Takumi said. The blue-skinned man moved across the bridge, uncharacteristically interested in the ship.

For the last thirty minutes, they'd hauled balls toward *Interceptor*. The little destroyer hadn't changed course or attempted to evade in any way the entire time. By now, they had to see *Chuck* was chasing them. Not that there was anything they could do about it. Once he was close enough,

Duval intended to put those very expensive plasma torpedoes to work.

"Its IFF is broadcasting." The pirate looked from Takumi to Duval, trying to make sense of who he should address. Should he talk to Duval or Takumi?

"Duval," Takumi said over his shoulder, "we have an interest in this ship. You can't destroy it; I need you to capture it."

Duval's eyes went slightly wide before narrowing dangerously. "We're not your personal boarding party, Takumi. Capturing a ship underway that doesn't want to be captured isn't easy if they know you won't blow her up."

"All the same, once you've destroyed the Navy ship, you *will* capture that freighter," Takumi said. His tone didn't allow for disagreement.

In his mind, Duval replied, *And if I don't?* But he dared not say it, because he knew the answer. The next time they went into port would be his last. Some other pirate would be in charge of *Chuck,* and he would end up in an unmarked grave with a bullet in his brain.

The ship was too much of an advantage. He found himself in the unenviable position of having the most powerful pirate ship in space, without the means to hold her without Takumi's help.

One more prize and he could take his share and execute his exit plan. He had a small one-man lane-capable ship stashed away on Niflheim. The next time they ported there, if he had the money, he'd be gone before anyone suspected. They could have their frigate and terrorize shipping to their heart's content. Eventually, the Consortium or Alliance Navy was going to clean up the Corridor and he wanted no part of it.

"Fine," he said to the man. "I'll see what we can do."

"You do that," Takumi said without looking his way. Duval

didn't miss the worried smile Kane shot his way. Like any pirate, she was loyal to a point. The point where it was worth more money to betray him than keep him alive.

"She's changing course," Kane said. Her hands brushed over the controls, showing any number of possible new vectors.

"New course?" he asked. She didn't respond immediately and he had to stifle his temper.

"She turned to port, forty degrees..." She paused as she checked the numbers again. Turning, she looked right at Duval. "Far enough to port that if we don't alter our own course, we could lose them."

"Dammit. Make the change," Duval ordered.

Jacob nodded, unsurprised when the new ship altered course just a minute after *Interceptor*. They were thirty million kilometers behind but building overtake velocity. If Jacob didn't accelerate soon, there would be no way to escape them.

"Owusu, what do you hear?" he asked.

"No change in acceleration, Skipper," he said. "They're probably going full speed already." They were too far out for lightspeed sensors, a little over ten light-minutes, but the space-time detectors could pick up gravitic noise up to twenty light-minutes out, depending on proximity to the systems primary. The larger the engine, the more power that pulsed through it, the farther the equipment could pick up the signal.

"If they do mean to engage us, what about *Dagger*?" Kim asked.

"They definitely mean to fight, which is good, because it's what we want. On our terms, though, not theirs. Load the professor and everyone from *Bonaventure* on *Dagger*. Send PO2 Oliv to command it and surgeon's assistant Desper to take care of Nadia." He looked behind him and saw Naki still guarding the bridge. "And PFC Naki... to watch after the prisoners," he said in a hushed tone. He wasn't worried about the disgraced captain, Mr. Morrison, so much as Daisy, the Caliphate spy. However, he was supremely confident in PFC Naki's ability to handle the situation. Along with Oliv, who was a top-notch petty officer.

"Aye, sir. I'm on it," Kim said.

———

"That's funny," Pablo said from the sensor station.

Duval's ears picked up. They'd doggedly pursued the ship for almost two hours now, closing the gap. At their current velocity and acceleration, they were going to blow by the destroyer, which was exactly what he wanted. The engagement would be over in seconds. However, he'd expected the Navy ship to act like prey and run. In the entire chase, the *Interceptor* had changed course only once, *adding* to Duval's velocity advantage.

"*Interceptor* dropped back, blocking *Dagger* from our view," Pablo informed him.

"Kane?" He asked his helm her opinion.

"If they know we're onto them, and they would have to be blind not to, then it's the smart play. Protect the package with the *Interceptor*'s guns. It won't help them in the end, as we know, but they don't know how outclassed they are and... it's their *duty*," Kane said the word as a pejorative.

———

Jacob leaned back in his chair, fear playing tricks on his stomach. It wasn't the fear of a fight, or even death, as he'd faced both those before. Before *Interceptor,* he'd thought his legacy, his *family's* only legacy, would be Pascal. When people saw his name, they wouldn't remember his mother, the heroic master chief who saved hundreds of her fellow crew before going down with the ship. His mom's legacy would be tainted by his actions, no matter the reason. He would forever and always be *the Butcher of Pascal.*

Maybe, though, just maybe... he could be remembered for something more, something better. For doing his duty to his crew, to the civilians under his care, and for the Alliance. If the professor's discovery was as big as he thought it was, then Jacob's name would be intertwined with it. His mother's legacy would be clear.

Dagger had the civilian freighter crew on board, Professor Bellaits, the spy, and Nadia, who was still in a medical coma. Along with PO Desper to take care of the wounded, PO Oliv to command the ship, PO Collins to fly her, and using the remaining *Bonaventure* crew to assist. He wished he could spare more, but it wasn't possible. *Interceptor* was dangerously low on crew as it was.

"Sir, *Dagger's* reporting all hands ready," Ensign Hössbacher said.

Jacob punched the button on his chair to give him comms. "Oliv, once we're clear, head full power to the Praxis starlane, and don't stop until you find Commodore Xin or you're in orbit of Fort Kirk on McGregor's world. Understood?" he asked.

"Aye, Skipper. Full speed to the starlane when clear, don't stop until we come across the picket or Fort Kirk. Understood," Oliv replied.

"Good luck, Oliv," he said.

"You too, sir," she replied.

He cut the call and glanced over at Owusu, who was hunched over, listening to the approaching ship.

"No change, sir," Owusu said.

"*Dagger* is rigged for silent running," Bosun Sandivol said from Ops.

Jacob nodded. It was time. "Helm, up bubble twenty degrees... initiate Fox Sierra...execute," he ordered.

"Aye, sir. Up bubble twenty degrees. Fox Sierra," Suresh repeated. Her hand gently pulled back on the stick until the ship's bow angled up, then she juiced the throttle, making sure to hide any emissions from *Dagger* in her wake. At the same time, *Dagger* cut all power and emissions, coasting silently through space. They would do so long enough to disappear in the vastness of Zuckabar. Jacob didn't know the exact details of the governor's plans, but if it were him, he would want all the witnesses dead.

Lieutenant Commander (frocked) Jacob T. Grimm wasn't about to let that happen.

CHAPTER FORTY-FOUR

Petty Officers Collins and Oliv watched the *Interceptor* blaze on without them, having changed course to fool the pirates into thinking the *Dagger*, their temporary home, was still in front.

Heart-pounding minutes passed by as they, along with PO Desper, PFC Naki, Professor Bellaits, and the former crew of the *Bonaventure* waited, staring at the plot, desperately willing the pirate ship to change course. If they were going to, it would only take a few minutes for their computer to update the *Interceptor*'s course change and then—

The pirates changed course.

Oliv let out a sigh of relief, echoed by the others on the bridge of the small ship. Had the pirates seen the separation, they would have come for *Dagger* immediately.

As *Interceptor* sailed away and up from ecliptic, *Dagger* went straight ahead on the same course. All she had were passive sensors, but when the pirates changed course, the angle of the passive sensors had changed.

Oliv's elation vanished as the *Dagger*'s computers identified the frigate. She reached for the comms but stopped herself—

any signal from her ship would be detected. She couldn't warn her captain, only hope and pray the Hellcat-Class Destroyer was as tough as their reputation.

"Oliv... what do we do?" Petty Officer Jennifer Collins asked from her position at the helm.

"Our duty, just like the captain," Oliv said with a stone-faced expression.

She leaned back in her chair, muttering to herself. Her ship, her crewmates, were about to go into battle, possibly be killed, and she was stuck babysitting prisoners and civilians.

———

"Range?" Jacob asked.

"Ten million kilometers."

He checked his screen. Plenty of time had passed—more than enough for *Dagger* to disappear. If the pirates were going to break off to follow her, they would have.

"Small victories, XO," he said. "Any idea what they are flying yet, Owusu?"

The dark-skinned midship shook his head. "No, sir. I checked the database on pirate activity and the closest ship I could find was a freighter outfitted with a frigate's gravcoil."

"They'd be pushing their luck running a freighter that hard," Kim said from her station next to the captain.

"Pirates aren't known for being overly concerned about safety, XO. Okay, Chief Suresh, I think we've had enough time. Let the shark off the leash," he said with a grin. "Flank speed." Then he looked over to Ensign Hössbacher. "Set Condition Zulu, sound battle stations if you would be so kind, Roy."

Chief Suresh grinned, not a frivolous one, Jacob noted, simply the grin of a woman who was doing the job she loved, in the way she loved.

"Aye, sir. Flank speed," she said. To every spacer who served, there was something sacred about flooring it.

"Battle stations. Aye, sir," Ensign Hössbacher said. The young man had flushed deep at the captain's use of his first name.

With two pirate ships closing in, Jacob had worried they would split up, one going for *Dagger* and one for *Interceptor*. It was why he kept the ship to three hundred gravities for as long as he had. There was no escaping the engagement; the pirate ship had too much of a velocity advantage. What Jacob wanted was to protract the battle, something pirates weren't keen on. As soon as they took a hit or two, their crew would demand the ships break off—he hoped. After all, you can't spend money if you're dead.

Every manual on fighting pirates he had ever read, every recorded fight between them and a Navy ship ended the same. Pirates never won. It was why the Alliance sent destroyers to fight them. They almost always ran, and they couldn't outrun a tin can. At least that was the theory.

Suresh pushed the throttle forward and the gravcoil pulsed with power as *Interceptor* shot through space at over five hundred gravities.

The battle stations klaxon wailed through the ship like a banshee. Every corridor, room, and crawlspace heard the alarm reserved for drills and actual battle.

"Battle stations, set Condition Zulu. Battle stations, set Condition Zulu," Ensign Hössbacher's voice echoed in throughout the ship.

The crew of the *Interceptor* rushed through the ship in controlled chaos, closing and securing hatches, scrambling into their ELS suits, and making sure every bolt and nut was locked down.

"Owusu, you have the con," Jacob said as he jumped up.

"Aye, sir, I have the con," Owusu replied from his station.

Jacob gestured for Kim to lead the way. She needed to get her suit and head for DCS, and he needed the suit stashed in his quarters.

"Skipper... Jacob... thank you," she said, stepping onto the ladder.

Jacob paused to reply but decided anything he said would be disingenuous. Instead, he smiled and nodded.

"Good luck, XO," he said.

"You too, Skipper," she replied.

Once in his quarters, he shed down to his Navy-issue skivvies. The only thing he had on that wasn't issue was the silver cross hanging at his neck.

He keyed the code on his locker and pulled out the stark white ELS suit. The skin-tight suit had one red stripe down the leg and his name and service on the chest. Once on, the complex nanite systems integrated and molded the outfit as if it were an extension of his own skin. He would not need to do detailed work with it on, but for those who did, the gloves felt like their fingers, not impeding sensation like normal gloves would.

He left his helmet off, carrying it under his arm as he returned to the bridge. No need to appear hurried. It would give a bad impression to the crew.

He'd sent PFC Naki with *Dagger* to guard the prisoners, much to the Marine's chagrin. There wouldn't be much use for a bridge guard, and while Naki could help with damage control, Jacob felt better with the two prisoners under his care. Not that the beaten Captain Morrison would try to escape... but the spy had shown a willingness to die for her nation. Jacob would much rather she not be allowed to try again.

"I have the con," he said as he strode onto his bridge.

"Aye, sir, you have the con," Owusu said. The ensign hadn't taken his eyes off the scope.

"Bosun, status?" he asked as he sat down in his command chair.

Bosun Sandivol tapped a few keys as the last of the reports came in. Generally, the Ops officer acted as a de facto second-in-command, with the XO manning damage control. If a hit took out the bridge, it ensured the ship maintained its command integrity.

With West detached to the Madrigal, he didn't have any other officers with the experience or knowledge to run Ops. It was out of the ordinary to assign the station to a non-com, but the bosun was an excellent spacer with detailed knowledge of the ship and her crew.

"All stations reporting ready, sir. One minute, fifty-nine seconds... not counting yourself, Skipper," he said with a barely concealed grin.

Jacob glanced around. In the time it had taken him to go from the bridge to his cabin, don his suit, and come back, the entire ship had assumed battle stations, ELS suits and all.

Jacob let out a long whistle. He pushed the "all hands" button on his chair and spoke.

"The bosun informs me that battle stations took one minute and fifty-nine seconds, beating the fleet average for tin cans by sixteen seconds. Well done. Next time we're in port, one additional day's leave will be granted for all personnel, and a second day for the ratings. I'm proud to be your captain." He figured the ratings would be cheering, since nothing was dearer to the enlisted spacers than leave. "We will be entering combat range with two unknown pirate vessels. I don't expect them to put up much of a fight, after all, pirates are cowards..." He paused for a second so the crew could chuckle. "However, Murphy being who he is, we are going to take every precaution and show these scumbags what an Alliance destroyer can do! Captain out," he said, closing the line.

"Bosun, assuming they have torpedoes, how long to engagement?" he asked.

"If they have anything made in the last fifty years, they can fire a salvo at a million klicks. Call it eighteen minutes to maximum range, entering gun range fourteen minutes later. Assuming our acceleration holds"—when damage started piling up, they both knew acceleration would not hold— "we will leave the combat envelope two-one minutes after gun range."

With her superior acceleration, they were rapidly making up for the velocity disadvantage. Once velocity was equal, *Interceptor* could disengage at will. Which they wouldn't want to do. He expected the pirates to surrender the first time he scored a hit.

Jacob nodded. Standard tactics for torpedo engagements were to use them against large, slow targets. The *Interceptor* was the least ideal target for torpedoes, as was the pirate ship. Which didn't mean they wouldn't fire them—they would—but they would also close for the kinetic kill. "Knife-fighting range," as his instructors at the Academy had called close-in gun battles.

"Alright, Bosun, drain the can." Jacob put his helmet on, sealing it shut.

"Aye, sir, draining the can," Bosun Sandivol replied. He waited less than a minute for all suits to show green. Once the station commanders reported all personnel were fully suited, he hit the button that slowly decompressed the ship. Anything could, and would, happen in combat. Crews had to be ready to repair ships components in almost any situation; draining the atmosphere from the ship guaranteed explosive decompression wouldn't be one of those conditions.

———

"What the hell?" Kane said.

"What now?" Duval muttered. He was having a hard time figuring out what this ship was up to. They didn't run when they could've and then they altered course, giving *Chuck* an even greater velocity advantage. Then they altered course again, seemingly at random, and finally, as if they saw *Chuck* for the first time, punched it.

"I think we got suckered, Duval," she said. They were at the very edge of effective lightspeed sensor range.

"How so?" he asked.

"I can't find *Dagger*. At this range, we should see *something* of the other ship, and we can't. There was no way they could pull five hundred *g*s to stay with the destroyer. She must have been left behind when they changed course, running silent so we didn't see them." She swore a long line of expletives that peeled paint as she hit buttons on her console.

Duval groaned. They must have shut *Dagger* down and gone doggo. Who knew where the ship was now? It was millions of kilometers behind them. Was it when *Interceptor* first went full power? Or one of the course changes. There was no way to know. But if he didn't do something, his pain in the ass would make him.

Almost on cue, "Duval," Takumi said, "we need *both* ships."

Duval opened his mouth to tell Takumi where he could stick his request when a thought hit him. He could dispatch *Raptor* to turn around and search for *Dagger* while he pursued *Interceptor*. His other ship had the money and the slaves in the hold, and this would be an ideal way to keep the ship that did belong to him out of harm's way.

"Kane, send to *Raptor* your best guess on where they are. Have them go after her," he ordered.

"They could be anywhere, Duval. I might as well close my eyes, spin around and poke the map," Kane said.

"Just do it," he muttered.

———

On board the *Raptor*, DeShawn smiled as Kane's message finished playing. He wasn't a hundred percent on board with taking down an Alliance Navy destroyer in the first place. Going after a civilian freighter was much more his speed. It was just... it didn't sound like Duval was giving the orders over there.

"Acknowledged, Kane. Helm, bring us about and let's start a search for the other ship. Since we're not hiding from anyone out here, go full active on the sensors."

The ship vibrated as the engines fought to slow her down. His computers showed him the bubble *Dagger* would likely be in, and each passing second the bubble expanded. He needed to find the little ship soon before it was too late.

———

"Sir," Midship Owusu said. "I have..." He gulped audibly. "I have a positive ID on the ship." His voice shook over the helmet comms. With combat only minutes away, everyone on the bridge was locked into their harnesses. Jacob waved and pointed at his screen.

"Let's see it," he ordered.

"I'm sorry I didn't identify it sooner," Owusu explained. "I didn't think to check the Consortium database. It wasn't until the other ship pulled away that the computer had a clean look at her power curve."

Jacob's heart leaped into his throat. This entire time, he'd thought they were dealing with pirates. Bold, brazen pirates, who thought because of connections or money, they could get away with attacking an Alliance ship in a friendly system but pirates all the same.

"XO, are you seeing this?" he asked. His voice came out a little more than a whisper.

"Aye, sir. I am," she said somberly.

"Suggestions?" he asked.

"I don't see we have many options here, sir. Charlie mike," she said.

He nodded at the screen her face was on. "Charlie mike," Jacob said.

How pirates managed to fly a top-of-the-line Consortium *frigate* was beyond him. In the end, though, it didn't change his mission. The frigate out-massed and outgunned *Interceptor* three to one. No *wonder* they were chasing *Interceptor* down. A destroyer stood little to no chance against a ship that could throw three times her weight in battle.

He took a deep breath, closing his eyes for a moment and letting the air out in time with his heart. This was what he trained for, what the crew trained for. Trusting in their training and each other was all they had. It didn't matter if the enemy was a pirate in a stolen frigate or a Caliphate heavy cruiser, he would do his duty to God and the Alliance.

"Chief Suresh, the moment the shooting starts begin evasive maneuvers on engagement. Don't wait for me to order it," Jacob said.

"Aye, aye sir," Suresh replied.

"Captain, stern torpedo rooms and all four turrets are ready," Bosun Sandivol reported. It was a double-check, just to make sure some last-minute malfunction hadn't taken them out.

"Ensign Hössbacher, don't wait for my orders to initiate ECM. As soon they launch, you go to work," he ordered.

"Aye, aye, sir," Ensign Hössbacher said.

"Bosun, drop the heat sink. I don't want to risk a build-up in the middle of a fight."

"Aye, sir. Dropping the sink," Bosun Sandivol said.

The ship shuddered as the hyper-condensed carbon cylinder ejected, carrying all the ship's stored heat out into the void. The thermal shined like a small sun—until it hit the gravwake and shattered into a million pieces.

Jacob's calmness surprised him. In Pascal, he hadn't had time to feel fear. Then it was over and that was that. He'd expected to be afraid now, but... no, he was calm. The time for fear had passed. He was ready. His ship was ready.

He hated the pirates and the governor for forcing the fight. Spacers on his ship were going to die today, and everyone that fell would be like a knife in his gut. He would forever wonder if he'd done the right thing. If he'd acted sooner, more aggressively, would they still be alive?

"Thirty seconds to firing range," Midship Owusu said.

There was just one last thing he needed to do.

Jacob T. Grimm closed his eyes and prayed.

"Launch, launch, launch!" Lieutenant Fawkes said as radar flared to life, showing the enemy ship firing.

Jacob opened his eyes and prepared for the fight of his life.

CHAPTER FORTY-FIVE

Every nation had its own approach to technology. The Consortium was the one nation sprinting forward with technological change, from genetic manipulation to new and experimental weapons.

The Alliance tended to rely more on proven systems, making small incremental upgrades, and Alliance ships were designed to allow for such upgrades over time. *Interceptor* herself was the last Hellcat hull laid down and had a newer style gravcoil, making her a full fifty *g*s faster than any of her sister ships.

Interceptor's MK XII torpedoes used a tube similar to her coilguns to launch, then switched to micro gravcoils for acceleration after they cleared the ship. Warheads were proximity detonated and guided by space-time detectors, seeking out a ship's gravcoil as their target. Since torpedo engagements usually didn't range farther than a million klicks, the ship that fired them could use lightspeed sensors to help guide them on target. Torpedoes, though, weren't terribly maneuverable.

Six Consortium plasma torpedoes blossomed on the screen, instantly accelerating at a thousand *g*s. Within seconds, they were going three times as fast as the destroyer.

Interceptor shuddered as the two rear turrets began firing their counter projectiles. Tungsten rounds shot through space, intercepting the plasma torpedoes one by one until none remained. The last one detonated two thousand kilometers off the port side stern, bathing the ship in red light as *Interceptor* sped away from the explosion.

"Well done, Fawkes. Best guess on salvo speed?" Jacob asked.

Fawkes shook his head. "No idea, sir. We'll know soon enough."

———

"Dammit," Duval muttered. He'd really hoped their first volley would finish the job. They were a million klicks out and gaining slowly on the little ship. The closer they got, the less time they would have to take out his torpedoes, but... why weren't they firing back?

———

"Second launch," Fawkes said over the suit comms. The frigate could throw a volley every thirty seconds. Jacob checked the range—nine hundred seventy thousand klicks. He did the math. His own stern torpedoes could fire every fifteen seconds, but there were only two of them. His eight versus their twelve per minute. If he rotated the ship, he could still maneuver, but their forward progress would be considerably slowed. Gravity moved through the coil bow to stern, and every time they rotated, their acceleration would dip.

If they drew in close enough, Jacob could unleash the Long 9 on them and end the fight. The frigate had to be within three hundred thousand klicks to give them the best chance of hitting. Even then, an astute pilot could still evade it. Not likely, but possible.

"Chief Suresh, Sierra Alpha, if you will," Jacob ordered.

"Aye, aye. Sierra Alpha initiated," Chief Suresh repeated.

Under her skilled hand, *Interceptor* rolled to port ten degrees for fifteen seconds before rolling back. Then she went to starboard. The gravity systems fought each other and Jacob had to lock his chair in place to keep it from swiveling with the alternating gravity.

"Fawkes, weapons free. Let them pay the price for chasing our stern," Jacob ordered.

"Aye, weapons free." The weapons officer flipped a switch and all four turrets went into rapid-fire as the ship maneuvered, giving them a clear shot for a few seconds out of every fifteen. The twenty-millimeter rounds could do serious damage to the enemy ship if they just drove straight up the stern.

———

"Is he drunk?" Duval asked.

Kane opened her mouth to respond when alarms screamed and the ship shook. "What was that?" Duval shouted.

"Hit, port side, minimal damage. He's shooting his turrets at us."

Duval scowled. A lifetime of hunting merchants had dulled his senses. Of course, they were chasing the Navy's tail in a straight line. "Evasive," he shouted at Kane.

A loud bang sounded and the bridge hatch sealed automatically. Duval had the sudden realization that neither he nor any of his crew had suits on. The Navy ship didn't have to destroy *Chuck*, just hole her.

"Rapid fire on the torpedoes! Rail guns fire!" he shouted.

———

"Here we go," Jacob mused. The pirates clearly didn't know how to operate their ship. Each second it took them to figure out was a second he had to blow holes in them and end the fight. He was starting to feel better about their chances of winning this engagement. Seeing the frigate had shocked him, but he was starting to realize they were operating a ship like a crew of newly minted midships.

"EMI spike. They're firing rail guns," Ensign Hössbacher said.

Where the Alliance used the much more energy-efficient coilguns, the Consortium preferred railguns. They took more power to operate, but the trade-off was that the shells were larger while still firing as rapidly as coilguns.

The pirate assumed, and rightly so, all it would take was one or two hits and *Interceptor* would be done. However, it wasn't as if they could fire at the ship with any kind of accuracy. The distance was too far and Jacob's ship too nimble.

The range of the two ships continued to close, but *Interceptor* was building her velocity. A few more minutes and they would be in knife-fighting range and the engagement would be over—one way or the other. *Interceptor* just had to hold together a little longer.

"They've gone to rapid-fire on their torpedoes. Range... eight-seven-three-zero-zero-zero klicks," Fawkes said without looking up from his scope, his face mask bathed in the blue light of his telemetry. Firing the ship's weapons was all math. A million complex calculations and nerves of steel.

"Let's up the pressure, Carter. Give them a volley," Jacob ordered.

"Torpedo rooms five and six..." *Interceptor* swung back

around and her stern was almost lined up with the frigate. "Fire!" Lieutenant Carter Fawkes said via his suit's comms.

Interceptor shuddered as twin two-hundred-and-forty-millimeter torpedoes launched out the back. Once they were far enough away, their own gravcoils kicked in, shooting them through space.

———

"Incoming," Kane yelled.

Duval had eyes, he could see. They were fast, closing the distance as *Chuck* raced to meet them. His own torpedoes had to sprint after *Interceptor*.

"Point defense!" he yelled.

The ship's torpedo defense computer lit up the space in front of them with rapid-fire multi-barreled railguns. A shroud of metal shot out, ripping the two torpedoes to shreds. Duval imagined what would happen to *Interceptor* once they were close enough. One aged destroyer was no match for his state-of-the-art frigate.

"Keep firing," he yelled.

———

The *Interceptor*'s computer-assisted, gunner-controlled turrets did their best. The enemy torpedoes only needed thirty seconds to cross the distance. Turret four rotated and fired. The barrel retracted from the recoil and the next twenty-millimeter nano-hardened tungsten projectile leaped up to fill the empty space. The barrel rammed forward, loading the round as the coils around it energized. Servos engaged and spun the turret four a few more degrees port. However, the crew had struggled with turret four, the weapon was constantly down-checked and overhauled as they strove to figure out what plagued the system. Lieutenant Yuki had thought she'd solved the problem when they stripped the turret down and rebuilt her.

She hadn't.

The servos froze as it spun to engage, halting three degrees shy of the intended target.

"Malfunction in turret four," Fawkes shouted. "Brace!" was all he had time to shout before a plasma torpedo detonated off their starboard side like a small sun.

Energy slammed into them, overwhelming the shields designed to protect from occasional bursts of cosmic radiation. What was left blasted through nano steel armor, vaporizing pieces of the hull and blowing into torpedo room two, instantly killing the four ratings and Petty Officer Kirkland.

Interceptor shook from the hit. Her forward acceleration momentarily interrupted from the lateral kinetic energy.

"Torpedo room two is offline, gravcoil undamaged. We've lost the forward radar array, sir," Lieutenant Yuki said from damage control in an all-too-calm voice.

Jacob checked DCS's assessment and it wasn't good. "XO, get to turret four. I want her operational, ASAP," he said.

Normally, it was engineering's job, but Kim knew the turret like the back of her hand.

"On it, Skipper," she confirmed.

———

Down in damage control, Kim leaped out of her harness, putting the faces of the people who had just died out of her mind.

Turret four was aft of her current location and on deck one, whereas DCS was on deck five. She tagged PO Hanz on the way out. "You have the watch. I'll be back as soon as I can," she said.

"Aye, I have the watch," PO Hanz replied. He glanced at Spacer First Class Baker and nodded. "We got this, Baker."

"Roger that, PO," the nineteen-year-old spacer said. Neither of them had seen combat before.

Kim ran through the deck, shouting for engineering to send her a tech. When she arrived at the number four turret, the crew had already removed the servo panel and added several extra bright lights to facilitate the repairs.

"Lieutenant, we already checked the mechanicals; they're working," Spacer Alvarez said. She wasn't wrong. Yuki had personally stripped down this very turret and gone over every inch. Every time they had a training exercise, it froze up. What was causing it now?

Interceptor shuddered again, the internal gravity wavering as the ship turned hard. The turret crew was harnessed in, but Yuki hadn't yet and she tilted sideways, losing her footing for a second before her boots magnetically held her in place.

"Stay in," she said as they went to unhook. Gravity aboard ship was predictable, but dangerous. The crew were hooked in via harnesses that would retract and hold them in place if needed. She pulled the line on her belt, hooking it in and sighing in relief as the harness took hold.

"Let's get to work," she said.

———

"Sierra Bravo, Chief," Jacob ordered. Alpha was a shallow S-curve through space, where Bravo was considerably deeper and would bring them almost perpendicular to their opponent before turning back. It slowed their relative acceleration but also gave each turret longer to fire on incoming projectiles and at the enemy ship. With turret four down, they needed the other three to make up the difference.

"Aye, Sierra Bravo," Suresh replied.

Despite Jacob's climate-controlled ELS suit, sweat gathered at his temples and under his arms. He had a brief moment of hesitation. What if he was wrong? What if allowing them too close would result in the destruction of his ship without gain? It was one thing to face death and the loss of his ship and crew if they could ultimately be victorious. The loss of a battle to *prevent* a war. But to lose both? No, he couldn't do that.

He shook his head, clearing his mind. He couldn't afford to think like that, couldn't afford to let doubt sway his confidence. Right or wrong, the path was set. All he could do was see it through and do his very best.

"Range?" he asked, not taking his eyes off their course.

"Seven-five-three-zero-zero-eight klicks," Owusu said.

"Torpedoes, commence rapid fire," Jacob ordered. It would deplete the rear arsenal within minutes, but Jacob didn't think they had minutes left in the engagement.

"Aye, rapid fire. Torpedo rooms five and six, rapid fire," Fawkes ordered.

In the cramped stern torpedo rooms, spacers hustled, sweat evaporating as their ELS suits fought to keep them cool and dry. The torpedo mechanism raised the weapons from the armory, but in order to rapid fire, four spacers grabbed the sides and heaved them into the tube.

Duval resisted the urge to run. The stupid little ship had scored several more hits on his frigate. Minor hits, but each one was like a ding on a prized aircar. A few dead pirates didn't concern him... but his own death did. And now *Interceptor* was spewing out two torpedoes every ten seconds. While his ship was state of the art, his crew were not. They were doing their best but they were pirates, not trained spacers. Most of them hadn't even served on a ship before, much less a state-of-the-art frigate.

Each hit brought the crew closer to breaking. And he wouldn't blame them if they did; he was right there with them, ready to bolt.

Chuck heaved, throwing Takumi off his feet. Two other men who weren't locked in smashed against the deck. Kane yelled as one of them tumbled over her.

"Hit," Pablo said. "Portside engine room... it's open to space..." His voice faded as the realization dawned on him. Everyone in the engine room was dead. "Acceleration dropping. We're losing thirty gravities," Pablo finished.

"Back off, back off!" Duval yelled.

Kane, still dazed from the man rolling over her, pulled the throttle back manually, bringing the ship's acceleration to zero.

One of *Interceptor*'s torpedoes was annihilated by counter rail gun fire, but the other made it through and detonated its payload. A dozen plasma pellets ignited as they shot out in a cone toward *Chuck*. Five of them missed outright, four more missed by the slimmest margin. The remaining three struck *Chuck* just below the bow, burning through armor, turning hardened steel into molten slag. Pressure released and three decks exploded into space along with a half dozen pirates.

Alarms screamed and wailed as systems overloaded. Three of the bridge stations exploded in sparks, and the lighting turned red as smoke filled the room.

"Hard over, Kane. Run!" he said. He hated the way his voice shook with fear.

"Duval," Takumi shouted. "We can't run. We have to

destroy that ship." He pointed at the screen from his position on his knees.

"Screw you, I'm not going to die for the Caliph—"

Takumi's maser whined as the power cell discharged. Duval wailed like a demon banished to hell before his head exploded from the invisible beam superheating vast amounts of water in his brain.

The blue-skinned man put his gun away before stumbling over to Duval's gruesome corpse. He unhooked the dead man and threw him out of the chair and took his place.

"Would anyone else like to advocate running?" he asked with deadly intent.

He looked around the bridge, meeting each pirate's eye so they knew who was in charge.

"Kane, you will resume course and follow that destroyer or you will be next, understood?" Takumi's posh Consortium accent was gone, replaced with his native Caliphate.

"Y-yes sir," she said, turning away from the mass of flesh that used to be her captain. All the pressure Duval had felt landed straight on her. Suddenly, failure wasn't an option, and any sign of retreat would instantly be dealt with. The helmswoman was distracted, half her brain trying to figure out how to escape death from the front *and* from behind her.

———

Interceptor didn't escape unscathed, though. When two ships closed and blanketed space with projectiles, often luck played a part. In this case, bad luck for the *Interceptor*.

Just as *Chuck*'s acceleration died, Chief Suresh brought *Interceptor* around, pulling out of a long S, when a forty-millimeter round slammed into her stern plate perpendicular to the hull. With no mitigating angle, the round smashed through the armor and exploded into the empty Marine country. Metal shredded as the round released its kinetic energy as explosive force sending fragments of the ship blasting up through the deck.

Two spacers caught in the path were instantly vaporized. Diagnostics Tech Trevors was cut in half as a shard the size of a hatch spun horizontally through the reinforced walls and into engineering.

Commander Beckett had time to scream as the same shard severed his legs at the shin. The ELS suit immediately doused him with painkillers and nanobots to stem the bleeding, stop the shock, and put him into a catatonic state until help arrived.

"What happened?" Jacob asked from his position on the bridge.

"Engineering took a hit, sir," PO Hanz said from his DCS screen. "Several casualties, and it looks like ring eighteen is cracked."

The gravcoil could operate as long as it was intact. Cracks and breaks would reduce the power, and therefore acceleration. They would also have to watch for dissonance—the variation of gravity from bow to stern that could break a ship in half.

"Their acceleration is climbing again," Owusu said. The harnesses strapped around their torso had done their job, keeping them all alive when the projectile hit, but the world was still a bit fuzzy to Jacob, like the moments after he woke up.

"Chief, helm status?" he asked, his voice sounding thick.

"We're down sixty-five gs, sir, and she's sluggish to port."

They were still faster than the frigate, but not enough to escape. Jacob had been so sure the pirates would retreat at the first sign of damage. Why would they risk their ship for this? Nothing they gained would be worth the repairs for the damage he was inflicting.

He needed a new strategy, one that caught them by

surprise. The way they used their systems, how they came right up his tail and then fell for the ruse with the *Dagger*, he should be able to trick them one more time. An incredibly bold idea occurred to him. It would never fool a real warship's crew, but against untrained pirates? It could work. *Fortune favors the bold, son.* His mother had said that a lot to him as a child, and she was right. It was time to be bold.

"XO," he said. The ship's computer routed his call to the correct suit.

"Go for XO," she replied, her voice noticeably strained.

"Status on the turret?" he asked. If his plan were to work, he would need every weapon the ship could fire.

"Self-test checks out, sir. She's spinning and... green!" Yuki said.

"Well done, Kimiko!" he said. Jacob pulled up his nav screen and made a quick calculation. "Chief, drop our speed by one percent every five seconds on my mark. Try to come around, but make it look like we can't. I want them fat and happy."

"Aye, sir," Suresh said with a grin. "One percent every five on your mark."

"They're resuming firing, sir," Fawkes said. "Only four tubes."

Jacob nodded, not taking his eyes off the screen. If this was going to work, he needed the frigate closer, close enough that whoever was flying it wouldn't have enough time to react. A real warship with such a weight advantage as the frigate would've stayed at three light-seconds distance, duking it out. The much larger frigate had the obvious advantage in such an engagement. Instead, she was four hundred and fifty thousand klicks and closing.

"Mark," Jacob said.

Chief Petty Officer Devi Suresh reacted instantly, dropping power by one percent every five seconds.

"That last hit must have cost them," Kane said with a predatory smile. *Interceptor* slowed on her screen, by almost one *g* per second. "We have them, Takumi. They can't turn to port—they must have lost lateral control," Kane said.

"Cease fire on the torpedoes. I don't want to get caught in our own explosions. Ready the main gun to fire, Kane," he said. "Put us on their rear."

Takumi was no naval officer, but he'd read the books. He knew what the Consortium guns could do to a smaller ship. A direct hit with the fifty-megajoule graser would punch through the insignificant ship like a pencil through paper. They had to be within three hundred thousand klicks, though, to guarantee a hit.

He watched the distance carefully, elation building with every kilometer they closed. He had done his duty to his Caliphate, and to Allah, well. He would be rewarded. And when they were done here, he would bring this ship to their secret base and have the ISB execute these disgusting pirates. It would be good to see them punished for their sins.

Victory would soon be his.

———

Jacob watched the same information as Takumi—the distance between the ships. They were down to three hundred and fifty thousand klicks.

"Cease fire on the torpedoes, Carter," Jacob ordered.

"Cease fire on the torpedoes, aye," Lieutenant Fawkes confirmed.

Railguns, however, suffered no such limitation and were still firing. It was either skill or luck, but Chief Suresh's maneuvers were keeping them clear of another devastating hit. For *Interceptor,* this was an all-or-nothing play.

"Chief, on my signal, hard over to starboard. Bring us about one-eight-zero and point her directly at the frigate, flank speed. Fawkes, have the Long 9 ready. Fire as we come to bear," Jacob said.

"Aye, sir," they replied in unison. Fawkes hit the button signaling the gun crew to stand ready.

"And, Carter?"

"Yes, sir?"

"Don't miss," Jacob added.

———

Spacer Second Class Mendez nervously cracked his knuckles right before PO Ignatius ordered the gun crew to lift. The Long 9 fired nine-kilogram slugs that had to be loaded by hand. Mendez and Spacer's Apprentice Perch heaved the heavy and awkward projectile up into the loading mechanism as the capacitors hummed with building energy.

"Hold," Ignatius said as the computer checked the coils. Any break or bend in the coils could severely damage the firing mechanism.

"Green. Push!" They forced the round into place.

The firing ram slammed the shot into place and the hatch closed. He tried to focus on his duty, not on how close the enemy ship was. This was why he signed up in the first place. A direction for his life, something to believe in. He just hoped it wasn't a cause to die for.

"Loaders, stand clear," Ignatius said over the comms. Mendez and Perch stepped back, reaching up simultaneously for the grab bar above their heads. Another round silently moved into place at their feet for them to lift if necessary.

———

Jacob pushed the "all hands" button on his chair. "All hands, brace for Close Quarters Battle. All hands, brace for CQB." It wasn't much, but some warning was better than nothing.

Then the range dropped. As soon as the reading registered, Chief Suresh hauled over on the stick. Gravity warred and every crewmember aboard her leaned to starboard.

———

Kane had the ship lined up on *Interceptor*'s six, and the computer overlaid the targeting information for her to follow. The graser, a massively powerful state-of-the-art gamma ray laser, was charged and ready to fire. Thankfully, none of the previous hits had damaged the sensitive system of mirrors and capacitors.

Like a hawk, she watched the range drop until... she snarled, squeezing the trigger. *Chuck* shook and the lights dimmed as the graser fired.

———

Interceptor turned at the exact right moment. Instead of a direct hit in the center of the ship, which would have destroyed her, the powerful graser sliced down her port side like a knife gutting a fish. The hull peeled back, hardened nano steel vaporizing like glitter under the intense gamma-powered laser. From torpedo room five topside stern, past main fusion, down the hull, opening up the barracks and finally glancing by torpedo room three, the graser vaporized everything in its path, including twenty-one ratings, six petty officers, and

Commander Stanislaw, who was urgently trying to save Diagnostic Tech Trevor's life.

Any delay in the turn and the shot would have blown *Interceptor* into so much superheated gas.

Despite warning alarms, exploding systems, and the thrashing the imparted energy inflicted on them, *Interceptor* came about. The gravcoil kicked in at flank speed, slowing them down as she turned. The ship shook as it hit its own wake.

All four turrets fired as she bore, shredding *Chuck*'s bow, punching though the hull and sending fragments of armor ricocheting through passageways, killing everyone they touched.

But those weapons alone wouldn't have finished her. The nine-kilogram, hyper-accelerated slug of nano-hardened carbon-tungsten was the ship killer.

The bow came around and lined up directly with the enemy ship. Lieutenant Carter Fawkes' hand hovered over the button, and when the target light flashed green, he slammed the button flat.

Gigajoules of energy flashed from the supercapacitors into the Long 9's coils, accelerating the 9-kilo payload. As it exited the twenty-nine-meter barrel traveling at thirty-percent the speed of light, the round shed its protective sheath. An arrow of armor-piercing doom flashed across space right at the enemy. Between *Chuck*'s velocity and the sudden mad deceleration of *Interceptor,* it took less than a single second to hit.

A second that Kane could have used to evade if she was focusing on flying the ship instead of desperately leaping out of the helm to avoid Takumi's reprisal.

The armor-piercing arrow struck the forward bow on the port side, exploding inward as the projectile transferred vast amounts of kinetic energy into the hull.

Chuck simply *shattered.*

The port side buckled in a ripple as armored plates and hull sections bent in on themselves, ending with the gravcoil snapping like dried kindling.

The ship tried to accelerate in two different directions, cracking her keel in half. Two seconds later, the fusion reactor overloaded, and the frigate known as *Chuck* vanished in an expanding ball of fire, consuming every living thing aboard.

CHAPTER FORTY-SIX

"Status?" DeShawn asked. His repeater told him everything he needed to know. *Chuck* was gone. How? *Interceptor* was a destroyer and *Chuck* was a frigate!

Nikko looked like he was in shock, pointing at the screen, which dimmed as *Chuck*'s signature faded. "She's gone?" he mumbled.

The rules of warfare said a destroyer had no business taking on a ship that out-massed her that badly. Sure, *Chuck* was no light cruiser, but still, tonnage mattered. Mass mattered. There was no way the Navy should have won that fight...

He could move in, take out what was left of the destroyer, but why? *Raptor*, and more importantly, the thirty million solar dollars in the hold, were his. Why risk it for revenge?

"Orders?" Nikko asked.

"Are you kidding?" DeShawn asked. "We run. What's the closest starlane?" When the helmsman didn't respond, DeShawn leaped out of the chair and smacked the man on the back of the head. "Wake up, which starlane is closer, Minsc or Praxis?"

Nikko shook his head, fingers flying across the screen. "We

have a decent angle on Praxis. Call it three hours if we start now."

"Get to it," DeShawn said. He sat back down, drumming his fingers on the arm of the chair.

After the course was set, DeShawn ran to the cabin he'd used. He had hours to contemplate what they would do next. Getting involved with Takumi was a mistake, he saw that now. Duval had worried too much about keeping the frigate and securing his own power. DeShawn wouldn't make the same mistake. He had thirty million in the hold and he planned on living long enough to spend it.

For two and a half hours, he thumbed through the files on *Raptor*, deleting anything incriminating while looking for her legitimate transponder codes.

"What about the women?" Nikko asked from the door leading to DeShawn's cabin.

The pirate glanced toward the room where he kept his pet, a snarl on his face. If they docked anywhere legitimate, they were subject to health and safety inspections, not to mention customs.

"We're going to have to space them," he said with a sigh. "Don't tell the rest of the crew; just go collect them, take them to the lock, and do it."

Nikko blanched at the declaration. "Uh, you sure?" he asked, his eyes glancing at the abused girl sitting in the corner. Her eyes went wide, but she made no move to fight or move.

It was one thing to take a crew out in a battle or boarding action, but quite another to walk a group of helpless women to their death. The obedience collars made them obey, but they still had awareness of what was happening.

"Don't get queasy on me now, Nikko. If we're discovered with obedience-collared women, it's the death penalty. You want to die?"

Nikko shook his head.

"Good. Neither do I. Get it done."

"DeShawn, you better get up here," the pirate stationed on the bridge called through the comms.

"What now?" he snarled. He glanced at Nikko and motioned for him to follow. They both made their way up to the bridge.

DeShawn froze as he looked at the main screen. He took a step back, then forward, not sure what he should do.

"It's not bloody fair," he muttered. "It's not damn fair!"

The computer, however, didn't care. It simply showed the Alliance Battle Group heading their way.

"They're hailing us. What do I say?" Nikko asked.

"Surrender. Tell them we surrender!" DeShawn had always imagined death before surrender, but now, faced with those options, he realized what a coward he actually was. And it was a bitter realization.

———

It was over. Jacob leaned back in the captain's chair, eyes closed for a moment as the after image of the frigate's destruction played out in his mind. It was close, so close. A second later, and it would have ended with *Interceptor*'s destruction.

As it was, they had no power, the gravcoil was down, and along with it, external comms. The ship was wrecked. Time to find out how bad.

"Damage Control, captain, come in?" he asked.

A cough came back, followed by a groan. "PO Hanz, here."

"Status, Hanz?" he asked.

Jacob looked around the bridge while he waited for DCS to give him a comprehensive report. They had made it, but the cost was high.

"Sir," Ensign Hössbacher signaled him. Did he sound happy? They were floating dead in space. If the other pirate ship came after them, there was precious little to be done about it.

"Wait one, Hanz. Go ahead, Roy," Jacob said.

"Message from the *Alexander*! She's in-system, sir! They've detained a fleeing ship and are in contact with *Dagger*. They would like to know if we need assistance?" Hössbacher spoke so fast, he tripped over his words.

"Yes, tell them to send help. Route the DCS reports to them as well," Jacob ordered.

It would take a few hours, hours in which more members of his crew could die. But it wouldn't be all of them, and some days, that was all anyone could ask for. Jacob leaned back in his chair, cradling the arm he injured in the final seconds of battle. If it was up to him, he would crawl to his quarters and sleep for a week. But he had other things to do.

"Okay, Hössbacher, let's see if we can get atmosphere back to sickbay—"

CHAPTER FORTY-SEVEN

Governor Rasputin growled as the reports came in. The vaunted "Black Legion" had failed. Over the last few years, he'd fed them merchant routes, shipping information, and a host of other things, all for a percentage of the take. Enough to start the black market operation running all through the Protectorate.

Then he had expanded his reach all the way to the Terran Republic, creating a human trafficking route where merchants would knowingly or unknowingly carry kidnapped women and children to Medial or other Caliph-controlled ports.

His bank accounts on Kremlin were overflowing with money from the operation, and now, mere months away from him declaring independence from the Terraforming Guild and the Alliance, it was all crashing down around him.

He hated pirates. If only he'd secured the small fleet of corvettes from his Caliphate contact. Eight of the ships would have had more than enough firepower to protect Zuckabar, and then he could have continued his criminal activities openly and amassed ten times the fortune.

The Navy had pieced it together, though, from the way he

used Longhorn Shipping to funnel stolen gear to his ships, to how he owned the *Bonaventure* and *Madrigal.* Any of those alone would see him executed.

In the ultimate act of irony, and it wasn't lost on Rasputin, his own greed and the greed of those below him had caused the mess. The gravcoil was worth a few paltry *million.* Had they simply repaired and returned it, the ship would have left the system.

Instead, he watched on video as Alliance Marines stormed the bottom floor of his headquarters. He walked over to the cooler concealed in the wall and opened the door, taking out a bottle of vodka he'd wanted to save for celebrating his victory.

Instead, it would be the last thing he drank. Settling himself back at his desk, he took out the ten-millimeter pistol, loaded, and racked the slide. He held up the bottle, letting the light sparkle through it before opening and filling the glass on his desk.

His wife would understand. She would inherit the system and his sons would one day rule. If not now, someday, Zuckabar would be free. They would receive a secret message soon, detailing everything they needed to know about his empire, and what he wanted for them and the system.

He downed the glass in one quick motion, savoring the way the drink burned his throat. Then, before he could change his mind, he pressed the gun to his head and pulled the trigger.

———

Lieutenant Bonds shouldered his rifle as the door opened. They had all heard the shot and knew what had happened. The governor wasn't going to stand trial for his crimes.

They spread out into the office, covering every direction as they were trained when clearing a room. Bonds walked up to the blood-soaked desk where the governor's body slumped forward. He approached carefully, leaning to the side to see if there was a booby trap or some other mechanism to kill whoever found the remains.

Once he was sure the body was safe, he called in the medical personnel from *Alexander*. He'd wanted to arrest the governor, badly. After everything the man tried to do... but he should've known a murdering scumbag would refuse the indignity of a trial.

CHAPTER FORTY-EIGHT

J acob cradled his guitar as he watched the tug push what was left of his ship into Kremlin Station's repair bay. Absently, he strummed the strings, wincing, as each was badly out of tune.

The fleet's arrival was fortuitous, he thought as he strummed once again. Not only had they stopped *Raptor* from fleeing, and in doing so rescued the remaining women from *Agamemnon*'s crew, they had also rescued *Interceptor* a few hours later.

His ship would have never made it without help. She was a wreck, and they couldn't turn on the gravcoil without risking destruction. Thankfully, the fusion plant had remained intact, but the power runs were damaged, cutting off vital areas from power they needed to survive.

Because of the heroic efforts of his medical and engineering teams, they had lost no crew post-combat. They had managed to power up medical, even going so far as restoring atmosphere to sickbay—which probably saved the most lives. The ELS suits were wonderful, but surgery in one was impossible.

All in all, though, he'd lost thirty-six members of his crew. Over a third. Including Surgeon Commander Stanislaw.

On the bright side, Commander Beckett would pull through. He was one of the many, many wounded loaded into a high-speed medical ship and sent out for McGregor's World immediately. They just didn't have the facilities in the Protectorate to deal with his injuries.

Not to mention Nadia... He reached over and touched her scarf, the expensive one she wore when they first met. He held on to it for her, promising himself he would return it in person.

She was still in a medically induced coma. Petty Officer Desper had explained to him it was for the best. Not only was it helping the nano-regenerative medications heal her, but it would also protect her mind until the right doctor could treat her. It would likely be months before she was able to fully function again.

It was a bitter pill to swallow. He liked her, a lot. But after what she went through, she would no doubt need time and distance. That wouldn't stop him from sending her letters, though. A friend could help her more than a romantic paramour.

At least they got the bastards that did it to her.

Once the professor had reported what happened on *Dagger*, Jacob had to stifle a deep, seething hatred of the Caliphate. No one should have to endure what she had. To do that to another human being. He only wished it was unimaginable.

Thankfully, the Caliphate spy had given them the information to locate the secret ISB base in-system. The admiral had blown it out of the stars, not even asking for them to surrender. She'd said it was common for the Caliphate to detonate nukes once invaders were in range. Jacob couldn't fault her logic for not risking her people.

Changes were coming, not just to the Navy, but to the

Alliance as a nation. The discovery of the Bella Wormhole, named by the professor for his late wife, would change the galaxy.

Not yet, but soon, ships would be able to move from Zuckabar to Praetor in hours instead of months.

Jacob couldn't feel bad about the governor's suicide. The man deserved his fate, as did everyone else involved in his schemes. How many thousands—maybe millions—of people did he send into slavery with the Caliphate? In the end, Jacob would never know. However, stopping it meant everything to him. No matter the cost, thousands of people who would have otherwise suffered a fate worse than death, were saved. That was a legacy he could be proud of. A legacy his mother would approve of.

The view from *Alexander*'s guest cabin was spectacular. The "window" zoomed in on *Interceptor*, letting him see the wrecked ship as it disappeared into Kremlin Station's repair bay. He loved that little ship. Reaching up, he touched the watch cap he wore. It had no unit patch and, since he was no longer a CO, it was the regular black instead of red. It felt... hollow. Commanding that ship had meant something, it had changed him. It was something real.

"Lieutenant Grimm?" the admiral's third officer asked. "Are you ready?" The rank stung him. He was only a lieutenant commander while in command of *Interceptor*, and with the ship in yard hands, his frocking was revoked and he was a lieutenant again. How quickly he had fallen into the role of CO. How much he already missed it.

"Aye, ma'am, ready." He followed the commander out and through the ship. The woman walked ahead of him in silence, not letting slip any hint of what was to come.

The memory of Pascal would never plague him again. He had come to terms with what had happened. He had faced adversity with honor in Zuckabar. He was proud of his ship, his crew, and himself. He knew his mother would be too. His actions would not erase the stain of Pascal entirely, but they would ease them. When people looked at his record, his family's record, his success in Zuckabar would outshine Pascal. No longer would his mother's sacrifice be forgotten.

He glanced at the bulkhead plaque and noticed they weren't heading for the admiral's office. "Ma'am, may I enquire as to where we are going?" he asked.

"I thought you might like to visit the Wardroom before we see the admiral," she said with a hint of amusement.

He wasn't hungry, but if she thought he should, he would.

They turned into the *Alexander*'s massive Wardroom, easily the size of *Interceptor*'s boat bay, and Jacob froze.

"*Interceptor*," Chief Suresh's voice bellowed out from the center of the room. The entire remaining crew lined up behind her. "Atten-SHUN!"

They leaped to their feet, snapping to attention with parade-ground precision.

"PRE-sent... ARMS!" Suresh bellowed.

From Lieutenant Yuki to newly-promoted Spacer Whips, they snapped a sharp salute.

The Navy didn't salute indoors, but some traditions, some honors, warranted the show of respect.

Pride filled Jacob's chest. It dimmed his vision and made his muscles stiff. He snapped to attention and returned the salute, meeting their eyes as he held it before bringing his hand down.

"Thank you," he said to them.

Chief Suresh yelled, "*Interceptor, first—*"

"—To fight!" they cried collectively.

Jacob turned to the commander, who had an openly appreciative expression on her face.

"I'm ready, Commander," he said.

"This way, Lieutenant." The way she said his rank sounded much more serious than before.

He caught Kim's eye as he turned to leave, and she nodded. His crew had honored him more than words could convey. Whatever happened next, he was ready for it.

She stopped outside the admiral's briefing room and gestured for him to go in. As he stepped through the hatch, he reached up and removed his watch cap. Crisply, like on a parade ground, he marched to the admiral's desk, snapped to attention, and reported. "Lieutenant Senior Grade Jacob T. Grimm, reporting as ordered."

Admiral Villanueva leaned back and adjusted her uniform, eyes unreadable. "At ease, Lieutenant," she said in a lightly accented voice. He fell into at ease, feet shoulder-width apart and hands clasped loosely behind his back. He wasn't nervous, or at least not overtly so.

"Lieutenant, you did a good thing here," she said, looking up at him. "I think the Navy owes you a debt of gratitude. I wish I could say you would be rewarded commensurate with your actions, but life doesn't always work out the way it should," Villanueva said.

"Understood, ma'am. At the end of the day, my crew acted with honor. You know it, I know it, and most importantly, they know it," Jacob said.

"Fair enough. However, the political ramifications here are overwhelming. You may not be aware, but several senators have wanted to annex Zuckabar for years, and now we might just be able to ram it through," Villanueva said.

"Politics aside, ma'am, I'm just glad we were able to stop the human trafficking going on through Alliance space," Jacob said.

A dark shadow passed over her face, not directed at him, but certainly a tempest. "I agree," she said.

He stood there, letting her come to the logical conclusion. There would be no point in reassigning him. Not with only a short time left in uniform. Jacob had proved his honor, loyalty, and courage. It would stay with him for the rest of his life. He took a deep breath in, prepared for her pronouncement.

"Because of the politics of the situation and naval regulations, I can't override a promotion board, Jacob," she said. The use of his first name surprised him. As far as he knew, he'd never met her before.

She softened as she said it, as if she wanted him to understand.

"Ma'am, whatever happens, I stand ready to serve," he assured her.

She shook her head. "We need more officers like you, Lieutenant. Badly." She glanced out the viewport toward Kremlin Station, then back at Jacob. "She's a tough little ship."

"The toughest, ma'am, but not so tough as her crew. As a point, ma'am, and I put it in the log, every decision was mine and mine alone. I hope none of this affects their careers in a negative way."

"You would say that, wouldn't you?" she mused. "It won't; there is no controversy here. You acted within the bounds of your duty as a naval officer. There will be no twisting of the facts as there was at Pascal."

He was sure, walking in here, this was the end of his career. It was only a few more months until the review board passed judgment on him and there was no way they would approve his promotion. The admiral already admitted she couldn't override it... so what was she waiting for?

"Twenty years ago, I was on a heavy cruiser serving in the last battle of the Great War. We'd taken severe damage, the ship was going down, and the captain had ordered all hands to abandon ship. It was a bad situation, deep in enemy territory, our fleet was pounded and our ship, mere minutes away from exploding. I'd taken a hit, my ELS suit was breached, and I was slowly asphyxiating. You know who pulled me onto a lifeboat?" she asked.

Jacob was stunned by the sudden change in direction. Did she... had she served with his mother?

When he didn't answer, she continued. "One Master Chief Melinda Grimm, your mother. When I first heard about Pascal, like many other people, I believed the lie, the rumors. I shouldn't have, and I'm ashamed I did. Know this, Lieutenant. I owe you a debt of gratitude. And it's about damn time I repaid it."

A beep on the hatch sounded behind him and he resisted the urge to turn.

"Enter," she said.

A man wearing a moderately expensive suit and sporting a black eye-patch walked in. As the man came to stand in front of him, Jacob noticed his military bearing.

"Lieutenant, outstanding work," he said with a smile.

"Thank you, sir..." Jacob reached for his name.

"Senator Talmage St. John, New Austin," he said, holding out his hand.

Jacob racked his brain, trying to figure out where he knew the name. Something to do with Navy oversight? However, he didn't ignore the man's handshake. It was firm and confident.

"Have you told him?" St. John asked the admiral.

"Not yet. I was waiting for you to arrive. It was your idea, after all. I thought you would like to be present," the admiral said.

"Thank you. I wouldn't want to miss this," St. John said with a boyish grin.

Jacob really wanted to ask what was going on. However, he was a lowly lieutenant and this felt bigger than him.

"Lieutenant Jacob T. Grimm," the admiral stated. The formality of her tone hit him, and he snapped to attention.

"Ma'am?" he asked.

She stood up from behind her desk, a small box in hand. "For conspicuous gallantry above and beyond the call of duty, I hereby award you the Navy Cross, the highest award I am authorized to bestow." She opened the anachronistic box and pulled out a metallic, cross-shaped award, hanging from a red and blue ribbon with a ship's silhouette on it. Reaching over, she pulled his lapel open and pinned it on him.

She stepped back and saluted, catching him by surprise, but years of reflex kicked in and he snapped a smart salute right back at her.

"Thank you, ma'am," he said, barely louder than a whisper.

"You earned it, as did your crew. Which, for them, I am awarding the Navy Unit Commendation. Not only can they wear it for their entire career, but *Interceptor* can display it as well. Senator?" She stepped back and the eye-patched man took her place.

Jacob forced himself to remain at attention. The shock and pride he felt threatened to overrun him.

"Lieutenant Grimm, under section seven of the United Systems Alliance Articles of the Navy, and with the permission of the president, and the Secretary of Defense, I am authorized to inform you that your promotion to lieutenant commander is approved. You will report to Command War College at Blackrock Naval Station no later than January first of twenty-nine thirty-four, standard reckoning," he said with a grin. He took Jacob's hand and shook it. "Congratulations, young man. You earned it."

"Yes, sir," he said, dumbfounded.

"If you pass your courses, and I'm sure you will," the admiral said, "*Interceptor* will be finished with her repairs about the time you graduate. Don't make me give her to someone... less deserving, *Commander*."

She reached in her pocket and pulled out another box. Snapping it open, she replaced his current rank insignia with a golden oak leaf.

Jacob glanced between them, unable to process what had just happened. When he finally caught up, he couldn't stop smiling. "No, ma'am, I wouldn't trade her for anything."

EPILOGUE

Admiral Wit DeBeck read the report for the third time. They'd gotten lucky. Too many of his assets were unable to give legally verified reports. When one of his spies discovered the human trafficking ring in Zuckabar, it had forced the head of ONI outside the box. A year of planning, maneuvering, and pulling strings to move the right pieces where he wanted them had all come together.

Commander Cole's death was an unfortunate necessity, one made possible by the knowledge he had falsified his coil malfunction for kickbacks from Longhorn.

Easier still was surreptitiously holding up the orders for a new commander or the promotion of the serving XO. Then he had to find the right officer to replace him and make sure Noelle came to the same conclusion on her own.

It was certainly a gamble, but it was his only one. Had *Interceptor* left the system, he would have had no options but to intervene. The hardest part, and it often was the most difficult, was making everyone involved feel like it was their idea. He had provided just the right amount of resistance necessary to push people forward.

The discovery of the Bella wormhole, though, that was a stroke of pure luck—along with Senator St. John forcing the vote in the Senate the night the task force departed. There was outrage as his fellow senators rushed to vote against it. The sudden and unexpected vote made the news. The media spread it around the systems, and they didn't portray Talmage in a good light.

Then the news broke.

Caliphate incursion, human trafficking, pirates, the loss of life... he smiled at the thought of how all those senators who had stood in the way of good sense scrambled to vote for annexation, passing it with zero no-votes—a first for the Alliance Senate. Hell, Talmage was still in Zuckabar when they voted.

This was a new beginning for the Alliance. War was coming. It wasn't a matter of if, but when. He knew for a certainty that the Caliphate was hungry to expand. He would not allow their barbaric ways to cause more people to suffer. Admiral Wit DeBeck would use every resource at his disposal to protect his beloved nation.

The comm buzzed. "Admiral, you have a visitor. A Chief Petty Officer Nadia Dagher?" his assistant said.

"Send her in," he replied, leaning back in his leather chair.

Nadia Dagher entered, her arm still missing and her silky black hair cropped short. She marched to his desk and stood before him, anger seething beneath the surface.

"Admiral, I want back in," she demanded.

She was his best covert operative. When she left ONI, he'd almost begged her to stay.

"I'm sorry for what happened to you. If I could have stopped it, I would have," he said with sincerity. For he truly was sorry.

Her body stiffened and she nodded like a machine. "Understood. I still want in. Let me fight this war," she asked.

Admiral DeBeck smiled inwardly. He wanted her in, but she was broken, and he needed her one hundred percent.

"Two conditions," he said. "One—and you're not going to like it—you can't come back until the doctors over at psych—"

She ground her jaw and clenched her fist. "That could take months!"

"Then it takes months, *Commander*," he said without a trace of emotion.

That froze her. "What?"

"That's the second condition. I need you to have enough rank to move through the Navy without running into issues. If you come back, you're coming back with a cover ID as an officer. Together we can make a difference, Nadia. We must. The fate of our Alliance depends on us. Are you with me?"

She glanced down at her feet for a moment, then her resolve hardened. "I'm with you, sir."

———

Lieutenant Commander Jacob T. Grimm will return as Captain of the USS *Interceptor*, DD 1071 in WITH GRIMM RESOLVE.

THANK YOU FOR READING
AGAINST ALL ODDS

We hope you enjoyed it as much as we enjoyed bringing it to you. We just wanted to take a moment to encourage you to review the book. Follow this link: Against All Odds to be directed to the book's Amazon product page to leave your review.

Every review helps further the author's reach and, ultimately, helps them continue writing fantastic books for us all to enjoy.

———

ALSO IN SERIES
AGAINST ALL ODDS
WITH GRIMM RESOLVE
ONE DECISIVE VICTORY

———

You can also join our non-spam mailing list by visiting www.subscribepage.com/AethonReadersGroup and never miss out on future releases. You'll also receive three full books completely Free as our thanks to you.

Facebook | Instagram | Twitter | Website

Want to discuss our books with other readers and even the authors? Join our Discord server today and be a part of the Aethon community.

LOOKING FOR MORE GREAT SCIENCE FICTION?

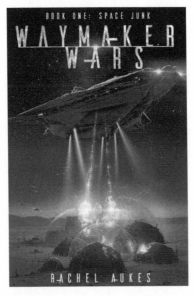

Drafted into a private army, he must fight monsters... or be hunted as one... A century after the Break destroyed much of the world, the wealthy island nation of Dios stands alone as a paradise for those than remain... so long as they aren't poor and homeless. For street orphan Grant Riven, life is a series of kicks to the face. Until exposure to a powerful mutating agent gives him super strength, passive-regeneration, and the ability to use powerful weapons. The downside? Lots of other people have mutated as well, except they're insane and want to eat everyone. After he's recruited by Cloud Nine Engineering, the most powerful corporation in Dios, Grant is labeled "Hallowed"–the fancy name for his new mutation–and drafted into a war against the Mutes, the cannibalistic mutants overrunning Dios. The deal is simple. In exchange for risking his life to fight monsters, Cloud Nine will provide him with the cure that keeps him from becoming a monster himself.

GET SPACE JUNK NOW!

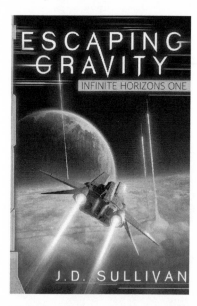

Dillon Mackey has always wanted to travel the stars...
When brilliant scientist and inventor Sherisza Rousilarru
offers him an apprenticeship aboard her starship, he leaps at
the chance to escape a boring future in the law. But she's not
the last of her kind for no reason. Dillon finds himself caught
up in intrigue and adventure across systems, empires, and
alien worlds he'd only dreamt of ever seeing. Just what other
secrets does his reclusive mentor hide? And will being her
apprentice make him a target of her enemies?

GET ESCAPING GRAVITY NOW!

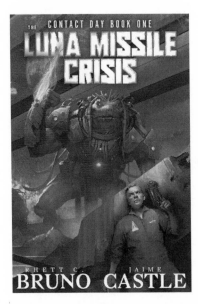

"Aliens, agents, and espionage abound in this Cold War-era alternate history adventure... A wild ride!"—
Dennis E. Taylor, bestselling author of We Are Legion (We Are Bob)

GET THE LUNA MISSILE CRISIS NOW!

For all our Sci-Fi books, visit our website.

ABOUT THE AUTHOR

Join Jeffery on his mailing list to receive the latest information about his writing. Find his other books on Amazon.com under Jeffery H. Haskell.

https://goo.gl/LJdYDn

Or via his website @ Jefferyhhaskell.com

Made in the USA
Middletown, DE
05 July 2023

34586892R00265